W9-CEA-956

Praise for Donna Grant

The Dark Kings series

"I haven't been this immersed in a series since J.R. Ward. Epic. Heartbreaking. Thrilling." —Rachel Van Dyken, #1 *New York Times* bestseller

"Vivid images, intense details, and enchanting characters grab the reader's attention and [don't] let go."
—*Night Owl Reviews* (Top Pick)

The Dark Warrior series

"The world of the Immortal Warriors is a thoroughly engaging one, blending powerful ancient gods, fiery desire, and touchingly human love, which readers will surely want to revisit." —*RT Book Reviews*

"[Grant] blends ancient gods, love, desire, and evil-doers into a world you will want to revisit over and over again."
—*Night Owl Reviews*

"Sizzling love scenes and engaging characters."
—*Publishers Weekly*

"Ms. Grant mixes adventure, magic, and sweet love to create the perfect romance[s]." —*Single Title Reviews*

The Dark Sword series

"Grant creates a vivid picture of Britain centuries after the Celts and Druids tried to expel the Romans, deftly merging magic and history. The result is a wonderfully dark, delightfully well-written [series]. Readers will eagerly await the next Dark Sword book."   —*RT Book Reviews*

"Another fantastic series that melds the paranormal with the historical life of the Scottish highlander in this arousing and exciting adventure."   —*Bitten by Books*

"These are some of the hottest brothers around in paranormal fiction."   —*Nocturne Romance Reads*

"Will keep readers spellbound."   —*Romance Reviews Today*

ALSO BY
DONNA GRANT

THE DARK KINGS SERIES
Dark Heat
Darkest Flame
Fire Rising
Burning Desire
Hot Blooded
Night's Blaze
Soul Scorched
Passion Ignites
Smoldering Hunger
Smoke and Fire
Firestorm
Blaze
Heat
Torched
Dragonfire
Ignite
Fever
Flame

HEART OF TEXAS SERIES
The Christmas Cowboy Hero
Cowboy, Cross My Heart
My Favorite Cowboy
A Cowboy Like You

THE DARK WARRIOR SERIES
Midnight's Master
Midnight's Lover
Midnight's Seduction
Midnight's Warrior
Midnight's Kiss
Midnight's Captive

Midnight's Temptation
Midnight's Promise

THE SONS OF TEXAS SERIES
The Hero
The Protector
The Legend

INFERNO

A Dark Kings Novel

DONNA GRANT

St. Martin's Paperbacks

NOTE: If you purchased this book without a cover you should be aware that this book is stolen property. It was reported as "unsold and destroyed" to the publisher, and neither the author nor the publisher has received any payment for this "stripped book."

This is a work of fiction. All of the characters, organizations, and events portrayed in this novel are either products of the author's imagination or are used fictitiously.

First published in the United States by St. Martin's Paperbacks, an imprint of St. Martin's Publishing Group.

INFERNO

Copyright © 2020 by Donna Grant.

All rights reserved.

For information, address St. Martin's Publishing Group, 120 Broadway, New York, NY 10271.

www.stmartins.com

ISBN: 978-1-250-18295-1

Our books may be purchased in bulk for promotional, educational, or business use. Please contact your local bookseller or the Macmillan Corporate and Premium Sales Department at 1-800-221-7945, ext. 5442, or by email at MacmillanSpecialMarkets@macmillan.com.

Printed in the United States of America

St. Martin's Paperbacks edition 2020

10 9 8 7 6 5 4 3 2

To each and every one of you who has fallen in love with the Dragon Kings.
For those who have just come to the series, for those who have been there from the beginning, for those who came in between—this one is for *you*.

Dear Reader,

I can't believe it's time for this book. I've been in the Dark World for so long that it's like an old friend who I always turn to. I've long held a love of dragons. No other mythical creature can be found in every culture all over the world. They've fascinated me for as long as I can remember.

I still recall the day I told my editor I wanted to write dragons. She didn't even hesitate before she told me to do it. At that moment, the Dragon Kings were born. They might be a spinoff of the Dark Sword/Dark Warrior series, but they've been waiting a very, very long time to have their stories told.

I look back to October of 2008 when I got my first contract with St. Martin's Press for the Dark Sword series. I knew it was going to be over six books, but I had no idea then that I'd move from setting the books in Medieval Scotland for the Dark Sword series to modern-day Scotland for the Dark Warriors. I also had no idea that I'd be asked twice to spin off the series.

The *Dark World* now includes the Dark Sword, Dark Warrior, Dark Kings, and Reaper series. It's been four series, eleven years, and fifty-four books and counting. I'm amazed, humbled, and truly thankful for each of you going on this incredible journey with me.

Which brings me to Constantine, King of Dragon Kings. From the very beginning, I knew he would be a character that readers would wonder if they should love or hate. I wanted each of you to see how difficult it is to be a leader, to have him make the arduous decisions—and live with the consequences. To me, there's nothing more real, more endearing than a character with flaws that we not only recognize but also see in ourselves.

I've gotten so many emails from readers telling me how much they hate Con after reading some books. Then I'll get more emails after others from fans telling me how much they love him and wish they could find a Con of their own. That's exactly the type of response a writer wants to hear. Mostly because I was right there with you, wondering what the hell he was doing, and screaming at him to make the right decisions.

I distinctly remember writing Ulrik's book and wondering if he would ever live up to expectations. That book nearly killed me to write. It was a constant roller coaster of emotions, leaving me mentally exhausted. And I can say with all honesty that Con's book has been even worse. There were days when I felt like I had to give a piece of my soul just to get the words on the page. This is the longest book I've ever written, and the most demanding, punishing, and grueling. Partly because it's the last book of this story arc, and a bit because Con has been such a force.

But mostly because I truly love these characters. I feel their pain and happiness, their triumphs and their losses. And when you've been with characters for this long, they're inevitably going to wring you dry of all emotions and then demand you give them more.

For so long, I couldn't wait to get to this book and get the words down. But when it came time to write, I hesitated. Not because the words weren't there, but because I knew this was the last book in an era that had defined my career in ways I can't even begin to explain. It's not the end of the Dragon Kings, Warriors, Fae, or Druids. I've been in this world entirely too long to say good-bye so easily. I can't tell you when I'll get back to writing the Dragon Kings, but I know I can't leave them. Not just yet.

There are more characters waiting to have their stories

told. More villains who think they can finally defeat the Kings and their allies. More love to be found, and couples to learn about, root for, and ship.

Until then, we have the Reapers. And boy, do they know how to kick some arse. Besides, I'm *dying* to write a specific Reaper's story. It's been a long time coming, and I know it's going to be another tough one, simply because I adore him so.

xoxox,

DG

DRAGON KINGS

For more information about the Dark World, please visit www.MotherofDragonsBooks.com

ANSON, KING OF BROWNS—*Blaze*. Possession.

ARIAN, KING OF TURQUOISE—*Dragon King*. Controls weather.

ASHER, KING OF HUNTER GREENS—*Dragon Fever*. Heals dragon fire burns.

BANAN, KING OF DARK BLUES—*Dawn's Desire/Dark Heat*. Hallucinations.

CAIN, KING OF NAVY—*Flame*. Cone of hot sand.

CINÁED, KING OF MOONSTONE—*Dragon Claimed*. Can learn anything.

CONSTANTINE, KING OF DRAGON KINGS, KING OF GOLDS—*Inferno*. Can heal anything.

DARIUS, KING OF DARK PURPLES—*Smoldering Hunger*. Power is secret.

DMITRI, KING OF WHITES—*Firestorm*. Thought cancelation.

DORIAN, KING OF CORALS—*Dragon Night*. Invisibility.

GUY, KING OF REDS—*Night's Awakening/Dark Heat*. Erase memories.

HALDEN AKA HAL, KING OF EMERALD GREENS—*Dark Craving/Dark Heat*. Sleep gas.

KELLAN, KING OF BRONZE—*Darkest Flame*. Finds metal.

KELTAN, KING OF CITRINE—*Fever*. Can cook anything.

KIRIL, KING OF BURNT ORANGE—*Burning Desire*. Freeze.

LAITH, KING OF BLACKS—*Hot Blooded*. Paralyzing gas.

MERRILL, KING OF ORANGES—Breath of searing light.

NIKOLAI, KING OF IVORIES—*Heat*. Projected thermography.

RHYS, KING OF YELLOWS—*Night's Blaze*. Calls shadows.

ROMAN, KING OF PALE BLUES—*Dragonfire*. Controls metals.

ROYDEN, KING OF BEIGES—*Dragon Lost*. Blinding light.

RYDER, KING OF GREYS—*Smoke and Fire*. Weakness.

SEBASTIAN, KING OF STEELS—*Dragon Burn*. Breath bolt of electricity.

THORN, KING OF CLARETS—*Passion Ignites*. Sound manipulation.

TRISTAN, KING OF AMBERS—*Fire Rising*. Get into someone's mind.

ULRIK, KING OF SILVERS—*Torched*. Bring back to life/ kill souls.

VAREK, KING OF LICHENS—Energy draining shadows.

VAUGHN, KING OF TEALS—Dream manipulation.

VLAD AKA V, KING OF COPPERS—*Ignite*. Can mask himself in dragon form.

WARRICK AKA WAR, KING OF JADE GREENS—*Soul Scorched*. Protection.

PART ONE

I knew what I wanted. And nothing was going to stop me.

—CONSTANTINE

PROLOGUE

In the beginning . . .

From his earliest memory, Constantine had been mesmerized by the beauty of the world. It didn't matter where
he went, every inch of it was stunning. From the vast
deserts full of sand, to the snow-covered peaks reaching high into the clouds. The grass that stretched end-
lessly from horizon to horizon, to the deep blue seas that
constantly beckoned him to explore, and all the places in
between.

Hot or cold. Wet or dry. He didn't care. He loved the
realm with every fiber of his being.

But not even that could compare to his devotion to the
dragons.

His father had brought him from the cave the day
after he'd learned to fly and told Con to look up. As soon
as Con did, the sun was blocked by the numerous Golds
that had taken to the sky to honor their new King.

Con's father joined them in their flight. Not wanting
to be left out, Con eagerly flapped his small wings and
found a current. His mother remained beside him, helping Con reach his father so the three of them could fly
together.

In that instant, in that very moment, Con knew that he would be the King of Golds one day. He didn't know how or when, or even where the thought had come from, but he was *certain*.

Years passed. Good years, and not-so-good years. He found friends, trained hard, and soaked up every bit of wisdom he could from those around him. The more knowledge he gained, the more he wanted.

Before he knew it, his mother was gone. It was just him and his father. Con grieved deeply, but during that time, he felt the first stirrings that he was meant for something more. It didn't take him long to realize what it was—he was to be the King of Golds.

Con said nothing to his father. Instead, he began watching the current King. He did it for as long as he could until Con could no longer ignore the insistence of the magic within him that demanded he claim what he had been chosen for.

He and his father flew over their territory to watch the sunrise as they had for many years. As they reached the spot where they always turned to head back, Con instead remained on course and went straight to the King without telling his father what he planned.

The King had seen Con watching him. He was a smart King, a good King. And he *knew*.

The battle was savage, violent. The King was ruthless. But so was Con.

Constantine knew the magic had chosen him. He trusted that and didn't give up, no matter how deep his wounds or how badly he ached.

By the time Con reared back to deliver the killing blow, the King was ready for it. Con saw it in his eyes. Even so, Con hesitated. He didn't want to kill. He loved life and protected every living thing around him. And he remembered flying in recognition of this very King so long ago.

It appalled him to have to take a life to become King.

"It's our way," the King told him. *"Take your place. You're strong. You'll lead our people well."*

Con closed his eyes as he ended the dragon's life to become the King of Golds.

When he lifted his lids, his father stood before him, pride shining in his eyes. After rejoicing for a moment, Con made sure that they gave the previous King a proper burial, a memorial as he deserved.

The next years were busy, but every morning, Con made sure to meet his father for their flight. Yet there was no denying that his sire was lonely and still grieved for his mother, deeply.

One morning, his father hadn't wanted to end their flight at their normal time. Despite the duties awaiting Con, he remained with his sire for the rest of the day. By the time the sun had set, his father's soul had joined his mother's.

Leaving Con alone.

Except he wasn't totally alone. He had friends. The first to visit was Ulrik. They didn't say a word. Simply sat in silence. It was enough that Ulrik was there. The brother he'd never had.

Ulrik was the only one who knew that Con wanted to be King of Dragon Kings. While others were finding mates and having families, Con had turned his focus on his clan. They were the strongest of the dragons, the ones others sought to have as allies. Con strengthened them more, tightening bonds between friends, and creating new allies.

When the day came that he felt the call of the magic inside him once more, he knew what it meant. This time, he was prepared. He'd spent his years as King of Golds, watching the King of Kings. So, when the magic pushed him, he didn't hesitate to challenge their leader.

And when he stood over the fallen dragon and watched as every Dragon King on the realm stood before him and lowered their heads in deference, he knew this was his destiny.

Life was good. Very good. As well as extremely busy, but Con loved every minute of it.

"You have females trying to get your attention," Ulrik said via their mental link.

Con turned his head from watching dragons train as Ulrik landed beside him. *"I'm aware."*

"Do none of them appeal to you?"

Con sighed. Ulrik had asked this many times, and quite frankly, Con was tired of answering it. *"You know they doona."*

"I'm hoping you'll finally tell me why."

Con looked toward the Dragonwood. *"Come with me."*

He flew off with Ulrik right behind him. Con didn't stop until he found the clearing in the wood where the magic felt the strongest to him.

Once they landed, he faced Ulrik and said, *"I can remember being just days old when I joined my parents in flight to celebrate our new King."*

"Aye. You've told me about it," Ulrik said, his obsidian dragon eyes observant.

"What I didna tell you was that, on that day, I knew I'd be King."

"Most younglings want to be King."

"I didna want it. I knew it. There's a difference."

Ulrik's eyes widened. *"I see. And your current role?"*

Con shrugged but didn't look away. *"What would you*

say if I told you that I also had a feeling some time ago that I would be King of Kings?"

"I know you've wanted it for some time. It was obviously meant to be yours."

"Then I hope you will understand what I'm about to tell you. I will have a mate."

Ulrik chuckled softly. *"I sincerely hope so. There's many a female dying for you to pick them."*

"It willna be a dragon."

Ulrik's smile died. *"How is that possible?"*

"I can no' explain it. It's just something I know. Here," Con said and touched his chest where his heart was.

Ulrik blew out a breath. *"Looks like we better prepare for the future, because if your mate isna a dragon, then something is coming."*

CHAPTER ONE

Dreagan

Something else had come.

How naïve Con had been to gleefully look forward to such an event. The mortals had changed everything.

Con stared at the rising sun, his mind drifting back in time. He wondered what his father would have said if he were here now. His sire had been wise, always thinking through every scenario to ensure that he took the best path.

If only Con had been able to do the same. Though hindsight was 20/20. Still, if Con hadn't known with such certainty that his mate wasn't a dragon, he might not have welcomed the humans so quickly.

Doona lie to yourself.

He closed his eyes and blew out a frustrated breath. No matter how much he hated it, his conscience was right. He detested killing so much that he wouldn't have done that to the mortals. And sending them off to find another realm would've been akin to murder.

"I had no other choice," he whispered as he opened his eyes to the first rays of light cresting the mountains surrounding Dreagan.

His aversion to taking a life had put him and his Kings where they were now—hiding and fighting for their very existence. He had no idea where the dragons were. Not a day went by that he didn't think of his Golds, wondering if they were safe and thriving. All the while, praying that he hadn't sent them to their deaths.

He'd been feeling a lot of regret lately. In fact, there seemed to be no end to it. But maybe, just maybe, if he were lucky, he could change a few things before his time was up.

Con wasn't sure if he was prepared for the challenge. And, quite frankly, he was having a hard time finding the courage to start. Yet all he had to do was think about his brethren, and he knew he'd do whatever it took to ensure their happiness and survival. Not because it was his obligation, but because the Dragon Kings and their mates were his family.

He inwardly winced when he heard a knock at the door. In all the millions of years that he'd been King of Kings, he had never refused a King entrance.

But that's exactly what he did now.

If he was going to begin righting all the wrong decisions he'd made, he couldn't talk to anyone. They would tell him that he had done the right thing before. That there was no need to change anything.

And they'd be lying.

That was the type of Kings he had. They were the bravest of dragons, the best of men. The only reason he had gotten through so many eons was because of them. They had needed him, and that allowed him to compartmentalize his sorrow and loneliness to focus on them.

It hadn't been the healthiest thing to do. He'd known that it would all come back on him like an avalanche of misery and torment someday. In truth, however, he'd honestly thought he would be dead long before it did.

That hadn't happened, though. Instead, he was faced with a deluge of regret, anger, desolation, sadness, heartache, and despair.

This was his punishment for not dealing with those feelings when they first came to him. He'd pushed them aside, telling himself that the Kings needed him, when in fact, they hadn't. *He* was the one who needed *them*.

All this time, he had been the weakest of them all. He had no idea why the magic had chosen him to be King of Kings, especially knowing all the wrong decisions he'd made that had brought the powerful dragons to what they were now.

"Con!" Ulrik bellowed in his head. *"I'm going to stand outside the office and bang on the door until you open it. Or would you rather I rip it down? You know nothing can keep me out."*

That wasn't true, and they both knew it. Every Dragon King had magic, but none was stronger or more potent than Con's—and he'd made sure that when his door was shut, the only way it could be opened was upon his command.

No one could tear it down—or rip it down—unless he allowed it.

"Con," Ulrik pleaded. *"I'm worried. Talk to me before you do something we'll both regret."*

"You really should answer him."

At the sound of the female voice behind him, Con whirled to find Death sitting in one of the chairs in front of his desk. She wore a black gown with long, sheer sleeves, reminiscent of her attire before she'd picked up her sword again. Her long, blue-black hair was pulled back at the sides to fall with the rest of her locks. He looked into her lavender eyes while he debated whether or not to order her to leave.

Erith was a goddess, which meant she had more magic than he. She ruled the Reapers, but more than that, she had been his friend for thousands of years. Although he hadn't realized it was her until recently, because she had changed her name and appearance just enough to fool him.

She blew out a breath, her eyes lowering briefly. "The Kings are concerned."

He turned his head to the side. "Do you know how many sunrises I've seen?"

"Probably as many as I have."

"I'm tired, Erith."

"Leaders like us can't get tired."

He scrubbed a hand down his face, feeling the whiskers against his palm. It had been days since he'd shaved, combed his hair, or even changed clothes.

"You look like shite," she told him.

Con wasn't feeling up for conversation, even with Erith. He turned his back on her and looked out the window.

A rustling of fabric from her full skirts sounded, and then she was beside him. "You have an amazing view."

"I doona want to be rude, but I'd rather be alone."

Just as he said that, Ulrik banged on the door again.

Erith crossed her arms over her chest. "It doesn't look like you're going to get that wish."

"Why can you no' leave me alone?" he bellowed.

Con couldn't believe he'd let his anger get the best of him. He was always in control of his emotions. *Always.* And he'd just snapped. It must have been loud enough for

Ulrik to hear, too, because even he halted in his knocking.

"Well. That's something," Erith said into the silence.

He squeezed his eyes shut. "I'm hanging on by a thread that is unraveling even as we speak. I need to be alone."

"No, you need friends," she insisted. "Actually, there's someone in particular you need."

His head snapped to Erith, his voice dropping low to show his anger. "Doona go there."

She raised a black brow. "Why is that?"

"You know why." Con fisted his hands as he fought the urge to hit the wall.

Her arms dropped to her sides as she gave him a sad look. "Do you know why I came to you that first time?"

A smile pulled at his lips when he thought back to the seventeenth century. "Nay. I believed at the time you were the one in need, but I get the feeling you're going to tell me you were the one helping me."

She laughed, her eyes filling with tears that she blinked away. "I admit that I might have told myself I wanted to meet you because you needed a little push, but the truth is, I needed a friend."

"We both needed a friend."

"It doesn't matter how many different names I used or excuses I made to visit you, I've always been your friend."

"And I, yours."

She licked her lips and took a step toward him. "Then please listen when I say there are many who want to help you."

"No one can help with what I have to do."

"That isn't true, and you know it."

Con shook his head. "Erith, I know what I have to do."

She searched his face for a full minute before her mouth fell open, and her gaze narrowed on him in a mixture of outrage and surprise. "You can't be serious."

"It's time. It's well past time. No one was meant to be King of Kings for this long."

She closed her mouth and slid her lavender gaze out the window. "Have you told the others?"

"Ulrik."

"Which explains why he's demanding to talk to you."

Con frowned as he realized that the banging from Ulrik hadn't commenced again. No sooner had that thought gone through his head, than he saw something out of the corner of his eye. When he turned to glance out the window, he spotted Ulrik outside, in dragon form, looking into the third-floor window. His nostrils flared, letting Con know he was pissed.

Erith let out a little laugh. "You've been a master of your emotions for so long that I think you've forgotten what it is to share things."

"None of the others really want to know the things I have to do or decide on."

"It's not their place to know such things. Just like it isn't with my Reapers and me. I never told Cael such things when he was leading the Reapers, but I do now."

Con slid his gaze back to her. "He's your mate."

"Now, yes. Once that happened, I had to open up and share things with him. It's called a relationship. But you don't have to be romantic with someone in order to share." She pointed to Ulrik outside. "The proof is right there. You told me Ulrik was more of a brother than a friend. Your brother is waiting for you to open up."

In response, Ulrik stomped his foot, shaking the manor.

Con drew in a breath and then slowly released it. "I appreciate your words." He looked at Ulrik and opened their mental link. *"I want to share, but I can no'. No' now."*

"As long as you know I'll be here when you can," Ulrik replied.

Con gave him a nod. With that, Ulrik spread his silver wings and leapt into the air, flying off.

"What's your plan?" Erith asked.

Con scratched the back of his neck. "Make sure the Others can no' harm us. We were so close to ending Moreann. If only we'd been able to do it. But once more, luck wasna on our side since Usaeil showed up and took her. I thought they were enemies."

"I'm not sure what is going on with Usaeil and Moreann. I might send one of the Reapers to find Brian, the Light Fae who was part of the Others. I have a feeling he can shed some light on things."

"Maybe. We know Noreen spoke the truth when she said that Moreann and Usaeil were enemies. I can no' figure out why Usaeil saved her from us."

Erith lifted a shoulder in a shrug. "It might have something to do with the binding spell they used when they joined forces." The goddess paused and glanced to the side.

If Con didn't know better, he'd think Erith was nervous.

"There's something else you should know."

Just what he needed. More bad news. Con braced himself. "What is it?"

Once more, Erith paused. She studied him for a moment, then lifted her chin and said, "The Light have a queen again."

"Usaeil came out of hiding? She retook the throne?"

he asked, suddenly eager to go into battle once more. After everything Usaeil had done to the Kings and . . . well, others, Con wanted her gone.

For good this time.

"No," Erith replied.

Con raised a brow, waiting for her to continue. "Then who?"

"Rhi."

The name hung between them, echoing in his mind like a bell.

"I didna know she wanted to be queen," he finally said.

Erith swallowed. "My Reapers and I might be responsible for pushing her in that direction. She'll be good for the Light."

"Need I remind you that her eyes flashed red?" he warned.

"There is darkness around her, but her light still shines brightly. I have faith in her."

Con shook his head angrily. "The moment Usaeil finds out that Rhi took her throne, she'll attack."

"I'm fairly certain that's exactly why Rhi did it."

Con wasn't sure whether or not to be happy about the news. So many emotions ran through him that he could do nothing but stand there.

"I know when Usaeil thought she had you as her captive, she took the gifts I gave you and used magic to throw them away because she believed they came from . . . well, someone else," Erith said.

Con swallowed, his thoughts still on Rhi being the Light Queen.

"I've been searching for them all this time, and I found these." She took his hand and turned it up before putting something in his palm. Erith met his gaze. "You're Constantine, King of Dragon Kings. Act like it."

Then she disappeared, leaving him alone. He looked down at his palm and saw the two gold dragon head cufflinks—her first gift to him.

CHAPTER TWO

Light Castle
Northern Ireland

This was wrong. No matter how Rhi looked at it, she didn't feel right pretending to be Queen of the Light. Because she *was* pretending. She didn't know the first thing about being a queen. She could lead an army into battle, but that was the extent of her skills. But this wasn't about being queen.

This was about drawing Usaeil out.

Rhi looked around the chambers Usaeil had used for her personal living area. The white and gold matched the rest of the castle, and while pretty, it wasn't Rhi at all. She preferred to either be in the small cabin on the beach, or back on the Fae Realm, living among nature.

No matter how much she craved such things, that wasn't within her grasp at the moment. It might never be again, and she had to come to terms with that—as difficult as it may be.

She gave an inward shake of her head as she thought about how she'd lived before. Shopping trips, expensive supercars, getting her nails done every other day and doing whatever she wanted. Those days were long gone.

Even if she survived the impending battle with Usaeil

and Moreann, the person she'd been before was no more. The darkness inside her had made sure of that.

I made sure of it?

She flattened her lips at the voice of the darkness within her. The darkness had offered her power. And she'd taken it.

Willingly.

Happily.

We make a good team. Look what you've accomplished.

She ignored the voice and focused instead on what her next step would be. No doubt it wouldn't take long for Usaeil to learn that there was a new queen. Ubitch might be many things—liar, backstabber, deceiver—but she wasn't stupid. She wouldn't rush to challenge Rhi.

Usaeil would plan for how to make her move. And she'd hit Rhi where she was most vulnerable—by targeting her friends.

Phelan.

Rhi closed her eyes as she thought about the half-Fae, half-Warrior who she thought of as a brother. Phelan and his wife, Aisley, had suffered so much. They deserved happiness and to be left alone. If that were to happen, then Rhi needed to take precautions. She had to assume that Usaeil would learn of Phelan, which meant that Rhi had to warn Phelan about what was coming.

She walked farther into the room. It wasn't until she halted next to a chair that she looked down at the hand that she'd rested on the backrest and saw what was left of her chipped nail polish. She could remove it with just a thought, but she didn't. She wasn't sure why, however.

A knock sounded on the double doors behind her. She wanted to ignore it, but that wasn't possible now. She had assumed the role of queen, which meant that she had to act like one. At least, for the time being.

"Yes?" she asked without turning around.

She heard a click as the knob turned and the door opened. The air around her seemed to swell, her body tingling all over. Before the guard spoke, she knew who had arrived. *Him.*

"My queen," the Fae said from behind her. "You have a visitor. The Dragon King—"

She held up a hand, halting the name the guard was about to say. Her heart hammered painfully in her chest, and it became difficult to breathe. He'd always done that to her. And he always would. No amount of time or distance could stop that.

She had survived the last couple of thousand years by compartmentalizing things—which involved putting their relationship and her love for him in a locked box in a dark corner of her mind. Being around him always put her off-kilter.

Then Balladyn's words came back to her. *"Your King still loves you."*

She wanted to believe her friend. She'd held onto her love, clung to the hope that one day she and her King might find their way back to each other. It didn't matter how dark the days got, how hard it was to shake off the loneliness, she held onto that hope with everything she had.

And what had it gotten her?

Not a fekking thing.

She didn't move until she heard the door close. But the feeling didn't go away. She lowered her arm and steeled herself because she knew he was there. Right behind her. Waiting to talk.

Minutes ticked by with neither of them speaking. She

wanted him to leave, but she didn't want to be the first to speak. She knew it was petty and childish, but it was what they had come to.

"Rhi."

The sound of her name from his lips made her heart skip a beat. The husky timbre, along with his Scottish brogue, always brought her to her knees.

There were times, like now, when it was tough to keep the past compartmentalized. Especially since the memories bombarded her constantly, making her remember the times she'd been deliriously happy.

With him.

Rhi struggled to get herself under control, to put the lid back on the box of her recollections and handle him as she had for the last few years. It had been the only way she could go to Dreagan. And it had worked.

Then why wasn't it working now?

You know why, the darkness all but purred.

This wasn't good. *At all.* She couldn't face him, couldn't talk to him. Because he wasn't just another Dragon King. He was . . . had been . . . everything to her.

No matter how hard she tried, she couldn't put her wild emotions into the neat little boxes from before. It didn't matter if it was the darkness's fault or hers, the simple fact was that she had lost the ability she'd had, the one that allowed her to talk to him, to face him.

To say his name.

She fisted her hands at her sides when she felt him take a step closer to her. Part of her wanted him to touch her, but another part knew that if he did, she'd lash out at him, releasing all the anger, resentment, and fury that she'd held within herself for so very, very long.

"I came to congratulate you," he said. "I can no' think of a better person to rule the Light."

"I can think of many," she replied, hating the icy edge to her voice.

"Your love for your people is what makes you so qualified. That and the fact that you doona want to be queen."

She blinked several times as tears suddenly filled her eyes. It wasn't fair that he knew her so well. That with just a few words, he'd not only given his support but also confirmed that her decision had been the right one.

His approval shouldn't matter. She didn't want it to matter.

But it did.

Oh, did it ever.

"I,"—he paused and blew out a breath—"I didna come to upset you. I only wanted to tell you that whatever happens with Usaeil and Moreann, I'll be there to fight with you. And I willna be the only King doing so."

She wished she could tell him that she didn't need him in the battle, but it would be a lie. She might have overcome the debilitating pain that speaking a lie had once brought her, but she still found it uncomfortable to do it with him.

"Usaeil is mine," she said instead.

"Aye."

She frowned when he didn't say more. Rhi fought the urge to turn and look at him. "You aren't claiming rights to Moreann?"

"There isna a Dragon King who doesna want his pound of flesh from her. Do I want to be the one to end her? I'd do it in a heartbeat, but I'd rather see her gone from our realm for good. It doesna matter who rids us of the empress, as long as Moreann and the Others are no more."

Rhi drew in a deep breath. "Thanks to Noreen, the Others are disbanded. Orun, Moreann's counterpart, is being held at Dreagan, and the mortal Druids aren't a threat. It's just Moreann and Usaeil."

"You forget, the empress wanted you."

Rhi hadn't forgotten any such thing. It had been on her mind since Moreann had told her how Rhi would be the one who got the Kings to leave the realm. Rhi wished she could deny it, but she couldn't properly get a handle on her emotions since she'd welcomed the darkness within herself to fight Usaeil.

Moreann had intended to use that so Rhi would get angry and begin to glow. To keep her from blowing up the realm, the Kings would've taken her away, thereby giving Moreann control of Earth. Knowing that they had intended to use her as a way to make the Kings lose control of their home made Rhi sick to her stomach. She was stronger than that. Or she had been. She needed to be again.

And soon.

"Do you think Moreann really has your brother?" he asked.

Rhi shook her head. "Even if she does, Rolmir has been dead for centuries. She merely has his body. Nothing more. My brother's spirit is laid to rest. That's enough for me."

"She was going to use that to get to you."

"Maybe." The truth was, there were a few people Rhi would do anything for—Phelan, Rhys, Balladyn, and . . . *him*. Rhi knew better than anyone that the only person who could be used against her, who would set her off in such a way that it would cause the Kings to take her to another realm, was, in fact, him.

He shifted his feet. "We will win this." When she didn't reply, he said, "You believe we'll win, aye?"

"I hope we do."

"We will, but you need to be careful. Usaeil willna take kindly to you sitting on the throne. You're too important. Doona let your guard down."

She shook her head, squeezing her eyes closed. "Don't say that."

"What? Doona say you're important? Why? It's true."

"It isn't."

He sighed again, this time louder. "I know I've done and said things . . . I want to talk about them, to—"

Her eyes flew open, and she spun around, looking into his black eyes. "No," she said firmly. "That's the past. It stays in the past."

He stared at her for a long minute before he gave a nod of his blond head. "I understand."

With another nod, he turned on his heel and walked away. She saw a flash of gold at his wrist. The dragon head cufflinks were back where they belonged. It was too bad she never would be.

Rhi didn't move until Con had softly closed the door behind him, then she fell to her knees, the tears she'd kept at bay rolling freely down her face.

CHAPTER THREE

Con strode through the halls of the Light Castle, feeling the eyes of the Fae upon him. Many were curious, some condemning, but most appeared pleased. Though when he looked at any of them, they quickly averted their gazes.

He didn't blame them. A Dragon King walking the halls of the castle wasn't a common occurrence. Not to mention, the last time a King had been here, it was to battle Usaeil, who the Light had adored for millennia.

The Fae were still coming to grips with who Usaeil was. Con wondered what the Light really thought of their queen, who had lied to them, pretending to be Light when she was actually Dark.

It showed how strong Usaeil's magic was that she had been able to keep up with that kind of glamour without anyone being the wiser. Even those closest to her, like Rhi and the rest of the Queen's Guard.

Just as Con reached the hallway that led to the main door, a figure stepped out from behind one of the gigantic, white marble pillars.

Con halted when his gaze landed on the Reaper. He

didn't know Torin well. In fact, he didn't know many of the Reapers. His connection to them began and ended with Erith, though he'd had a few conversations with Cael. All in all, he liked the Reapers. But that impression could be colored because of his friendship with Erith.

"Bold move," Torin said in his Irish accent as he leaned a shoulder against the column and crossed his arms over his chest.

"I think I did more harm than good."

Torin shook his head, his shoulder-length black hair moving back and forth. "I think you did the right thing."

Con wasn't in the habit of talking to anyone about his personal life. But maybe that was the problem. "So, you know?"

Torin gave him a droll look. "Really? With the interest that's been paid to Rhi over the last few years, how can you ask me that?"

In other words, Torin knew. But how much did he know? "Did you know it was me?"

"I had it narrowed down to you and a couple of other Kings. I knew when Rhi took the throne that the arse who had broken her heart would come."

Con deserved that and more, but it still bothered him to hear it. "Aye."

Torin swore beneath his breath. "I shouldn't have said that. The fact is, I don't really know what happened. I just know Rhi's side of things, and that Usaeil instigated it. If Erith knows, she hasn't told any of us."

Con waited until two Fae moved past before he said, "There's nothing to apologize for. I hurt Rhi. Usaeil, well, the queen likes to think she had something to do with my decision, but no' in the way she believes."

"Do you want Rhi back?"

Con turned his head away, both unable and unwilling

to answer such a question. After a moment, he said, "I suppose you were sent to look after Rhi?"

"I was sent to keep an eye on things, but also to look after Rhi."

"We'll be fighting against Usaeil and Moreann," Con said as he looked at Torin. "Notify me if either makes an appearance."

"Don't worry. I'll make sure you and the Kings know."

Con gave him a nod of thanks. "I appreciate it."

Torin pushed away from the pillar. "You might not want to say it, but I know you still care for Rhi. It's there in your eyes and the way you speak about her. If you want her, fight for her."

"If I thought I had a chance, nothing could stop me."

"What makes you think you don't have a chance?"

Con laughed, though there was no humor in the sound. "Let me give you a piece of advice. If you're ever fortunate enough to find love, and I mean real love, the kind that transcends time and space, hold onto it as if it's the only thing keeping you alive. Because it is. Put your love and the person you hold most dear first before anything else. Because if you doona, if you try to do right by others, you'll lose the verra thing that can make you happy."

"You let her go because of the Kings."

"I put my position as the dragons' leader above my own wants. Above hers. I purposely destroyed the best thing that ever happened to me. You want to know why I doona think I have a chance? Because of that. Because whatever love she once had for me, I crushed beneath my boot heel when I severed our relationship."

Torin was silent as his silver eyes looked away.

Con glanced over his shoulder, looking back the way he'd come after seeing Rhi. He'd gotten good at keeping his face devoid of emotion, but each time she was near, he fought the raging desire within him. The need to have her. To hold her against him, to feel her soft lips against his.

"And if there was anything left of her love," he continued, "my . . . affair . . . with Usaeil ended that."

Torin ran a hand through his thick hair, his silver eyes coming to rest on Con. "I'm sure you had your reasons."

He did, but Con wasn't going to share them with Torin. Or anyone else. He still wasn't sure why he'd come to Ireland. Actually, that wasn't true. He did know. He'd wanted to see Rhi, to see how she was doing, as well as to gauge her emotions. In reality, he should've remained at Dreagan.

Con didn't say anything else as he moved past the Reaper and out the doors into the rain. He didn't care that his suit was ruined. The weather matched his mood, which seemed fitting.

This area was without mortals since the Light used magic to repel them. Thankfully, there were no humans around to see Con shift. And he wasn't keen on the Fae watching him, either.

He walked farther north from the castle until he reached the end of the land. He stood on the cliffs, looking out over the turbulent sea with its white-capped waves. He never let himself consider what his life would've been like had he not pushed Rhi away, and he wasn't going to start now. As he'd told Erith, he was already hanging on by barely a thread. It wouldn't take much for him to break, and he couldn't let that happen. Not yet, at least. There were things he needed to see to first.

Con lifted his face to the rain and closed his eyes. Then he spread his arms wide and leaned forward. There was a brief instant where he floated before he began to plummet toward the stones below.

He opened his eyes as he fell, watching the rocks and water get closer and closer. Then, at the last minute, he shifted and spread his wings to glide over the water. Once he was away from the boulders, he dove beneath the waves and began the swim back to Scotland.

Rhi might think the Others, as a whole, were gone, but Con wasn't going to underestimate anyone. Moreann, as the leader of the Others, had put things in place to ensure that the dragons were gone so her people could have the realm and the magic.

Con didn't think she'd give up so easily. In his mind, it didn't matter if Usaeil and Moreann were friends or enemies. Sometimes, enemies made the best allies. Because of that, he needed to look at all angles for how the two of them could work together to strike at not only the Kings and the Fae but also the Warriors and Druids.

The two mortal Druids on Earth who were part of the Others were also a concern. He already had Noreen and Cain locating them and letting those Druids know the Others were finished. Because the sooner the Others were well and truly dismantled, the better.

But that wasn't going to happen until Moreann was dead.

Con wished his only problems were Usaeil, Moreann, and the Others, but they weren't. There was still the issue of Melisse, as well. He knew that Henry and Melisse had spoken several times. Con was relieved that Henry hadn't asked him about Melisse again, but Con knew it was coming. Henry was too smart to not figure it out. What concerned Con was whether he would be angry or not.

Then there was Rhi. The other Kings had kept their

opinions about him and Rhi to themselves. Well, mostly. All except for Ulrik. He didn't expect that to continue since Rhi had many friends at Dreagan—Kings and mates alike.

Only two Kings knew about the changes he'd gone about making at Dreagan over the last year. Kellan because he was the Keeper of History and wrote down everything that transpired. And Vaughn because he drew up the legal papers.

If Con died tomorrow, everything was in place for the new King of Kings to take over and step into his role, both privately and publicly, without anything standing in the way. And Ulrik would do a damn fine job.

Ulrik had always been the best of the Dragon Kings. He'd walked through ten kinds of Hell to become the Dragon King he was now, and Con saw for himself just what kind of leader Ulrik could be.

It was the reason Con had remained with Usaeil those weeks, letting her believe that she kept him prisoner. It had killed him to stay away from Dreagan and pretend to be in love with her, but he'd seen how smoothly Ulrik ran things in his absence.

If there had ever been any doubt in Con's mind about Ulrik's ability to lead, it was quickly wiped away. The magic of the realm wouldn't let him name his successor, but he knew who the strongest was, and it was Ulrik.

Con swam deeper, using his wings to push himself through the cold water. But no matter how deep he went, he couldn't escape the thoughts running through his head. He had a plethora of things to think about, but his mind went to the only one that mattered—Rhi. It didn't make any difference how many times he told himself not to think about the past, the memories filled him anyway.

He remembered how easily he and Rhi had fallen in

love. In fact, it had been love at first sight. He hadn't believed in it, but the moment he'd laid eyes on her, his heart had been hers. Then she'd smiled at him, and it had taken his breath away.

She was the most beautiful thing he'd ever beheld. There was nothing before or since. There would never be anything as beautiful as she was. If he hadn't allowed the mortals to stay, the Fae might never have come, and he wouldn't have met her.

With her, the days were bearable again.

With her, he truly saw the world for the first time.

With her, he found a sense of serenity and tranquility that he'd never felt before.

He'd had a good life, a happy one. But with Rhi, the colors were brighter, food sweeter. Nothing had mattered but her. He would've gladly given up his role as not only King of Dragon Kings, but also as King of Golds, just to have her love.

And that's when he'd begun to realize that what he had was something his Kings might never experience. There was a chance that they might find love with a Fae, but he knew it was slim. The spell he created after the war with the mortals prevented the Kings from feeling anything for humans, and there were no dragons anymore.

Not a single one of them had said anything about the time he spent with Rhi, or the fact that she practically lived at Dreagan. But they would have. Eventually. It may have taken centuries, maybe even millennia, but it would've happened.

After everything they'd been through together, Con couldn't do that to his men. If they suffered, then so would he. He'd tried to tell Rhi his thoughts, but he could never find the right words. One time, he did bring it up,

made a mess of it. And she hadn't understood.
when he realized that he couldn't tell her. Because
anted her to stay. And if he told her, if he made her
erstand, he had known she would walk away.

He didn't want to let her go, didn't want to end the
beautiful, fabulous love they had. For months, he'd tried
to find a way to have Rhi and keep things steady for the
Kings, but no matter how hard he looked, there was no
such balance to be found.

He had to choose: either Rhi or the Kings. Because
of his love for his brethren and the realm, the magic had
chosen him to be a King as well as King of Kings. With
his choice made, Con then had to find a way to break the
news to Rhi.

That's when Usaeil had come to him.

And because he'd known he wouldn't be able to look
into Rhi's silver eyes as he broke her heart, he'd sent
Darius.

There was no doubt, he was a coward. He didn't deserve Rhi or to be a Dragon King.

But he would make up for his mistakes. He had to.

He owed it to too many.

CHAPTER FOUR

She had survived his visit.

Well, sort of.

Rhi sat up and sniffed as she wiped away the remnants of her tears. Why hadn't she been able to compartmentalize Con as she usually did? Why had every carefully laid stone she'd placed in the wall around her heart suddenly crumbled as if it had never been there?

If she couldn't control her emotions, then she couldn't return to Dreagan. Or have any contact with the Dragon Kings. It had taken her several millennia to even consider going to Dreagan after Con had ended their relationship. Now, with the looming battle with Usaeil and Moreann, Rhi didn't have that option.

"You don't need the Dragon Kings," the darkness told her.

As much as she wanted to believe that, it was a lie. She wished she was powerful enough to take out her two enemies on her own, but she wasn't. It was the one time she wished she had Erith's power. If Rhi did, she wouldn't hesitate to end her enemies.

But she wasn't Death. She was merely a Light Fae,

who had made some bad choices, and had been betrayed by someone she'd believed was a friend.

Thoughts of that betrayal made Rhi think about her father. She wished she didn't have to, but there was something in the past that she needed to learn. There was no denying that he'd been a part of the Others. What she couldn't understand was *why*. Her father had been the wisest, most patient, and accepting person she'd ever known. Reconciling the male she remembered with what she had learned about him recently didn't make sense.

If only she could talk to him. If only she could ask him what had pushed him to such a decision. But she didn't have that luxury.

Rhi climbed to her feet. The moment her eyes landed on the furniture, she became furious. In a blink, she removed every piece from the queen's chambers. With the walls and floors bare, she walked from room to room, her thoughts slowly drifting back to her childhood. It was a safer train of thought than thinking about Con and her erratic emotions.

Safer *and* wiser.

But no matter how hard she tried, Rhi couldn't dredge up the deep memories she searched for. There was only one other option for her. She had to return to the home her parents had made on Earth.

Rhi was about to teleport out, but she hesitated, once more remembering that she was acting as queen now. She went to the door and opened it to find two Queen's Guards stationed outside. She looked at each of them and said, "I'll return shortly. Have everyone on high alert, and keep the castle guarded."

"Are you expecting someone?" the one on the right asked.

Rhi opted not to keep the facts from them. The truth was what everyone needed now. "Usaeil isn't dead."

The shock showed on their faces as their mouths went slack.

She understood how they felt. "She used a spell to keep herself alive. She'll be back to claim the throne."

The other guard shook his head. "She can't. She's Dark."

"That didn't stop her before," the first guard stated.

Rhi took a deep breath. "Usaeil is a master at using glamour. Tell everybody that if any of the Queen's Guard questions anyone's identity, keep them separated and call for me."

"Send one of us to handle whatever you're attending to. You shouldn't leave."

She happened to agree, but it wasn't as if she really wanted the throne. This was only temporary until she could meet Usaeil in battle again. "I'll be quick. I'm counting on each of the Queen's Guard to do their duty."

"We will," the two said in unison.

Rhi forced a smile she didn't feel and closed the door. She pressed her forehead against it, preparing herself before she teleported. Then, with a deep breath, she jumped to her old home.

When she arrived, she stood with her eyes closed. It had been so long since she'd been here. Fat raindrops landed on her head. She dashed one from her nose. Then, slowly, she lifted her lids. Just like that, she was a kid again, running wild among the beauty of Ireland.

The mountainside looked the same as it had a millennium ago. Even the rock wall that had been erected still stood, though she could see it had been repaired in places. Her gaze drifted farther down the hill, taking in the vibrant green all around her and the mountain peaks in the distance.

So many times, she'd stood in this exact location as a young Fae, wondering what kind of life she would have. She'd known from an early age that she would be more than a wife or mother. The idea of taking care of a house while there was adventure to be had didn't appeal to her. Thankfully, her parents had never held her back. They'd urged her to follow her dreams, which she'd done without hesitation. And with much abandon.

As good as those memories were, she needed to shift them to a different time—when she'd first met Con. That day was burned into her memories.

The craggy mountains. The torrential downpour. The lightning that had zigzagged across the sky in a spectacular display of artistry and power. The smell of summer that the rain couldn't diminish.

She'd stood on the mountain peak, thinking how similar Scotland was to Ireland, though she had to admit that Scotland held a note of wildness. It felt utterly untamed while urging her to explore its many glens and bask in the feral nature that stood before her.

To this day, she wasn't sure what had pulled her gaze up to the thick rain clouds that blocked out the sun and darkened the day. She had spotted something large moving amid the clouds. In the next heartbeat, she saw the dragon slice through the rain as if he controlled it.

She had been mesmerized, her gaze locked on the golden scales. The dragon moved with a grace that belied its massive size. For several minutes, she simply stared, transfixed, unable to think as she watched him fly through the clouds like water.

He wasn't the first Dragon King she'd seen, but he was the only one who held her captivated. She didn't know why, only that she got a great deal of pleasure from watching him.

Then, his gaze landed on her. Even from a distance, she could see the royal purple of his eyes. She felt something run through her, something hot and electric.

Something primal.

She wasn't supposed to be in Scotland. She certainly wasn't supposed to be anywhere near Dreagan, but she'd heard so much about it, she couldn't stay away. The gold dragon flew over her, making her tilt her head back and then turn to keep her eyes on him. He swung around quickly before landing behind her.

Rhi knew that he could kill her with one breath of dragon fire. But she wasn't afraid. She stared into his purple eyes as he folded his wings. She was glad when he remained in dragon form. He was magnificent, and being this close to him was a thrill like no other.

She smiled when he sat, wrapping his tail around himself. Rhi had the insane urge to ask him for a ride. It was a ridiculous thought, one that would likely get her killed.

"I'm Rhi," she told him. "I can't stop watching you. I envy your ability to fly."

When he didn't immediately crush her—or incinerate her—she found she wanted to talk more. It didn't bother her that he hadn't spoken. It might be better this way.

"Dreagan is magnificent. I see why the Kings chose it."

He blinked but otherwise didn't move.

She shrugged. "I'm sure I'm going to get into trouble for being here, but I wanted to see Scotland. Next thing I knew, I found myself here. I know it's the magic calling me. I should've been strong enough to stay away, but there's something about this area that is so . . . striking."

In the distance, she heard a sound that a mortal might mistake as thunder, but she knew what it was—a roar from a dragon. She glanced over her shoulder, wondering if the gold dragon had called for others. As soon as the thought went through her mind, she dismissed it. There wasn't a dragon on Dreagan who needed help doing anything.

Her head swung back to the beautiful beast. "I'd like to be your friend. Or at least do whatever is needed so I can return. Ireland is beautiful, but . . . something here calls to me."

Rhi pulled in a ragged breath as she resurfaced from the memories. She hadn't realized it at the time, but it hadn't been the magic or the beauty of the land that'd called to her. It had been Constantine. As if his soul and hers had been reaching out to each other, across time and space.

She closed her eyes, but there was no shutting out the memories, not when she'd let them in.

"No," she whispered, the anguish in her voice making her wince.

At this rate, it wouldn't be hard for a young Fae just coming into their magic to strike her down, let alone someone powerful. Rhi knew she had to get control if she was going to have any chance of winning against Usaeil.

She forced herself to turn around and look where the house had once stood. There was nothing left of it now, not even a single brick to show the lovely place that had once been her home.

Her father had come from a well-off family. They'd always had plenty of money, but her parents preferred to live more simply. They hadn't lived in a grand manor, but Rhi hadn't cared. She'd been loved, and that mattered more.

However, her father's wealth and connections made him sought after by those of the court. Her mother had wanted no part of court life, but even then, she had often accompanied her husband when he had to go.

No matter how hard Rhi looked back to those days, she couldn't remember her father ever saying much about what went on at court. In fact, he'd rarely even spoken about Usaeil, even when he'd had dealings with the queen. Rhi had come to the conclusion that her father had intentionally kept things from the family. Therefore, she had no choice but to shift her memories to when she and Con had begun dating.

It wasn't difficult to recall the first time she'd told her parents about Con. Her mother had been thrilled that she'd found love. Even her brother had been happy. But her father had been subdued. It wasn't until after dinner that she had approached him.

"Why aren't you happy for me?" she asked.

He shrugged as he stood outside and looked at the night sky. "Because I foresee tough times for you both. You aren't a dragon, and he isn't Fae."

"Why should that matter? We love each other."

"You're just getting to know him. It's all sunshine and roses now."

She moved to stand in front of him so he had to look at her. "He's a good man, Da."

"You mean dragon."

"Does it matter if he treats me well and is good?"

Her father stared at her for a moment before his silver gaze slid away. "Neither of us can know what the future holds for you. I want you to be happy, my darling.

You deserve that. And if it's with a Dragon King, then you have no choice but to follow your heart."

While he said the things she wanted to hear, his expression didn't match his words. "But?" she pushed.

He blew out a breath. "You would do better finding a Fae to love."

"You're telling me that a Dark would be better than a Dragon King?" She knew she was being insolent, but she was furious.

Her father lowered his head before he looked at her once more. "I know how cruel the world can be. I'm merely cautioning you to think ahead. Every relationship in the beginning stages is amazing and bright and wonderful. It's when things get difficult that you see someone's true colors."

"He isn't the kind to back away easily. He's the King of Dragon Kings."

Her father's mouth went slack. "Constantine? You're telling me you and he are . . . ?"

His words faded away as she nodded happily. "So you see? He's perfect."

Her father had said nothing else as she babbled on about how wonderful Con was. But looking back on that memory now, Rhi realized that her father hadn't argued more because he was in agreement with her relationship. He'd gone silent once he'd learned who it was that she'd fallen in love with.

All the signs had been right there.

She just hadn't seen them in her happiness.

CHAPTER FIVE

The moment Con broke the surface of the water and took to the sky, it almost felt as if he'd shed the chains that had been around him since the moment the dragons left the realm.

He soared straight up into the clouds and didn't stop until they swallowed him. He heard the distant hum of an airplane and deviated from his course so they wouldn't collide. He'd never thought there would be anything but birds that he would have to share the skies with. How wrong he'd been.

How very, very wrong.

It didn't take long for him to reach Dreagan, and yet he didn't immediately return to the manor. He flew over the vast, sixty thousand acres of Dreagan and tried to forget the world he lived in. He thought back to when dragons ruled, when their roars filled the silence, and the realm was as close to Utopia as it could be.

Dragons fought. Dragons stole. Dragons killed.

But they hadn't destroyed the very world they lived in. They protected it, and the Kings who ruled each clan kept those who got out of line in order. Each time he heard a mortal mention Utopia, his thoughts went back to the time before the humans, before the Fae. When life had been simpler.

He dipped a wing and swung around. As he did, his gaze landed on a mountain peak he had intentionally avoided for centuries. It was the place where he'd first seen Rhi. Just thinking about it now made his heart heavy, thinking of what he had chosen to give up.

But the memory was a good one, one he willingly sought out. And in an instant, he was taken back in time . . .

Exotic. Arresting.

Ravishing.

He'd seen many beautiful Fae, but not one touched the Light who watched him now. The ends of her long, black hair lifted slightly in the breeze. She wore all white, the garments hugging her trim frame, showcasing her figure. He had no idea how long she had been watching him, but once he saw her, he was unable to look away.

And he needed to take a closer look. He flew over her, fully expecting her to teleport away since no Fae—other than Queen Usaeil—ever visited Dreagan. Though they weren't technically on Dreagan land but rather near one of the borders.

Instead of running, the female remained, her eyes locked on him. He inwardly smiled as she turned when he flew over her. Before he realized it, he had swung around and landed near her.

She had been stunning from a distance, but up close, she stole his breath. Con had never been tongue-tied before, but this Fae caused it to such a degree that he decided not to shift into human form.

"I'm Rhi. I can't stop watching you. I envy your ability to fly."

She had no idea what she did to him. He tried to think of something to say, but no words came. He was too addled by not only her beauty but also her fearlessness.

Rhi. Her name rolled through his mind, causing him to grin inwardly. The name suited her.

"Dreagan is magnificent. I see why the Kings chose it," she continued with a smile.

He realized then, right that second, that she was the one he'd been waiting for, the one he'd known in his heart would eventually find him. He hadn't believed in love at first sight, but he knew that's what this was.

He'd found his mate. Finally.

She shrugged. "I'm sure I'm going to get into trouble for being here, but I wanted to see Scotland. Next thing I knew, I found myself here. I know it's the magic calling me. I should've been strong enough to stay away, but there's something about this area that is so . . . striking."

Dragons called in the distance, wondering where he was. Rhi looked over her shoulder at the sound. Through his mind link, he told his Kings he was fine and to keep their distance. He didn't want to run Rhi off.

Her head swung back to him. "I'd like to be your friend. Or at least do whatever is needed so I can return. Ireland is beautiful, but . . . something here calls to me."

If he'd been able, he might have told her that he was the one who'd called her toward Dreagan, but he didn't think it was wise. Not yet, anyway.

He realized she was waiting for him to answer. But answer what? Then he remembered that she had said she wanted to be his friend and wished to return to Dreagan. He nodded, letting her know that she could.

Her eyes glittered with excitement. "Thank you. I'll be back."

Before he could respond, she was gone.

Every day after that, he returned to fly over the area. It took three days before he saw her again.

Con landed on the mountain, wishing he could go back in time. If he still had the pocket watch Erith had given him, he could. Unfortunately, Usaeil had tossed it away with his cufflinks. He wasn't sure how Erith had found the cufflinks, but he was glad that they were back.

The third gift Erith had given him, one of the very first Montblanc pens, never left his office. Thankfully, Usaeil hadn't been able to touch that. Still, it angered him that he hadn't realized that Usaeil had such drastic intentions.

Hell, he hadn't even been aware that she had taken the items until he'd gone looking for them. That's when she had gleefully told him that she had gotten rid of them. And why. It was on the tip of his tongue to tell her that they hadn't come from Rhi as she assumed, but he knew that wouldn't help matters.

Usaeil's intense jealousy blinded her to everything—especially reason. Con had used that to his advantage when he let Usaeil believe that she had kidnapped him a few months ago.

He shifted into human form but didn't bother with clothes. Con didn't care that he wasn't on Dreagan. He should. After all the millennia of carefully staying hidden and making sure no King flew unless it was at night or during a storm, he found himself breaking all kinds of rules lately.

Maybe because he knew there was a very real chance that the Kings would be gone forever soon.

"This is a side of you I've no' seen since your father passed."

Con didn't turn around at the sound of Ulrik's voice.

"I saw it, you know," Ulrik said as he came to stand beside him.

Con blew out a breath. Ulrik had worded it in a way that meant he'd have to ask exactly what he meant. "You saw what?" he asked in a bored tone.

"The first time you met Rhi."

Surprise and disbelief had Con swiveling his head to face his oldest friend. "What?"

Ulrik gave him a sheepish smile when he glanced at Con. "It was one of the first times I dared to venture near Dreagan. So much time had passed without any mention of dragons that I wanted to be sure all of you were still here. I saw her watching you. The look on her face . . . wow. It was really something. She was smitten instantly."

Emotion choked Con, even as his lips tipped up in a grin.

Ulrik turned his head to him. "Then you saw her. I could tell by your reaction that she was your mate."

"I knew it, as well."

"It made me think back to when you became King of Kings and how you'd said your mate wasna going to be a dragon."

Con chuckled softly. "Aye. And finally, there she was. Why did you no' tell me before this that you were there?"

"I doona know," Ulrik said with a shrug. "I knew it was something private between the two of you. I was going to leave it that way until I saw you come here. I probably should've left you to your memories."

"It's better that you didna, actually." Con ran a hand through his hair as he used magic to call one of his suits to cover him. "I went to see her."

Ulrik's lips twisted. "I thought you might after Erith's visit."

"She told you?"

"Nay. Kellan did."

For the Keeper of History to find Ulrik, Kellan must have been really worried.

Ulrik gave him a penetrating stare. "So? How'd it go with Rhi? What happened?"

"It went as well as could be expected. She's . . . no' willing to talk. No' that I blame her. I thought after all her visits to Dreagan and how we've been almost friendly for a few years now, that things might be different. I was wrong."

"Give her time. She's still verra much in love with you."

Con thought about her affair with Balladyn. Jealousy rose up in him in a flash, but he curbed it. After all, what right did he have to be resentful of Rhi finding comfort in someone else's arms? It had been thousands of years since they had been a couple.

Then there was the fact that he had gone to Usaeil.

That was his greatest regret. It had come from a time of profound loneliness. He'd just wanted to ease himself, but Usaeil had been the worst possible choice. He had actually believed that she would keep their relationship secret. He'd realized too late what she planned. That's when he called everything off, but Rhi had already found out by then.

Con expected Rhi to flay him alive, but she had been calm. So calm, in fact, he'd begun to suspect that her love for him had finally faded—something she swore would never happen.

Then again, he had professed the same thing.

But his love had never died.

Ulrik cleared his throat, getting Con's attention. "If you can no' talk to her, write a letter."

Con looked out over the mountains of Dreagan. "My chance with Rhi is gone. I should never have taken Usaeil to my bed."

"That was a dick move."

"In all these years, I've never slept with anyone else. If only I would've been able to hold out."

Ulrik shook his head and waited until Con looked his way before he said, "The two of you were no' together. It had been a few *thousand* years, in fact. Rhi knows this. She might no' like it, but that's more because it was Usaeil than anything else."

"It was only supposed to be one night," Con said. "When she began talking about things I knew she'd otherwise never speak to me about, I thought I might use it to our advantage. The Dark were a problem, and I'd hoped to use Usaeil—or her connection, at the verra least. But it all backfired."

"We all make mistakes."

Con shook his head. "I've no' made mistakes. I've made catastrophes."

"Then fix them."

Con wanted nothing more. In fact, Rhi was all he thought about lately, when he should be focusing on Melisse, Moreann, and Usaeil.

"You didna see Rhi's face. She's changed, and I doona think it has anything to do with the darkness inside her. This is different," Con explained.

Ulrik sighed loudly. "There isna a King at Dreagan who doesna know who your mate is. We've all watched the two of you interact as if nothing happened. That has given everyone hope. Because you two belong together."

Once. It was just one more thing Con had fucked up

beyond repair. But he knew there was nothing he could tell Ulrik that would get that point across.

So, he said, "I'll see what I can do."

Though, in his heart, he knew Rhi no longer loved him.

CHAPTER SIX

Somewhere on Earth . . .

She was empress. How in the hell was Usaeil holding her? Moreann hadn't ensured her survival for all these thousands of years, only for some Fae to stop her now. The fact that Usaeil hadn't killed her yet meant something. But what? If Usaeil wanted to work together, then she wouldn't have locked Moreann away.

Moreann paced the spacious room. The bed was big and inviting, the chairs before the hearth a cozy setting. The ornate rugs upon the wood floor bore a spectacular array of colors and craftsmanship. The pictures on the walls were an art collector's dream.

And Moreann hated everything.

The mortals she'd brought to the realm might be of her race, but the humans who now ruled were nothing close to what her people were. From the food to the clothes to their activities. It was wrong.

All wrong.

When she thought about what this realm could give her people who were even now dying out, it made her sick. The mortals were vain, inconsiderate, and self-absorbed.

They took and took from the realm without thought of consequence.

Her people would never do such a thing. They had taken care of their realm, protected it. Safeguarded it. It wasn't anyone's fault that the magic had stopped sharing its gift with some.

Moreann had searched high and low for a reason as to why more and more were being born without magic. And yet, she found no answer. How could she help her people if she couldn't get answers?

Then, she had found Earth. The sheer amount of free-flowing magic was mind-boggling. It not only gave the Dragon Kings power, but also the Fae and Druids. And she was sure there were other magical creatures upon the realm that she hadn't found yet.

In other words, there was more than enough magic for her people. She just needed to get rid of everyone else on Earth first. It had seemed like a monumental feat until she met Usaeil. They had wanted the same thing, and while Moreann had no intention of sharing the realm with the Fae, she also understood that she needed the Light Queen.

"That didn't work out so well," Moreann murmured aloud.

She wrapped her arms around herself and stopped to stare at the door. Usaeil hadn't been by in a few days. Something was going on, of that she was certain. Usaeil was different, though Moreann couldn't quite put her finger on why.

Usaeil had always been powerful, her magic as Queen of the Light enough to make Moreann take notice of her. But Usaeil's magic was different now—and it had nothing to do with the fact that she was really Dark. She was still powerful, but . . . more.

Well, Moreann did know one thing: Usaeil certainly wasn't working with the Dragon Kings as she had once thought. The looks on their faces when Usaeil had shown up right before they tried to kill Moreann had been priceless.

Her smile dropped when she realized that all her planning, all her sacrifices, had been for naught since Earth was still under the Dragon Kings' control.

What would she have to do to win?

As much as she hated to admit it, the answer lay with Usaeil.

They had never been friends, though they had been friendly. The mortals had a name for it. What was it? Oh, yes, *frenemies*. It was apt. The very thing she would call her relationship with the queen.

Moreann's smile came back as she thought about Usaeil. The Light Fae was no longer queen, not after the epic battle between her and Rhi. It really was too bad Rhi hadn't been a part of the Others like her father. She would've been exactly what Moreann needed—just as Anand had been.

Anand had had one thought through it all, and that was to protect his family, specifically Rhi. His love for his children took precedence over everything else, including his honor. He'd wanted a place for his family, wanted to ensure that they survived.

Looking back on her first moments with Rhi, Moreann realized she'd handled their first contact poorly. She hated to admit that she'd done anything wrong, but the proof was there. The very last thing she had been told by the most powerful Druid in her realm, Lornavon, was that there were two paths Rhi could take. One would involve Rhi joining the Others, and the other involved Moreann forcing Rhi's hand by threatening Rolmir's soul, thereby ensuring that Rhi would lose control and Con—as well as the rest of the Dragon Kings—would have no choice but to take Rhi away to protect the realm.

With the way Rhi had held onto her love of Con throughout the centuries, Moreann hadn't imagined that Rhi would join the Others. So, Moreann went forward with the second plan.

She had forced the Druids to look to the future, made them kill themselves by doing such magic. But it had been necessary. They hadn't been wrong before. Everything they'd predicted went according to plan.

Sort of.

The Kings had managed to thwart her and the Others time and again, when that shouldn't have been possible. She should've been in control of this realm by now. She'd had the future laid out before her, knew exactly what to do and when to do it to ensure that the Dragon Kings were defeated.

So, why was she the one behind a locked door?

Moreann's eyes narrowed. She was empress, able to control time to become immortal. She commanded millions of Druids. There was no reason her path had led her here when so many counted on her.

Unless . . . no. That wasn't possible. She would've known if one of the Druids had lied to her. Their minds were all linked.

Her arms fell to her sides as she realized that, in order for one to lie, they *all* had to lie.

And by lying to her, they would've known exactly where she would end up.

CHAPTER SEVEN

MacLeod Castle

Isla stood on the edge of the cliffs with her arms wrapped around herself as the sea raged below. She'd been apprehensive for days, with no explanation. She couldn't sleep, couldn't eat. She kept searching for the reason, but no matter how hard she looked, she couldn't come up with one.

"Och, love," Hayden said as he came up behind her and slipped his arms around her, sharing his warmth. "Here again, aye?"

"I can't stay in the castle with everyone looking at me," she told him.

He placed a kiss on her jaw. "We do have a house. You can go there."

She shook her head. "I can't explain what keeps drawing me here. I've just got this feeling that something big is about to happen."

Hayden shifted to his side, turning her as he did so she looked into his ebony eyes. His shoulder-length blond hair blew around his face from the wind, but he ignored it, keeping his gaze on her. "Have you heard from the Ancients again?"

"No." And that bothered her, as well. The Ancient Druids didn't speak to every Druid. She still didn't know why they had chosen her.

Nor did she know what they wanted.

Hayden's lips flattened. "Sonya has been talking to the trees, hoping they know something. But as of yet, they've no' shared anything relevant."

"Oh," Isla said, trying to hide her disappointment.

"Gwynn hasna heard anything from the wind, and Evie hasna gotten anything from the rocks, either."

There was no denying it now. "Everything has gone silent. It's like they've stopped sharing with us."

"No' true, love," Hayden said as he smoothed a lock of hair from her eyelashes. "The trees are still talking to Sonya, the wind to Gwynn, and the rocks to Evie. They just are no' telling us what we want to know. If they were no longer talking to the others, then that would be cause for worry."

She pulled out of his arms and turned to walk a few steps away before she whirled to face him. "Hayden, the last time I heard from the Ancients was months ago. That was something very important. Then nothing. Nothing!" she screamed as she threw up her arms in defeat.

Isla shook her head as her hands slapped her legs when they lowered. "Yet I feel something . . . here," she said and touched her chest. "Like a gnawing inside me. Something saying we need to be prepared."

"For?" Hayden asked softly.

She blew out a shaky breath. "War."

In two steps, Hayden had her in his arms again. He held her tightly, his hands stroking her back in a calming fashion. "Would it help to know that I've already asked Fallon to get in touch with the Dragon Kings?"

"Yes." She leaned her head back to look at her husband. "This involves them."

"I know. Just as it will involve the Druids, which means it involves the Warriors."

She put her hand on his cheek. "I fear this involves everyone on this planet."

"We've survived Deirdre and the other *droughs* who wanted to kill us. We'll survive this, as well," he stated.

Isla turned her head to look out at the sea again as she pressed her cheek against her husband's chest. They'd had a good life together. She had done some horrible things before, when Deirdre had controlled her, but somehow, she had found redemption—and love—in Hayden's arms. She didn't want to lose that. They'd had hundreds of years together, but it wasn't enough. She wanted eternity.

But that might be the one thing she couldn't have.

"We've not forsaken you."

Isla jerked at the multitude of voices in her head. Suddenly, the sound of distant drums filled her ears, a sign of the Ancients. She felt Hayden's arms tighten around her, even as she closed her eyes and gave herself to whatever the Ancients wanted to tell her.

"The Druids are no longer safe. Look to Skye. Protect them."

And just as suddenly as the drums and voices had arrived, they were gone.

Isla opened her eyes and lifted her head. It took her a moment to focus again.

Hayden peered down at her, a worried expression on his face. "The Ancients?"

"Yes," she said with a nod. "We need to go to Skye. The Druids need protecting."

Hayden's blond brows snapped together. "The Skye Druids are some of the strongest on this world. Why would they need protection?"

"I think if we go, we'll find out."

"Then let's go," he said as he took her hand and turned toward the castle.

With every step they took, Isla knew that whatever peace their group at MacLeod Castle had found, it would soon be gone. And they would have to work to find it again.

CHAPTER EIGHT

When Rhi returned to the Light Castle, she was happy to see that the guards had taken their duties seriously. And she let them know how pleased she was.

The guards had questioned only a handful of people, and it didn't take any time at all for her to see that none of them were Usaeil. Though Rhi didn't put it past Usaeil to try such a thing.

Which made Rhi think. Usaeil had put up wards and spells to ensure that no one could teleport into the castle, and most especially, her chamber. However, that didn't apply to Death or the Reapers because their magic exceeded Usaeil's.

Rhi knew she couldn't keep Usaeil out. Her magic wasn't that strong, but she could ensure that she was alerted the moment Usaeil stepped foot on the property, no matter what disguise she wore.

Without telling a soul, Rhi started at the four corners of the land where the castle rested. She put up wards there, the cornerstones to her spell. From there, she teleported to the very top of the castle and cast a magical net that would let her know when and if Usaeil came.

Rhi faced each of the cardinal directions, strengthening the spell with every turn as it rained down on the castle, encasing it in magic. When she finished, she went to every window and door—there were many—and put up more spells.

By the time she was done, she was exhausted, but at least she would know when Usaeil arrived. None of the spells would stop her from getting in, but Rhi didn't want her stopped, she just wanted a heads-up when Usaeil came for her.

Rhi wouldn't have needed to go to such lengths if she knew where Usaeil was hiding. If she did, Rhi could go to her and finish this thing between them. But she didn't, so she had no choice.

As she paced the empty queen's chamber once more, Rhi knew that Usaeil would likely suspect that such spells and wards had been put up. Either that would stop her, or it wouldn't, since Usaeil believed her magic could overcome Rhi's spells.

That was certainly a possibility.

A few months ago, Rhi wouldn't have hesitated to say that Usaeil's magic was stronger than hers. But she wasn't so sure of that anymore. The darkness inside her gave her an edge—one she hadn't had before.

Granted, Usaeil also had the darkness inside her, so Rhi didn't have that much of an advantage. Still, she knew her magic had grown. Now that she was seeing how much she could do, how far she could push herself, she was learning just how much she had.

Her first test had been in the Fae Realm. Rhi hadn't meant to begin healing it. Honestly, it had been an accident. She'd thought it was long past saving, but once she realized what she'd done, she pushed even more of her magic into it. She had known that she could destroy and create realms. But to heal one? That took significantly more power.

Especially a planet like the Fae Realm, where the scars of war ran deep after centuries and centuries of battle. There hadn't been a single living thing remaining on the realm. Everything had given up and either died or left. But, somehow, her magic had managed to coax the world back to life.

If she could do that, then surely, she could end Usaeil once and for all. After, she'd turn her attention to Moreann.

Just thinking about the leader of the Others brought back thoughts of her father. Rhi's visit to their home had confirmed what she'd been too oblivious to see back then—her father hadn't wanted her with Con. Had he and Usaeil been in league with each other to end their relationship? Had it been her father's idea? Not that it mattered. That was in the past. It was over.

She needed to focus on what other things she may have overlooked with her sire because she would've staked her life on the fact that he wasn't part of the Others, when in fact, he had been. She wondered if her mother had known. Surely, she must have, but Rhi couldn't be sure.

And Rolmir? Had her brother known, too?

Rolmir and their father had been very close, though she did remember a few arguments between them. On those rare occasions, Rolmir went to Balladyn's.

Balladyn. Why hadn't she thought of him before this? He might have seen something.

"Balladyn," she called. "I know you can hear me. I need to ask you about my family."

Rhi waited as the seconds passed, and Balladyn didn't appear. He was a Reaper now, which meant he couldn't do as he pleased. But surely Erith wouldn't keep him from Rhi. Or would she?

"Balladyn," she tried again.

The air in front of her moved. Suddenly, a man appeared, but it wasn't Balladyn. It was Torin, another Reaper. "He won't be coming, so you can stop calling."

Rhi rolled her eyes. "Did you ever hear of knocking?"

"What? You don't like us just popping in?" he asked sarcastically.

"Not in the least."

"Yeah. It is rather offensive, which is why I love it."

She wrinkled her nose. "I thought Rordan was the smartass."

"Yikes," Torin said, twisting his lips. "Don't tell him that he's rubbing off on me."

"Oh, trust me. I won't." She crossed her arms over her chest. "Care to tell me why I can't talk to Balladyn?"

"Perhaps because of where you are," he said and looked around.

Rhi rolled her eyes again. "Oh, puh-lease. These are my chambers. People don't just barge in."

Torin raised a brow, a flat look on his face.

She ground her teeth together. "Fine. Reapers do, but others don't."

"The point is, he needs to keep his distance from this realm."

"I need to speak to him. It's about my family and the Others."

Torin ran a hand over his chin. "I'll see what I can do, but I'm pretty sure I know the answer."

"I'll be happy to plead my case with Death. If she'll come here."

Torin's silver eyes widened as he looked at her in

shock. "You have some balls speaking that way about Death. She has more power in the tip of her little finger than the whole of the Fae combined. Why would you want to push Death?"

"Because I no longer care about my life. I need answers, and the only one alive who can give them to me is Balladyn."

Torin made a sound in the back of his throat as his head briefly tipped to the side. "There's someone else who might be able to help."

"You seriously think Usaeil is going to tell me what I want to know?" Rhi asked with a snort.

"I was referring to Con."

Rhi's witty comeback dissipated at the mention of the King's name. In one second, she was deflated, her heart aching to see him, while at the same time, she wanted to get as far from Con as she could. How could she have such conflicting emotions for someone who had once meant the world to her?

Torin took a step closer. "Ask Con. You might be surprised by how much he knows."

"Then why hasn't he told me?" she demanded.

Torin shrugged. "Maybe he doesn't realize you need the answers."

Dammit. She hated that Torin had a point. The last place she wanted to go was Dreagan, but she certainly didn't want Con back at the Light Castle.

"Balladyn and my brother were best friends," Rhi said. "Balladyn will know more than anyone else. I need to talk to him."

Torin nodded slowly. "As I said, I'll see what I can do. In the meantime, talk to Con."

Rhi was thankful when the Reaper was gone. Or at

least she was until she realized that she was left with her thoughts again. Could she go to Con? Did she dare? If she wanted answers, she didn't really have a choice.

She went back to the guards at her door and warned them that she had another errand to run. Then she went to Dreagan, though she didn't teleport to the manor. She opted instead for the Dragonwood.

Mainly because she wasn't certain the Kings hadn't ensured she couldn't get inside the manor as they had done with Usaeil. She was surprised that she could still get onto Dreagan land at all.

The moment she appeared, the Kings would've been notified that a Fae had broken their barrier. She leaned back against the nearest tree and closed her eyes. It was peaceful in the Dragonwood. The magic within had a lot to do with it, but it was also a genuinely safe place, and the animals that called it home knew that. So did any other beings who walked the vast forest.

The longer she stayed, the more she relaxed. It made her think of a long-ago time when she and Con had met in the Dragonwood one night. They'd watched the humans dancing around a roaring bonfire, playing bagpipes.

It had been a sensual night filled with lovemaking, cries of pleasure, and vows of love.

Her eyes snapped open when she began to relive the vows. Her gaze landed on none other than Con. He stood about twenty feet from her. He wore a navy suit and a pale blue dress shirt. His blond hair was tousled as if he'd run his hands through it many times.

His face was a masterpiece of beauty. Perfectly proportioned, utterly masculine, and heartbreakingly handsome. She had once licked every inch of him, stroked his cheek, and kissed him for hours.

"You were humming."

She started to deny it, but then stopped. She had no idea if she'd been humming or not. "I always did like it here."

"Come whenever you want. I opened Dreagan to you a verra long time ago."

Rhi looked away but made herself meet his gaze once more. "I have some questions I'd like to ask."

"I'll answer them if I can."

"Did you ever speak to my father?"

Con gave a single shake of his head. "I did no'."

"What about Rolmir?"

"He came to see me a few months after we got together."

Rhi tried not to react to the news, but it unsettled her. She'd had no idea that her brother had come to Dreagan. "What happened?"

"Rolmir wanted to tell me that he held no ill will toward me."

That made Rhi frown. "Why would he say that?"

"A Dragon King and a Fae? Did you think that wouldna cause waves among your people?"

She shook her head, shrugging. "It didn't among the Kings." Rhi fully expected him to agree with her, but he didn't. "So, I was wrong about that, as well?"

"I didna say that."

"Point in fact, you didn't say anything."

Con merely stared at her.

"Fine. I'll ask the question. Were the Kings upset about you being in a relationship with a Fae?"

"My brethren liked you, but they knew—as I did—that there would be opposition among the Fae."

"But not the Kings?" she pressed.

Con broke eye contact first as he glanced to the side. "It was different for the Kings."

"Different how?"

"We realized that if we were to ever find happiness, it would be with someone other than a dragon since they were gone. And we knew it would not be with mortals."

"Because of the spell used," she finished with a nod. "Which left the Fae."

"Which left the Fae," he confirmed.

CHAPTER NINE

She was here. Con didn't allow himself to read too much into Rhi's visit. Obviously, she was there for information, but that was fine with him. The fact that she'd come to Dreagan spoke volumes. He honestly didn't think she'd step foot here again.

Not that he'd blame her.

Rhi had been through more than nearly anyone on the realm. She deserved a respite. And happiness.

She gave him a dark look and demanded, "What?"

He lifted one shoulder in a half-shrug, confused. "What?"

"You're staring at me. Stop it."

He didn't look away. "I tend to look at those I'm conversing with."

The dramatic way she rolled her eyes told him that she knew he was full of shite. "You never said the Kings weren't happy about . . . us."

He tried not to take offense at the difficulty in which she said *us*. But he did, nonetheless. A part of him wished they could go back to pretending that they had never been a couple. It hadn't been easy, but it was certainly less painful than what was happening now.

Not that anything about their breakup had been uncomplicated. Removing her from his life had been more painful than sending the dragons away. It had, in fact, been like tearing out his heart and tossing it away.

It was why he'd begun the red journals. They had been his way of getting out all the things he wished he could say to her before he actually said them. Journaling had made some days bearable.

Others had been sheer torture.

"Con."

He blinked. This time, he did slide his gaze to the side as he struggled to remember her last comment. He met her eyes once more as he drew in a deep breath. "None of the Kings had an issue with you."

"You keep saying that, but I think it's shite. How about the truth?"

The truth? Bloody hell, he wasn't sure he could give her that. Not now. He came up with an alternative, something in between with enough truth that made it easier to say.

"We were no' exactly friendly with the Fae, no' even the Light. The Kings couldna have anything with mortals because of the spell. It was inevitable that a King and a Fae would get together. I didna think I'd be the first."

She watched him closely. "You still haven't said how the other Dragon Kings felt about our union, however brief it was."

"I have. You've just no' been listening. There isna a King at Dreagan who didna immediately like you. You have that ability, though you may no' believe it. Had it been anyone else, I doona think they would've felt the same."

Rhi shifted her feet and looked at the ground for a heartbeat. "The way you say the words makes me think the Kings were fine with your involvement with a Fae, but I know that isn't the case. You're choosing your words very carefully, and that tells me you're trying not to say something. Do everyone a favor and just spit it out."

Con wanted to refuse. He wanted to come up with some smooth line that would convince her that he spoke the truth. But he couldn't. He was too tired. And frankly, perhaps it was time she knew all of it.

Every last horrible bit that he'd held within himself for thousands of years.

"I was aware of how your father felt about me," he began.

Rhi cut him a look that halted his words. "How can you say that if you didn't talk to him? Did my brother tell you something?"

"It was the things Rolmir left out that told me all I needed to know. If your father had no issues with me, then your brother wouldna have come on his own. Or he wouldna have felt compelled to come at all."

"True," she murmured, her lips pinched.

Con shifted to the side and looked through the trees. What he was about to say, he hadn't said, even to himself. He couldn't look at Rhi as he voiced the words. He'd gotten so used to bottling up his emotions that he was afraid to let them out now. Scared of the storm of feelings that might consume him.

More than that, he was terrified of Rhi learning the truth. He'd hurt her so much, the last thing he wanted was to cause more harm now. But it was his fault that they were in this moment. He had made the decisions. And he had lived with the consequences.

"When the dragons left, and after I banished Ulrik,

the rest of us came here to our mountains. I was the only one who didna sleep. The endless days with no one but myself was the worst time of my life. But I had the Kings to focus on. It's how I got through it. Eventually, some of them began to wake, and things got easier."

He took a breath and released it. "The humans didna know we existed. Everything about dragons was myth or legend to them, and that's how we wanted it. Life was . . . good. We found a balance, of sorts. Then, the Fae came." He looked over his shoulder at her, meeting Rhi's silver eyes briefly. "After what happened with the humans, I almost ran the Fae out that verra day."

"Why didn't you?" she asked.

Con shrugged and put his hands in his pockets. "I really doona know. I was sorry that the Fae Realm had been destroyed, but it was the Fae's own fault. I didna want them doing that here. Despite my misgivings, I allowed the Fae to make a home here. It didna take long for the Dark to begin causing trouble."

"As they always do."

"Before I knew it, we were at war again. I wanted to end things quickly, but I also knew that we had to keep the mortals from learning that dragons were still here, as well as keeping them ignorant of the Fae. That made our task that much harder. The war should've been over in days. Instead, it lasted much, much longer. I know many believe that the only reason we won was because the Light joined us."

Rhi blew out a breath behind him. "That's not true. There isn't a Fae alive who doesn't know that you could've wiped us out easily. It's the reason Usaeil decided to join the Kings."

"I was prepared to spend eternity alone. I figured that was my Fate. Then I saw you atop the mountain peak that day." He listened, hoping she would move toward him or make some sound, but there was only silence. Con ran a hand over his mouth. "Everything changed when we met. Instead of dreading each day, I began looking forward to them. I—"

"I don't want to hear any of that. Get on with things," she interrupted.

So, that's how it was to be. He should've known. Not that he blamed her. "I was happy. Verra happy. It took me a while to realize that I was the only one walking around Dreagan with a smile. At first, I pretended that I didna notice, but after weeks of it, I could no longer deny it."

Rhi snorted loudly behind him.

He frowned as he faced her. "Something funny?"

"No," she stated, her expression filled with ire.

Con debated whether to push her. Finally, he decided to continue. "That was about the time your brother visited. Knowing what I did about your father and seeing the other Kings, it dampened my happiness."

"When does Usaeil factor into this?" Rhi asked pointedly, her arms crossed over her chest.

Had he really thought this was the right time to talk to Rhi? Obviously, he'd been wrong. But there was no backtracking now. "A few months later."

"When you gave me no clues that you were having these feelings?"

"Nay," he admitted quietly.

She nodded, a brow raised. "Exactly. Finish."

No one took him to task quite like Rhi. Then again, he expected no less from his mate. By the stars, how he loved her. But those words could only be said in his head now. And that was his fault.

"Usaeil came on a particularly bad day. I began to see a few of the Kings with looks of envy on their faces when they saw us together. It didna last long, but I knew it was the beginning. That's when I came to the realization that there was a good chance I couldna have both you and my position. I fought it, telling myself that Fate wouldna put you in my life only to take you away. Usaeil came with her own reasons for why we shouldna be together. I knew some of them were utter nonsense, but some were valid."

"Like?" Rhi pressed.

Con clenched his jaw. "You were one of the top Queen's Guards. She had plans for you."

"And you thought you knew what was best for me. Better than I did?" she asked with a roll of her eyes. Then she shook her head in exasperation. "That's rich."

"Of course, it sounds silly to you now, but at the time, when everything was stacking up, and Usaeil began listing the reasons our affair should end, I could see no other way."

Rhi dropped her arms and took a step toward him, fury rolling off her in waves as her eyes briefly flashed red. "What you should've done was talk to me. But that wouldn't make sense, would it? That would mean you couldn't be the martyr."

"You think I wanted this?" he bellowed, no longer trying to hide his emotions.

She laughed, but there was no mirth in the sound. "You're bloody right, I think you wanted this. It's easier for you to let something go than to hold onto it, to fight for it. For us!"

"It wasna easy," he said through clenched teeth. He'd never been so furious in all his life. Here he was, trying to explain where he'd been mentally and emotionally, and she was throwing it back in his face as if none of it mattered.

"Sure as hell looks it to me. You saw a few Kings jealous of you having someone. So what? Did it never occur to you that they would eventually have someone, as well? Then Usaeil delivered a load of shite because she wanted you. You never saw that, did you? Of course, you didn't. She gave you what you needed to get what she wanted."

Con moved a step closer. "Give me some credit. Usaeil's visit and words might have coincided with my decision, but that's all it was. I wouldna let someone sway me in such a way."

"Ha! You expect me to believe that? Not going to happen." She took another step closer to him, her anger palpable. "She hasn't stopped telling me how she was responsible for splitting us up."

"She's a fucking liar! You know that."

Rhi's eyes narrowed. "Not about this. I'd have believed the same thing in her shoes."

Con started to release a string of curses, but he bit it back and looked heavenward to get control of himself. Letting his emotions rule him would get him nowhere. When he lowered his gaze, he moved yet closer to Rhi. "I had a duty to the Kings. I was their leader, the one who kept us on a path that would keep us going. We'd lost everything, Rhi. *Everything*. All I wanted was to have the dragons return. And you." He paused and shook his head at the situation. "It all seemed so simple then. A couple of the Kings had taken Fae lovers, but nothing lasted longer than a week. I make the decisions, and the consequences lay at my feet. With the spell in place so none of us would feel anything toward humans, I had diminished the pool from which we could find mates."

"You didn't give it time," Rhi said softly.

He swallowed and shrugged. "Maybe no'. But the one thing I became adept at doing was looking at every scenario. And there were verra few that ended with them no' taking their anger out on both of us because they were alone. We're Dragon Kings, but we struggled to find ourselves without our clans. The next best thing was a mate. There are Kings here now who will never be mated because their other half is neither human nor Fae. They're dragons."

"You're telling me you ended things because you didn't want to be the only King mated?"

She asked the question too quietly. Con knew that it didn't matter how he answered it, she was going to be furious either way. "Aye."

"And your reasoning for sending Darius to do your dirty work when you broke it off?"

Con lowered his gaze to the ground. If there was one thing he wished he could take back, it was this. But he couldn't. He looked up at Rhi. "Because I knew the moment I looked at you, I wouldna be able to go through with it. Whenever you were near, I had to touch you, kiss you. I'd already tried to end it myself, several times, but I couldna."

She walked right up to him so only inches separated them, her face full of scorn. "You're a coward."

He found himself drowning in her silver eyes, but before he could find any more words, she was gone.

CHAPTER TEN

"That didna go well at all," Rhys murmured in disgust as Rhi vanished.

Ulrik gave a shake of his head from their vantage point in the Dragonwood. "No' in the least."

"What do we do?"

"There isna anything we *can* do."

Rhys's aqua ringed dark blue eyes turned to Ulrik. "I disagree."

"What do you suggest, then?" Ulrik asked, because he was at his wits' end.

"Phelan."

"You've lost your fucking mind," Ulrik said and turned away before Con saw—or heard—them.

Rhys hurried to catch up while looking over his shoulder at Con, who still hadn't moved. "I doona think so. Phelan is one of the only people who can talk any sense into Rhi. I'd give it a go if I honestly thought it'd help. But she willna listen to anything I have to say because I'm a King."

When Ulrik believed they were far enough away from Con that he wouldn't hear, he halted and faced Rhys.

"How long has Phelan asked us to tell him who Rhi's King is?"

"Since he discovered that a King had broken her heart."

"And did anyone tell Phelan who it was?"

A muscle jumped in Rhys's jaw. "You know we didna."

"Why?"

"Because it wasna our place," Rhys ground out.

Ulrik shook his head. "Nay, you were protecting Con."

Rhys started to argue, then turned away and raked a hand through his wavy, dark brown hair. "Shite. This is a bloody mess."

"Con protects us. He always has. And you all protected him."

"He never told us why he ended it with Rhi."

Ulrik slid his gaze through the trees to where he'd left Con. "You suspected. We all did."

Rhys blew out a breath as he dropped his chin to his chest for a heartbeat. Then he turned his head to look at Ulrik. "Aye. We did."

"And none of you told him to go back to her." It wasn't a question. Someone had to put the truth out there—as hard as it was to hear.

Rhys frowned. "He wouldna have listened to us."

"If it came down to it, I wouldna be able to let Eilish go. She's my mate, the other half of me. The missing part that I longed for since I began thinking of a mate."

Rhys was silent for a few moments. "I've done a great many things for the Kings and Dreagan. I'll continue to do them because this is my home. But could I give up Lily? Never."

Ulrik swallowed as he struggled to get the next words

out. "Con did what neither of us could do. He did what no other King would dream of doing."

"He's stronger than all of us combined."

Only Ulrik knew that Con was barely hanging on by a thread. He didn't want to share that with the others just yet. No doubt that time would come sooner rather than later, but it wasn't now.

"A King like Con can only shoulder so much," Ulrik replied.

Rhys flattened his lips while shaking his head again. "I spent so much time trying to forget what happened to us. I sought out women as my means of escape."

"Every King had or has such an escape."

"Does Con?"

Ulrik had to look away. Con wasn't only his King, he was also his best friend, the brother he'd never had. He didn't want any King believing that Con wasn't up to his duty, but it was time the others began to realize just how much Con had sacrificed for each and every one of them, and how much he suffered.

"Ulrik," Rhys pressed.

Finally, Ulrik met Rhys's troubled gaze. "I doona know how Con survived the first thousand years alone while the rest of you slept. I was too busy dealing with my own issues after being banished from Dreagan and no' having my magic so I could shift. I know that I barely survived. I can no' imagine that it was any easier for Con."

Rhys made a face and looked away, his unease evident.

Ulrik continued. "Eventually, Con began writing in journals. I only recently discovered that. I've no idea how long he's done it, but based on the number I saw, it has been for a verra, verra long time."

"Bloody hell," Rhys murmured.

"He had two different sets. A leather one he used for his thoughts on Dreagan, his role as King of Kings, and everything to do with us. And red ones he used for Rhi."

Rhys shifted his feet, visibly distressed as he—like Ulrik—tried to imagine what it had been like to know that your mate was out there, but not be able to get to her because you had given her up.

Ulrik cleared his throat, emotion choking him. "After the last mating ceremony, I noticed that Con wasna at the party. I found him in his chambers. He'd destroyed everything. His clothes were in disarray, and he was well on his way to getting drunk as he threw the red journals into the hearth, burning them."

Rhys's head jerked to Ulrik. "Did he burn all of them?"

"I doona know."

"We need one. Maybe showing Rhi will let her see how much he pines for her."

Ulrik shrugged one shoulder. "Maybe. It could work. We'd have to get a journal away from Con first, and I doona think he'll let that happen. I didna even realize he had them."

"Neither did I. He's always kept to himself. I thought that was how he wanted it."

"He spends time by himself because he doesna want any of you to see how much he worries or hurts. When he's alone, he allows all the emotions he hides from everyone to show."

Rhys snorted. "That's insane. Does he think we willna believe him strong enough if he shows emotion?"

"When have you ever seen him show emotion?" Ulrik asked.

Rhys thought about it for a moment and then shrugged. "It's a rare thing. It's how I've always known him to be."

"Because that's how he's always been. It wasna something that was taught to him, or even something that someone told him he should do. It's just Con."

"I didna know. I'm no' sure any of us did."

Ulrik slapped Rhys on the back and dropped his hand. "That's how he wanted it. I've known him since before he was King of Dragon Kings or even King of Golds. He had verra few that he called *friend*. No' because he didna want them, but because so many didna understand him."

"But you did."

"Aye. I didna care that he wasna like me or others. He was honorable and loyal. Someone I could confide in about anything, knowing he wouldna tell a soul. He's one of the most giving dragons you'll ever meet."

Rhys grinned. "He once said the same thing about you."

Ulrik smiled as he thought about his friendship with Con. "Despite everything that transpired between us, he will always be a brother to me. I hated him for banishing me and taking away my magic, but only because I couldna face the fact that I'd brought all of that on myself. I told him all of this already, and he's forgiven me for everything I did."

"What do we do now? Out of all of us, Con deserves to be happy. I used to hold out hope that it could happen between him and Rhi again, but after what I just witnessed, I'm no' so sure."

"Con told Rhi things that he hadna before. There isna a scenario that would've turned out differently. Trust me. That's what Con does. He would've thought of every angle, every word that might have turned things his way. I saw the resignation on his face."

Rhys pulled a face. "Then he shouldna have said anything."

"The truth has been kept from Rhi for long enough. It's time she—and everyone else—knows the facts."

Rhys squeezed the bridge of his nose with his thumb and forefinger. "When she came to Dreagan and told Con that Usaeil had been the one to end them, I was so angry. But she came to Con." He dropped his hands. "Why? Why would she do that when she must have been hurting?"

"Because she loves him. And where else could she go? She wanted confirmation from him, and while she might no' admit it, she needed him."

"It doesna make sense to me."

"When has love ever made sense?" Ulrik questioned.

Rhys threw up his hands in defeat. "Never. It makes people do and say stupid things."

"But it also gives people the strength to carry on when they would otherwise falter."

"Hope. Love gives us hope," Rhys said.

Ulrik nodded slowly. "It's that hope that Con has been holding onto for so long."

"He's changed. It's recent, but he isna the same."

"Nay, he isna." And that's all Ulrik would say on the matter.

Rhys stared at him for a long moment. "Just tell me if we need to be worried."

Ulrik lowered his gaze to the ground as he thought over the last few weeks with Con and the conversations they'd had. Finally, he looked at Rhys again. "He's in a place he hasna been before. For the first time, we're the ones who need to be strong for him."

"In other words, we need to be worried." Rhys's expression turned concerned. "Did you intend to tell anyone?"

"No' until I had no other choice. Right now, Con

doesna see a way out for himself. The only one who can pull him out of this is Rhi."

"Then she needs to know that."

Ulrik was shaking his head before Rhys finished speaking. "That can only happen if she finds her way there herself. Con will know if she's forced, and it'll do more harm than good."

"We can no' just sit back and watch this train wreck without doing something," Rhys stated angrily.

Ulrik gave him a flat look. "What do you think I'm doing out here?"

Rhys narrowed his eyes at him. "How did you know that Rhi was here?"

"Magic," Ulrik said with a grin. "I cast a spell to alert me every time Rhi appears and where. And before you ask, nay, I wouldna have brought you had I no' run into you on the way here."

"You doona want me to tell the others, do you?"

"I doona like keeping secrets, but Con doesna need everyone checking in on him or asking him questions. And he would find out that everyone knows. It's better this way."

Rhys nodded, his lips twisting ruefully. "I agree with you."

"There is one thing we need to prepare for."

"What's that?"

"Phelan."

Rhys winced. "Och, that willna be good. He's going to be furious with Con."

"And with everyone else for no' telling him."

"You still doona think we should go to him now?"

Ulrik hesitated as he thought over the options. "Nay, I doona think we should."

"Con told Rhi the truth. She's now Queen of the Light,

and we've no word yet on Usaeil or Moreann. This is a fucking fabulous week," Rhys said sarcastically before he turned and stalked away.

Ulrik watched him go, then retraced his steps to find Con still standing in the same place. No doubt he was deep in thought, rooted in his memories of better times with Rhi. The more Ulrik saw, the more concerned he became. Con was going down a path of no return, and he needed to make an about-face soon before they lost him forever. If only Ulrik knew what to say or do to achieve that.

Con had never failed them. Ulrik wasn't going to fail Con now.

CHAPTER ELEVEN

What was she supposed to feel now? Anger coiled within Rhi like a snake, ready to strike at Con—or anyone—who had wronged her as she paced the empty queen's chambers at the Light Castle.

But was she right?

She wasn't sure anymore. Everything was so jumbled and tangled into a motley collection in her mind that she couldn't discern one emotion or thought from the other. How was she supposed to fight Usaeil or Moreann in such a condition?

The answer was simple: she couldn't.

Her thoughts were everywhere except where they needed to be. Without warning, she flashed back to her recent meeting with Con. She'd known it was a bad idea to go to Dreagan, but she hadn't had a choice. She'd hoped to come away with information about her family, which she had. But she'd gotten so much more than that.

The one question she'd had from the moment Darius had told her the relationship was over was: why? It didn't matter how many times she pleaded for an answer or in what way, there had never been a reply. It's what had propelled her into such despair that she'd only wanted the pain to stop.

When she met Con, her once happy and carefree life had exploded with ecstasy and joy unlike anything she'd ever known before. That brief time had been the absolute best of her long life. And without warning, it had ended.

She understood misery. At least, she thought she did. She'd been taken by surprise by the depth of her heartache and despondency. Worse, she hadn't wanted to come out of it since Con wouldn't be there to comfort her.

Rhi remembered making the decision to leave the realm and venturing into the Fae Realm without paying attention to where she was. It wasn't a good place. She hadn't necessarily wanted to end her life, but she knew she couldn't remain on Earth. Rhi simply had nowhere else to go. She went to the only other place she knew— and in so doing, had put her very life on the line. The planet had turned on them, killing everything. It seemed a fitting place to be. Except she'd had no idea that a few Dark were there, as well. They attacked her.

Since Rhi hadn't been prepared, she'd been wounded. Her body had begun to fail on her. Except she hadn't died. To this day, she didn't understand it. All she knew was that the raging storms that alternated between rain and wind seemed to match her mood. She didn't know how long she stayed there.

One day, she woke, and she was back on Earth. She didn't know how she'd gotten here, but she wasn't alone. Balladyn was by her side. He hadn't asked questions, hadn't said a word. He'd merely reached for her. She'd gone into his arms and finally let the tears fall until there were none left to cry.

When she raged at the world and the unfairness of

it all, he'd remained beside her, giving her comfort and helping her find her way again. He'd forced her to live again. She'd fought him every step of the way, but he didn't relent, didn't stop pushing her.

Then, one day, she finally began to live again.

During that time, she hadn't a clue that he loved her. Balladyn never said anything. He had been her friend as she mourned her lost love. She honestly didn't know if she could've done the same if the positions were reversed.

He'd loved her for all those years and hadn't told her. When she believed him dead during one final skirmish with the Dark, she'd honestly thought her life was over. She had lost everyone. Her family, her friends, and Con.

But, somehow, she'd managed to carry on.

Then, hundreds of years later, she went back to helping the Dragon Kings. She still didn't know why. Actually, that was a lie. She knew why. It was always the same reason—Con. She might have told herself and anyone who wanted to know some fabricated tale about helping friends, but the real reason was Con. She had to see him. It had been the worst—and best—decision of her life.

Being around him allowed her to finally put away her feelings for him. She became an expert at compartmentalizing her memories and sentiments. And it had worked.

For a while.

She got to see her friends at Dreagan, and she made new ones. They asked for her help, which had been something she'd never thought would occur.

And, she'd found Balladyn again. While he had turned Dark, her friend was still alive. And that had been enough for her. However, it wasn't for him. He had trapped her and bound her with the Chains of Mordare because he blamed her for his becoming Dark. It was ludicrous, and she'd told him so, but it was easy to hold onto hate.

Being in that prison, feeling the darkness creep into her, had been one of the most dreadful experiences of her life. The chains prevented her from using her magic and allowed the darkness to take root within her.

She had refused to turn Dark, refused to give in to the seductive and wicked things the darkness offered. She began second-guessing herself, wondering if she was even strong enough to stand against the darkness. Rhi hoped that someone would save her, but she realized the only person who could save her was herself.

Then, in a surprising twist of Fate, she'd broken the un-breakable Chains of Mordare. The force of it had knocked her unconscious, and—as she found out later—had taken out a huge section of the dungeon in the process.

A Dragon King had rescued her, but it hadn't been Con. It had been Ulrik. More and more, the Kings turned to her. Many times, she offered to help, but there were other times when they came to her. She felt as if she were making progress and really getting on with her life.

She and Balladyn eventually made peace—of sorts. He'd declared his love, and she, realizing that she didn't want to spend her life alone, took a chance. She loved Balladyn, but she wasn't *in love* with him. She could've had a nice life with him, but it wouldn't have been the same kind as she would've had with Con.

The rug was jerked out from under her yet again when she learned about Con and Usaeil. She was hurt and angry. But when she wanted to lash out at him, she realized she couldn't. For one thing, they had been over for hundreds of years. And two, she had moved on with Balladyn—and Con hadn't said a word about it.

How could she go to him and say anything about

who he was with—even if it was Usaeil? It hurt, by the stars, did it hurt. But she had done the same to him. And she knew she'd hurt him, given his disregard of Balladyn.

Yet when she had turned to Con to save Balladyn, he hadn't hesitated. It had been within his power to let Balladyn die, but Con had given him life instead.

When she had been hurt, it had been Con who carried her from the fight with Mikkel to Dreagan and spoke to her, bringing her back to consciousness. He was always there in some form or fashion. Always.

Yet she'd never had any answers as to why he'd ended their affair. Now that she finally knew the truth, she wished she didn't. To realize that he had chosen the Kings over her was a blow she hadn't been expecting.

It had been easy to lay the blame at Usaeil's feet before, and he could've let her continue believing that. Usaeil certainly thought she was the reason they'd broken up. But Con had told Rhi the truth, every ghastly syllable of it.

Now, she understood the saying the mortals had about ignorance being bliss. She felt worse now that she knew the truth, though it didn't let Con off the hook. In fact, it made her even angrier with him.

But should it? He was King of Dragon Kings. From the beginning, he'd made no bones about telling her how important his brethren and Dreagan were to him. Then, she'd fallen head over heels for him, and like anyone in her position, she'd put him first and believed that he'd done the same for her. That hadn't been the case.

To be fair, however, the Kings had suffered quite a bit. But she didn't understand why they couldn't have remained together. She clenched her fists, putting a stop to her thoughts of Con. She'd go around and around until her head ached if she continued in this vein. No, she needed to think about the reason for her visit to Dreagan.

Now she knew that Rolmir had spoken to Con. She'd never known that her brother had gone to Dreagan, though it seemed like something he would do. However, she didn't have any more knowledge of her father than she had before. Actually, that wasn't true. Con had said he knew that her father hadn't approved of them.

Con was very good at reading people, and after the things she'd recalled in her memories that matched his feelings, there was little doubt her father hadn't wanted them together. But would he have gone to such lengths as to join the Others to stop it?

She might not know his reasoning for becoming an Other, but the simple fact was that he had. It was time she came to terms with that. His reasons didn't matter, only the fact that he had done it. If he were still alive, she would be fighting against him. Thankfully, that wasn't the case. In her mind, the Others were all but finished now. With the help of Noreen, Cain's mate, they had been disbanded.

It was ironic that Con had ended their relationship because none of the Kings had mates. Now, he was one of the few who *didn't* have a mate.

"He still loves you."

Balladyn's last words to her filled her mind once more. She wanted to believe that Con might still love her, but she'd held out hope for so long, she couldn't do it any longer. It hurt too bloody much.

She wanted to move on. Then again, she'd wanted to move on for centuries now, and she hadn't been able to. What did that say about her? She'd even had a chance to be happy again. A part of her really wished she'd been able to love Balladyn as he loved her, but she hadn't. And she cared about him too much to lie.

For so long, Rhi had known exactly what to do. She'd had a purpose in the Queen's Guard, and she'd wanted to be captain. She'd found her way again with the Kings, and even the Reapers, but that had only led to more heartache and pain.

Had she wronged Fate somehow to be set upon such a path? If there was a way for her to make up for whatever she'd done or said, she would do it in a heartbeat. But no one was here to tell her how to fix it.

Balladyn was gone now. While he wasn't dead, he was a Reaper, which meant that she might never see him again. The fact that Death had allowed him to talk to her briefly had been a gift. Though she now knew he wouldn't answer her if she called for him—even if it was because there was a chance he knew something about her father that could help in her quest to end the Others for good.

She made her way into the bedroom and stared at the emptiness that matched her mood. She was acting queen, perhaps she should look the part in order to convince Usaeil and everyone else that she took this position seriously. Rhi snapped her fingers. A large bed appeared with a white headboard that had gold studs along the top.

Since she had no desire to wear anything other than her usual black, she decided to add that color into the mix. Another snap of her fingers had a black and white harlequin patterned comforter appearing on the bed, complete with pillow shams and decorative pillows in black, black and gold, and white. A long, white bench rested at the foot of the bed.

It had been a while since she had done such decorating,

and she discovered it was rather restorative. Rhi continued decorating in the bedroom, adding a white table with black and gold accents, along with two matching chairs. Near the large windows, she chose a plush black rug and dozens of white, gold, and black pillows in an array of sizes spread around the black, high-backed chairs with gold legs.

When she finished with the pictures and turned to her closet, she had a smile on her face.

Maybe this was exactly what she needed.

DONNA GRANT

CHAPTER TWELVE

Isle of Skye

There was something about Skye that drew people. Most didn't know why, but Isla did. It was the call of the Druids. If there was even the tiniest bit of magic within a person, they felt compelled to go to Skye.

She wished her visit wasn't one based on worry. It wasn't her first time on Skye, and she knew it likely wouldn't be her last. The Skye Druids were formidable enemies and the best allies.

"Do you feel anything?" Hayden asked as they got out of the Range Rover.

She shook her head as they met at the front of the SUV. "If you're asking about the Ancients, they've been silent since we left the castle."

"I doona have a good feeling about this," he murmured.

Evie tucked her curly, brown hair behind her ear as the wind picked up. "I love this place."

"I know," Malcolm told her as he put an arm around her.

Isla met Evie's blue eyes. All the Druids from MacLeod Castle had wanted to come, but it was decided that only one other would accompany Isla. She had chosen Evie since she could speak to stones, something several others on Skye could do.

Malcolm and Hayden walked ahead to scout the area. Every Warrior at the castle had been on high alert since Isla had told them that war was brewing. Each of them had fought at least one powerful *drough* and had come out victorious, but none of them wanted another war.

"What are you looking for?" Evie asked in a whisper.

Isla shrugged and wrapped her arms around herself. A chill had settled over her, curling its cold fingers around her the moment the Ancients had spoken this last time. "I don't know. The Ancients said the Skye Druids needed protecting."

"Every time you say that, I can't help but think that something has happened to them."

"Wouldn't we have heard through the trees, the wind, or the rocks?" Isla asked.

Evie shrugged. "Maybe it isn't reaching us. Or perhaps something is preventing it."

Isla gathered her long, black hair over one shoulder and braided it to keep it out of her face since the wind was whipping it everywhere. As she did, Evie suddenly turned and walked away.

They were far from a main road. Isla hadn't known where to go, but something had told her not to go straight to the Skye Druids, though now she doubted her feelings. She kept her eyes on Evie, who continued walking through the tall grass and wildflowers until she stopped and squatted down.

"Malcolm. Hayden," Isla said as she started running to Evie.

Malcolm reached Evie first with the incredible speed

all Warriors had. He put out a hand, stopping both Isla and Hayden as they approached. Malcolm's gaze was locked on his wife as he observed her.

Isla and Hayden silently moved closer to find a brook. The water rolled over smooth stones of all sizes. Evie had placed her hand on one of the stones, her eyes closed. Several minutes passed before Evie jerked her hand back. Malcolm was there, gathering his wife in his arms. She clung to him, but her head turned to Isla.

"What is it?" Isla asked.

Evie was visibly shaken. "We have to be careful. There's danger here for all Druids."

"On Skye?" Hayden asked, frowning. "This place has always been a refuge for Druids."

"Not anymore," Evie said.

There was more, Isla was sure of it, but it didn't seem Evie could put it into words right now. She needed time to digest what she'd learned, but it changed nothing. The Ancients wanted the Skye Druids protected, and they had come to Isla to make sure of it.

"That's all I need to hear," Hayden said as he took Isla's hand. "We're going back."

She pulled him to a stop and shook her head when he looked at her. "No. We're not."

"Isla, I'm no' going to lose you."

"And I don't want to lose you, but we have to do this."

Malcolm released a sigh. "She's right. Trust me, Hayden, I'm with you on wanting to return to the castle, but something has happened here that caused the Ancients to speak to Isla about it. We need to find out what it is."

Isla jerked her chin to Evie. "Watch over her, Malcolm."

"We aren't splitting up," Evie said. "We stay together."

Hayden's lips twisted. "I agree with that."

Isla caught Evie's gaze. "Are you up for this?"

Because you've already seen what we haven't, was left unsaid.

"Yes," Evie said as she lifted her chin.

There was still a healthy dose of fear in her eyes, and it shook Isla to her core. "Okay," Isla agreed.

Hayden shook his head. "Look, I know Evie saw something that frightened her, but I'm no' going anywhere until I know what it is we're heading into."

"Evie would tell us if we were walking into a trap," Malcolm said defensively.

Isla turned toward Hayden and put her hands on his chest. When he looked down at her with his black eyes, she said, "Malcolm is right."

"He might be, but that doesna erase the fact that something happened," Hayden said.

Evie's voice rose over Malcolm's, silencing him. "Hayden's right. You should all know. Two Druids are missing."

Isla had feared they were dead, so at least the news wasn't that dire. Still, it wasn't good that Druids were missing. "I think it's time we find Corann."

"I like the sound of that," Hayden stated as he turned Isla toward the SUV.

Hayden got behind the wheel and glanced her way when she closed the front passenger door. Isla gave him a nod. He started the engine and began the drive to the hidden location where some of the Skye Druids lived.

Many chose to live out in the open for anyone to find them. It was their way of welcoming other Druids who came to the isle. Many more wanted to live in isolation, away from those searching for Druids or magic.

Corann, the leader of the Skye Druids, had created an environment for both sides. Isla didn't have a clue how old he was. He was mortal, of that she was sure, but he somehow continued to look as if he were in his sixties.

The Warriors were immortal, and all those who called MacLeod Castle and the surrounding area home hadn't wanted visitors. So, Isla had created the shield around the castle that hid it and those within it from the outside world. Any mortal who stayed within the shield was, for all intents and purposes, immortal.

Since the Warriors didn't want their wives to leave and possibly die, it had become somewhat of a prison. The Dragon Kings stepped in and gave each of the Druids a ring, which allowed them to be immortal with their Warriors. Could Corann have something similar? Isla wasn't sure.

She rubbed her finger along the ring on her right hand as they neared the Druids' hidden compound. No one rushed out to greet them, but that wasn't abnormal. However, Corann was usually there since he somehow always knew when visitors arrived.

"I doona have a good feeling about this," Malcolm said.

Hayden put the vehicle in park and shut off the engine. "Nor do I."

Isla opened the door and stepped out. A feeling of dread came over her so swiftly that she nearly dropped to her knees because of it. She gripped the door to keep herself upright. Before she knew it, Hayden was by her side.

His black eyes searched hers. "I feel it, as well."

"We need to find Corann," she said.

He nodded and waited for Malcolm and Evie to join them. The small village was quiet. No dogs barked, no children played. It looked utterly deserted, except for a few horses and cattle in a distant field. When Isla looked in the opposite direction, she spotted a herd of sheep.

"Maybe they've gone to the Fairy Pools," Evie said in a whisper.

Hayden kept his voice low as he told them, "We're no' alone."

They walked through the center of the village, and with every step, Isla felt her anxiety rise—along with her panic. This was the one place not even Deirdre dared to mess with because the Druids were so powerful. What could've happened to create such an atmosphere?

The four of them came to a halt when a woman stepped into the road. Her vibrant red hair was like a flame against the blue skies and her gray shirt. She was young, probably in her mid-twenties. Isla lifted a hand in greeting, but the woman didn't return the gesture.

Isla began walking to her. She moved slowly, as did Hayden and the others, until only a dozen feet separated them. "Hello," Isla said.

"Leave," the woman stated, her green eyes locked on Isla. "Leave now."

Isla shook her head. "I can't. The Ancients sent me."

The woman issued a loud snort. "Too little, too late."

"What happened to the Druids who are missing?" Malcolm asked.

Green eyes slid to Malcolm. "How do you know about that?"

"The stones told me," Evie explained.

The woman's shoulders relaxed slightly. She swallowed and shook her head. "Bad things are happening here. You should leave before it's too late. Go now."

"We're no' going anywhere until we speak to Corann," Hayden stated.

The woman's eyes moved to him. "Then you'll be here for a very long time. He was one of those taken."

It felt as if someone had kicked Isla in the stomach. "There's no way Corann could've been taken."

"He was."

Evie walked to the woman and smiled. "I'm Evie. My husband is Malcolm, and that's Isla and Hayden. We're from MacLeod Castle."

"I know who you are," the woman said. She drew in a shaky breath. "I'm Rhona."

Isla went to her and smiled. "Would you please tell us what happened? The Ancients didn't convey much. They only told me the Druids here needed protection."

Rhona glanced at the cottages and buildings surrounding them. "This used to be a place of safety, but it isn't anymore."

"When was Corann taken?" Malcolm asked.

The redhead clasped her hands together before her. "Yesterday. He went out looking for Daniel, who hadn't been seen in over twenty-four hours."

"Do you know where they could've gone or where they may have been taken?" Hayden asked.

Rhona shook her head, the ends of her long red hair lifting with a gust of wind. "A few of us went looking for Corann, but we found nothing."

"Let's start by having you show us the direction you took," Evie suggested.

Isla nodded. "That's a good idea."

Rhona pointed to the right. "That way."

"Will you join us?" Isla asked.

It was obvious that Rhona wanted to refuse, but at the last minute, a resigned expression came over her face. "I'll take you, but I won't stay out there."

"We'll protect you," Malcolm said.

Hayden released his god then, his skin turning deep

red, small horns protruding from the blond hair atop his head. His eyes went completely crimson, filling in with color from corner to corner. He clicked his red claws together before a fireball appeared in his hand. "Aye. Let whatever is out there come for us. I dare them."

Isla watched Rhona as Malcolm also released his god, his skin and eyes turning maroon with sparks of electricity firing off him. He gave a nod to Rhona.

The Druid was apprehensive but turned and said, "Follow me."

CHAPTER THIRTEEN

He was an idiot.

A bloody fool who deserved everything he'd gotten and anything that was yet to come.

Con shoved the file on his desk. No matter how hard he tried, he couldn't think of anything but Rhi and their conversation. He put his elbows on the desk and dropped his head into his hands.

The parts of himself that he always managed to control—be it his temper, anxiety, or anything else— were unmanageable now. He fought to curb his anger and keep from shifting into his true form, raging at the heavens. He struggled to keep his sorrow in check, strove not to let the past—or the present—torment him.

He'd always been a master of his emotions.

Always.

But not anymore. He could feel his authority slipping away. Or maybe he'd never had control. Perhaps it had all been an illusion, a lie he told himself to keep going.

He slammed his hands on the desk in a bid to stop his inner voice from talking. But it didn't listen.

Con spun his chair around and angrily got to his feet.

He looked out his window, gazing at the beloved land that had always consoled him. Even that did nothing for him now.

A knock came from his door. Con dropped his chin to his chest. Why couldn't everyone leave him alone as they usually did? Why must they all want to check on him? It wasn't like he'd gotten any better since he'd walked into the manor an hour ago.

"It's Fallon. We need to talk."

He slowly turned to the door. With a thought, Con released the spell that locked the door and let it swing open. Fallon's face was drawn, worry filling his dark green eyes. The leader of the Warriors said nothing as he walked into the office and softly closed the door behind him.

Then he faced Con and released a long breath. "I come with dire news."

"Is everyone okay at the castle? Do you need us?"

Fallon shook his head and held up a hand to halt Con's words. "It isna anyone at MacLeod Castle." The Warrior's lips pressed together, and he looked away briefly. "Ever since Isla heard from the Ancients about a threat, all the Druids at the castle have tried to use their gifts to learn something."

"I gather they've no' had any luck," Con said.

Fallon put his hands on the back of the chair before him. "No' a single one of them. I'd wondered if perhaps all was good again."

Con inwardly winced. "My apologies. I've been a bit wrapped up here. I should've told you about Usaeil being alive and about Moreann, the leader of the Others."

"Doona be," the Warrior stated. "I know how it is to be a leader and have the weight of all of that on my shoulders. This didna involve the Warriors."

"But it did involve the Druids. At least in how Moreann and the Others found the Druids on this realm to join them."

Fallon shrugged. "My point is that I doona feel any ill will toward you. Honestly, I was quite happy to no' have the Warriors and Druids brought into things, though I knew it was only a matter of time until we were."

"You had enough to deal with over the past few centuries. We didna help because you and yours had it well under control."

"Thank you," he said with a brief grin. "It certainly never seemed like it."

Con chuckled, knowing exactly how Fallon felt. "I've been there. Hell, I'm there now. But I doona think you came to talk about such things. I see the concern in your eyes. What's going on?"

"The Ancients spoke to Isla again."

Now that got Con's attention. "What did they say?"

"That the Skye Druids needed to be protected."

Con frowned as he walked around his desk. "Is she sure of what she heard? The Druids on Skye are no' the ones I'd be worried about. It's all the other Druids around the world."

"That was my thought as well, but Isla was adamant. She, Hayden, Evie, and Malcolm drove to Skye first thing this morning. As soon as I heard from them, I came here."

"Tell me," Con urged.

Fallon blew out a breath. "Two Druids have been taken in two days. Corann went out looking for the first Druid yesterday, and he hasna been seen since."

Fury ripped through Con. He didn't have to search his mind since he knew exactly who was to blame. "It's Usaeil."

It was Fallon's turn to frown. "What do you mean? Usaeil and the Light Fae had an agreement with the Skye Druids. She would never harm them."

"That was before Usaeil began killing Druids to take their magic, making her even stronger."

Fallon's face fell. "Bloody hell," he murmured. His brows raised briefly. "I would've worried about the Druids on their own. But . . . those on Skye? That doesna make sense."

"We learned a few months ago that Usaeil was adding Druid magic to her own. One of the mates here is a Druid, and she was able to stop Usaeil's attack against her because Gemma has the ability to halt Druid magic. And since she stopped Usaeil—"

"Then Usaeil used Druid magic," Fallon finished. He walked around the chair and slowly sank into it.

Con put his hands in his pants' pockets. "Henry and Esther also found a Druid killed by Usaeil in Spain."

"No Druids are safe, then."

"The combination of Fae and Druid magic was enough for Usaeil to withstand dragon fire meant to kill Moreann."

A muscle in Fallon's jaw jumped as determination filled his green eyes. "Tell me what you know about Moreann and the Others."

"Moreann is the one who brought the mortals to Earth. Everyone on her realm is born with magic, but suddenly, that began to change. She found our realm and brought some of the people without magic here to see what we'd do."

Fallon grimaced. "And you let them stay."

"Aye. It was her first step in bringing us down and taking over the realm. Noreen, a Fae and previous member of the Others, came to us for help. She's the one who told us that Moreann used some verra powerful spells to make herself immortal. My guess is that is one of the reasons the magic began fading on their realm."

"It makes sense." Fallon bent his leg and rested his ankle on his other knee. "You trust Noreen, I'm guessing."

"She's mated to Cain."

"I see," Fallon said with a nod. "If anyone would know Moreann's secrets, it would be someone from within the Others."

"Usaeil was part of them. The original Fae, actually, but she and Moreann had a falling out. Moreann is the one who took Usaeil's body before Rhi could sever her head. That allowed the resurrection spell Usaeil put in place to revive her, which is how she's still alive."

Fallon ran a hand down his face. "Bloody hell."

"With Noreen's and Rhi's help, we set a trap for Moreann. We would've killed her, but Usaeil showed up at the last minute and took her, besting our magic."

"Since I know that dragon magic is the most powerful on this realm, then Usaeil must have had Druid magic mixed with hers."

"Aye, I'm thinking a significant amount. The fact that she's continuing to kill Druids tells me that the magic doesna stay. It must get depleted when she uses it."

Fallon dropped his foot to the floor and sat forward. "She'd need a continuous supply of Druids, then."

"And the stronger those Druids are, the longer the magic will last."

"That must be why she decided to strike at the Skye Druids. We'll help, but the Druids there are no' keen on outsiders."

Con drew in a deep breath. "Understandably. There *is* one who can help, however."

"You mean Rhi. Shall I call for her? Surely, she'll come if she knows it's important. You did mention that she aided you recently."

"Before you do, there is something else you need to know."

Fallon got to his feet. "Is she all right?"

"Oh, aye," Con told him. "Rhi is fine. She's taken over as Queen of the Light."

"Well, damn. I can say that I'm pleased by that news, especially after she disappeared. But I get the impression there's more."

Con lowered his gaze. "There is. Much more. Rhi is . . ." He stopped and made himself look at Fallon. "She's rather . . . irate . . . with me."

"Rhi has never really cared for you. I always assumed it had something to do with you interfering in things between her and her lover."

"You could say that." Con simply looked at the Warrior, letting Fallon come to the conclusion on his own.

"Shite," Fallon said after a long moment. He ran his hand through his dark brown hair and looked away before his gaze slid back to Con. "*You* were her lover?"

Con couldn't find his voice, so he nodded instead.

"Now it all makes sense. Bloody hell," he said, his voice heavy with surprise. "Do you no' think Rhi will help?"

"She will because she cares. However, I think, given the circumstances, the request would be better coming from you."

Fallon swallowed, disbelief still etched on his features. "It's none of my business, but . . . why?"

It wasn't any of his business. Con could tell Fallon that, and he started to, but then he didn't. He turned his head to the side and looked at the floor. "I've recently told a couple of Kings, and I'm sure the others know by now. And I just told Rhi the truth today. It wasna Usaeil who ended things for us, though Usaeil likes to believe she was responsible."

"You loved Rhi, did you no'?" Fallon asked.

Con's throat tightened with emotion. He glanced at Fallon. "Verra much. It's why I couldna break it off with her myself. I knew if I tried, I'd never be able to do it. She called me a coward for how I handled things. She's right. I was."

"I doona claim to be your friend, but we've had enough dealings over the years for me to come to know the person you are. Every decision you make, everything you do is for the Dragon Kings and Dreagan. If I had to guess, the decision to end things with Rhi was, as well."

Con nodded slowly. "None of the others had mates. I could see the beginnings of jealousy, and I didna want to make an already impossible situation worse by flaunting my love in front of them."

"So, you put aside your happiness."

"It was the hardest thing I've ever done."

Fallon shook his head. "You're a better man than I am. I wouldna have been able to do it, but I can see why you did. I'd have wanted to do the same thing. Except I wouldna have had the strength to do it."

"I've carried the truth for too long. And the secret. Actually, all of the Kings have. I know Phelan has asked multiple times."

"He's even asked Rhi, so if he wants to get mad, he'll have to be angry at her, as well. I'll handle Phelan."

Con frowned as he said, "You doona have to. I'll listen to everything he wants to say to me. I understand that he thinks of Rhi as his sister."

"Fuck me." Fallon ran a hand through his hair again. "I know how much Rhi loved her King. Now that I know it was you, and I look back on the moments I saw the two of you together, it was right there the entire time."

Con chose to remain silent. What was there to say?

"You two will get back together," Fallon stated with certainty.

Con blew out a breath. "I'm afraid no'. She feels I betrayed our love and her."

"You were doing what you believed was right."

"That doesna matter. I love her. I'll always love her, but there is no chance for us. I've known that for a while, but I've no' wanted to admit it. Now, I have no choice."

Fallon swallowed and gave a nod of acceptance. "We might need the Kings on Skye."

"Then we will be there."

It was something to do, other than thinking about everything with Rhi. Though Con knew he'd have to see her again.

Maybe that was the very reason he was going.

CHAPTER FOURTEEN

Rhi spread out her hands in front of her, palms down, and looked at the horribly chipped nail polish—or what was left of it. She should take it off, but she couldn't bring herself to do it.

Nor could she seem to get her nails done again.

She wasn't sure what was wrong with her, but she didn't like looking at her nails. Maybe because it reminded her of how silly she used to be, thinking about what design she'd get, or what colors to use instead of more important things.

A tremor went through her when she heard her name being called from a great distance. She recognized Fallon's voice. The leader of the Warriors didn't call for her. If he was saying her name, then it must be important.

She looked around her rooms. Her mark was on them now. And with the spells she'd put in place, it didn't matter if she was at the Light Castle or not, she'd know if Usaeil ventured too close. But she wasn't going to just disappear as Usaeil had done again and again. She opened the door to inform the guards that she was leaving once more, only two new guards stood there.

One was a female who reminded Rhi of herself. The other was a male she couldn't help but notice had a thing for the female. For just a moment, Rhi thought about chatting with them, but she realized the folly of it at the last minute and instead told them that she would return shortly. The Queen's Guard, as well as the Light Army, knew to remain on high alert until things with Usaeil were finished once and for all.

Rhi used her magic to jump to the location where Fallon's voice had come from, but she made sure to arrive veiled in order to see who all was there. It took her half a second to realize that they had brought her to the Isle of Skye. She spotted Isla and Hayden, as well as Evie and Malcolm, along with Fallon and his wife, Larena, the only female Warrior. With them were Con, Rhys, Kiril, and Banan.

She ignored Con, who looked her way. He'd always been able to tell where she was, veiled or not. She had once found it endearing. Then again, that had been when they were together. Now, it just irritated the hell out of her.

Rhi moved to stand in front of Fallon and lowered the veil. "Quite a gathering you've got here."

"I'm glad you came," Fallon said. "We need your help."

Rhi quirked a brow. "Is that right? What could be so important that the Warriors, Druids, and Dragon Kings would call for me?"

"Usaeil," Con replied.

She paused before sliding her gaze to the right to meet his black eyes. While she wished she was past everything she'd recently learned from him, she wasn't. And seeing him now, hearing his voice, wasn't helping matters at all.

Unfortunately, she had no other choice but to talk to him—as she had for years.

"How?" she demanded.

Isla was the one who answered. "The Ancients brought me. They said the Druids needed protection."

"That's crazy. It would take an idiot to think they could get past the magic of the Druids here to hurt one."

"Two, actually," a woman said as she walked up. She had long, red hair and green eyes. "One is Corann."

"This is Rhona," Isla said. "She's the one who showed us the last place Corann and Daniel, the other missing Druid, were seen."

Rhi had known that Usaeil was killing Druids, but she'd never dreamed that Ubitch would come to Skye and break the bonds that she herself had formed thousands of years before. Then again, Rhi should've seen this coming.

"I underestimated her again," Rhi said.

Rhys crossed his arms over his chest. "We all did. Just as we've long thought that those at MacLeod Castle were safe. We can no' assume anything anymore."

"We're doing what we can to strengthen the shield around the castle, as well as putting up new wards," Fallon said.

Con then added, "We'll also add in our magic, if you'd like."

"Absolutely," Larena said with a nod.

"We're going to need to help each other," Evie replied.

Suddenly, everyone was looking at Rhi. She lifted her chin. "You don't need to ask. Of course, I'll help." Her gaze then returned to Con. "There is someone else we should ask."

"Great," Rhona scoffed. "Get ahold of anyone you can think of to help put a stop to Usaeil. Whatever loyalty we held toward the Fae is now gone."

Con stepped forward, blocking Rhona's path when

she started to leave. He didn't threaten her, simply stood in her way. Then, in a calm voice, he said, "Your pact with Usaeil is broken. It isna broken with the Light Fae."

"If they couldn't contain Usaeil, then why should we continue guarding the Fairy Pools?"

Rhi was shocked by Con's move. She hadn't thought he would defend her people for anything. Just one more thing she'd been wrong about today.

She cleared her throat to get Rhona's attention. "I know you're upset. Every Druid on Skye is upset. So are we. Otherwise, none of us would be here. We want to help, and we'll stop Usaeil. I nearly had her last time, but she got away. I'm going to make sure that doesn't happen again."

"Fine," Rhona said with a shrug. "I make no promises, however. If someone can take Corann, then they must be extremely powerful."

Rhi knew Rhona was right. Corann didn't display his power, but it was there. Someone with that kind of magic didn't keep such a strong community of Druids together unless he had the wherewithal to do it. Corann wasn't just intelligent, he also had immense power, just the kind of Druid Usaeil would need.

"Using the power of the Skye Druids is how she got to Moreann," Rhi mumbled.

Kiril's lips flattened before he said, "Aye."

"We think she might be gathering several so she can take whatever magic she wants when she needs it, instead of hunting," Banan said.

This couldn't be happening. Usaeil should be dead, her wicked deeds finished. Why was Rhi failing time and again when it came to Usaeil and Moreann? But now wasn't the time to think about that. She needed to focus on stopping Usaeil and finding the missing Druids. The Skye Druids needed Corann.

Rhi turned her head to Rhona. "I assume the Druids have set up barriers around the isle to stop Usaeil."

"We have," the Druid replied.

"It won't work." Rhi looked around at the others. "She's too strong. The only thing we can do is have spells that will alert us if she's here. I have them up at the Light Castle."

Larena grinned as she glanced at Fallon. "I do love the way Rhi thinks."

"Should the Druids take down the spells to stop her?" Isla asked.

"No," Rhi and Con said in unison.

Rhi didn't look toward Con as she turned to Isla. "Let Usaeil think that's all there is. If no spells are there to stop her, she'll suspect a trap. We can even begin to spread the word that Skye is closed to anyone with magic who isn't a Druid."

Malcolm's blond brows drew together. "Why? Could a Druid no' have taken the others?"

"Not someone like Corann," Rhona answered. Her head swung back to Rhi. "I think that's a great idea. We can get that going immediately."

"Do it," Rhi urged her. "And if any of us come here, we need to make sure we're no' seen."

Rhona nodded in agreement. "The roads and ferries are already being watched. We'll make sure we see the Warriors and Druids leave. None of the others on the isle know the Dragon Kings or Fae are here."

"It needs to remain that way," Rhys said.

A muscle ticked in Fallon's jaw. "Where is the best place to meet?"

"Here. This is my property, and I own another ten acres," Rhona told him. "I live alone, and I like my privacy, so there's no one else around."

Rhi listened intently, pleased that things were sorting themselves out at least somewhat. "That is all well and good, but there's still the fact that we need to find Usaeil. We couldn't locate her after her body was taken from the Light Castle. How are we to find her now?"

"You're the key to that," Con said.

Rhi smiled, understanding what Con was saying. "Then it's time I make my new reign something that will reach her ears."

"You shouldna be alone," Rhys said.

Rhi shot him a dark look. "If I die, then you know who killed me. And you'll know where to find her."

"The Light throne," Banan replied.

Rhi then looked toward Fallon. "I'd offer my magic at MacLeod Castle, but she'll recognize it. It's better if Usaeil believes my attention is elsewhere."

Fallon smiled at her. "I understand."

"What about Moreann?" Hayden asked.

Con's lips twisted. "I wish we had an answer for her, but we doona. Wherever Usaeil is, Moreann is. Whether they're joining forces, or Usaeil intends to kill the *mie*, I couldna tell you."

"Maybe it's time we ask Broc to look for them," Malcolm said to Fallon.

Fallon nodded. "It couldna hurt."

"We should all set out to search for them," Rhona said. "Eventually, one of us has to find them, right?"

Kiril made a sound in the back of his throat. "I sure the hell hope so."

"I don't want to leave," Isla said into the silence.

Rhi looked toward the petite Druid and smiled. "For this to work, you have to, because your husband isn't going to let you remain without him."

"Damn straight, I'm no'," Hayden replied before he kissed Isla's forehead.

Evie cleared her throat. "Then we should head back to the castle. If we need to return, Fallon can get us here quickly."

"How do I contact you?" Rhona asked as she looked between them all.

Rhi was the first to answer. "Just say my name. I'll come immediately."

Con held out his hand, palm up, and a mobile phone appeared. He handed it to Rhona. "There're two numbers in there. One is a direct line to Dreagan. The other rings MacLeod Castle."

"Thank you," the Druid said. She shot everyone an apologetic look. "I wasn't very friendly at first."

Hayden held up his hand to stop her. "We understand, lass. Your home was invaded, people you know and care about taken. Any of us would've acted the same."

"I don't know what we'll do if Corann doesn't return," Rhona added.

Isla smiled at her. "You're the only Druid who stepped up. It makes me think you'd be a good candidate to take his place."

"Not me," Rhona said with a shake of her head. "It'd have to be someone else."

Isla and Evie said farewell to Rhona before they began the trek back to their SUV with Hayden and Malcolm. Fallon and Larena then said their good-byes and teleported away.

Rhi spotted Ulrik's silver cuff on Con's wrist. He and the other Kings spoke briefly to Rhona and then gathered to leave. Just before he disappeared, his gaze landed on her.

It took Rhi a second to get herself back under control, and to realize that Rhona was still there. She looked at the Druid and said, "We'll defeat Usaeil. One way or another. Be strong and keep the community together. As Corann would do."

"I will," Rhona promised.

Rhi then jumped back to the Light Castle. She needed to make a big splash to get Usaeil's attention.

CHAPTER FIFTEEN

It really wasn't going to get any better with Rhi. Con would have to come to terms with that. Only he wasn't sure he could.

Then again, he doubted he'd be around long enough for it to be an issue.

He strode up the stairs after returning from Skye. Unfortunately, the Kings who had accompanied him were following him now. So much for being alone. At least none of the others were stopping him.

As soon as he walked into his office, he came to a stop. His gaze moved around the room, touching on each of the Kings there. Ulrik sat behind Con's desk, leaning back in the chair with his ankles crossed on the surface.

"Feel free to take care of the work while you're sitting there," Con told him.

Ulrik grinned. "You wouldna come to us, so we came to you."

"I see that."

Con leaned against the doorframe and crossed his arms over his chest. Usually, meetings such as this took place in Dreagan Mountain in the largest cavern. But this wasn't just any meeting, and he should've expected this.

"Is this some kind of intervention?" Con asked.

"You could say that," Banan said as he walked past Con into the office.

Ulrik reached down beside him and picked up something before he placed a bottle of whisky on the desk. "I thought this might go better with some flavor."

"Get on with it," Con demanded.

Hal said, "You've always been somewhat detached, but it's gotten worse."

"Much," Guy added. "It's unsettling because it's obvious you're struggling and willna let us help."

Banan snorted. "No' even letting us in the office."

Con almost pointed out they were in now, but he didn't.

"There's no denying this is about Rhi," Kellan stated.

Con met the Keeper of History's celadon eyes. "Is it?"

Kellan's eyes narrowed. "We both know it is."

"We're here to help," Tristan said. "In any way you need."

Kiril grinned. "Even if it's giving you a swift kick in the arse, as we're doing now."

Laith blew out a breath. "We appreciate what you did for us. I'd like to say that it was unnecessary, but I'm no' sure I can. I'll be the first to admit that I was a wee bit jealous of you and Rhi, but it had a lot to do with the fact that the dragons were gone, and we were in hiding. I didna ever expect any of us to be happy again."

"And there you were," Rhys continued, "smiling like I'd never seen you smile before. You were gloriously happy. We want you to know that none of us ever wanted to deny you that."

Con lowered his gaze to the floor. "I know."

"Nay, you doona," Rhys stated.

Warrick pushed away from his spot along the wall and walked to Con. He stopped, his cobalt gaze holding Con's. "You're no' acting like a King, which isna you. We want our King back."

With that, War stalked out of the office. Those who had spoken followed. Con barely had time to process what had happened before the others continued in the vein of the talk that had begun.

He listened to each and every one of them as they told him in no uncertain terms to buck up, attempted to bolster his confidence, or let him know that they didn't want him to go anywhere. Con had no idea how long it went on until the office finally grew quiet. When he looked around, there were only two people inside—Ulrik and Henry. Con hadn't even known that Henry was there.

Ulrik dropped his feet to the floor and poured three glasses of whisky. He rose and passed them around. "I think we all need this."

"Me more than you," Con pointed out.

Ulrik quirked a black brow. "You brought this on yourself."

"Maybe." Con lifted the glass to his lips and let the smooth liquor glide over his tongue and down his throat.

Henry looked at the amber liquid in his glass. "Every King here protected you and Rhi. None of them told me you were her lover, and I asked multiple times." The Englishman's hazel eyes lifted to Con. "None of them agreed with what you did, and there were times they told me that Rhi's King should do something to get her back. They're right. You should."

"I'm afraid that time is long past," Con said.

Ulrik shook his head. "I'm with Henry. There's still a chance."

Con didn't bother to argue the point. He knew the truth, even if they didn't.

"I've not been here long," Henry continued. "But even I've noticed the steps you've taken to protect Rhi from herself and others. I saw the lengths you went to when she was wounded. You love her, and she knows that, even if she can't or won't admit it right now. She will eventually."

Eventually. Con wouldn't last that long.

Henry shook his head. "You're a great man and King, Con. You offered me a home when you didn't have to. You've never once denied a single King their mate, even when you had reservations. You did that because you know what it is to be without Rhi. You didn't want any King to experience that pain."

"The fact that you've gone this long without Rhi is a testament to your strength of will and character," Ulrik said. "We see you, old friend. We always have. You've long thought you hid the pain, but we only let you think that."

Con couldn't look at either of them. His emotions rose up to choke him, and damn if his eyes didn't water a little. He hadn't wanted any of their words, but he couldn't deny that he had needed them.

"I'm not a Dragon King," Henry said. "Hell, I'm not even Scottish."

Con slid his gaze to Henry. "You're family. You've done more for us than I can ever repay."

"Then I hope you don't mind me saying that I know the plan. The one with Rhi making it known that she's now Queen of the Light to lure out Usaeil."

"I figured you would know about it," Con said with a shrug.

"It won't be enough."

Con frowned. "Sure, it will. Usaeil cares for nothing but power."

"That's where you're wrong," Ulrik chimed in.

Henry nodded his head of brown hair. "Exactly. It's going to take more. Will Usaeil be irritated that Rhi is on the throne? Without a doubt. But it won't be enough to bring her out into the open."

Con looked between the two of them. "Then what will?"

"You," Ulrik announced.

Henry met his gaze, nodding. "That's right. Usaeil kidnapped you in order to have you. If she thinks you and Rhi have let the past go and have rekindled your love, she won't be able to stand it. She'll show herself, giving you and Rhi a chance to end her once and for all."

Con parted his lips, trying to think of a reason this plan wouldn't work, but there was none. In fact, it was the best thing he'd heard all day.

"There's just one problem," he said.

Ulrik tossed back his whisky and swallowed, smacking his lips afterward. "Convincing Rhi it's the way to go."

"Precisely," Con replied.

Henry smiled then, the corners of his eyes crinkling. "This is your chance. Prove to yourself—and her—the lengths you'll go to for her. This could be your way back into her heart."

It could work. It really could.

Ulrik chuckled. "I can see the wheels turning in his head. Con's definitely on board."

"She'll have an argument for everything you say," Henry said. "Be prepared to respond in a way where she either thinks it's her idea, or that it's the only way to end things with Usaeil."

Ulrik refilled his and Con's glasses. "If nothing else, tell Rhi that the sooner they get Usaeil out of the picture, the sooner you'll return to Dreagan. Because this will have to take place at the Light Castle."

"Just think," Henry said, his smile widening, "Usaeil learning that Rhi not only has the throne but Con, as well. The very thing Usaeil wanted—the King of Dragon Kings and the Queen of the Light mating."

Con felt his lips turn up in a smile. "That will infuriate Usaeil."

"Yes, it will," Ulrik said with a wink. "And if anyone can convince Rhi to do this, it's you."

Con wasn't so sure, but he was going to find out. The three raised their glasses, clinking them together before tossing back the whisky.

"Thank you," Con told them. "I'll be thanking the others, as well."

Ulrik slapped him on the back. "What are friends for other than to kick your arse when it's needed?"

"You helped me. I wanted to do the same," Henry said.

Ulrik set his glass on the desk. "Well, my job is done. I'm going to find Eilish and have naked movie night."

"It isna night," Con pointed out.

Ulrik just grinned. "It never hurts to get started early. Doona leave without telling me. Otherwise, I might have to make an appearance at the Light Castle."

Con waved at him as Ulrik departed. Then his gaze turned to Henry. There was something in the Englishman's gaze that let Con know that Henry had figured out the secret about the weapon.

"Why did you want me to find the weapon when you could've found it yourself?" Henry asked.

Con sighed and reached for the bottle of whisky.

"When I became King of Kings, I was sworn to keep the weapon a secret, never telling anyone what it was or where it was hidden. I never liked the secret. Melisse is a person, no' a thing. I often wished I could ask her why she had been frozen. However, I'd been told that if woken, she would destroy all of us."

"Did you let her go?" Henry asked.

"Nay. But I didna follow her, either. I've always known where she was. As for why I tasked you with the job, all I can tell you is that it was a feeling. Every time I thought of going to find her or sending another King, it felt wrong. I also thought it might help if she had a friend who wasna a King. She has no reason to trust us, but she could trust you."

Henry held out his hand for the whisky and poured more into his glass. "You could've killed her at any time when she was here."

"Aye. I was told that if I ever felt we were threatened, that it would be better to take her life than put ours in her hands."

"But you didn't kill her."

Con walked to his chair and sat, leaning his arms on his desk. "I hate taking life, any life. There have been times I've no' had a choice, but I did with her."

"What if what you were told is true? What if she does end the Kings?"

"I asked myself that same question, but one thing I've learned in my long, long life, is that I can never go wrong by trusting my instincts. And my gut told me that Melisse deserved a life."

Henry thought about that for a moment. "She's incredible. I also seem to know where she's at, though I can't explain it. I don't have magic."

"Does it matter how it works?" Con asked.

One side of Henry's lips lifted in a grin. "No."

"Good."

"Is she a Druid? Mortal?"

Con glanced down at his desk. "I doona know why the two of you needed to meet, or what's in store for you. I did what I felt was right, and I sincerely hope you can convince Melisse to meet with me soon. I've told you more about her than I have anyone else, but I willna tell you what she is. That will be for Melisse to share."

CHAPTER SIXTEEN

Rhi walked the halls of the Light Castle. She didn't feel any different than the last time she had been here before Usaeil banished her. But everyone treated her differently now.

Naming yourself queen tended to do that.

She had yet to be approached by anyone who had put in a bid to take the throne, though she knew it was coming. No one who craved that kind of power gave it up so easily.

A few Fae stopped her to chat. She readily exchanged conversations because while she had never liked the machinations of court, she had learned to decipher them and work them to her advantage. And she was using every bit of that now.

She kept a smile on her face despite not feeling it. Not only was she still coming to terms with the truth that Con had finally decided to share, but Moreann and Usaeil were still out there. Then there were the Others, and last but not least, the Druids being taken and killed by Usaeil.

Her life had been simple once. Even when she joined

the Queen's Guard and took on a multitude of duties, she didn't stop to think about all the things someone in charge had to deal with.

"Someone like Con?"

The voice of the darkness surprised her. She hadn't heard it in hours, but she should've known that it wasn't gone. It was there, waiting for when she let down her guard. But no matter how she felt about it, the simple fact was that the darkness was right. Con dealt with the same things she was dealing with now—and more. He had been doing it for eons. How did he do it? How did he care about anything without being crushed under the weight of it all?

Her mind halted as she realized what she was doing. No. She wouldn't go down that road. If she did, she would find herself feeling for him again.

"It isn't good to lie to yourself," the darkness told her. *"You can't feel again for someone when you never stopped loving them."*

Rhi ducked into the first door she found and grabbed her head as she squeezed her eyes closed, hoping it would stop the voice and her thoughts. Seconds passed as she concentrated on her breathing. She lowered her arms and leaned her head back against the wall.

After another minute, she opened her eyes and saw shelves of books. The library. It was a place she used to come and walk, simply because she liked being around books. She didn't care what was inside them. There was something about the knowledge and creativity that went into each one, be it a history or a made-up story.

She walked farther into the library and looked up at the great glass dome above her. Sunlight glittered through it, casting an array of different colored lights in all directions. She slowly walked between the shelves, letting her fingers run along the spines of the books. With each step, she found a calm she hadn't felt in a long time. Gradually, she realized that the books were helping to center her.

Row upon row she walked, soaking up the tranquility and quiet. The library was huge, and she moved from one end to the other. She smiled when she thought about the many times she had found Balladyn in the library, his nose in one book or another. He'd been fascinated by the history of their kind, and he searched out books to give him more knowledge. Her thoughts then turned to the library he'd put together at the Dark Palace. She hoped that whoever took the throne didn't throw away the books.

Rhi walked around a shelf and came to a stop when she saw the door. It hadn't been shut all the way. Was this a new place? She couldn't remember there ever being a back room to the library.

Curious, she walked to the door and opened it. The room within was small, holding only a pedestal with a thick tome upon it. She crept closer, a frown forming when she saw the way the words moved around the pages.

"Well, this is new," she murmured. "Is this some trick by Usaeil to make sure only she can read this?"

Rhi set her hands on either side of the book without touching it. The words moved at such a rapid rate that it was difficult to make any of them out, but she knew it must be an ancient Fae language that had been lost to time.

No matter how hard she tried, Rhi couldn't make heads or tails of the pages. And she hadn't even looked at any of the others. Maybe she should start at the beginning. She touched the book, getting ready to close it so she could open it to the first page, when the words stilled. After a brief pause, they moved to different locations and then remained there.

Rhi ran her hand over the page in wonder. She was about to flip to the front of the book when she saw two words that all but screamed at her—*Dragon Kings*. After that, the indecipherable words were suddenly readable to her. With her heart thumping in her chest, she closed the book and turned it to the front. She slowly opened it again, half expecting the words to be moving once more, but they weren't. One page after another, she began to read. She only got a few pages in when she heard her name. It took her a moment to answer because they were calling for Queen Rhiannon.

She left the book open to the page she'd just read and walked from the room. She looked inside until the door was properly shut, double-checking it and then locking it with four different spells, each more complex than the last. Whatever that book was, whatever information it held, she was going to read every word. If the Dragon Kings were mentioned, then it must be important.

She ran through the library on silent feet and hastily reached the door. There, she paused and took several deep breaths before she lifted her chin and strolled out as if she had been walking the corridors the entire time.

"My queen," one of the guards called when he spotted her. "You have a visitor waiting in the throne room."

She couldn't imagine who would come see her. "Do you know who it is?"

"The King of Dragon Kings, Constantine."

Two visits in so short a time. Rhi wasn't sure what to think. "Thank you," she told the guard as she shifted directions and headed toward the throne room.

Her blood rushed in her ears. She tried to convince

herself that it was about the book, but this felt different. The only reason for her anxiousness was because it was Con. Maybe instead of pretending that she didn't love him, she should accept how she felt. She might then be able to get over him.

As she approached the throne room, she found that her hands were clammy, and her blood felt like ice in her veins. She was nervous. Nervous! The last time she'd felt like this was when she'd been with the Warriors at Charon's bar, and Con had arrived.

The guards opened the doors for her. As they parted, she saw Con turn toward her. He stood a few feet from the throne as if he had been looking at it.

Rhi waited until the doors were shut behind her before she spoke. "Admiring my new addition?"

"I think it suits you better than the previous owner."

Was he intentionally not saying Usaeil's name? If so, she was thankful. Rhi walked past him and sat. She crossed one leg over the other. "What brings you back to the castle?"

"Your castle," he corrected.

Her brows snapped together. "Excuse me?"

"If you want everyone to believe you're the queen, then you must act like it. This is your castle."

"You never said Dreagan was yours."

Con shrugged, his black suit jacket shifting with the movement of his shoulders. "Depends on who I speak with, but Dreagan was never mine. It was meant as a home for Dragon Kings. The Light Castle was always meant to be the monarch's home, with others staying here as he or she allowed."

Rhi drew in a long breath and then released it. "I suppose you're right. So, what brings you back to my castle?"

He grinned, one of those crooked, heart-stopping smiles that used to make her go weak in the knees. It was a good thing she was sitting down. Otherwise, she would've made a fool of herself.

When they had been together, Con had smiled often, but over the last few years, she had seen it so rarely that this one had taken her by surprise. Kind of like being knocked in the back by an elephant.

"Your plan to gain Usaeil's attention is going to need additional help," he said.

She tried not to roll her eyes, but she failed. "You mean *your* help."

"I do." He put his hands behind his back and simply stared at her with those unreadable black eyes of his.

No one had ever asked her why she loved the color black so much. The answer had been there all along. Not only was it a color he favored, it was also the hue of Con's eyes. To stare into them was to stare into an abyss, one that had loved her and sheltered her like none other.

Until he broke her heart.

She brought her thoughts back to the present. It didn't take her long to realize what he was suggesting. "You want Usaeil to think you and I are back together."

"No' just together, but on our way to being mated."

Rhi's stomach plummeted to her feet with such force that she had to grip the arms of the chair to keep from bending over. Mated. She had told Con at one time that it didn't matter to her if they ever completed the ceremony since she knew he was the one for her.

He had merely smiled and then gave her a long kiss before telling her that their hearts and souls were already bound, but the bond needed to be completed formally to make her his, and him hers.

From that moment on, Rhi had longed to be mated to him. But it had never happened.

She looked away, no longer able to meet his gaze. "You're asking a lot."

"We'll pretend anytime there are others around," Con explained. "When we're in private, you doona have to speak to me. In fact, I'll leave, if that's your wish."

She could barely get through having him in the same room with her, and now he was asking her to act as if they were together again in front of others? That was the cruelest thing he could possibly think of.

"My claiming to be queen will be enough to bring Usaeil," she said as she slid her gaze back to him.

Con gave a small shake of his head. "How soon do you want this done with Usaeil? You being queen might do it, but it's going to take time. Meanwhile, she's going to continue killing Druids, doing who knows what with their magic. Not to mention, Moreann is still with her." He paused for a beat. "However, if you throw me into the mix, it'll be like a slap to Usaeil's face. She told the Light that she and I were to be mated. But it isna her that I chose. At least, that's what everyone will think."

Rhi hated that he had such good arguments, even though she knew she couldn't put herself through it. But she didn't get a chance to respond.

"We'll get Usaeil dealt with quickly," Con continued. "You'll take her down as you were supposed to. That will stop the Druid deaths and allow you and the Light Fae to mend the fractured relationship with the Skye Druids. As for Moreann, the Kings will focus on her, but you're welcome to join in that hunt, as well. I know you'd like your brother's body returned."

The only thing stopping Rhi from agreeing to this

was the simple fact that she would be putting her heart in jeopardy being so close to Con.

However, the thought of the world without both Usaeil and Moreann was too good to resist. She would be strong enough to withstand any feelings that might arise from pretending to be Con's again.

"Riiiiight," the darkness said with a loud snort.

Rhi could do this. She *would* do it. This wasn't just about her. This was about all the Fae, mortals, and Dragon Kings. This was about every living soul on the realm.

And when she looked at it that way, she only had one choice.

She rose to her feet and said, "All right."

CHAPTER SEVENTEEN

Con struggled not to smile. He hadn't thought it would be so easy to convince Rhi to go along with his plan, but it seemed he'd been wrong.

"However," she said before he could rejoice too much, "I have some stipulations."

"Of course." He kept his disappointment hidden. He had won a small victory in getting Rhi's agreement. He should be pleased with that.

But he wanted more.

She was likely going to make sure that he was reminded she didn't intend for that to happen.

Rhi's silver eyes were hard as she stood as unmovable as the mountains on Dreagan. "I will play your lover to make everyone far and wide believe that we're once more together, and I will be *very* convincing."

His gut clenched, wondering if he had made a mistake. If he went by her voice alone, he was in for a torturous time. But it would be worth it. She might fake it, but he wouldn't. Maybe, just maybe, if he were really lucky, he might sway her thinking, get her to give him another chance by the time it all ended.

But he'd have to be extremely lucky.

"I understand," he told her. "I'll also be verra convincing."

She gave him a flat look. "The moment we're alone when no one else can see us, then we're back to this," she said, moving her finger between them.

Con bowed his head in her direction. "I agree to that."

"I'm not finished."

Perhaps now wouldn't be a good time to tell her that he'd always loved it when she got bossy, and her Irish lilt intensified. No, he'd keep that tidbit to himself.

"You will do what I say, when I say it," she ordered.

Con raised a brow. "This plan benefits both of us."

"Maybe, but I'm not going to be the one doing everything."

"You're no'," he replied, frowning. He didn't like that she thought of herself as being on the losing end all the time.

Rhi shrugged one shoulder. "Regardless, I'm going to make sure of it."

"Anything else?"

"I won't be going to Dreagan anytime soon. You'll remain here, proving your love and devotion of me to the Light."

Con had expected to remain at the castle the majority of the time, but he hadn't thought he wouldn't be going back at all until the business with Usaeil was finished.

"Is that a problem?" Rhi asked, a gleeful look on her face as if she'd anticipated that he would argue.

"No' at all. However, that means the Kings will need to come here."

"Perfect. The Fae need to see that there are no hard feelings between our two species."

The triumphant feeling Con had gained was rapidly dissipating. "A fine plan."

"Since you'll be living here, that brings me to our living arrangements. I'll have some rooms readied for you."

It was Con's turn to raise a brow. "You think we can show everyone a display of affection, but go to different rooms? They willna believe we're actually together. More importantly, Usaeil willna believe it."

Rhi's nostrils flared as she glared at him. "Fine. There are multiple rooms within my quarters. I'll choose one of them for you." She took a step toward him. "When we retire there, you'll never venture into *my* room. Do you understand?"

"Perfectly."

"I'm glad we're in agreement."

Con inwardly snorted. He might not be going to her room, but he was going to make sure she came to him. He couldn't believe he'd given up before. Just talking to her, admitting that he still loved her, made him realize what an utter buffoon he'd been.

He wasn't just a Dragon King, he was King of Kings. And he was going to claim the heart of the only female to have ever captured his. Rhi was his mate. He would do whatever it took to win back her love. He'd grovel, he'd beg, he'd bring the very moon to her if she asked. Whatever her heart desired, he'd give it to her.

Because Rhi deserved that and so very much more.

It didn't matter how long it took. He'd spend the rest of eternity wooing her, winning her back.

"Our show should begin immediately," he told her. "This is my second visit. This will make it official."

Rhi hesitated, uncertainty crossing her features. Finally, she released a loud sigh. "Fine."

"Shall we make our announcement now?"

"Yes," she said, much too eagerly. "The sooner Usaeil is gone from our lives, the better."

Con wasn't entirely comfortable with Rhi's sudden enthusiasm, but he had pushed things. He now had to deal with whatever happened next. "Shall I call in some Kings?"

"Not yet," she told him as she walked toward the door. "It's better if it's just the Light for the moment."

He turned and followed her, stopping when she came to a halt. He watched her carefully as she seemed to ready herself.

"This isna about us," he said. "This is a means to get back at Usaeil for all she's done to both of us and the entire world. Keep that in mind."

Rhi's head turned to him. "You understand that's the only reason I'm doing this? Whatever was between us is gone."

"You've made that clear." Bloody hell, her words hurt, but she'd earned her right to throw as many barbs as she wanted at him after what he'd done to them.

She looked back toward the doors. "Play your part well, King."

He didn't get a chance to respond as Rhi motioned with her hands, and the doors opened. She halted near the guards and told them to call everyone immediately.

Con remained beside her and just a few inches behind. Rhi was queen here. He wouldn't overshadow her, and he wanted the Fae—as well as Rhi—to see that.

It didn't take long for the Light to gather. Once they saw Rhi and Con standing together, the rest arrived in a hurry, each of them vying to get a look at the couple that stood on the steps above them.

Rhi raised her hand to quiet everyone. She stood regally in all black with gold earrings dangling to nearly her shoulders, the metal mixing with her black hair. Her gaze scanned the crowd, letting the silence grow until everyone was on tenterhooks, waiting to hear what she had to say.

Con was impressed. He studied her, watching the minute movements that others missed, but he knew her well enough to know that she was waiting for just the right moment to speak. She might not want the position of queen, but Con knew she had been born for it.

Finally, Rhi spoke. "I've only been queen for a few days. I've spoken with some of you today, and starting tomorrow, I'll begin having audiences with anyone who wishes to speak with me. However, I didn't call you here just to tell you that. I have news."

She turned her head to Con and met his eyes as she smiled. His heart skipped a beat. He remembered when she had showered him with such looks. There was genuine warmth there, though he cautioned himself that, right now, Rhi was putting on a show. Eventually, he hoped that she would freely give him such a smile, instead of doing it to get under Usaeil's skin.

Con winked at her and took her hand in his. Let her think he was putting on a show, but in truth, he was going to take advantage of every moment he had to touch her.

"*We* have news," Rhi corrected as she faced the crowd once more. "Some of you might remember that a very long time ago—and all too briefly—before the Fae Wars, Constantine and I were together. We've found each other again."

Con brought their clasped hands up to his mouth and kissed her fingers. Rhi glanced his way, refusing to meet his gaze. He didn't care that she didn't really look at him. It was enough that he felt the little tremor that rushed through her at the touch of his lips.

"And your queen has finally agreed to be mine," Con announced into the silence. "As we were always meant to be."

Rhi smiled and nodded. "The Queen of the Light and the King of Dragon Kings will be bound, uniting our two species."

A deafening cheer rose up from the crowd. The happiness of the Fae took Con by surprise. He and Rhi smiled, laughing and appearing like a couple in love for all who watched. Con couldn't help but look at Rhi.

As if feeling his stare, she turned her head to him once more. Their gazes met, and for the briefest of moments, the years they'd been apart disappeared. They were the couple who had been deeply in love, who couldn't go a single day without seeing each other.

But just as quickly as that feeling arrived, it vanished.

Rhi relaxed her fingers, but Con didn't loosen his hold on her hand as the Fae continued cheering. If there had been any doubt in his mind about how the Light felt about Rhi, the proof was there before him now. She was beloved.

"When will you be married?" someone shouted.

The room quieted to allow Rhi to speak. She gave a small shrug. "Con and I have waited eons for this moment. We won't put it off long. It'll happen soon."

More cheers erupted. Rhi waved at everyone and turned to walk away, her hand still joined with Con's. He followed her into the throne room. The moment the door closed behind them, Rhi jerked her hand away.

Con kept in step with her, moving through a back panel in the wall that led to a set of stairs that would take them to the queen's chambers. "That went well."

"It did. If Usaeil has any friends here, it won't take

long for word to get back to her. If we're lucky, this facade will be over in a day or two."

Con quickly looked her way when they reached the stairs. "It would be good to have Usaeil gone so we can concentrate on Moreann, but your people don't deserve to be yanked one way and then another so quickly."

"What are you saying?" she asked, a deep frown puckering her brow.

"That we should come up with a plan for how we'll cancel the engagement and eventually end our union."

Rhi snorted loudly as she reached the top landing and opened the door to her chambers. "Couples break up all the time. Ours was very sudden, if you remember."

"Aye," he said as he closed the door behind him, inwardly wincing at the anger in her voice. "But this isna just about me and you now. This is about your people."

She turned and looked at him. "I'm queen right now to draw out Usaeil. I'm with you right now to draw out Usaeil. Once she's dead, I'm going to give up the throne, and then it won't matter what happens to either of us in the eyes of the Fae."

"You can no' be serious," he stated.

Her brows shot up as she gave him a pointed look. "About dropping your arse as quickly as I can? You're damned straight, I am."

Con sliced his hand through the air. "I'm talking about you giving up the throne. Did you no' hear the people out there? Did you no' see them? They love you. You're meant to be queen."

"I don't want it," she said and walked away.

He followed her once again, not failing to notice that she was making him trail after her on purpose. And he was just fine with that. "Usaeil abused her power. You

willna do that. There isna anyone I know who deserves
to sit on that throne more than you."

"I can think of two," she said as she stopped and spun
to face him. "Phelan and Xaneth. But I know Phelan
doesn't want it, so that leaves the last heir through Usaeil's bloodline—Xaneth. Well, there's Thea, Usaeil's
daughter, but she's with a Reaper, so I'm pretty sure that
rules her out."

"I agree, Xaneth would be a likely candidate, but we
both know he's still missing. He may remain that way for
millennia—if Usaeil hasna already killed him."

Rhi threw up her hands in nonchalance before opening a door. "I don't care. I've made my decision. And this
is your room."

He looked past her to the large room that was devoid
of furniture. Con drew in a breath to continue their conversation when he heard a door close behind him. He
looked over his shoulder to the vast expanse that separated them and the door to her chambers that she had
shut.

"Aye," he murmured. "I've got my work cut out for
me."

CHAPTER EIGHTEEN

Somewhere on Earth . . .

Usaeil glared down at the prone body of her nephew, lying on the bed. Xaneth was still locked in his mind, battling forces she had put there—and all without the use of his magic. She had taken great pleasure in tormenting him at first, but now, it had lost some of its appeal.

Xaneth was the last member of her family. Somehow, he'd had the wherewithal to not be found by her Trackers, who took out everyone else in their bloodline. Then Xaneth had made the mistake of telling her who he was after she'd had him track down Thea.

Usaeil turned away from the bed and looked out the windows to the majestic mountains beyond, and the calm river that wound through them. Thea had been the only offspring that she hadn't killed. Most, she terminated in the womb. Usaeil still wasn't sure why she'd allowed Thea to live.

Yet, live she had. Thea had thrived among mortals as a Halfling. It was ironic that Usaeil had gone looking for the daughter she'd given up the same time Thea had met the Reapers.

Xaneth had found Thea as instructed. Usaeil hadn't

known what to do with her. Part of her wanted to kill
Thea as she had the rest of her children, but she held her
hand once more—and considered bringing Thea with
her to the Light Castle so she could follow in Usaeil's
footsteps.

It had been a brief and utterly idiotic idea. Usaeil
didn't plan to ever stop ruling. She'd ended her children
and any blood relatives so no one would be able to claim
the throne.

During all of that, Xaneth had turned on her and
released Thea to the Reapers. That was the first time
Usaeil had learned that the Reapers—as well as Death—
were real.

The group of them had actually teleported inside the
Light Castle, something no one should've been able to
do. It told Usaeil how powerful their magic was, especially Death's. Truth be told, Usaeil had been terrified.
But they hadn't stopped her from killing Thea, nor had
they taken her soul.

And *that* told Usaeil that as powerful as they may be,
they couldn't come close to touching her might. Whatever fear she held for the Reapers and Death had dissipated in an instant.

Her head turned to the side so she could look at
Xaneth once more. He was the only one who could claim
the throne she had vacated when Rhi had attempted to
kill her. Not that Xaneth would ever break free of the
spell she had him under. He wasn't strong enough to figure it out—or counter her spell.

Usaeil hadn't checked on the Light or Dark Fae since
she'd taken Moreann. She wanted them to flounder for a
while before she stepped in as the Queen of the Fae, not
just the Light. It was her destiny, and it was nearly within
her grasp. Once she had that, Con would have to give her

the respect she deserved. No one else on this realm could equal his power but her, and he would see it.

She didn't want to love him. In fact, she thought of it as a weakness because it could be used against her. However, she also realized how much power Con had. Nobody could harm Earth if they stood together.

Con cared about the humans despite what they had done to the dragons. He thought of his Kings before anything else, which meant that Usaeil would use both of those instances to reach him. He would then come to see that she had some good in her, and eventually, he would love her.

The sound of screaming reached Usaeil from down the hall. Moreann wasn't taking too kindly to being held, but Rhi didn't care. The Druid would remain there for as long as Usaeil saw fit.

She spun from the window and left her nephew's room to descend the stairs. When she reached the main floor, she spotted one of her Trackers giving something to another. Usaeil strode to the door and held out her hand.

"Where did you come from?" she demanded of the Tracker.

"Castle," he replied.

She unrolled the paper as she eyed the Tracker. She had them all around the world, veiled as they followed her enemies or spied on places like the Dark Palace and the Light Castle. She wanted to place some near Dreagan, but the Kings would no doubt discover them before the Trackers could give her any information.

Usaeil looked down at the message that read:

Rhiannon has taken the throne and declared herself queen.

Usaeil ground her teeth together as she reread the

line a second time. "That bitch. Of course, she would. I always knew she coveted my position. Well, I hope she enjoys it because she won't be there long."

Then she realized there was more to the message.

Constantine has come twice. The second time, Rhi announced that she and Con would be mated.

Anger like Usaeil had never known before erupted within her. She threw back her head and screamed her rage as she lowered her arms and spread her fingers with her palms facing out. She released magic, uncaring who or what was struck.

This couldn't be happening. Con was hers. She'd made sure of it long ago when she broke up his and Rhi's relationship. For thousands of years, the two of them hadn't rekindled their affair. They were supposed to be finished.

Usaeil lifted her head and stared at the Tracker that had brought her the news. She sneered at him as she lifted a hand and swiped it through the air, taking his head with her magic.

Rhi had her throne.

Rhi had her power.

Rhi had the love of the people.

And . . . Rhi had Con.

Usaeil couldn't allow this to continue. All of that was hers. Rhi was a usurper, who needed to be reminded of her place—which was beneath Usaeil's boot heel.

When she closed her hands into fists, there was nothing left but bits and pieces of the Trackers who had been near her. Even the house was destroyed. She snapped her fingers and fixed the building. She then stepped over the remains of the dead Trackers. It was time she took back her throne.

Suddenly, she stopped. She needed a plan, one that

would give her a dramatic entrance, but also one that would cause all Fae to tremble with fear at her approach.

"Maybe the Light shouldn't be my first stop," she said aloud.

Usaeil dressed in her sexiest red outfit that hugged all her curves and showed ample cleavage before she teleported to the Dark Palace and walked up the wide steps to the huge doors. Once inside, she simply stood and looked around. For several minutes, no one paid her any heed. Not that she expected any different. The Dark had other . . . appetites, as was evident by the cages filled with humans, who would happily have sex with a Dark, all while unknowingly having their souls drained in the process.

And to think that, at one time, Usaeil had thought that disgusting. She quite liked it, actually. It was the very way she'd come to be pregnant with many of her offspring, including Thea. It was too bad she hadn't been able to bring Con's seed to life. If she'd been able to fill her womb with his bairn, she knew he'd have never left her.

Finally, one of the Dark pushed away from the wall and walked to her. He eyed her with his red eyes, his black and silver hair short and slicked back from his face. She remained still as he looked her up and down.

"Slumming it, aren't you?" he asked.

Usaeil propped a hand on her hip. "You should be on your knees when you speak to your queen."

He laughed, his gaze narrowing on her. "Oh, you'll do great here, love."

"I'm not joking. Get on your knees, and you'll refer to me as Queen Usaeil."

His handsome face went slack. "Usaeil? The Light Queen?"

"Do I look Light to you? In fact, I haven't been Light

in thousands upon thousands of years. I had my family killed to ensure that no one could take my throne. And now, I'm going to rule both the Light and the Dark."

"But,"—he hesitated—"we heard the Light have a new queen."

Usaeil smiled then. "Not for long."

The Dark's smile was slow as he lowered himself to one knee. And he wasn't the only one. Others had been listening to the conversation. They, too, bent a knee.

"Hail Usaeil, Queen of the Dark!"

She smiled as the cheer rose, causing many more in the palace to take notice. She glanced down at the Dark who had first approached her and motioned for him to rise. "Come with me," she said as she made her way to the stairs to take over the chambers that had been Balladyn's. "What's your name?"

"Coslar," he replied.

"Well, Coslar, you're going to remain with me until I'm bored with you."

"That won't happen, my queen."

She snorted loudly and pushed open the doors to her new chambers. "Oh, it will. I can promise you that. Now, see to it that the guards take up their positions immediately throughout the palace and on the grounds. Then, you'll return and tell me who all has been vying for the Dark throne."

Coslar hurried to carry out her orders. While he was gone, Usaeil got rid of all the masculine furniture and decorations in the suite. She wanted everything having to do with Balladyn gone for good. With that thought, she also removed the colors he'd chosen. They might be favored by the Dark, but she didn't care.

She was a queen, something the Dark had never had. It was time they realized that she did things differently.

She would be their queen, but she would unite the Fae eventually. Sooner rather than later, if she had anything to say about it.

Usaeil magically installed black wood floors and a large Persian-style rug in deep burgundy and gray. Two overstuffed armchairs in deep gray sat opposite a black leather Chesterfield sofa. Between them stood a wooden coffee table, its top made from a slice of oak. She stood back to look at her work.

"The guards are in place," Coslar said when he returned.

Usaeil sat in one of the chairs and tested its comfort. Satisfied, she motioned to the sofa. "Take a seat. I'm sure you have a lot to tell me."

He sat and spread one arm along the back of the couch. "Why me? Others probably know more than I do."

"I'm sure you'll be able to discover anything I need you to."

"I can," he assured her. "But you still haven't told me why you chose me."

Usaeil crossed one leg over the other and placed her hands in her lap. "I've been a queen for a very long time. I learned the ins and outs of court when I was just a child. With one look, I can tell who people respect and who they don't. When we were speaking, I wasn't the one who first got their attention. It was you. And not because you got down on one knee. You're the kind of man who gets attention wherever you go."

"All Fae do."

"Perhaps," she replied. "From humans. But if you can do that to the Fae, then you hold power. I'm guessing you already knew that, though, didn't you?"

His smile was slow as it spread over his face. "That I did."

"You've used that to your benefit, as well."

"I certainly have."

It was her turn to smile. "Just what I wanted to hear. Now, give me the details of those who want the throne."

PART TWO

"It begins and ends with the Dragon Kings."

—UNKNOWN

CHAPTER NINETEEN

There were few things Rhi gave up on. Sleep that night was one of them. Con was too close. Knowing that he was across the vastness of the queen's chambers still meant that he was closer than he had been in millennia.

And it disrupted her sleep.

She knew that no matter what she did, as long as he was in the castle, she wouldn't rest. She returned to the library instead. Well, she did after she destroyed Usaeil's spell, preventing any Fae from teleporting in or out of the castle.

They were Fae. Fae used magic. Preventing them from doing what they did every day of their lives was idiotic. Usaeil might have done it to ensure that no enemies could surround her, and while it sounded like a good plan, Rhi didn't agree. A Fae could be surrounded by their enemies at any time. Usaeil just liked to control others, and preventing Fae from jumping in or out of the castle was just another way to do that.

Once Rhi had broken Usaeil's spell, she was able to teleport to the back room of the library without anyone knowing. Until she knew what the book was, she'd rather no one knew about her whereabouts or what she was reading.

She looked up, taking note of the room itself. The ceiling was so high that it disappeared into the darkness. Some kind of magic allowed a soft light to spotlight the pedestal and the book upon it. When it sensed someone in the room, the light brightened to appear like sunlight.

The walls were a simple white, and the floor matched the white marble of the rest of the library. No other adornments or decorations were within the room. Rhi's gaze returned to the tome. Because it was the only thing a person was supposed to see upon entering.

She walked to the book and lifted it in her hands. It was heavy, as if the words and knowledge within were weighty—and she suspected that was exactly the case.

Rhi called a small settee that would fit in the room. It was comfortable, allowing her to recline as she read through the many pages instead of standing or sitting on the floor. Though there was little room for anything or anyone else in the chamber.

Before she opened the book, she gazed at the cover. Some bindings within the library were so ornate, it had likely taken months for a Fae to craft them, even using magic. Some had gold as decoration, some silver. Some even had gemstones adhered to the covers to bring attention to them.

But not this book. It was as simple as the chamber. It was covered in leather. Someone had gone to a great deal of effort to craft such a fine piece of hide, but it was leather just the same. And, oddly, there was no title on either the front or the spine. The more she looked at the tome, the more intrigued she became.

She took in a deep breath, letting the leather scent fill her nostrils. The binding of the cover creaked as Rhi opened it. This time, she took more notice of the pages. She rubbed her fingers against them. They were thin and light. Not heavy, like linen, at all. Several pages were left blank at the beginning. Instead of picking up where she had left off, she decided to start from the beginning.

"It begins and ends with the Dragon Kings," she read aloud. "They shepherd in death and give rise to life. To have them as an enemy is to ensure your demise. But to have them as an ally means untold destinies await."

Rhi swallowed and let those words sink in. Was this book the reason Usaeil had eventually joined the Kings against the Dark in the Fae Wars? Had she read this and realized what could be given to the Light if they became friends with the Kings?

That didn't sound like Usaeil at all. She had never been keen on books, and, in fact, used to get irritated at Balladyn for always being in the library.

If Rhi had to guess, Usaeil either hadn't known about the book, or she hadn't read it.

A frown furrowed Rhi's brow when she thought about how the words had moved about the page when she first found it. Was that part of the book? Did it do that to ensure that not everyone could read what was within the pages?

"Why me?" she asked the tome.

There was no reply, of course. Then again, the answer was probably within the pages. She leaned her head to the side and looked at the thickness of the book. It was wider than her hand. Stood on end, the volume was easily half a meter tall. She had no idea who'd written it or why it had been hidden. Though she was glad she'd found it.

Rhi went back to reading and, in seconds, became absorbed in the pages as the narrator talked of the grandeur of the Dragon Kings, the beauty of dragons, and how their realm was one that offered those the Kings allowed to live there life, abundance, and magic.

But not all the pages were filled with niceties. The narrator went into great detail about how powerful the dragons were, how the earth would shake when they clashed on the ground.

Dragons might love the sky, but they will fight anywhere. Be it land, air, or even the seas. Yes, dragons love to swim. Some have even chosen that as their domain. They are terrifyingly violent. Their mere presence commands respect, as well as awe.

They are, in a word, formidable.

I've seen them clash in the air, their magic colliding so that storms formed. I've seen them clash upon the ground with such force that mountains crumbled, and vast swaths of land broke away. I've seen them fight in the waters so that great tsunamis rose from the seas and swallowed islands, decimating anything close to shore.

But for all their savagery, there is another side to them—one of giving and kindness. They're all about clans and family. They look after one another in ways that all other species in the universe could learn from.

No clan turns their back on one of their own. Ever. There are tempers and battles, but the Kings of each clan are quick to rein them in before they can get too extreme.

Dragons aren't like the rest of the species in the vast universe who do any number of horrible things to one another. However, I don't want you to think that dragons are perfect. They're far from it.

But they are ruled by an inner voice that none of us have ever heard—or can hear. I've tried, believe me, I've tried. I want to hear whatever it is that governs not just the dragons, but also the Dragon Kings—and most especially, the King of Dragon Kings.

The few dragons who are bad seeds—because you can't have good without evil—are dealt with swiftly and justly. Stealing is not tolerated within a clan but done to another clan can see the dragon rewarded within his own. Lying is something that not even the dragons can get away from.

But if you want to know what honor is, you need only look to one individual—the King of Dragon Kings.

He is the one who will sacrifice everything—even his own life—to protect the dragons and the realm. A more selfless individual, I've never known. Years of study didn't tell me how a dragon became King of his clan or how one becomes King of Kings. I finally had to ask.

The answer: the magic of the realm.

Coming from a species of individuals where the greatest power and command are the ones who rule, I was shocked by this. The idea, however, is an intriguing one. The rulers aren't chosen by bloodline nor are they given the honor by force. Instead, the magic searches the heart of each and every dragon. It then looks into the deepest reaches of their minds to see what kind of dragon they are.

Only the purest of heart, the ones with honor, patience, and kindness are considered. Only then is their magic and power factored in. Because only the strongest of the strong can best the current King to take his place.

The first time I saw a dragon challenge a Dragon King, I stood in awe, watching the battle. It lasted for nearly an entire day, and in the end, the clan had a new King.

Not all new Kings must issue a challenge. Some are killed in battle, and the new one simply takes over. I was told that a dragon feels the magic within him, telling him it's time to become King. In an odd twist, there are actually some who don't want the position. Some because they like their current King, and others because it means challenging—and killing—either a friend or family member.

It's all so barbaric for a species that I would consider ahead of its time.

Then there are those who so desperately want to be King that they believe they feel the magic, when in fact, they do not. They issue a challenge, and the King has no choice but to fight. Of course, the King keeps his position, but in order to do that, he has to kill the one who challenged him.

It didn't matter what battle I watched, there wasn't a single King who enjoyed killing. The ones who did, well, the magic didn't choose them. Somehow, the magic of the realm knows who to pick in order to keep the balance on the realm and peace within the ranks.

No matter how much I admire the Dragon Kings, there is one who awes me—the King of Kings. He's set apart from the others. One of them, but also not.

The Dragon Kings are a tight bunch. No one can truly know what it means to be a King unless you have the position. Which explains their close friendships. And that surprises me because there is a chance any time during their reign that it'll all come to an end. That doesn't matter to them. They form those bonds anyway, showing yet again their big hearts and their affinity for inclusion, not exclusion.

Now, the King of Kings isn't ever excluded. The other Kings often try to bring him in on things, but he always declines. His responsibility isn't to just his clan, but *to all clans and the realm. That kind of responsibility could crush lesser individuals. I think that's why I respect the King of Dragon Kings so much.*

When he issues an order, the other Kings obey it instantly. But he doesn't let the power go to his head. Instead, the Kings will often come together to discuss topics and vote on them. In the end, however, it is the King of Kings' decision. Though I find it fascinating that he doesn't mind when other Kings disagree with him.

If only the rest of those out in the many realms would model themselves after the dragons, so much could change.

Most importantly, the Fae.

Rhi blinked. She looked up from the pages, shock rolling through her. A Fae had come to Earth and seen the dragons before Usaeil? Before the Fae had destroyed their world? She'd never heard such a thing.

Her gaze dropped back to the pages as she reread the passage on the King of Dragon Kings. There was no way that whoever this Fae was had written about Con, but as the narrator spoke, that's who Rhi envisioned.

Because she knew firsthand the lengths Con would go to for his Kings and the realm. He'd done it time and again. And he'd continue to do it until the day he breathed his last. Con was the epitome of honor. Rhi didn't want to think that, and she certainly didn't want to feel it, but she did. It was part of the reason she'd fallen in love with him to begin with.

She squeezed her eyes closed when she remembered the Fae writing about how the King of Kings stood apart from the other Kings. One of them, but separate. That was Con to a T.

Softly, she closed the book and returned it to the

pedestal. She wanted to read more, but her heart couldn't take it. Not after the day she'd had, and Con once more in her life—even if it was only to draw Usaeil out.

"Steady," she warned herself. "You won't be able to survive another broken heart."

Especially since the one she had wasn't yet healed.

CHAPTER TWENTY

Dreagan

Ulrik looked at the faces of the Dragon Kings, their mates, and Henry, who stood in the cavern of Dreagan Mountain. Silence filled the space as they all waited to hear why he'd brought them together.

His gaze shifted to his mate, Eilish, who stood to the side. She was the only one who knew what he was about to say. She gave him a smile and a wink as an offering of love and encouragement.

Before Eilish, Ulrik had been adrift. He'd thought he knew what he wanted, but he'd known nothing. Not until he held her in his arms and tasted her kiss for the first time. That moment of discovering that she was his mate still made his breath catch. She was his other half, the one who balanced him as no one else could. Eilish showed him love. She gave him the strength to see the path he really wanted—which had been home to Dreagan.

He wouldn't be here without her. He knew that, accepted it then, now, and always. The thing was, she didn't need him. She was strong in spirit, intellect, and magic. She could continue on her own without him. She often teased him that she didn't need him, but said she wanted him, craved him, hungered for him.

Some Fae—and even a few Kings—believed mortals were inferior because they had such short lifespans. The truth was, they were stronger than the dragons or the Fae, even without magic. Because a King couldn't survive without his mate, not once they had been found.

Ulrik had no idea how Con did it. He suspected that Rhi returning to Dreagan a few years ago had helped matters. Then again, the fact that Con had gone to Usaeil might mean that Rhi's appearance had made things much, much worse for his friend. For a King to find their mate and not be able to have her was like being slowly flayed alive every hour of every day that he was without her.

The magic of the realm made the dragons the strongest magically, but it also made them the weakest when it came to love and matters of the heart. Something only dragons knew.

Ulrik blew out a breath and looked at the others. "We know Rhi has taken the Light throne in order to draw Usaeil out into the open. I wasna the only one who knew that wouldna be enough for someone like Usaeil."

His head swung to Henry, who once more stood in the back. A part of the family, but neither a Druid nor a Dragon King. No doubt Con had a plan for Henry, the JusticeBringer. Ulrik really wished he knew what it was, because he suspected it was going to be epic.

Ulrik nodded to Henry before he continued. "There was an ulterior motive for Henry and I approaching Con. For too long, our King has suffered while we've found our mates and brought them to Dreagan." Ulrik looked at Rhys. "Some of us know what it feels like to believe we've lost our mate, only to be lucky enough to get her back."

Lily wrapped her arms around Rhys and hugged him tight as the King of Yellows kissed the top of her head.

"Con hasna been so lucky," Ulrik continued. "We've kept his secret from mates, Henry, the Druids, and even the Warriors. Especially Phelan. We were no' the only ones. Rhi never shared the truth, either. However, the time has come. The secret is out. Fallon knows the truth. More importantly, Con recently told Rhi the truth of *why* he ended things. Now, it's time you all know what Con has held within him for so verra long. He ended their relationship for us. Because none of us had mates yet, and he didna want us to be jealous and have it cause a rift within Dreagan that couldna be mended."

Ulrik had to pause as his throat clogged with emotion. He looked at Eilish again, who wiped away a tear and gave him a nod. "We've each nudged Con over the years to go back to Rhi, to mend what was shattered. He never did. Con hasna been himself for quite some time. He hid it well, but being without Rhi took a heavy toll. One that I fear he might no' come back from."

"How heavy?" Thorn asked.

Ulrik pressed his lips together. "The heaviest."

"He can no'," Darius stated.

Ulrik shrugged. "I'm in agreement. I doona think anything we could've said would've changed his mind. Circumstances, however, have changed. Henry and I realized that it would take much more than Rhi sitting on the throne to draw Usaeil out immediately."

"But Con being with Rhi would," Asher said.

"Exactly. Con seemed to see that our reasoning was sound. He went to the Light Castle to find Rhi a few hours ago, to try and convince her of the same thing. I expected it to take a lot more for him to swing her to the plan, but it didna. Rhi is on board. They've announced their relationship and upcoming mating." Ulrik licked his lips. "Con has told me that Rhi is acting, but he isna. He plans to win her back, however long it takes."

Dmitri rolled his azure eyes. "About damn time."

"I second that," Anson said.

Ulrik looked over the group, touching on each of them. "Rhi wants Con to remain at the Light Castle as a display for the Fae and Usaeil. Things will continue at Dreagan as they have. We're still searching for Usaeil and Moreann."

"What of the weapon?" Sebastian asked.

Ulrik looked at the King of Steels. "Henry has that well in hand, per Con's order. Usaeil could arrive at the Light Castle any moment, so we must be ready. Then there is the issue of Skye and the missing Druids. There will come a time for us to rest, but that isna now. It's going to take all of us to win against our enemies."

Nikolai asked, "And Con? What can we do for him?"

"Support him as he's always done for us," Ulrik answered. "He willna survive without Rhi. No' any longer. He's desperate, and he's even more cunning and ruthless when in that state. I doona imagine he'll make it easy for Rhi, but we all know he has a lot to make up for."

Dorian twisted his lips and held up his hand he had interlocked with Alexandra's. "We're ready and waiting."

"We all are," Roman said.

Cináed nodded. "If we can no' help Con win back Rhi, then we can make sure Dreagan and all who are here are safe."

"I dare anyone to attack Dreagan," V said, his ice blue eyes filled with determination.

Keltan glanced from his mate, Bernadette, to the other Kings. "Con has sacrificed for us and Dreagan. It's time we do the same for him."

"Just what I was about to say," Royden added.

Cain caught Ulrik's gaze. "We willna let Con down. Whatever it takes."

"Whatever it takes," Ulrik repeated.

He'd known he would be able to count on his brethren, but hearing their words reinforced his thoughts. If Con only knew how much he was respected and loved. He had no idea, but they were going to show him.

It was Vaughn who asked, "What's the plan?"

Ulrik grinned as he looked at the group. "We begin preparing for Con and Rhi's ceremony. I want all the Fae—Light and Dark—to know that we support the couple's union. That we want them together. A few of us need to go to the Light Castle."

"I'll go," Merrill said.

Varek nodded in agreement. "I'll join him."

"I'll let Con know the two of you are coming. We doona want to overwhelm the Fae or Rhi, but I think it's good that we make an appearance there."

Kendrick twisted his lips. "I doona want to be the one to bring down the group, but have we thought about what will happen if Rhi can no' defeat Usaeil? There's a good chance Usaeil and Moreann will team up and attack Rhi."

"Then we'll be there as backup for Rhi, just like last time," Rhys stated.

Kendrick nodded. "Aye. I'd just like to point out that we need to take a page from what Con has always done. We need to think about all the scenarios."

"He's right," Ulrik said, hating to even think about it. "Con is hanging on by a thread now. If Rhi dies . . . well, then there will be nothing holding him together. No' even us."

Kellan crossed his arms over his chest. "Then Rhi can no' die."

...oona think she will, but we should be prepared,"
...added.

...Ulrik gave a nod. "Merrill and Varek will go to the
...ght Castle. Kendrick, you, Sebastian, Guy, and who-
...ver else wants to join them, start putting a plan together
for what needs to happen if Moreann is indeed with Usaeil when she attacks. Rhys, Kiril, and Banan, keep your
attention on the Isle of Skye and the Druids there. We
doona need Usaeil taking more of the Druids to boost
her magic."

"What of Erith and the Reapers?" Cain asked.

Ulrik released a breath. "You and I will have a talk
with them." He paused as his mind began to sort the rest
into groups, each responsible for one part of the plan or
another, be it guarding Dreagan or attacking when the
time came—because it would come.

He even had the mates in groups. Those with magic
guarding those who didn't, with special attention placed
on Claire, who still carried V's child. Ten minutes later,
everyone filed out of the cavern to begin their work. Eilish blew Ulrik a kiss as Bernadette reached her, and the
two left together.

"You doona seem keen on talking to the Reapers,"
Cain said.

Ulrik twisted his lips as he shrugged. "It all hinges on
Erith. I understand her reasoning for keeping the Reapers secret from the Fae. If we want her help, then we
need to have an option for them that will allow her to
agree."

"It's Con," Cain said with a frown. "They're friends.
Look at the lengths she went to just to help Con all these
years. Why would she no' do it now?"

"Because this goes beyond her."

Cain's brows rose briefly as he shook his head. "I say, let's get this over with."

"Erith. Cael," Ulrik called.

In the next instant, the couple appeared before them. Erith's lavender eyes were locked on Ulrik. She moved her gaze to Cain before returning her focus to the King of Silvers. She didn't seem at all surprised to have been summoned.

"Thank you for coming," Ulrik said.

Cael crossed his arms over his chest. "We were about to come anyway. Word reached us that Rhi and Con are back together."

"It's a ruse, at least on Rhi's part," Ulrik explained. "Con has every intention of winning her back."

Erith nodded her head of long, blue-black hair. "I'm happy to hear that, but you didn't call us here to celebrate."

"Nay," Cain replied. "We wanted to talk to you about joining us when the time comes."

Erith and Cael exchanged a look. She released a long breath, her lips pressing together for a heartbeat. "There wasn't a Reaper who agreed with my original decision to keep out of things. I had my reasons, but I was wrong. Had we joined the Dragon Kings sooner, there's a chance that Moreann wouldn't have gotten her hands on Usaeil's body to bring her back, nor could Usaeil have saved Moreann from all of you. I won't make that mistake again. Whatever you need, we will be there. The Dragon Kings shouldn't be the only ones protecting this realm. Everyone who calls it home should. And that's us. Specifically, me."

"And me," Cael added.

Ulrik grinned, relief pouring through him. "That makes

me verra happy. I'm sure you've already thought of ways to help so the Reapers willna be seen."

Erith's smile was slow and filled with resolve. "Oh, we certainly have. I've already got one Reaper at the Light Castle, and two at the Dark Palace." Her smile dropped. "Which brings me to the news *I* have to share. Usaeil has taken the Dark throne."

Ulrik's guts twisted. "We should've expected that. She wants to unite both the Light and the Dark under one ruler—her. Looks like she chose the Dark to rule first."

"It's her way of getting back at Rhi," Cain pointed out. "With Balladyn gone, of course, Usaeil would take the throne."

Erith laughed softly. "Usaeil has no idea what's coming for her."

"I can no' wait," Ulrik replied with a grin.

CHAPTER TWENTY-ONE

It wasn't the first time Con had woken up somewhere other than Dreagan, but it was the first time he wasn't in a hurry to return. And the reason for that was the Fae who had stolen his heart long ago.

He'd spent all night lying upon the bed, staring at the ceiling as he thought about Rhi and how he might win her back. It wasn't going to be easy, but he didn't care. He'd do whatever it took to have her. Because without Rhi, he was nothing.

The last time he'd truly been alive, actually felt anything, was when they were together. When he'd decided to end their affair and walked from his chambers a few days later, he was just a shell of the dragon he'd once been. He put on a good façade for the Kings. So good, in fact, that no one had questioned him until recently.

Then again, he had kept up the pretense until he couldn't anymore.

He swung his legs over the side of the bed and stood to watch the sunrise through his window. Ireland was pretty, but it wasn't Scotland. Then again, he didn't care where he was as long as he was with Rhi.

What an utter fool he'd been all these centuries. He'd actually thought he could go on without her. The fact that he'd done it for so long was simply because of his brethren. Without them, he'd have ceased long, long ago.

He'd tried to put Rhi out of his mind. Some days, he actually succeeded, but those were rare and few and far between. He might have ended things, but a piece of her had remained with him, buried in his heart, reminding him of how happy he'd been. How happy *they'd* been.

After Darius told her the words Con hadn't been able to, Rhi had left Dreagan. Con had thought it'd be easier if he didn't see her again. And he tried, really tried. But only a short time passed before he went looking for her. That's when he discovered that she wasn't on the realm. She'd left.

There was only one place he knew where she would've gone. He'd searched all over for a Fae doorway, even knowing that they were only visible to the Fae. But he searched anyway because a knot of fear rode him. He'd known instinctively that she was in danger.

To this day, he still didn't know how he'd found the doorway. He'd chalked it up to loving Rhi and using every bit of his magic to locate it. Once he did, he went through it without hesitation. It was the first time a King had left the realm, but he hadn't thought of anything but her. When he finally found her, near death, what was left of his heart had shattered all over again.

He'd put every ounce of magic he had into healing her. He didn't breathe easily again until he saw her wounds disappear. Then, he returned her to Balladyn. The Fae had said nothing, had simply taken Rhi from Con's arms and walked away. He'd gone back to the doorway, intending to return to the Fae Realm to find out who had hurt his mate, but for some reason, the portal was gone.

The sight of Rhi that day had told Con just how much both of them were hurting. He knew then that he had to stay away from her. If he sought her out again, it would only hurt them both more. He had to let her heal and move on.

Though there was no moving on for him. She was his mate. It was as simple as that.

But he wanted her to be happy. The only way he got through the days was by writing in his journals. Centuries passed, but his love never faded. Many times, he'd wished he could see her, wanted to know how she was. Then he thought better of it, thinking that she might have found someone else. And that was something he couldn't handle.

Then, one fateful day, he walked into a pub and saw Rhi at the bar with one of the Warriors. Con was gutted, his breath locked in his lungs while his body refused to do as he commanded. He wasn't sure how he got any words out, but somehow, he managed it. With the way he acted, he was sure everyone there had known how he felt, but miraculously, they hadn't.

After that, he began searching for any signs of Rhi. Con knew he was walking hand-in-hand with madness, but he didn't care. Seeing her had revived something long dead inside him. His heart had beat once more, and desire had churned within him.

Rhi began turning up at Dreagan. But with that came the realization that she wasn't his. The way she treated him, ignoring him in most cases, told Con everything he needed to know. She loathed him.

To help his heart, he tried to ignore her. Each time she came to Dreagan, it hurt him more and more, so he lashed out at the very person he'd hurt. He hadn't meant to cause Rhi more pain, but that's exactly what he'd done in an effort to help himself.

He'd tried to make amends once by finding her cabin in Italy and leaving clothes, jewelry, and nail polish for her. It hadn't worked.

Con then kept this distance from her as much as he could, even though she'd pop into his office whenever she wanted, taunting him with her sly smile and mouth-watering body. He'd come to terms with the role he had in her life. He might not have her as his own, but at least he got to see her. It was a special kind of torment he put himself through, but he knew what it was like to not have her in his life. Something was better than nothing.

When she got hurt fighting Mikkel, Con hadn't been able to release her. He'd even spoken to her while she lay unconscious. During that time, he'd let his guard down. No one saw him, no one heard him, but it had done wonders to help heal his ragged soul.

His thoughts halted when the door to his room opened behind him. He turned and found Rhi standing in the doorway, her hand on the knob. Her black hair was pulled away from her face, showing her cheekbones and full lips. Her silver eyes pinned him in place.

His gaze roamed over her trim form from the sheer, silver, long-sleeved top to the black leather pants that hugged her legs, down to the black stiletto boots with their cluster of silver spikes on the toes.

"Did you sleep well?" she asked.

Con lifted his eyes back to her face. "Aye. You?"

"Do you want anything for breakfast?"

"I can go without if you're no' eating."

She shrugged. "Do whatever you want."

"Merrill and Varek are coming today."

"I knew you'd send for some Kings."

"I didna send for anyone. They want to show the Fae that they support our union," he told her.

Rhi flattened her lips. "Whatever."

When she started to turn away, he hurriedly said, "I'm sure you have questions for me. Things you've no' asked. Ask them now."

"I don't need to know anything."

"Sure, you do," he prodded. "There are likely a million questions running through your mind. I'll answer whatever you ask."

She looked at the ceiling and sighed. "I don't care about the past. I'm over you."

But he wasn't over her. She turned away. Con blurted out, "I wanted to rip Balladyn apart when I found out the two of you were together. It was all I could do no' to bellow my rage."

His words stopped her. For several seconds, she didn't move. Then, slowly, she turned back to him. "You dare to say you were angry with me? You're the one who went to Usaeil."

"Aye." It was one mistake he'd never be able to make up for. "From the moment you left, I didna feel any desire for anyone. My body was dead. Then you came back into my life, and with you, the desire. I tried to satisfy myself, but it wasna enough. Because it wasna you."

Rhi gave him a dry look. "Which is why you went to Usaeil?"

"I knew you'd never let me touch you again, which only made me crave you more. I became so desperate that I went looking for you one night. I was prepared to do anything, say anything, just to hold you again. But it wasna you I found. Instead, Usaeil found me. I knew it was a mistake, but I also believed I could use it to my advantage. I was wrong. So verra, verra wrong. That's when I ended it. Or tried to. Usaeil was . . . persistent."

"Obsessed," Rhi interjected. "She's always been obsessed with you."

Con was happy that Rhi was at least listening to him. He knew she hadn't forgiven him, but the fact that she hadn't walked away was something. "I didna know that before. I just wanted to relieve my body, and in the process, I began something that ultimately led us here."

"Playing the martyr again?" Rhi asked with a raised brow. "I hate to burst your bubble, but this wasn't only about you. It was also about me."

"I'm no' trying to play anything. I'm trying to explain things."

Rhi shrugged. "Like I said, I'm over you. There's no need to tell me any more of this stuff. I don't care."

"Then why did you end it with Balladyn?" The minute the words were out, Con wanted to take them back. But he couldn't.

They hung there between them as Rhi glared at him.

"I ended it with Balladyn because he wanted me to become Dark. Again, it had nothing to do with you."

Con had been grasping for something, anything that proved that Rhi might still care for him. Even a little bit. And by doing that, he'd been kicked while down. She knew just how to hurt him. Not that he blamed her. He deserved it.

Whatever words he'd thought to say after that evaporated. He could only stare after Rhi as she spun on her heel and walked away, leaving the door open. He didn't know if he was supposed to follow her or not.

Con looked down at his wrinkled dress shirt and slacks. He'd taken off his jacket and shoes to sleep, but he needed a change of clothes. The Kings didn't use magic for every little thing like the Fae did, but he didn't have a choice now.

The clothes upon him vanished as he walked into the bathroom and turned on the shower. He took his time cleaning his body and hair. When he finished, the mirror was fogged, the steam hanging in the air like a thick curtain.

He hung up the damp towel and walked naked into his room. He was two steps out before he realized that Rhi was lounging in a chair near the door, her legs crossed, and her foot swinging. He came to a halt from surprise. She stilled, her eyes slowly caressing his body.

The moment her gaze landed on his cock, it thickened, standing up at the sight of her. Rhi immediately looked away, but not before he saw desire flash in her silver depths. Con briefly thought about going to her to see if he could get more of a reaction, but he decided not to push things. He'd gotten more than he'd ever hoped for. Because no matter what she kept telling him, Con knew that Rhi still wanted him. Her body couldn't lie. He just needed to convince her heart and mind.

Con used magic to clothe himself in a black suit with a silver dress shirt to complement Rhi's eyes and her attire. He walked to stand before her, waiting until she looked up at him.

"What do you think?" he asked as he held out his arms.

She shrugged one shoulder. "It'll do."

He hid his smile until she rose and turned her back to him. She'd let him see a chink in her armor, and he was going to take full advantage of it. Just not right this minute. She could back out of their plan, and that simply wouldn't do.

"What's on the agenda for today?" he asked as he followed her out of his room.

"I'll be taking audiences with the Fae in the throne room."

"And me? Would you like me with you?"

She stopped and blew out a breath before she turned her head to the side when he reached her. "Yes. That's why I came back to get you. And you might as well tell Varek and Merrill to join us. You're right. The Light need to see that the Kings are on board with this."

Con grasped her arm as she began to walk away when he heard Ulrik's voice in his head, relaying a message. When his friend finished, he blinked and focused on Rhi's face. "I've news about Usaeil."

"Then I suppose you'd better spit it out."

Con studied Rhi's calm face. "She's taken the Dark throne."

"I thought she might," Rhi said as if she were discussing the weather.

That took Con aback. "Why did you no' say anything?"

"Slipped my mind, I guess," she said and continued walking.

He sighed, knowing that whatever ground he believed he'd gained that morning was only a tiny crawl forward on the razor's edge of the slope he had to climb to win her.

CHAPTER TWENTY-TWO

How was she supposed to concentrate on anything after seeing Con naked? Rhi could barely remember her own name. It had been so long since she'd run her hands over that hard body of his, felt the ridges and valleys of his muscles.

Been surrounded by his warmth.

Known his tongue on her body.

Felt his length inside her.

There were few nights where he didn't come to her in her dreams, kissing her, caressing her . . . loving her. He'd bring her right to the edge of orgasm before she woke, her body screaming for release.

Even when she managed to climax, it wasn't enough. Her body had never been as satisfied as when Con had made love to her. He'd known exactly how to put his hands on her, exactly where to touch her so that she experienced the most pleasure. Nothing else had ever come close to that.

Not her own hands, not a toy, and sadly, not even Balladyn.

She shouldn't be angry at Con for going to Usaeil. He

had needs, just as she did. But no matter how many times she told herself that, it still felt like a betrayal. And it was one of the reasons she had gone to Balladyn. Her dear friend hadn't deserved that. He had loved her. By accepting Balladyn as her lover, Rhi had given him false hope. Without meaning to, she had hurt him as deeply as Con had hurt her.

Rhi was glad when she finally reached the throne room so she could turn her mind to other matters instead of thinking about Con. She'd told him she was over him. If only that were true. She took her seat and glanced out of the corner of her eye to see what Con would do. She hadn't told him where to stand because she had wanted to gauge his reaction.

Without missing a beat, he moved to the side closest to the window and leaned his hip upon the sill. She could feel his gaze on her, but she refused to look his way. He rattled her. Deeply. And she didn't want him to know it. After all this time, he still had such an effect on her.

Her eyes sought him out, she listened for any sound from him, her body longed to get close so he could touch her again. When he took her hand yesterday, it had felt wonderful to have his fingers wrapped around hers. She hadn't wanted him to let go, but at the same time, she hadn't wanted to touch him, either. It hurt too badly. A reminder of what they'd once shared.

She kept telling him that they were through in the hopes that she might come to believe it herself. His words that morning as he explained about Usaeil replayed in her mind over and over. With as obsessed as Usaeil was, Rhi could see how the queen would put herself in Con's way, especially if Usaeil knew that he was in need. Con wouldn't have stood a chance.

Rhi wasn't sure how she felt about any of it. She had

imagined all sorts of ways that Usaeil and Con had become lovers but had never thought about the reason he explained. Perhaps because she'd assumed that Con had actually wanted Usaeil instead of being so needy thinking about her that he'd taken the first thing available to ease his body—Usaeil. Did that help matters? She couldn't say for certain. The one thing she did know was that Con wouldn't lie about such things. It wasn't in his nature.

Her attention moved to the first Light Fae who entered after Rhi told the guards to open the doors. For hours, she listened to complaints and issues that the Fae hadn't had resolved in years.

She became so absorbed in finding solutions that she never saw Merrill and Varek enter the throne room. She happened to look up and found the two Kings standing on either side of Con, as the three watched her.

Rhi swung her head back to the Fae before her, but that one look had her mind occupied with Con. Again. She wondered what he was thinking as he watched her. Maybe she'd ask him. But as soon as the thought went through her head, she knew she wouldn't. She didn't care what he thought.

"*Liar*," the darkness said in a seductive whisper.

When Rhi next looked up, it was dark outside. She rose to her feet, stopping the next Fae from approaching. "That's all for today. I'll resume tomorrow morning."

The guards immediately closed the doors, shutting her in. Rhi sank back into the chair and dropped her head into her hands. She was exhausted, both mentally and physically. And emotionally, if she were honest with herself.

"This is why you'd be the perfect queen," Con said, his voice close.

She looked up, shocked to find him standing beside her. He'd moved with such stealth that she hadn't even known he was there. Rhi cleared her throat and sat up straighter. "I'm just trying to make up for the things Usaeil didn't do."

"Because you care for the Light."

"Of course I care. They're my people."

Merrill asked, "What if they were Dark? Would you still listen to their grievances? Still attempt to help?"

Rhi's gaze swung to the King of Oranges. "If I was their queen, yes."

"No' all Light could say that," Merrill said with a smile. "It's good to see you, Rhi. And might I add, you look good sitting on the throne."

She smiled despite herself. "Thank you."

Varek grinned at her. "I'm impressed. You were patient and firm today, but also hard when you needed to be. Con's right. You were made to be queen."

Unable to help herself, Rhi's eyes returned to Con. He leaned one arm on the back of her chair. It felt as if he were crowding her, but it was only her imagination. She could tell him to back off, but then he'd know how much his nearness disturbed her. She needed him to think she didn't care for him anymore. Otherwise, she might take Balladyn's words to heart and throw herself at Con.

And damn the consequences.

"What do you think your people thought of the Kings being here?" Con asked.

Rhi shrugged and called a glass of water to her. She drank it down before she answered. "I saw them looking your way a time or two. They didn't seem offended that you were here. Thank you, by the way, for keeping your distance. You were here, but you let me handle my business."

"Because they're your people," Con replied. "I'm glad I got to observe you and the Light today. They're in awe of you."

She waved away his words. "I think it's more that they've had Usaeil as queen for so long, they aren't sure what to do with me."

"I agree with Con," Varek said. "You didna see their faces as they looked at you when you were speaking to another. They respect you, Rhi. That isna something you can command. It's something that's earned, and you've definitely earned it with the Light."

Rhi shot him a smile. "I have no idea what I'm doing. I'm stumbling around."

"You're stumbling in the right direction," Merrill said with a chuckle.

Con's black eyes were intense as they watched her. "She certainly is."

Rhi grew uncomfortable under such scrutiny. "It's late, and we're alone now. There's no need to pretend anymore."

"Who says I'm pretending?" Con replied.

Before she could come up with a reply, he walked away, Merrill and Varek following him through the passage to her chambers. She hadn't thought about where the other two Kings would sleep, but no doubt Con would put them in her quarters with him, which would be perfect. The more of them that were here, the easier it would be for her to ignore the ever-present voice that told her to stop pushing Con away.

Rhi remained in the throne room for several minutes. She wanted to be alone, needed to just take in the day. She had solved five disputes, righted a wrong, and listened to numerous other issues that would take more than a few minutes to figure out.

Still, it felt good to help her people. She couldn't believe that Usaeil had stopped doing such things. Maybe if Rhi hadn't quit the Queen's Guard, she would've known what Usaeil was up to. Then again, the queen had been good at hiding things.

Finally, Rhi pushed to her feet and walked back to her chambers. She could've teleported, but it felt good to move her limbs after sitting for so long. When she reached her door, she opened it and stepped inside to find it quiet.

With three Kings about, there should be more noise and conversation, but it was so quiet, she could hear a pin drop. Rhi glanced at the door to Con's room as she made her way to her own. The other doors in her chambers were open. She took a quick stroll past them to find all of them empty.

Rhi walked to her room and softly closed the door. She then reached the bed and fell face first onto it. She spread her arms out as she turned her head to the side and lay there with her eyes closed.

It took her a moment to realize that the delicious scents she smelled were coming from her room. She lifted her head and looked around until she found the tray of food sitting on the table out on the balcony. A light breeze came through the opened glass doors, causing the sheer black curtains to move gently.

She pushed up and crawled over the bed to the other side. Then she hopped down and hurried to the table. Once seated, she dug into the variety of food before her. She ate until she couldn't move. Then she sat back and looked at the glittering night sky.

In that instant, she realized that she was happier than she had been in quite some time. In fact, there was a smile on her face, and it wasn't just because she had eaten a delicious meal. She wasn't really sure what the cause was. It could be many factors. Being back with her people, taking over as queen, or solving problems.

"Or Con," the darkness offered.

Rhi didn't want to admit that he could be the cause. But sadly, she didn't have a choice.

Her mood now soured, she removed the tray with magic and walked back inside. She rolled her head, trying to ease her aching shoulders. A bath would be perfect. Except when she went to the tub, it was already full, steam rising from the water while dozens of candles filled the room, bathing it in golden light.

There was no denying who was responsible. She stormed to her door and threw it open before marching to Con's. She stopped when she neared it and said, "This won't help your cause. Food and a bath? Really? I expected better from you."

Rhi whirled back around and slammed the door to her room before removing her clothes and sinking into the tub. She wasn't going to waste it since it had been drawn. But she knew Con was trying to get under her skin. This was his attempt to soften her. But . . . why? Why did he now suddenly want to help her, be with her, share truths that she had once begged to know?

They had an understanding. He'd left her. She hated him, and therefore, he hated her. They worked together when they had to, and it had benefited both of them.

But . . . could he want more?

Hope sprang up so quickly at the thought, that it made Rhi's breath catch. It was dangerous to even consider such a thing. She had barely survived the first time Con had ended things. She wasn't about to open herself up to that again, no matter how much she wanted it.

"Even if it is forever this time?"

She didn't know why the darkness would ask such a question. It had nothing to do with evil, and everything to do with good. Love was light and peace, it was warmth and affection.

But . . . what if they could have forever? The Kings had been taking mates for years now. Con could be happy, which meant, they could be together.

She closed her eyes at the thought. No. She couldn't go there, not even in her mind. It hurt too badly, because it was everything she'd ever wanted, ever dreamed of. It was bad enough having to touch Con and pretend that she loved him in front of others. Because it wasn't make-believe. She did still love him. She'd never stopped, no matter how much she'd wanted to, no matter how much she'd tried to make it happen.

This couldn't last much longer. Usaeil would come for her throne. The fact that she'd already become Queen of the Dark meant that Usaeil was making plans. All Rhi had to do was guard herself and wait. Because if, by chance, she did win against Usaeil a second time, she wouldn't be strong enough to walk away from Con if she kept thinking of them together.

And if she fell, taken down by Usaeil's hand . . . well, then that's how it was meant to be. At least her heart would no longer hurt.

CHAPTER TWENTY-THREE

Con had known it would take more than getting Rhi food and drawing a bath for her to win her over, but he'd thought she would at least thank him. Instead, she'd gotten angry.

He smiled. The only reason for her to be mad was if she felt something. And if she felt something, that meant she still cared enough to let emotion rule her.

"Och, lass. You've no' seen anything yet. Just wait," he whispered, long after she'd stormed back to her chamber.

There was a soft knock. Con walked to the door and opened it to let Merrill and Varek inside. Both were quiet until he shut them in.

"We found Rordan," Varek said.

Merrill sank into one of the overstuffed chairs and stretched out his legs to cross his ankles. "It's just as we thought. The Light seem to be on board with you and Rhi. In fact, Rordan hasn't heard any kind of grumbling about Rhi being queen. The Light are happy."

"I think the Fae are waiting to see what she does," Varek added.

Con nodded slowly. "I tend to agree. Rhi has always been someone they've looked up to. She might be infamous, but she's loved. Yesterday and today proved that."

Merrill twisted his lips. "I wasna here yesterday, but I saw today with my own eyes. She handled each and every Fae who came to her with respect and patience. Even when they tried to manipulate her, she quickly and effortlessly made sure that didna happen. She was something to behold."

"Aye. She was." Con hadn't been able to take his eyes off her. He'd known Rhi was special, but seeing her today in the role of queen only confirmed what everyone had known for some time—Rhi was made to be queen.

Varek eyed him as he took the other chair next to Merrill. "Did you speak to her tonight?"

"She was tired," Con replied. "I'm letting her rest."

"Approaching her when her guard is down might be in your best interest."

"Trust me, tonight isna the night." Con turned away as he remembered her words. "But it will be soon."

Merrill asked, "How did Rhi take the news about Usaeil and the Dark?"

"As you'd expect. She didna bat an eye. In fact," Con said as he turned back to face them, "she said she expected such a move."

"A slap to Rhi by taking Balladyn's place," Varek said. He wrinkled his nose. "Usaeil does know how to strike a low blow."

Con shrugged. "It didna hurt Rhi as Usaeil might have hoped. The fact that she went to the Dark lets me know that she's learned about Rhi and me."

"Then why no' just come here?" Merrill asked.

Con looked at the two Kings. "Because Usaeil willna come alone. She intends to bring the Dark Army."

"Another civil war?" Varek asked with a frown.

Con quirked a brow. "What does Usaeil want more than anything?"

"To rule the Fae," Varek replied.

Merrill's eyes widened as he said, "Ah. She intends to let the Light know that, and if Rhi still wants to fight her, then it'll make Rhi look bad by pitting the Dark against the Light again."

"Exactly," Con said.

Varek sat forward. "Does Rhi know that?"

"I'm sure she does. I've no' spoken to her about it yet, but I will. She's too smart no' to have thought of it herself." Con rubbed his hand over his jaw. "Especially if Rhi suspected Usaeil would go to the Dark."

Merrill pushed to his feet. "Dreagan is secure, in case you were wondering."

Con looked from one to the other. "I wasna. I know it's in good hands."

"We just want you to know that we've got your back."

"Thank you," Con replied, sincerity in his voice.

Varek stood and exchanged a look with Merrill. "We'll retire for the night. Rordan found us some rooms near his. Good luck with Rhi. We'll be around if you need us."

Con gave them a wave before they departed. After they were gone, he almost called them back when the silence of the room grew to be too much. But he decided against it. He removed his jacket and lay on the bed, turning out the lights. The moment his eyes landed on the dark ceiling again, he knew he couldn't handle another night of letting his thoughts rule him. He jumped up and strode quietly from the room.

Con took his time investigating the queen's quarters. He had been here a few times to see Usaeil, but he'd only ever been to the throne room and her bedchamber. Now, he got to see the rest of it. He quite liked that Rhi had redecorated, putting her own mark on the place.

There was still more to do, but the fact that Rhi was doing something told Con that she was forcing herself to move forward—even if it was just for show. She might think that was the only reason, and if that's what it took, fine. But he knew that it was healing her in ways she didn't realize.

When he found himself in front of her room, he paused, debating whether to knock or not. But he knew she wouldn't let him in. He could say that he wanted to talk about the plans for Usaeil, but the last thing he wished to do was bring up Usaeil's name. It was only a reminder to Rhi of what he'd done.

Con raked a hand through his hair. If only he could take it all back. But he couldn't. It was a mistake, and he had to find a way through it somehow.

He walked through the main doors to the queen's quarters and strode down the wide corridor. Rhi had an entire wing to herself. It was nice and private, but it took some time to get to the rest of the castle.

For the first time, he looked at the castle in a new light. Before, he'd just seen it as a place where Usaeil held court, somewhere the Light gathered. Now, he saw it as Rhi's home. Whether she wanted to admit it or not, she led the Light in an entirely new direction.

But what did that mean for them? He had every intention of winning her back, but if she was Queen of the Light, and he was King of Dragon Kings, where would they live? They couldn't choose one place over the other without destroying their people. Then again, he was thinking about a problem that wasn't even an issue yet since he still had lots of work to do to win Rhi back.

Despite it being late, many Fae were still walking the castle. They nodded at him, and he responded in kind. None of them stopped him, and he was thankful. He wasn't in the mood to talk.

His steps carried him through the great hall and into parts of the castle he'd never seen. After about an hour of wandering, he found himself in the library. He'd only seen it once, long, long ago when the castle had first been constructed.

He walked through the quiet stacks, his gaze perusing the many titles. Rhi had an affinity for the tomes. When they had been together, he'd found her in the library at Dreagan many times. It hadn't held nearly the number of books that it did now, but she had loved it just the same.

Con was near the back of the library when he saw a flicker of light coming from a space between the floor and a wall. When he walked closer, he realized that it was a door. He put his ear to it and listened. No sound could be heard other than the soft turning of a page every now and again. Just as he was about to pull away, he heard Rhi's voice.

Stunned, he stood there, waiting for her to say more, but she didn't. He had no idea how long she had been in the room, or what she was reading, but at least he knew where to find her if he needed her.

Instead of discovering what she was doing, Con returned to his chamber and thought about how he was going to woo Rhi. She didn't want or need trinkets. What she needed was proof that he would choose her, that she came first. And he would need to do that several times over just to convince her.

If it meant that he gave up being King of Kings, then so be it.

The moment that thought went through his head, pain

zinged through his chest, causing him to clutch it. It had been so long since he'd felt such a sensation that he didn't recognize it for several minutes.

When he did, he leaned his hands upon the window-sill and hung his head. It was the magic of the realm talking to him, telling him that his decision about being King of Kings wasn't his to make. It was the realm's, and the magic had already made it.

Con closed his eyes. "I gave up Rhi once. Please, doona ask me to let my mate go again. I can no' do it."

The magic didn't reply, not that he expected it to. It didn't care if he found love or not. All it wanted was the right dragon to rule.

"There are several Kings who could take my position. Ulrik, for one."

Still, the magic didn't answer. Con sighed loudly and opened his eyes.

"You're right. I wanted this position, and you chose me for it. I'll continue to guard the realm and rule the Kings as I've always done. But I'm also going to have my mate."

His announcement solidified his resolve. He took a deep breath and straightened. If he tried hard enough, he could have it all. It might mean making sacrifices, perhaps living at the Light Castle part of the time, but he didn't care. He'd have Rhi, and that's all that mattered.

Con found himself smiling, a true one this time. An expression that he hadn't worn in quite some time. He didn't care about Moreann, or what was left of the Others. He didn't care about Usaeil or what she might try to do.

Because he knew that as long as he and the Dragon

Kings stood as one, nothing could defeat them. And if their allies joined them, they'd all be stronger for it.

Con removed his shoes and the rest of his clothes and climbed beneath the covers. He didn't need sleep, but he shut his eyes anyway. Immediately, he found himself dreaming of the first time he'd met Rhi. Of seeing her standing atop the mountain with her long, black hair swirling around her head in the wind. She had been the most beautiful thing he'd ever beheld, and thousands of years later, he could still make that claim.

He was fortunate that she hadn't discovered happiness with anyone else. Fate had given him another chance. He'd actually had it for years now, and he'd squandered it. He wouldn't let another second pass without doing his best to get her back.

The dream suddenly changed. Instead of Rhi, Usaeil filled his vision. She stood staring at him with her hair nearly solid silver, her red eyes blazing with fury.

"If I can't have you, then no one can," she declared.

Con saw the magic orb come at him. He lifted his hands to block it and forced himself to wake. He sat up, breathing heavily. He looked around his chamber. When he didn't find a trace of Usaeil, he ran to Rhi's room. He threw open the doors and scanned the area for Usaeil.

"Bloody hell, Con," Rhi grumbled angrily as she sat up in bed. "What are you doing?"

"Usaeil was here," he said and continued searching the room.

Rhi jumped from the bed and grabbed his arm to stop him. "What do you mean, Usaeil was here?"

"I saw her." Con stilled at the touch of Rhi's hand. It seared him straight to his soul. His gaze finally met hers, and that's when he noticed that she was naked.

Standing before him in all her glory. A hunger so great shot through him, he had trouble finishing his thought. "I was dreaming, but it wasna a dream."

Rhi shook her head. "Usaeil couldn't have been here. I've a spell in place that alerts me if she breaks it."

"Unless she was only here in spirit."

CHAPTER TWENTY-FOUR

The sight of desire reflected in Con's black eyes made Rhi's breath seize in her lungs. He looked at her as if he wanted to devour her. For a moment, she forgot what was between them, what he'd done to her—to them. In that second, she nearly went to him.

She glanced down and realized that she was nude, which was her preferred way to sleep. Rhi immediately called clothes to herself. While the outfit covered her body, it did nothing to stop the heat that rushed through her veins, or the need that centered itself between her legs.

In an effort to get control of herself, she took a step away from Con. If only he wasn't so gorgeous. If only she didn't crave his kisses or dream of his hands on her body. If only she could forget what it was like to be loved by him.

If only. . . .

Rhi cleared her throat and made herself look into Con's face. He wasn't even trying to mask his desire, but even if he did, the large bulge in his pants that outlined his arousal would let her know he wanted her.

He was like a drug, because no matter how much she knew she shouldn't go near him, shouldn't let herself want him, she did. Oh, did she ever. Her body overruled her heart and mind, and that simply wouldn't do. At this rate, she would throw herself at him and void everything she'd said since he arrived at the castle.

"What did Usaeil say?" Rhi asked, finally remembering why he was in her room.

Con stared at her, unmoving for several heartbeats. She didn't know if he was struggling to find words, or if he was debating whether to yank her against him and kiss her senseless.

A part of her really, really hoped Con kissed her. Just thinking about it made her gaze drop to his mouth. And what a mouth he had. Wide, full lips that were too sensual for a man but looked perfect on his face. The Fae were known for their beauty, but none of them held a candle to Constantine. He was stunning, a true work of art in both his true form and that of a human.

Con swallowed, the sound loud in the silence. She had no idea how long they'd been standing there, each lost in thought. It could have been minutes or hours. Even days. It didn't matter.

Rhi knew that she was treading dangerous waters. Con had always had a way of making her forget everything when he was near. It didn't help that he had touched her as no other before—or since. He knew her body, knew how to bring her to heights she hadn't known existed.

Her eyes snapped back up to his. "Well?" she demanded.

"Usaeil said that if she couldna have me, no one could."

His voice was rough, as if he were struggling with his desire. And Rhi really hoped he was. It would make her suffering more bearable. She wanted Con to ache for her, to want her so desperately that he couldn't go on without her. It would only be a smidgen of what she'd carried for the thousands of years since they'd parted ways.

"Usaeil can't kill you," Rhi pointed out, trying her best to keep the conversation going.

Con's eyes lowered to her chest. Her nipples hardened, poking through the thin shirt she now wore. Damn him. Rhi fought not to cross her arms in an attempt to stop her body's response.

"Nay, Usaeil couldna. But the Others might be able to," Con answered.

Rhi frowned, her body's reaction forgotten. "The Others are disbanded."

"Are they?" Con shrugged. "We assume so. Noreen thinks so, but Brian is still unaccounted for."

Rhi rolled her eyes. "That Light Fae is a coward. We'll never see him again."

"Usaeil could find Druids anywhere to fill the mortal side of the Others. As a matter of fact, she already has. Maybe she isna killing them."

"I wish that were true, but I don't think so. I think Usaeil is killing the Druids for their powers. And need I remind you that you have Orun? Without the other Druid from Moreann's planet, there can't be a group."

Con drew in a deep breath and then slowly released it. "True."

Rhi waited for him to continue, but he didn't. He shifted his eyes to the side, and his gaze went distant, as if he were lost in his thoughts. She clenched her teeth in an effort to be patient and wait for him to tell her what he was thinking, but then again, this was Con. When did he include her if he didn't have to?

"What are you thinking?" she finally asked.

Con's black eyes slid to her. "Corann."

"I think Usaeil is saving him for last. He has the strongest magic. No doubt it'll last a while when she comes after us."

"*If* she kills him for his magic."

Skepticism filled Rhi. "What are you thinking?"

"Corann has been alive for a verra long time."

"What about it? Some humans live longer than others."

Con quirked a blond brow. "Every mortal on this realm is a descendant of someone from Moreann's planet. Every one."

"You think Usaeil and Moreann would talk Corann into joining them? He's a *mie*. You know, a good druid," she said, her voice heavy with sarcasm.

"Aye."

Rhi's eyes widened, letting him know she was waiting for more. When Con didn't continue, she sighed loudly. "That's all you have to say?"

"With the right motivation, a Druid will readily become *drough*."

"Corann isn't that easily manipulated."

Con gave her a flat look. "He would be if it meant that the rest of the Skye Druids would be left alone."

All the air rushed right out of Rhi as she whispered, "Bloody hell."

"I have no proof of any of this."

"I don't need any to take this scenario seriously. Especially when it involves Moreann and Usaeil. Both of them have managed to surprise us, and I'm tired of it."

Con nodded slowly. "I am, as well. The fact is, Usaeil is backed into a corner now. It should make her easier to deal with, but it actually makes her more dangerous."

"Because she has nothing to lose," Rhi finished.

Con lifted a shoulder as his lips twisted. "Exactly."

"But she does have something to lose—the Dark throne."

"That's true, but she hasna put the time into the Dark as she did with the Light."

Rhi closed her eyes as she rubbed her right temple with her index finger. "We're looking at this wrong." Her eyes opened, and she met Con's gaze. "Usaeil wants power. And you."

"She never had me," he said in such a low tone that dripped with fury, that Rhi took a step back.

"Usaeil wants you, regardless of whether she had you or not," Rhi stated. "And we know she wants to unite the Fae. I'd like to think we pushed her into taking the first step to becoming Queen of the Dark, but I don't think we did. I think she was going to do it anyway. We may have just upped her timeline."

Con considered that for a moment before he nodded. "All right. Say that's right. Then her next move should be coming here and trying to take back the Light throne."

"Which won't happen because I'll make sure of it. However," Rhi emphasized when Con tried to interject, "I'm going to make sure that I don't send us to war. There will be a battle, but she'll be the one to initiate it, not me."

"You need to be careful. She knows what to say to rile you."

Rhi wrinkled her nose. "Maybe. Then again, for all she knows, we're back together."

Just saying it sent a tingle running through Rhi that made her want to smile.

"When Usaeil comes, I'll be standing right beside you so she can see us together," Con added.

Rhi couldn't help but smile. "That will certainly anger her."

"She'll be expecting it, so there willna be the big explosion of fury that you're hoping for."

"I'm sure I can get her there," Rhi replied with a smirk.

"Just as I'm sure she feels about you."

Damn him. She hated when Con was right. Rhi folded her arms over her chest and tapped her toe. "If I'm going to pretend to be queen, then I need to act like one. I just hope I can pull it off."

"You can."

"You have more faith in me than I do."

"Because this isna just about you or me or the Fae. This is about the entire realm, as well as justice. Usaeil can no' continue without being punished for what she's done to her family, countless other Fae, and the Druids she's killed to take their magic."

Rhi hadn't been looking for a compliment—or had she? Whether or not she was, Con had given her a doozy that left her reeling and feeling warm inside.

"We need to expect that Usaeil could arrive at any time. She'll want to catch you unawares," he continued. "Make sure the Light Army and the Queen's Guard are prepared. I would also suggest that you alert the Light and tell them what could happen."

Rhi licked her lips. "But we don't know what will happen. Usaeil could come on her own instead of with an army."

"She could. But she willna. She'll want a show of force behind her, something to prove to anyone who looks that she can rule the Dark. Since she governed the Light for so long, it demonstrates her ability to rule the two sides as one."

Rhi dropped her arms as she blew out a breath. "I'm convinced, and that's just with you speaking. Maybe she should rule us all."

"You can no' mean that," Con stated in a harsh voice. "Stop second-guessing yourself. You took the throne because you knew you could do a better job than she did. Aye, a part of it might have been to get back at Usaeil, but deep down, it's because you knew the people needed someone they could depend on. You have no ulterior motive. You simply want to do the right thing."

"You make me sound so . . . perfect. When I'm anything but," she told him in a soft voice.

His brows snapped together. "I didna say you were perfect. No one is. What you are, however, is the right person to be queen."

"I'm doing all of this, mostly because of what Usaeil did to me. But also because she's Dark, pretending to be Light. She lied to us for thousands of years."

"I know."

Rhi drew in a deep breath and said, "And now I'm doing the same thing."

"Because you hear the darkness within you?" Con asked, a blond brow raised in question. "For the majority of your life, you were blessed that your light was so bright that no darkness could penetrate it. Unfortunately, a wee bit got in. So what if you hear the darkness now? You're no' Dark. And you're no' Usaeil."

Rhi glanced at the floor and swallowed. "I let the darkness in. I welcomed it in order to best Usaeil."

"Nay, you didna. You thought you did, but you didna need the darkness. You were strong enough to do it all on your own. If you need proof of your power, look at what you did to the Fae Realm. Usaeil knows your strength, which is why she does everything she can to make you feel inferior. When in reality, she's inferior to *you*."

Rhi eyed him, unsure whether she could believe his

words. Con didn't know the things the darkness had said to her—or what she'd said to the darkness.

He didn't know how good it had felt to give in to it when she met Usaeil on the battlefield the first time.

"I'm not the person I once was," she said and turned her back on him.

CHAPTER TWENTY-FIVE

"I know exactly who you are," Con replied.

But Rhi kept her back to him. "You should go."

He walked around her until he stood before her. "Why? Because you doona like what I'm saying? Too fucking bad. You're going to listen because someone should've been telling you this all along. *I* should've been telling you this."

"Telling me what? That I'm good?" She rolled her eyes. "Don't waste your breath."

"Do you really believe you're the only Fae—hell, the only being—on this realm who battles the evil within you? Everyone does. Every single one of us fights that battle daily. If I'd been in your shoes, I would've let the darkness in, as well."

"Don't you dare lie to me," she spat at him. "Of the two of us, we both know you never would've done such a thing. The magic never would've chosen you as King if that were the case."

He snorted loudly. "Do no' mistake the magic as perfect, because it isna. Sometimes, the dragons chosen changed during their reign because of things the magic couldna see. That's called life, Rhi. It's called living and making decisions that you have to live with. So what if your eyes flashed red?"

"What?" she asked slack-jawed.

Con could've kicked himself. He hadn't meant to let that little bit of information slip, in case Rhi hadn't known.

"My eyes turned red? When?" She moved closer, eying him as she did.

"After Usaeil's body disappeared. I saw your eyes flash red before you teleported away."

Her head turned away so he couldn't see her expression. Con wanted to get to a better position to observe her, but he remained where he was. Rhi didn't want him to see her face, and he would respect that. Even if he didn't like it.

"Why didn't you tell me?"

He briefly closed his eyes and gave a shake of his head. "I knew you were strong enough no' to let the darkness take you completely. I know you, and I knew that you were no' in a good place mentally or emotionally from everything that Usaeil put you through with the banishment. You're stronger than you realize."

"Sometimes, people get tired of being strong."

Con knew that better than she did, but he didn't say that. "Whether we want to be strong or no', sometimes, we doona have a choice. We do it because we must."

Her head swung back to him. "I don't want to turn into Usaeil."

"You willna."

"You sound sure of that, but you can't make that promise."

He started to reach for her but stopped himself in time. "I am sure, and I can make that promise because

I willna let you become that. But it willna come to that because you'll always stay true to yourself."

"Maybe," she said in such a low voice that he almost missed it.

Con didn't want to leave her. He wanted to remain with Rhi and continue talking. They had been conversing without any hostility between them, which was something that hadn't happened when they were alone. It was a step, a tiny one, but progress, nonetheless.

"I'll alert Merrill and Varek that Usaeil could be getting to us through our dreams," he said and began to walk away.

"Don't leave."

He'd only gotten two steps when her voice reached him. He halted and turned back to her. Whatever excitement filled him was quickly quashed when she said, "We need to go over every possible course of action that Usaeil will take. And two heads are better than one."

Con wished that she wanted him to remain for other reasons, but she wanted him to stay, and that was something. He gave a nod of agreement and went to one of the chairs in the room to sit. Rhi remained standing. She paced as she began listing the various ways Usaeil could come for the throne on her own, with the Dark Army, with Moreann, and other various combinations of each.

All the while, Con's eyes followed her from one end of the room to the other. Rhi's hair fell in thick midnight waves, begging for his hands to grab a handful and pull her head back to expose her neck before he kissed it.

That had used to drive Rhi mad with desire. She had never held back from him, giving him everything she had. The passion between them had been explosive.

Primal.

He'd never experienced anything like it before. It was

how he'd known for sure that Rhi was his mate. While the sex had been fantastic, it was more than that. They fit together in all ways. Like puzzle pieces that had been made for each other.

Neither of them cared that they came from different species. Nothing mattered but the love between them and the happiness they shared. But he had ruined it all. He might have had a good reason, but it didn't make it right. The suffering he'd put both of them through hadn't been worth any of this.

Rhi walked past him, her gaze on the floor. "Stop it."

He frowned as he turned his head to follow her. "Stop what?"

"Looking at me like that."

"Like what?"

She halted and spun around to glare at him. "You know exactly what I mean."

He did, but he wanted her to say it. "Afraid to speak it aloud?"

"You're impossible," she said with a roll of her eyes. "And if you can't be professional about this, leave."

Con crossed his arms over his chest. "Professional? Were you professional all those times you called me names when you were at Dreagan? How about jumping into my office veiled and listening to my conversations?"

"You knew I was there."

"Aye, I did, but the others didna."

"You could've told them."

"I could have, but I chose no' to."

Her silver eyes narrowed. "Because you didn't want them to know that you've always been able to tell when I come to Dreagan whether I'm veiled or not."

"You're right."

"Which is bull—what did you say?" she asked perplexed.

She had expected him to deny it, and when he hadn't, it stumped her. Con held her gaze and shrugged. "I said, you're right. I didna want them to know. There isna a King at Dreagan who didna know you were my mate. They told me often what a fool I was to have let you go. If they'd known I could sense you, they would've doubled their efforts to bring us back together."

"I told Rhys it wasn't going to happen. I've told many of them that," she declared.

Con hid the hurt her words caused. "I doona blame you. What I did wasna right."

"You should've told me yourself."

"I'm sorry. I know the words are too little, too late, but I need you to understand that it was never to hurt you. I was d—"

"Doing it for the Dragon Kings," Rhi said over him, her anger evident. "I know. You've already told me."

"What would you have done in my place?"

She threw up her hands. "Oh, jeez, Con, I don't know. Maybe talked to you about it instead of making a decision for both of us. I would've seen if we could come up with some kind of solution."

"What solution?" he pushed as he dropped his arms and sat forward. "What would you have done with a manor full of Dragon Kings, and even more still asleep in their mountains? They were angry at the world and missing their clans and family. Thankfully, the spell stopped them from turning that animosity on the humans, or there likely would've been another war. What would you have done if you'd just told your lover good-bye for the day and wore a smile as you entered the manor, only to find several of your brethren looking at you with jealousy while others looked miserable?" He got to his feet, his anger getting to him. "Could you have continued with your happiness, despite what was happening to those around you? Could you have ignored the discontent running through the manor? Because I couldna. No matter how much it killed me to end things, no matter how much I knew that I'd never again be happy, I had no other choice!"

Rhi stared at him for a long moment, her brow puckered as his words rang in the room. "There is always another choice."

"No' that I saw. In every scenario of us together, I saw the Kings falling apart. In order for Dreagan to survive, we had to stick together."

"So you chose misery?"

"I chose the happiness of my brethren."

Rhi released a breath. "And in the process, tore two people apart."

"You were never far from me. Whether in my dreams or random thoughts during the day, you were always there. Always."

"I wish I could say that was enough, but it isn't. You tore out my heart."

"And you took mine with you. Doona believe for one moment that you're the only one who has been miserable. You doona know how hard it's been to get through each day without you. Then, suddenly, you were back in my life. And with your arrival came a fresh kind of pain. Yet, I accepted it. Because I got to see you."

She moved to him, stopping just short of touching him. "Thank you for finally telling me all of this, but it's too little, too late."

A bellow began in Con, but he held it back. "It's never too late for the kind of love we have."

"Had," she corrected. "You killed it when you ended us."

"That isna true, and you know it."

She looked to the hand he'd raised that was reaching for her. Her gaze stopped him cold. Then, her silver eyes swung to him. "I would've done anything for you. You were everything I wanted, all I ever dreamed of. Nothing mattered but you. I would've gone anywhere, given up anything, just to have you. We made vows to each other."

"I know." As if he could ever forget. "We bound ourselves to each other."

"Those words were as binding as the ceremonies you perform for the Kings and their mates. Yet you forgot them when you chose your brethren over me."

Con clenched his fist and lowered his arm to his side. "I never forgot those vows. I didna take another to my bed until Usaeil. Can you say the same?"

Rhi lifted her chin. "I don't need to justify my actions to you. You were the one who let me go. What I did with anyone after is none of your business."

He'd always suspected that she had taken lovers. After all, it had been a very long time since they had parted ways. But to hear her say it nearly brought him to his knees. Balladyn was one thing, but he didn't want to know about any others.

"What?" she asked sarcastically. "Did that hurt? Good. Feel a little of what I've felt all these years."

In a blink, his pain turned to fury. He grabbed her by the shoulders and held her tight. "So, it's all right for you to have lovers, but no' me?"

"Yep. What are you going to do about it?" she taunted.

Con told himself to let her go. He knew the longer he held her, the more he'd tempt himself. He'd made headway with Rhi, and to do anything to jeopardize that was stupid.

But her heady scent of jasmine reached him. Whatever sane thoughts he had evaporated as he lowered his head.

CHAPTER TWENTY-SIX

It felt so good to be held by him. *He* felt so good.

Rhi knew it was wrong. She knew she should push him away or jerk out of his grasp, but she couldn't seem to make herself do it.

Then his nostrils flared, and suddenly, desire filled his eyes again. She'd barely withstood it when he hadn't been touching her. Now, she didn't stand a chance.

Yes. Please, yes.

The thought repeated itself over and over in her mind as his head began to lower to hers. Her eyes closed on their own just before she lifted her face to his, and their lips met. For a brief instant, neither of them moved.

Then the passion took them. His lips moved over her mouth, enticing and exploring. She didn't have the will-power to withstand the onslaught of need, of wild, un-abashed desire that consumed her.

She wound her arms around his neck and sighed as his hands slid to her back and held her against his rock-hard chest. Then he moaned low in his throat. It made her stomach flutter, and heat pool between her legs.

The kiss was an inferno of yearning, of hunger that

they both remembered. Every part of her sank into him, willingly giving herself to the need she could no longer ignore. He deepened the kiss as his hands roamed over her back. A little voice in the back of her mind told her that she would regret this later, but it was quickly silenced by her body. Rhi let the world fall away as passion swept through her.

Con's fingers tangled in her hair and pulled her head back, exposing her neck. His hot mouth trailed down her throat. He paused at the base, his tongue licking at the vein that pulsed rapidly there.

She dug her fingers into his back as he rocked his hips against hers. Suddenly, she needed to feel his skin beneath her palms. She was so lost in the passion that she didn't think about her magic while she clawed at his shirt.

Then, his mouth was back on hers, kissing her senseless. He turned them, backing her up until she was pinned against the wall. His hands were between them. She whimpered when he moved away from her, then she heard material ripping, and looked down to find he had torn her shirt in half.

Their gazes met, sounds of their harsh breathing filling the room. This was the time she should end it, the time to come to her senses and walk away.

But that wasn't what she wanted, and it certainly wasn't what she needed.

Once more, she reached for his shirt, but she couldn't get to it. Con had slipped his fingers into the waistband of her pants, and with one yank, tore them, as well. His onyx eyes blazed with longing, and it made her heart miss a beat. She loved this primal part of him, the part that wanted her with a need that meant nothing would separate them.

It took little effort for him to tear both her bra and

panties from her body until she stood bare before him. She leaned her head against the wall behind her and let him look his fill.

The way his eyes traveled slowly down her body made desire tighten her sex. And just like that, he had her on the edge of orgasm. He'd always had the ability to look at her like that and immediately send her spiraling out of control.

His hands shook from the hunger pounding through him. Con stared at the woman before him, awed by the siren she was. All it would take was a word from Rhi, and he'd be on his knees. That's the kind of control she had over him.

There was only one person in the entire universe who could save him—and she stood before him now. Con's gut clenched because he knew she was breathing life back into him. It was a second chance few ever got—and he certainly didn't deserve it.

But he was going to take it anyway.

Her soft skin begged for his touch. He lifted his hand and let his fingers trail from behind her ear, down her neck, and over her collarbone to the outside of her breast. He cupped her, letting her mound fill his hand before he gently ran his thumb over her nipple.

She sucked in a breath. He glanced at her face to find her eyes closed, and her lips parted as her hands flattened against the wall. How he'd missed caressing her. He'd always loved the way Rhi filled his palms perfectly. More than that, he loved how sensitive her nipples were.

He leaned forward and wrapped his lips around the other turgid peak to suckle gently while his thumb and forefinger rolled the other bud. All the while, Rhi's hips rocked against the leg he had shoved between hers.

But soon, even that wasn't enough for him. Con kissed down her body as he lowered himself to his knees. When he reached her belly, he looked up to find her gazing down at him, her chest rising and falling quickly.

He held her gaze as he lifted one of her legs and moved it over his shoulder. Then he leaned forward and softly ran his tongue over her sex. Rhi's answering sigh was just what he needed to hear.

Con licked and laved, taking his time and letting the taste of her fill him. Her sighs turned to soft cries. Then, her fingers slid into his hair so she could hold his head against her. He could feel her on the edge of a climax. With a flick of his tongue, he sent her over the edge.

Her scream of pleasure had him inwardly smiling. But he wasn't finished with her yet. With her body still convulsing, he pushed a finger inside her and began to pump it in and out of her.

"Con!" she screamed as another orgasm began just as the first was fading.

He didn't stop licking her or moving his finger until her hand loosened on his hair. He placed a small kiss to her navel and then lowered her leg to the floor before he straightened.

As soon as he did, she snapped her fingers, removing his clothes. Rhi pushed away from the wall and put her hands on his chest. Slowly, her gaze lifted to his face.

Whatever worry he had about her sending him away vanished at the sight of the desire reflected in her silver depths. She pushed him backwards, step by step, never breaking contact with him. When his legs hit the bed, she gave him one final push that sent him falling onto the mattress. She put a knee on the duvet and crawled over him like the seductress she was.

"My turn," she whispered with a sly grin.

Con swallowed and watched her as she looked down his body before traveling back up. He met her gaze and let his head drop back when she caressed a finger down his chest to his stomach. Stopped just short of touching his aching cock.

He wanted her so desperately that he contemplated taking control and joining their bodies. But her touch felt too good. And it had been so very long since she'd had her hands on him in this way. Only a fool would pass up such an opportunity.

She could spend eternity running her hands over Con's amazing body and still never get enough. From his broad shoulders, thick chest, and chiseled abs to his narrow waist, he was gorgeous.

Rhi leaned down and flicked her tongue over his nipple and felt the tremor that ran through him at her touch. She smiled and looked up at him.

"Minx," he said, but there was a smile in his voice.

"Oh, I'm just getting started."

He moaned in response. She held his gaze as her hand traveled back down his body before her fingers wrapped around his thick arousal. It jerked in response as he closed his eyes and let the passion consume him.

She knew exactly how he felt since he'd done the same to her not minutes before. Rhi moved until she was between his legs. She looked down at his impressive length and ran her hand up and down it, feeling the heat and hardness.

Then she leaned forward until her lips were a breath from touching him. She looked up and saw him watching her through eyes narrowed into slits. If there was one thing that she loved to do, it was to take him into her mouth. The fact that he'd loved it just as much meant that she had done it often when they were together.

How she'd missed having him in her hands and at her mercy. It was the only time he gave up complete control, and she'd always treasured that.

She parted her lips and slowly brought her mouth to him. As she took him into her depths, his hands fisted in the covers. But it was the raw, unadulterated need in his voice as he whispered her name that brought tears to her eyes and made her heart swell.

No matter their past, the one time they had always been completely honest with each other was during sex. There were no walls, no secrets. Only complete surrender.

She continued working him as her mouth moved up and down his length. His hips began to lift in time with her strokes. Rhi was prepared to make him orgasm just like this, but she should've known Con would have other plans.

Before she knew it, he sat up and grabbed her. With ease, he lifted her until she was straddling him. Her sex clenched as she waited for him to enter her, but he didn't move. Instead, he gazed at her with such an intense look that it took her breath away.

She wanted to ask him what he was trying to communicate to her, but she couldn't seem to find the words to break the hold that he somehow had over her. She was trapped in his black gaze, ensnared by his desire.

Then, slowly, he lowered her. The moment the blunt head of his cock touched her, she sucked in a breath. He filled her, stretching her as her body took him deep inside.

Nothing had ever felt so perfect or so right as everything did right at that moment. It brought back all the other times they had shared their bodies, and both had known they had something special, something that didn't happen every day.

And the proof was here once again.

She might try to deny it, might make bold claims about her feelings, but her body and her heart knew the truth. It was Con. It would always be Con.

Unable to hold still any longer, Rhi began rocking her hips. Con's hands rested on her waist, urging her faster and faster until even that wasn't enough.

He flipped her onto her back, their bodies still joined. Rhi locked her ankles around him as he began to thrust. The feel of him sliding in and out of her hard and fast was everything she'd needed, everything she'd longed for.

And like he'd always been able to do, he propelled her toward another climax. He rose up on his knees, still pumping his hips as he reached down and swirled a finger around her clit.

The orgasm was swift and intense as it swept through her like fire, leaving her sated but also craving more. When Con leaned over her again, Rhi wrapped her arms around him and squeezed her eyes closed as his hips pistoned faster and faster until he climaxed with a shout.

Tears gathered in Rhi's eyes because she knew that by giving in to the desire now, she had provided Con with the opening he needed.

When their breathing returned to normal, he pulled out of her and rolled onto his back as he tugged her against him. Rhi said nothing because there was nothing to say. Not when she felt so good.

"I'll hold onto you for the rest of time," Con whispered. "I'll never let you go again."

Rhi pretended to be asleep since she didn't know what to say to that. Or even if she *should* say anything.

CHAPTER TWENTY-SEVEN

Con came awake immediately. He hadn't intended to sleep, but something about holding Rhi in his arms lulled him. They had rolled over so that he now molded himself against her back as she lay on her side.

Few times since he'd ended things between them had he actually lain in a bed. It wasn't as if they had only ever made love there, but they had often ended the day in his bed, their bodies tangled together as they held each other and talked for hours.

He hadn't been able to see a bed without thinking of Rhi, and all the special memories they had created together. And now that they were in a bed again—this time hers—he wasn't going to waste a single second of it.

Con closed his eyes and listened to the sound of her breathing. He smiled, knowing she wouldn't have fallen asleep if she hadn't felt comfortable with him. Her words had been harsh, but her fiery kisses and the passionate way she'd touched him said something altogether different.

Her head rested on his arm, while his other was

draped over her side. Their feet were intertwined, and there wasn't a single millimeter of space between them. This was one of those times Con never wanted to forget. He was deliriously happy. He didn't for a moment think that things between him and Rhi were fixed, but he knew that they were definitely headed in the right direction.

His eyes opened when she made a soft sound in her sleep and leaned back against him. Her moods were so volatile lately, though he couldn't blame her. She might have been amorous a little while ago, but she could wake up and kick him out of the castle.

And that simply wouldn't do.

He needed to remind her of the chemistry they had, of how great they were together. But more than that, he had to prove to her that he wasn't going anywhere. Ever. That he would stand beside her for the rest of time. Or at least for the rest of his life.

Rhi was his everything. His mate, his soul, his better half. Whatever name you put to it, that's what she was. He would show her that she came first for him. And, somehow, he would have to figure out a way to continue governing the Kings while putting her first. It wasn't going to be easy, but something as important as Rhi was worth any difficulty.

Con's cock hardened. A taste of her after so long had left him famished for more. He shifted his hand slightly and cupped a breast. He slowly began to circle her nipple with his finger. It didn't take long for the tiny nub to pucker.

Her hips rocked back instinctively. He managed to move his leg just enough so that hers separated, and he could slide his hand down to the junction of her thighs.

His fingers slid through the trimmed black curls and found the folds of her sex. He parted them so he could tease her clit. Her breathing changed, rushing faster and faster through her lungs, causing her chest to rise and fall more rapidly.

Con then dipped a finger inside her and found her wet. He bit back a groan even as his balls tightened in response. But his finger inside her wasn't enough. He needed to be closer, to join their bodies.

No longer worried about waking her, Con moved her leg over his and took his cock in hand so he could guide it to her entrance. The moment he came in contact with her wet heat, he thrust his hips, burying himself within her.

Rhi gasped and dug her nails into his hip. "Oh," he moaned.

He held her still as he drove in and out of her. He was so close, and he wasn't going to reach the end without her. Con once more teased her clit.

She cried out, her back arching from the pleasure. Her earlier cries still rang in his ears, and he was going to make sure she screamed again. If he had any say in it, she'd be doing that several times a day for eternity.

There was something incredibly sexy about being woken by your lover's hands or mouth. Rhi couldn't remember what she'd been dreaming of, but it had quickly changed to images of Con rubbing her body. Except that hadn't been a dream, it had actually been happening. She hadn't woken until he filled her.

The way he touched her, working her body as his hard arousal slid in and out of her, was toe-curling. But before she got too used to that, he had her on her hands and knees, her hips grasped tightly as his tempo quickened. He drove deeper, making her fist the blankets as the pleasure intensified.

He kept her on the precipice of orgasm for what felt like years, the pleasure building and building until he pinched her nipple. And just like that, she fell over the edge.

White light flashed behind her eyes as ecstasy so pure, so intense consumed her. It felt as if she were floating upon a cloud, her body humming with bliss.

As reality returned, Con's fingers dug into her hips as he moved faster and faster until he gave a shout as he climaxed, his seed filling her.

Rhi found herself smiling. She was happy, truly happy. She didn't let memories of the past or problems of the present intrude—not yet, at least. There was enough time for all of that later. For now, she was going to enjoy these moments.

They fell to the side together, their bodies still joined. Con wrapped his arms around her and pulled her against him as he rested his cheek near hers.

"Wow," she murmured. "That was amazing."

She felt him smile. "Mm-hmm. That it was."

"You fell asleep."

He chuckled softly. "I can no' remember the last time I did that."

A little thrill went through her at his confession. It made her never want to leave her room, much less her bed. But then she remembered her new role and the duties that awaited.

"No' yet," Con whispered.

She frowned. "What are you talking about?"

"You stiffened, which means you're thinking about things you need to do. I'm asking you to hold off for a wee bit longer."

"I don't plan on getting up just yet."

"Good, because I wasna going to let you up," he said and playfully nipped her lobe.

Rhi smiled and found herself holding onto his arms. It made her think of all the times she and Con had been in this exact position before. Unfortunately, other memories returned, and she also recalled how he had broken her heart.

Con sighed, though he didn't loosen his grip. She didn't bother asking him what was wrong. She knew. He was somehow able to determine what was going through her mind just by holding her.

It would be so easy for her to fall back into him. So, so easy. But she couldn't do that. Not only because of the past, but also because of Usaeil. Rhi couldn't allow herself to become that invested in Con again.

"You've always been that invested. Stop lying," the darkness told her.

"Last night and this morning were great, but it changes nothing," she said into the silence.

Con was silent for a heartbeat. "It changes everything, and you know it. But I'll wait until you can admit that. I'm no' going anywhere. I promise you."

"You made a lot of promises before."

"I explained why I did what I did."

She turned in his arms so she could look into his eyes. His wavy blond hair was in disarray, his eyes heavy-lidded, which only made him sexier. "I appreciate the explanation, but it doesn't magically heal my scars."

"Scars like yours can no' be healed. I know this. But that doesna mean I'm going to give up on us and our love."

Rhi fought the tears that suddenly filled her eyes. She touched Con's face, her heart urging her to let go of the hurt and pain of the past and grab hold of the present as well as the future Con offered.

"We have bigger problems than what's between us. You should be focused on that."

"I am," he stated.

Rhi lowered her hand. It hurt too much to touch him, and being in his arms was a sweet torture that would haunt her for weeks to come. But it couldn't happen again. Her words to Con were also a warning to herself.

"Doona pull away from me."

The pleading in his eyes was something she'd never seen before. It tugged at her heart in a way that caused cracks to form, weakening the wall she'd put around herself in an effort to keep him from getting too close.

"I was a fool before. Doona let my past mistakes color your thoughts of the present. Please."

Rhi couldn't handle it anymore. She rolled out of his arms and rose from the bed. She kept her back to him for a few moments to compose herself before she faced him.

"I don't regret sharing our bodies. We're good at that, and it was nice to feel that kind of pleasure again," she began.

Con sat up, his muscles shifting and moving as he did. "But?"

"This isn't the time or place for the conversation you want."

"Why? Because you doona want to hear something that could change your mind about us?"

She'd hurt him. Yesterday, that might have made her feel good, but now, she didn't like that it had happened. "I'm being realistic. I can't let anything in that will distract me from defeating Usaeil once and for all. We both know what she could do to this realm."

"She willna defeat the Kings. I can guarantee that."

"What about Moreann? The Others did some pretty damaging things to the Kings already. You can't forget about that."

Con rose from the bed like a god come to take revenge on those who dared to tread upon his realm. "You actually think I could?"

"I'm just reminding you."

Black eyes went cold with fury as he glared at her. His typically low, deadly tone was replaced by one of barely controlled violence. "You doona need to do such a thing. I'm the one who has ruled for millions and millions of years. I'm the one who remained awake while the rest of the Kings took to their mountains to sleep after we sent our dragons away. I walked Dreagan, alone for eons, and had to deal with my grief myself. I didna have anyone to turn to, anyone to talk to. I had to be strong, to be the one who didna put his feelings ahead of what was best for everyone else. I had to be the voice of caution and reason for the others. I had to set aside my love for you, my mate, for them. So, doona dare think that after taking the throne for a few days, you have any idea what it's like to sacrifice for others, or that I doona have the Kings prepared for *any* eventuality."

Con then turned on his heel and strode from the room.

Rhi could only stare after him, shocked by the depth of his anger after seeing him so controlled for so long. First, he'd lowered his guard last night, but passion had always caused him to reveal his true self to her.

But the fury? That was different. She quite liked seeing him lose control.

Rhi snorted. Con hadn't lost control. He'd allowed her to see his outrage on purpose. Was it because she had hurt him earlier, or was it something else?

"It doesn't matter. We need to be concerned about Us-aeil and Moreann, nothing else," she told herself.

But she leaned to the side to look out her door. She hadn't heard him go into his room. Had he left? Her stomach clenched in dread. He'd promised to stay.

She fisted her hands and quieted her mind. So what if Con left? She didn't need him.

A tear fell onto her cheek.

"But I do," she whispered.

CHAPTER TWENTY-EIGHT

MacLeod Castle

Phelan looked around the great hall, browsing the faces around him. All the Warriors and Druids had gathered. Though no one had told Phelan exactly why they'd been called, he knew it must be about the Ancients talking to Isla.

Aisley reached over and slid her palm against his so their fingers locked together. "It'll be fine."

"You say that as if I doona know," he whispered back.

"You often remind me of that. I just thought I'd do the same."

He looked at her and smiled. She was a Phoenix, the last of her kind, and his wife. Even after all this time, he could still recall how he felt when he believed that she'd died. But after burning her body, Aisley had returned to him.

"What?" she asked with a grin.

"I love you."

Her smile softened. "And I love you."

"Whatever this is, we'll get through it."

She nodded her head of wavy, black hair, her fawn-colored eyes serious. "Yes, we will. We survived Declan and Jason. And this time, we have the Dragon Kings."

"I think we're here because of the Kings," he said in a low voice.

Aisley looked around the hall at those gathered, everyone speaking softly except for three couples—Isla and Hayden, Evie and Malcolm, and Fallon and Larena.

Fallon finally took a step forward, causing everyone's attention to turn to him. "As most of you know, Isla heard from the Ancients a few days ago. They urged her to go to the Isle of Skye. Hayden and Malcolm accompanied Isla and Evie, and what they found there caused them to contact me. After which, Larena and I immediately traveled to the isle and discovered that Corann and another Druid had been taken."

"Why are you just now telling us?" Lucan, Fallon's youngest brother, demanded.

Quinn, the middle brother, nodded, and his pale green eyes narrowed in anger. "I second that."

"There are reasons," Fallon told the group. "We were no' the only ones who went to Skye after learning of the missing Druids. Con arrived with a couple of Kings. That's when we learned it was Usaeil who had taken Corann and one other Druid."

Phelan's brows snapped together. "That means the Fae are involved."

"Aye," Fallon said with a nod as his dark green eyes locked with Phelan's. "Rhi also made an appearance."

"Is she all right? Last I heard, no one had seen her," Phelan stated, his anger and concern churning together as he glanced at the two other couples who had been to Skye. "Why did no one tell me?"

Larena's calm voice broke the silence. "She's taken the Light throne."

Phelan's heart hammered in his chest, but he realized what was going on. "She did it to draw out Usaeil."

"Aye," Fallon said with a nod. "However, the Kings knew that wouldna be enough to get Usaeil to attack."

Phelan waited for them to finish. When they didn't, he searched his mind. Unfortunately, his emotions were in such chaos after learning that Rhi wasn't just all right but now Queen of the Light, that he couldn't form a thought.

Then it hit him.

"Constantine," he murmured. "Usaeil wants him, so if she believes he and Rhi are together, it will certainly call her out."

"Aye," Fallon said as he observed Phelan carefully.

Phelan shrugged, not understanding why it would matter if Rhi and Con pretended to be together. Now, if Con had been her King then . . .

His thoughts trailed off as he put two and two together.

Aisley gripped his hand with both of hers. "Breathe, baby."

"It was Con," Phelan said in a soft voice, hardly able to believe it. He wanted to reject the idea, but given the way everyone stared at him, he couldn't. "Con," he said louder, fuming. He surged to his feet. "Con, who has repeatedly asked for her help, who began an affair with Usaeil, who hurt Rhi again and again. And again."

Isla was the one who said, "And Rhi went back to Dreagan, again and again. It was Rhi who offered to help the Kings first. She who chose not to tell you, or any of us, who her King was. You need to remember that."

Phelan took a step forward when Aisley was suddenly

before him. She cupped his face with her hands and held his gaze. "Baby, I know you're angry. If Rhi had wanted you to know it was Con, she would've told you. You can't blame all of this on Con."

"I bloody well can."

Aisley shook her head. "You can't. You also have to think that Rhi agreed to let everyone know that she and Con were back together to use it against Usaeil. If Rhi can do it, then you can accept the past and her decisions."

Phelan peeled back his lips, not at all happy. It seemed that everyone was okay with what was going on, but he wasn't. Not by a long shot. "Fine."

Aisley raised a black brow and leveled him with a flat stare. "Then why haven't you tamped down your god?"

That caused Phelan to pause. He lifted his hands and saw the gold skin and claws of his god, Zelfor. He ran his tongue over his teeth and felt the fangs, as well. He'd been so incensed that he hadn't even realized he'd released his god. That kind of lapse could easily allow his god to take over, something every Warrior there had gained command of years ago.

He immediately got himself under control, his gold skin fading, and the fangs and claws disappearing. Then he released a breath.

"Con wanted to be the one to tell you," Fallon said. "However, I decided to tell everyone at once."

Aisley moved to Phelan's side and looked at Fallon. "Obviously, there's going to be a war. What do you need from us?"

"We'll know soon enough. The Kings are on their way," Fallon replied.

Phelan sincerely hoped it was Con. He wanted to punch him. Phelan might not be able to best a Dragon King, but he could certainly cause a little pain.

As one, everyone felt the intrusion at the barrier around the castle. Galen went to the window and looked out.

"It's Ulrik, Rhys, Kiril, and Banan," he said over his shoulder.

Fallon gave a nod and walked to the door to open it. Within seconds, the four Dragon Kings entered the castle.

Ulrik's gold eyes immediately landed on Phelan before jerking to Fallon. "You told him."

"I did," Fallon replied.

Ulrik's lips flattened. "Perhaps that was for the best." The King of Silvers then returned his attention to Phelan. "How are you taking it?"

"I just found out a few minutes ago. How do you think I'm taking it?"

"That well, huh?" Rhys stated sarcastically. "Wonderful."

Banan's gray eyes scanned the room. "I know each of you have feelings regarding Con and what he did to Rhi, but you should know that he did it for us."

"That he did," Kiril said, nodding his head of wheat-colored hair. "He didna think it was right that he be happy while the rest of us suffered. He never expected the spell to fail, the one that kept us from feeling anything for the humans. And with our dragons gone, our only chance at finding mates was with the Fae—which we were no' exactly friendly with at the time."

Ulrik crossed his arms over his chest. "Con did what he thought was best for the Dragon Kings. He sacrificed his and Rhi's happiness for his brethren. Whether you agree with that or no', I can promise you that no one has hurt as much as Con has all these thousands of years."

"Ulrik's right," Fallon said. "Con is a stronger man than I. I could never have let Larena go."

"You should also know, that if a dragon loses his mate, it can kill us," Rhys added.

Phelan swallowed hard and looked at Aisley. "I know what it is to believe you've lost a mate. When I thought I lost Aisley, it nearly killed me. Con *willingly* let his mate go." His eyes swung to Ulrik. "How did he do it?"

"By burying his pain and putting all of his energy into protecting the Dragon Kings and this realm. But it's taken a toll, more than any of us realized until recently. Rhi returning to Dreagan has been especially difficult for Con. If he can no' win her back, then I doona think he'll survive. A King isna truly whole until we have our mates."

"Con has sacrificed more than anyone," Aisley said. "I can't imagine the pain he's dealt with all these years."

Charon asked, "And Usaeil? Why did he go to her?"

"She caught him at a weak moment," Banan explained. "Con had no' had any lovers since Rhi. Usaeil bided her time and found Con at an especially difficult moment. Then, she lured him. He tried to make the most of the situation by getting information from her, but he realized almost instantly that that wasna an option. That's when he called it off."

"Shite," Logan said.

Ulrik dropped his arms. "I'm no' here to justify Con's actions. We're here because we doona know if Usaeil and Moreann are working together now or no'. With Con at the Light Castle with Rhi, we're here to ensure that everyone is on guard. Usaeil has taken the Dark throne. Her goal is to unite the Fae and rule both."

"That willna happen," Phelan stated.

Kiril shrugged his shoulders. "It might. Usaeil has

significant power, especially now that she's taking the magic of Druids."

"I'm sorry. What did you say?" Marcail, Quinn's wife, asked.

Kiril's shamrock green eyes met her gaze. "To make her magic stronger, Usaeil has been killing Druids and taking their power. It doesna last long, so she's been taking more and more Druids."

"But Corann is extremely powerful," Gwynn said. She and Logan exchanged a look. "He shouldn't have been able to be taken."

"That's how powerful Usaeil is," Fallon said. "And that's why we need to be careful. She knows of us, and it's only a matter of time before she comes here."

Ulrik nodded. "Fallon's right. If she kills Corann, his magic will last longer than other Druids. Which means, she'll turn to the strongest Druids on the realm. She'll look here and at Dreagan. She can no' be allowed to take any more Druids, no matter how powerful they are."

"Agreed," Sonya said. "We'll do what must be done to keep her out."

Rhys's lips twisted ruefully. "Actually, we thought it might be better if all of you came to Dreagan."

All eyes swung to Fallon. He considered the option before he said, "Let us talk amongst ourselves. We've no idea when Usaeil will attack. It could be tomorrow or next year. We have lives here."

"We're aware, but it's better to be safe," Banan warned.

Ulrik blew out a breath and looked at Broc. "We're also here for another reason."

"You want me to find Usaeil," Broc replied.

Ulrik shrugged. "Usaeil, Moreann, Corann. We doona care, just so we can get to one of them. The Skye Druids need Corann."

"What are you no' telling us?" Ian asked.

Ulrik hesitated before he said, "Every mortal on this realm has Moreann's people's blood in their veins. That means they have ties to Moreann."

"In other words, Moreann could convince Corann to join the Others if she promised him that the Skye Druids would be safe from whatever the plans are," Isla stated.

The great hall grew quiet as each considered what could happen.

Broc then stepped forward. "I better begin looking immediately."

CHAPTER TWENTY-NINE

He'd let his temper get the better of him. Con stood on the edge of the cliffs and watched the deep blue sea churn before him. Something about Rhi had always made him lose control.

It didn't matter if it was with his emotions or his body, she'd always had that authority over him. At one time, the fact that Rhi had been able to shake up his life in such a way had been like a high. He hadn't been able to get enough of her or discovering all the ways she could unsettle him.

Because no one else had ever been able to do that. Only her.

"Only Rhiannon," Con whispered into the wind.

Maybe he'd been a fool to think that he could win her back. He knew for certain that she still felt something for him. Otherwise, she wouldn't have reacted the way she did in his arms—or screamed so loudly in pleasure.

All this time, he'd held out hope that Rhi might still care for him. Even if it was just a wee bit, it would be enough for him to work with. He could woo her until she fell in love with him again.

She'd told him that she didn't feel anything for him. He hadn't believed her, not when she'd said the words, and certainly not when he'd had her in his arms. But now . . . he was beginning to doubt himself. There was a chance that he was seeing and hearing the things he desperately wanted to see and hear instead of the truth.

Con reached for the gold dragon head cufflink on his left wrist and twisted it. The gift made him think of Erith, and for just a second, he almost called out to her. Thankfully, the moment passed.

He wasn't used to taking his problems to anyone, much less a goddess who had bigger issues. There had only been two people in the entire realm he'd ever shared his troubles with—Ulrik and Rhi.

Ulrik might be back at Dreagan, but Con had dumped a lot on him. Ulrik wouldn't turn him away, Con knew that. But he also knew that there were bigger issues for Ulrik and the rest of the Dragon Kings to focus on right now.

"What a view," Merrill said as he walked up.

Con didn't respond as he glanced at the King of Oranges.

Merrill didn't take his eyes from the water. "I can almost believe I'm in Scotland. Then I hear one of them speak, and it ruins everything," he said with a grin before he finally looked at Con.

"I understand why Ireland holds a certain appeal to some."

"Aye," Merrill replied. "If my mate were here, then I'd want to be here, too."

Con looked down before he lifted his eyes to the horizon. "Do you wish for a mate?"

There was a beat of silence before Merrill answered candidly. "Sometimes. There are nights when I see those mated at Dreagan go off together, and when I'm in my chambers alone, I wonder if I'll ever find that. Sometimes that feeling is fleeting, and other times it lasts for days." Merrill shrugged. "In times of war, like now, I'm thankful my attention isna divided between my mate and my duties to you and Dreagan. Do you regret finding your mate?"

"I wish I could say that I doona have regrets in my life, but I can no'. Seems I have more regrets than anything."

"You didna answer my question."

Con blew out a breath as he looked at Merrill. "I doona regret finding Rhi. She . . . was a missing piece that I didna even realize until I found her. The joy we shared, the passion, and the love . . . words can no' describe the depth of those things."

"You say that as if you doona think you deserve them."

"Maybe I doona." Con shrugged one shoulder. "All of you followed my example when I allowed the humans to remain."

Merrill rolled his eyes dramatically. "Stop. Just stop. You can no' assume the weight of that all on your own. You might have said that we should open our home to the mortals, but had any of us doubted that, you would've listened. But none of us did. Because that isna who we are."

"Allowing the mortals to remain is when our troubles began," Con argued.

"Who is to say that wasna supposed to happen? Who's to say that this horrible path you believe we're on, wasna already set out before us?"

Con frowned as he shook his head. "We've done nothing to deserve such a Fate."

"I'm no' saying this is happening to us because of something we did. Perhaps it is all about the humans and giving them a place to thrive. I doona know of any other species who would have let them do that. Certainly no' the Fae—no' even the Light."

"You're no' wrong there."

Merrill shifted to face Con fully. "And I'll tell you this. There isna a King at Dreagan that I wouldna lay down my life for, but in my mind, there is only one who could've gotten us through all that shite to where we are today. You. You were chosen by the magic to be King of Kings. Remember that when you doubt yourself. It chose you. No' Ulrik, no' Kellan, no' me or anyone else. You."

Merrill then gave Con a nod and walked away.

Con watched him go, unsure what had just happened. Normally, Con was the one giving such talks. He frowned as he turned back to the water, only to find Varek standing there.

"So, Merrill gave you one of his pep talks," Varek said with a nod. "He does that when he thinks someone needs it. Bastard keeps doing it to me."

Con frowned at Varek, looking into his deep brown eyes. "Obviously, Merrill thinks you need it."

Varek snorted. "But he directed it at you today."

"Point taken." Con blew out a breath.

"Merrill isna wrong, you know."

"About?"

"Everything," Varek said. "But if you tell him I said that, I'll have to kick your arse."

Con found himself struggling not to smile. "Your secret is safe with me."

"I doona know what happened between you and Rhi last night, but I do know the two of you belong together.

I knew it when you first got together, and I know it now. Doona let her go."

"I may no' have a choice."

This time, Varek sighed loudly. "She's been hurting for so long that I doona think Rhi remembers what it is like to be happy. She did the same thing you did—buried her pain. It's time both of you realize that and face the future. I'm no' going to lose my King, and you can no' lose your mate. I have no idea what it is you need to do, but you'll figure it out. You always do."

Con turned his head to look at Varek. "You really think so?"

"Without a doubt. You're Constantine."

Once more, Con watched another of his Dragon Kings walk away. He gave a little shake of his head. He couldn't remember another time when any of them had given him such words, but he liked it. In truth, he hadn't realized how good it was to hear such things. He didn't need the words, but that didn't mean he wouldn't take them.

Several minutes ticked by as Con watched the ebb and flow of the sea before him. He had no idea how long he stood there before he realized that he wasn't alone.

"About time you became conscious of me," Erith said, a smile in her voice.

Con cut his eyes to her as she stood beside him. "My mind is filled this day."

"With Rhi."

"Aye," he said, not bothering to deny it.

Erith blew out a breath. "Then you might want to know she's watching you."

Con stiffened as he fought not to turn and look at the castle to see if he could find Rhi. "Doona jest with me."

"I wouldn't do such a thing."

He felt Erith watching him, but he didn't turn her way. Con wasn't sure he wanted her to see the turmoil in his eyes. Because she would. She'd always had that ability.

Finally, Erith said, "I'm your friend, Con. I've always been your friend. From the first time I came to see you and gave you those cufflinks. And I will be your friend until the end of time. You can talk to me, you know."

"I doona talk to anyone."

"And that's the problem. You hold it all in and figure out everyone else's problems, but not your own. You've done a good job of it, and you could continue doing it. But why would you? You're not alone. You've never been alone. You have your Dragon Kings, and you have me. We're all here for you."

Con squeezed his eyes closed for a moment. "I doona know where to begin."

"How about what brought you out here? I'm guessing it was Rhi."

"Aye," he stated. "I thought I had a chance with her. I now think I was mistaken."

Erith faced him, her arms crossed over her chest as she glared at him. He turned his head just enough to catch the look on her face.

"What?" he asked, confused by her irritation.

"You're intelligent. Which is why I can't believe you can be so . . . dumb."

At this, Con faced her. "What the hell do you mean?"

Her brows shot up on her forehead. "Rhi. Of course, she's going to try and convince you that she doesn't want or need you. You didn't just break her heart. You tore it from her chest and ripped it into tiny shreds, pieces that she's been trying to pick up for centuries."

"I know I hurt her," Con admitted as he took a step toward Erith, his anger getting the better of him again.

"It nearly killed me to let her go. It's taken everything to keep going every bloody day without her all these years. Every day, I have to stop myself from going to her. Every. Single. Day."

"Why? Why didn't you go to her the moment Hal and Cassie fell in love?" Erith asked with a shrug of confusion.

Con lowered his gaze to the ground. "Because Rhi deserves better than me. I didna put her first."

"You're King of Dragon Kings. You have to think of your people," Erith said in a softer voice. "I know why you did what you did. At the time, you believed it was your only decision. And I agreed with you. Still do."

His gaze jerked up to meet her lavender orbs. "You do?"

Erith nodded sadly. "You forget, I watched all of you for a while. I, too, saw the way the Kings reacted to Rhi. It wasn't that they didn't like her or that you had found someone."

"They were discontented by the knowledge that they might never find their mates."

"Exactly. You saw that. You were able to see past your happiness to see your brethren. Not many leaders can do that. It's what sets you apart from all others. You did what you had to do for the Kings. Now, it's time for you to do what you need to do for yourself. Rhi is your mate, and you're the only one for her."

Con drew in a deep breath of salty air. "There is nothing I wouldna do for Rhi."

"Then prove that to her. She understands you. She may not admit it or let you know, but she does. Why else would she be watching you now?"

"Tell me, how is it you always know when I need a friend?"

Erith smiled and shrugged. "That's what friends do for each other. We've both spent so much of our lives apart from others, thinking of everyone but ourselves. I needed a friend. That's why I first came to you."

"I'm glad you did."

"Me, too. Now, go get your mate," Erith said before she vanished.

CHAPTER THIRTY

He hadn't left. The relief Rhi felt when she finally found Con standing at the edge of the cliffs was monumental. She placed a hand on her stomach, which roiled viciously as she stood atop the castle.

No matter how hard she tried to keep him at a distance, Con had managed to worm his way into her heart again.

"Again?" the darkness asked with a snort. *"He's always been there. You don't stand a chance against his love, and you know it. This pitiful display is just that—pitiful."*

Rhi rolled her eyes. The darkness was nothing if not blunt. However, it also spoke the truth. When she had thought Con left the Light Castle, Rhi had been frantic. Just knowing that he was here to stand beside her had given her courage she hadn't realized she lacked until that moment. She had no idea how to be a queen or a leader. She simply did what she had seen Con do on several occasions.

She wondered what he was thinking about while staring at the sea. Was it her? Did he regret coming to the

Light Castle? He stood still as a statue, steady and sure as the wind blew around him. Con remained immovable, even when Merrill and Varek approached.

Rhi was about to go to Con after Varek walked away, then Death appeared. For just a second, a flurry of jealousy rushed through Rhi, but she knew it was silly. Erith and Con were friends—and everyone needed friends.

Con didn't share his problems with just anyone. He wanted the Kings to have faith in his ability to lead, which is why he kept so much to himself. And when Ulrik had been banished, Con had lost the one friend he'd always been able to turn to.

Rhi had filled that role for a short time. Con had opened up to her and told her things he hadn't even told Ulrik. She had done the same with him. But when Con ended their relationship, there had been no one for him. That's when Erith stepped in.

While Rhi knew very little about Death, she saw the similarities between Erith and Con. It was no wonder Erith had sought him out as a friend. They had developed a friendship that both of them needed.

Rhi slid her gaze away from Con, but it only lasted a heartbeat before she was watching him again. Her body still hummed from the pleasure he'd given her during the night. Even when she slept, she'd dreamed of him kissing her, touching her.

Loving her.

She wanted Con back in her life as her lover. It seemed like such a simple thing. All she had to do was tell him. He was with her now, offering her the very thing she wanted.

But she was scared. Scared of putting her heart out there again, scared of being rejected once more. Scared of him turning her away anew. She wasn't scared of dying. She was terrified of admitting her love again, because she wouldn't survive a second heartbreak. Rhi knew this for a fact. In many ways, she wasn't sure how she'd lived through it the first time.

Hope.

Her eyes closed as she accepted the truth. She had done everything since that horrible day on the slim chance that he might want her again.

She'd never questioned his love. The fact that he hadn't told her himself that he wanted to end their relationship told her just how much he loved her. She hadn't been able to see that until this very instant, but she knew it was true.

Con projected this imposing figure to all, and in many, many ways, he was that and more. But she also knew the side of him that he'd never shown to anyone. The one where he questioned everything, including himself. He'd allowed her to see his vulnerability, something he didn't even like to admit to.

For someone so commanding, Con really was a big softy. All he wanted was to protect those he cared about and to love and be loved. It seemed so simple, and she had believed it was.

Until it wasn't.

"You only thought of yourself."

The darkness was right. She *had* only thought of herself after the breakup because she had been hurting so badly. Without any explanation from Con, she'd done the thing most anyone would—she'd blamed the person responsible.

But she hadn't looked deeper into the reasoning. Not then, and not in the thousands of years since. Not until this very second. Perhaps if she had, she would've come to this realization much sooner.

"Not likely," she murmured to herself.

For too long, it had been easy to blame everything on Con. She hadn't looked at how her involvement with him might have affected those at Dreagan. She considered some of the Dragon Kings friends, so she had automatically assumed that they had no issue with her, which was folly on her part, especially after everything they had endured.

Con had been right earlier. She had been acting Queen of the Light for only a matter of hours, and she already assumed she knew what a ruler did. She knew nothing.

But she was learning quickly.

The moment Erith left Con, Rhi started to go to him. But she hesitated. She wasn't sure what to say or how to approach him. All she'd done since he arrived at the castle was push him away and tell him how she didn't love him anymore.

Rhi closed her eyes and searched her mind for the right words. After a few moments, she gave up. It never worked when she tried to rehearse whatever she wanted to say. It was better to just go and say it.

But when Rhi opened her eyes, Con was gone. Her gut clenched briefly, but she knew he was still at the castle. If Con wanted to leave, he would've done it earlier, not gone to the cliffs.

It might be better if they didn't talk yet. She still needed to sort out the new feelings within her. She was so turned around that she might throw herself at Con and tell him that she never stopped loving him.

Rhi turned and stepped off the edge of the roof. She then teleported to the throne room. When she walked in, Con was there, speaking to the Queen's Guard. He gave her a nod and then made his way to the window where he'd sat the day before.

She debated whether or not to talk to him, but the guards waited for her to tell them she was ready to begin seeing the Fae. Con didn't meet her gaze as Varek and Merrill came into the room. Rhi faced the two Kings and gave them a nod as she sat on the throne.

The day passed just as quickly as the last, but she was always aware of Con. She felt his gaze on her several times, and she looked his way on a couple of occasions, as well. Their eyes met briefly, but she couldn't tell his mood since he had closed himself off again.

The day was winding down. Rhi was even more exhausted than the day before. She lifted her hand in a motion to the guards that she was finished when she heard her name being called in her mind. She stiffened at the sound of Phelan's voice.

"What is it?" Con asked.

She hadn't heard him cross the room. She turned her head so she could look into his black eyes. "Phelan."

"Is he in trouble?"

"I don't think so."

Con's lips flattened. "He must know, then."

Rhi inwardly winced. She had purposefully kept from telling Phelan—or anyone, for that matter—that Con was the one who'd hurt her. She hadn't intended to do that. In fact, she had been all too ready to spill everything to Phelan and anyone else who asked. But when it came time to do it, she couldn't. Rhi didn't know if it was to protect herself, Con, or both of them. Though it really didn't matter.

"I need to see him," Rhi said.

Con nodded. "Do you want me to accompany you? Or would you rather go alone?"

She knew it might be better if she talked to Phelan alone, but she wanted Con with her.

"I'll no' go anywhere," Con said into the silence. "I'll wait here for you."

"I think you should come with me."

His gaze searched hers. "Are you sure? He's no' going to be happy."

"He needs to see that we're fine, not just hear me say it."

Con nodded slowly. "He's protective of you. If I were him, I'd want to kill me."

"It's a good thing he can't, then," she teased. When Con didn't smile, she sobered. "I know what you're saying. I agree."

"Then I'm ready when you are."

She didn't ask about Merrill and Varek, but she did take a moment to let the guards know that she'd return shortly. Then she made her way to Con. In order to take him with her when she jumped, she had to touch him.

Her heart thumped loudly in her chest as she put her hand on his arm. He subtly shifted so her palm met his. He wrapped his fingers around her hand, his gaze on her the entire time. She gave him a small grin before she teleported them to Phelan.

A heartbeat later, they stood in the great hall of MacLeod Castle. Her gaze landed first on Fallon and his wife, Larena, before she saw Ulrik, Rhys, Kiril, and Banan. Rhi saw movement out of the corner of her eye. She turned her head to find Aisley. Rhi smiled at the Phoenix, and Aisley returned the grin. But there was no sign of Phelan.

"He's outside," Ulrik told them.

Con looked to her. "Should I talk to him first?"

"No. We're doing this together," she told him.

Rhi was aware of how everyone in the hall watched them. But it was Ulrik's gaze lowering to her and Con's linked hands that made her remember they still held onto each other. She didn't release him, though.

"Excuse us," she told everyone and started forward.

Con moved with her as the group parted, and they walked through them and then out the door of the castle. Once outside, Rhi paused and looked for Phelan. It took her a moment to realize where he was.

"The caves," she said with a wry grin.

"Excuse me?"

She swiveled her head to Con. "The first time I met Phelan was in one of the caves in the cliffs below the castle. That's where he is now."

"He wants to talk alone."

"I want you to come."

"And I want to be there, but I think you should consider Phelan."

Rhi shook her head. "This isn't about him. This is about you and me keeping the truth from him all these years. We do this together."

Con shrugged. "So be it."

Rhi immediately teleported them to the cave. Just as she expected, Phelan was there. He stood with his legs spread wide and his arms crossed over his chest. He noted her hand joined with Con's, but Phelan didn't comment on that.

"I didna expect you both," he said.

Rhi rolled her eyes. "You most certainly did."

Phelan lifted one shoulder in a shrug. "I just want to know why you didna tell me it was Con?"

"Everyone wanted to know who it was," Rhi told him. "You think I kept Con's name from you to protect him?"

"Did you?" Phelan demanded.

Rhi looked at Con for a heartbeat. "Maybe. It was also to protect myself. I didn't like talking about the past, and not telling you it was Con allowed that. Everyone knew not to bring it up."

Phelan released a long breath as his arms dropped to his sides. "You're family. If this is what you want, then I'll support you." His gaze then shifted to Con.

There were no words exchanged, but Rhi saw the silent understanding pass between the males. She wanted to ask what it meant, but she didn't.

"We should get back to the hall. Broc is trying to find Usaeil," Phelan said as he walked between them on his way out of the cave.

Rhi looked at Con to find him staring at her. "Well, that went better than I'd hoped."

CHAPTER THIRTY-ONE

Usaeil's Manor

Corann paced back and forth in his cell. He'd been caged like an animal for days, and his patience was wearing thin. He still couldn't believe that Usaeil had taken him, though he shouldn't have been surprised after what he'd witnessed on the isle with Gemma and Cináed.

He'd made use of the time he had to prepare those on Skye in case Usaeil ever came for them, but he hadn't done enough. The way she had busted through his spells as if they were nothing showed him just how powerful she was.

Corann gingerly touched the knot on the side of his head that she'd dealt him when he attempted to stop her. She had laughed, gazing at him as if he were mud beneath her boots.

And that's exactly what he was.

For too long, he'd been the Druid with the strongest magic on Skye. Even when he came across Fae now and again, he'd been able to keep up with them somewhat. He might be getting up there in years, but his magic wasn't waning.

In all the time he'd led the Skye Druids, he'd never

thought that Usaeil was so powerful. She'd hidden it from him, just as she'd hidden her true nature. He realized that now, though it was too late.

He had no idea what had happened to his people. Usaeil refused to tell him anything, and the grotesque beings she called Trackers didn't talk to him, either. It had been hours since Corann had seen Usaeil. He wasn't even sure she was in the house anymore. After she'd put him in her dungeon, she'd promptly killed Daniel, the Druid she'd taken from Skye before him.

Corann had made the mistake of trying to use magic against her. That's when he learned that there was something about the bars around him that prevented him from doing anything. In fact, it made him no more of a threat than any other mortal walking around.

But he knew he wasn't alone. There was another woman in the manor. He'd heard her yelling for Usaeil a few times. The female was a floor or two above him in the main house. She was obviously a prisoner as well, but there had to be a reason she wasn't in the dungeon with him.

Or was she?

In order to best Usaeil, Corann needed to think like her. And Usaeil had proven that she liked to trick people into believing one thing when she was really doing the opposite. He stopped in the middle of his cell and lowered himself to the floor. Then he closed his eyes and listened to the house. It took him longer than it should have to hear anything, which proved how good Usaeil's defenses were.

But sound did finally reach him. He might not be able to use magic traditionally, but he'd learned how to use it with his mind long ago. It allowed him to get the layout of the house. The main floor was above him, and then two more above that. Many Trackers roamed around. Some were in the house, but most were outside. There might even be more, but his senses didn't reach that far away from the structure.

Corann returned his focus to the dwelling itself. He wanted to see if he could determine who all was in the home, including Usaeil. He began in the dungeon and discovered that he was the only one alive, though many souls roamed.

He wanted to aid them in finding peace, but that would have to come later. He continued up to the main floor but found only Trackers. He was nearly finished with the second floor when he came to a room that seemed empty, but he was sure that someone was inside.

It wasn't a soul, but a person who was shrouded in some haze that he couldn't penetrate. There was no sign that it was Usaeil, but he noted the room in his mind so he could return at a later time and try again.

On the third floor, he found the woman. She was furious, her anger rolling off her in waves. Again and again, she tried magic to bust down the door—Druid magic.

Corann almost tried to see if his mind could reach hers so he could speak to her, but at the last minute, he hesitated. There was something about the woman that sent warning bells off in his mind. When the female began to scream Usaeil's name, he knew it was the same voice he'd heard before.

He opened his eyes and took a deep breath. Whoever the female was, she was incredibly powerful. Usaeil must want her for something, but what? At the sound of someone approaching, Corann lifted his chin and waited for the person to show themselves. It wasn't long before Usaeil strode into his line of sight.

"Growing old is awful," she said as she eyed him.

Corann shrugged. "It's a part of life. Everything must die."

"Not everything. Not me."

"Even you."

She smiled then. "How cute you are, thinking you know all about me. You even think you know the Fae."

"I do."

"You know what I allowed you to see, and none of it was real. There was no need for you to guard the Fairy Pools. I could do that with a spell."

Resentment began to swirl, but he refused to rise to the bait. "Then why ask the Skye Druids to protect them?"

"I like to keep my options open." Usaeil shrugged indifferently. "I wanted to make sure I had a relationship with some of the most powerful Druids on this realm in case I needed them. And it didn't take much for them to agree. You either when it came time for you to rule."

"I follow traditions."

Usaeil laughed and tossed her silver and black hair over her shoulder. "You should've asked questions."

"So you could lie again?"

"Mortals are so easily duped, but especially Druids, who believe they have a greater purpose. Do you know what your purpose was, old man?" Usaeil asked, barely able to contain her glee.

Corann wanted to get up because his back ached, but he didn't move. "I doona care."

"Sure, you do. You were brought to this realm by a Druid to cause the demise of the Dragon Kings."

At this, Corann frowned. "You lie."

"Actually, this time, I'm not lying. I have the woman responsible in custody. She comes from a realm where everyone is a Druid. When some were born without magic, she knew something was wrong. She searched for another realm with magic and found this one. That's when she rounded up a bunch of you without magic and dumped you here."

"I know this story," Corann interjected. "The Dragon Kings allowed the mortals to remain since they had nowhere to go. They lived in peace for a short time before war broke out and the humans and dragons killed each other. The Dragon Kings sent their clans away, and the Druids went to Skye."

Usaeil's smile had grown as he spoke. "Ah, well, you see, the power you have didn't come from those brought here. It was given to you by the magic of this realm. And while everything else was going on, the woman—her name is Moreann—found me."

Moreann. Corann's blood turned to ice in his veins. He knew that name. It had long been said by the Ancients, like a warning. It's all they ever said to him. One name—Moreann.

"We made a pact," Usaeil continued. "I agreed to help her defeat the Kings. Everything that's been happening to the Kings has been because of her."

Corann sneered at her. "You're part of the Others."

"That's right."

"I thought you wanted Con. Does that no' go against your vow to Moreann?"

Usaeil shrugged but never took her gaze from him. "Things change. I changed. I decided I didn't want the Kings gone. Instead, I'm going to unite the Fae. I'm Queen of the Dark, and soon, I'll retake my throne with the Light, as well."

"Someone took it?" he asked, forcing a smile because he knew it would infuriate her.

And he was right.

Usaeil's red eyes narrowed. "You think that's funny? You should see what I do to people I want to hurt."

"You doona scare me."

"I should," she warned.

Corann held her gaze, refusing to budge. He was frightened, but he would battle against it. To give in was to concede victory to Usaeil.

She chuckled. "Moreann is the leader of her realm. She's immortal, thanks to her magic. We could've been good allies, but she tried to rule me, and I'm not some-one to be ruled. I'm someone who leads."

"Is this how you lead? By slaughtering the Light and deceiving them?"

"The Fae are cattle. It doesn't matter if they're Light or Dark, they'll follow the strongest ruler, and that's me. They've been left to their own devices for entirely too long. They need a strong hand, one that doesn't give in to every whim."

Corann lifted a brow. "And me?"

Once more, she smiled. "Ah, you're just what I need to go up against Rhi. Do you know that meddling Fae has taken my throne as well as Con? But I got him once. I'll get him again."

"Con doesna want you. He loves Rhi and always has. Even I know that."

Usaeil shook her head. "You're wrong. Con just doesn't realize what I'm offering."

"And you're going to change his mind?"

"Yes."

"By killing Rhi?"

Usaeil's face brightened. "Exactly."

Corann didn't bother to tell her how that was going to backfire. First, he wasn't sure if Usaeil could defeat Rhi. The Light Fae was deceptively powerful, and he suspected Usaeil was not aware of that. As for Con, if Usaeil did somehow manage to take Rhi's life, then there wasn't a place in the universe that Usaeil could go that Con wouldn't track her down and get his revenge.

"What of Moreann?"

Usaeil rolled her eyes. "What about her?"

"Do you think she'll sit back and let you change her plans?" He suspected the female he'd found in the manor was Moreann, but he wasn't going to tip his hand just yet.

"Oh, she won't be bothering anyone. Actually, I doubt she'll live much longer."

"Is that so? You plan to attack her, as well?"

Usaeil squatted down so that she was eye-level with him as she looked through the bars. "Trying to prod information out of me, are you? Well, let me save you the trouble. Moreann is my prisoner. She actually believed that she could keep me chained and locked away, but I showed her. Now, it's my turn to get my vengeance, and it's going to be beautiful. It's almost too bad you won't be here to see it because it's going to be epic."

"What about the Druids here?"

Usaeil pulled a face. "What do I care about the Druids? Or mortals, for that matter? The only ones who will occupy this realm are the Fae and the Dragon Kings. The Fae will finally give the Kings their children. We're going to save the Dragon Kings."

There was no doubt in Corann's mind that Usaeil was completely off her rocker. But he had no idea what he was going to do about it. The fact was, his time was most likely limited. So, if he was going to think of anything, he needed to do it soon.

Usaeil smiled as she cocked her head to the side. "You've had a good life. Too bad it's over."

CHAPTER THIRTY-TWO

"You're still standing," Ulrik said as Con walked up beside him in the great hall of MacLeod Castle.

Con glanced at his friend and saw the barely contained smile. "Verra funny."

"I was referring to Rhi putting you on your arse, no' Phelan," Ulrik leaned over to whisper.

On the other side of Ulrik, Rhys, Banan, and Kiril snickered. And they weren't the only ones. Few Warriors *weren't* grinning, their heightened senses having picked up Ulrik's words.

Con leaned close to Ulrik and said, "I definitely recall Eilish setting you on your arse a time or two."

Ulrik's smile was wide as he turned it on Con. "That's what makes her so damn wonderful."

"Aye," Con said, thinking of how perfect Rhi was for him.

She had released his hand when they returned to the castle, and he found himself fighting not to reach for her. Having her in his arms the night before had been amazing. Not only had he felt at peace, but his mind was also able to clear in a way that he hadn't been able to do in eons.

Now, Rhi stood across from him in the hall, talking to Isla and Aisley. He couldn't take his eyes from her. Con couldn't help but think of all the wasted years recently, all the times when he could've gone to her, when he should've told her the truth about everything and tried to win her back.

Why had he waited so long? But he knew the answer. The only thing he'd ever feared was living without Rhi. He'd done it because, in the back of his mind, he'd always thought there might be a day when they could find each other again.

When she returned to Dreagan, he'd known there was a good chance he'd lost her forever. And he couldn't take the step that would give him a definitive answer—even if that answer might have been yes. There was a greater fear inside him that she would reject him.

With that rejection, he wouldn't have been able to continue on. He would've died, leaving the Kings to find someone else to fill his role. And no matter what Merrill and Varek said, Con knew there were plenty of other Kings who could fill his shoes. Ulrik was one of them.

Rhi suddenly looked his way. She paused midsentence, her brows drawing together as she shrugged at him.

"You're frowning," Ulrik told him.

Con wiped his face of emotion and gave her a nod. Rhi returned to her conversation while Con made himself look away. Everywhere his eyes landed, he saw the Warriors and Druids staring at him.

He shifted, uncomfortable with their gaze, but he should've expected it. He was the infamous King who had sent his mate away. They couldn't understand it, but he didn't expect them to.

Larena came to him with a smile. "I'd like to apologize for everyone staring. It's beyond rude."

"It's fine," Con told her. "They're trying to make sense of it all."

"So am I," the female Warrior confessed.

Fallon gave her a dark look as he admonished her. "Larena."

Con caught Fallon's attention. "It's all right. Really."

Their conversation was halted when Broc walked down the stairs. He didn't look at anyone until he reached the hall and went to stand beside his wife, Sonya. The Druid immediately clasped her hands around one of Broc's.

"Please tell us you have good news," Fallon said.

Broc's deep brown eyes met Con's. "I can find nothing on Usaeil or Moreann, but I'm no' surprised about the Druid. I've never met her, so that can factor into the scenario."

"And Corann?" Isla asked.

Broc swallowed. "I sense him, so I know he's still alive, but I can no' pinpoint his location."

"That's good that he's alive, right?" Evie asked everyone.

Rhi shrugged as she exchanged a look with Con. "Yes and no. It could be because Usaeil is waiting to use his magic."

"He's alive," Con said. "We're going to take that as a win for the moment because we all need it. Broc, you said you can no' pinpoint the location, but what about the area? Is he still in Scotland? Or somewhere else?"

Broc's lips twisted ruefully. "I get the feeling he's far away."

"Usaeil wouldna keep him in Scotland," Ulrik said.

Con shook his head. "I was hoping she might try, thinking we'd look elsewhere."

"I can keep trying," Broc announced.

Sonya nodded as she looked up at Broc. "And I'll continue talking to the trees. They should eventually tell me something."

"They're keeping it from you for a reason," Con stated. He drew in a breath and released it as he looked around the room. "Before this, the trees would warn you of any harm coming your way, right?"

"Aye," Sonya replied.

Con flattened his lips. "None of you are hearing from the trees, wind, or stones because they're protecting you."

"We've battled strong Druids before," Marcail announced.

Ulrik shifted his feet. "That you have, but what's coming is worse. I agree with Con. I think everything is trying to protect you. Whether that's to keep you out of things altogether or no', you can no' go against that."

"We shouldna be here while you fight Usaeil and Moreann," Ian said.

Rhi walked into the middle of the room. "Perhaps you should. There's no doubt that all of you are strong separately, and together you're near unstoppable. However, we're still figuring things out. Stay here and remain vigilant for Usaeil. Have an escape planned if she shows up."

"To Dreagan," Con added.

Rhi gave him a nod. "Yes, to Dreagan. Until then, remain here while we continue sorting things out and coming up with a plan."

"We should be a part of that plan," Phelan interjected.

Con looked at the Warrior. "You will be if you're needed, trust me. It's going to take all of us."

Fallon sighed loudly. "I doona like it, but it appears as if we doona have a choice. We've always had an advantage with the trees, wind, and stones talking to the Druids. Without that, we doona have anything."

"No' true," Broc said. "You have me, and I'm going to keep searching for Corann."

Con gave a nod. "Be safe."

Ulrik, Banan, Kiril and Rhys left, but Con waited as Rhi gave Phelan and Aisley each a hug. They spoke for a moment before Rhi walked to him and held out her hand. Con liked how she didn't hesitate to reach for him. He intertwined their fingers and continued watching her as she spoke to the others.

He was so focused on Rhi that Con never saw Phelan approach him. The Warrior came up behind him and whispered, "I can no' believe I never noticed how you watch her. It's obvious you love her, and while I doona agree with what you did, I can understand it. But if you hurt her again, I'm coming for you."

"I'd die before I caused her pain again," Con said as he turned his head to the side.

Phelan gave a nod. "I'm glad we understand each other."

The Warrior stepped away when Rhi turned to Con. With a farewell wave, Rhi jumped them back to her quarters in the Light Castle. It was the first time they had been alone since that morning, and Con wasn't sure what to say. He didn't get a chance to do anything as Rhi faced him.

She looked down at their joined hands and then slowly released him. "I was out of line this morning."

"You only said what you felt."

"Which was out of line." She swallowed. "You're right. I know nothing about ruling. I was trying to push things back on you. I've done it for so long that it's become a habit now, and . . . I'm sorry."

Con wanted to pull her into his arms so badly that he ached with the urge. "I hurt you, and you wanted to get back at me. I deserved it. There's no need to apologize. I'm the one who should be begging you for forgiveness."

"A few days ago, I would've agreed. But now?" She shrugged and turned away to walk a few paces while picking at her thumbnail before she faced him again. Her arms dropped to her sides as she met his gaze. "You gave me answers I'd long sought and I threw them back in your face. It's no wonder you didn't want to tell me the truth."

"I didna want to tell you because I knew it would hurt you again."

Rhi shook her head of black hair. "Well, it did, but it was better than thinking of all the different reasons you could've wanted to end it. I had answers, but I wasn't in a good place to hear them. I . . . I should've listened instead of blaming you."

"It was my fault. All of it. Including Usaeil."

Rhi winced at the mention of her enemy. "I can't get angry at you for Usaeil when I had Balladyn."

"Aye, you can, because I was furious with you about Balladyn," he confessed. "I tried to tell myself that you had a right to be happy, but it didna help. I might have ended our relationship, but my heart never let you go. Seeing you at Dreagan was both a joy and the worst kind of torture because I couldna have you. But knowing Balladyn got to hold you was . . . hell."

Rhi's eyes glittered as she hurriedly looked away. "I was only thinking of myself when I went to Balladyn. It was wrong of me. I couldn't give him what he wanted."

"What was that?" Con pressed, hoping she might admit to it.

She licked her lips and shrugged. "My heart. Every day you and I weren't together, I blamed you, wondering what I'd done to tear us apart. I was so angry that you wouldn't come to me so we could talk about it and work it out." She slid her gaze back to him. "We used to tell each other everything, which is why it hurt so much that you just cut me off."

"I should've talked to you."

"No," Rhi stated with a firm shake of her head. "Had you done that, I would've done everything I could to talk you into ways we could remain together and not upset the dynamic at Dreagan."

"And I would've listened."

"Then everything you'd worked so hard to give the Kings would've fallen apart. You were the only one thinking rationally. You put your own personal wants and needs to the side and saw the bigger picture. I couldn't have done that. Not then. Not now. It's why you were chosen to be King of Kings."

Con briefly closed his eyes. "I wanted to put you first."

"A good leader, a *true* leader, doesn't do that. I know that now. And, sadly, I should've realized that about you when it happened."

"You were hurt."

Rhi's shoulders lifted in a half-shrug. "I've had time to put aside my anger and think about things, but I didn't. And when the Kings began to find their mates, I waited for you to come back to me. When you didn't, it made things worse."

"I wanted to," Con confessed. "Every time I saw you, all I wanted to do was pull you into my arms and kiss you. The times you came to me when Usaeil hurt you, I wanted to tell you that I loved you still. Always."

Her brows drew together. "Why didn't you?"

"I was afraid you'd reject me. I'd thought it would be enough to see you at Dreagan, but it wasna. The more you were there, the more we spoke, the more my heart ached for you. And the more my soul craved its mate. I made many mistakes, but I'm here now. And I'm never going to leave you again. That is, if you'll have me."

CHAPTER THIRTY-THREE

A tear fell down Rhi's cheek. She had been waiting thousands of years to hear those words. She wanted to fly into Con's arms and hold him tight for eternity.

His black eyes grew troubled as he studied her. "Rhi?"

"You're immortal. Usaeil can't hurt you."

Con's frown deepened. "I doona like the way you're talking."

"It's true, though." Rhi quickly brushed away the tear. "No matter how much magic Usaeil takes from Druids, she can't harm you or any of the Dragon Kings."

"You're forgetting about Moreann," he replied.

Rhi sniffed, hating the raw emotions that governed her. She wanted to rejoice in hearing that Con still loved her. And she wanted to cry because she had the awful feeling that no matter what, they'd never be together.

"You told those at MacLeod Castle that it would take everyone in the upcoming battle with Usaeil," Con said. "That includes you."

"The truth is, I'm not sure I can defeat Usaeil a second time. Not if she has Druid magic, as well."

Con's lip lifted in derision. "That's shite. One of the

reasons she was always jealous of you was because of the power that came so easily to you. You had it, and didna even know it, much less know to use it. Look what you did to the Fae Realm. You're healing it."

"I can destroy and create worlds," she said with a shrug. "We both know that."

"Aye, but healing takes even more power. Even you have to acknowledge that."

She rubbed her hand across her brow before she turned away and walked to one of the chairs. Rhi sank into one of the new ones and slouched down so her neck rested on the backrest. "Fine. I acknowledge that. It still doesn't mean I can best Usaeil. I knew when I fought her the first time that there was a chance I wouldn't live through it."

"I saw you. The fire in your eyes said otherwise. Especially when she killed Balladyn."

"He's not dead," Rhi confessed.

Con's lips turned up at the corners. "Erith told me."

"It's fitting, isn't it?" Rhi asked with a smile. "He gets a second chance since he was betrayed so viciously by Usaeil."

"I didna like him because of his love for you and your affection for him, but even I can admit he did good as King of the Dark. I think he'll make an excellent Reaper."

Her smile dropped. "All I could think about on the battlefield that day against Usaeil was that you were with her. I thought I had truly lost you."

"The vows we took bound me to you, heart and soul. No' even death can keep me from you."

There was something in his comment that caught her attention. Before she could ask him about it, Con spoke.

"You will find that same fire within you the next time you and Usaeil meet."

Rhi drummed her fingers on the arms of the chair. "I let the darkness in so I could fight her."

"Good. Use it again."

"What if it takes me?"

Con chuckled as he came to sit in the chair near her. "If the darkness hasna taken you by now, it never will. You'd have to give in to it."

"I did."

"Nay. You only think you let it in. You believed that Fae were either good or bad. You never considered that every being has both inside them, and they choose which to be. You think you let the darkness in, when in fact, you only accepted that part of yourself."

Rhi shook her head as she scowled. "That's not true. I heard the darkness. It spoke to me. It still speaks to me."

"Does it?" Con asked, brows raised. "What does it say?"

She shrugged, not wanting to admit to anything. "Various things."

"And you believe it's the darkness?"

"Absolutely."

Con smiled. "Maybe it is. Most likely, it's your conscience telling you the things you need to hear."

"No," Rhi said with a shake of her head. "I know what my conscience sounds like. This is the darkness."

Or was it? She wasn't sure anymore.

"It doesna matter. My point was to tell you that you've always had light and dark inside you. A mix of both, something I've never seen in another Fae. The light within you has always shone so brightly that you never noticed the dark until you had no other choice but to acknowledge it. Once you did, you believed it was taking over. What you've no' perceived is that *you* have control over whether you let it take over or no'. For instance, when your eyes flashed red after Usaeil's body was taken. It was just for a moment, but it happened. Then you disappeared. That's when everyone began searching for you, but I knew you wouldna be found unless Erith went looking for you."

At the mention of Death, Rhi rolled her eyes. "What is it with her? Why is she so interested in me?"

Con lifted one shoulder in a shrug. "We might find out one day. But getting back to things, where are you?"

"The Light Castle," Rhi said hesitantly. "Why?"

"Would you be here if you were Dark? Would you have taken the throne and used glamour as Usaeil did to betray the Light?"

Rhi was indignant that Con would even ask such a thing. "Never."

"Exactly. You didna become Dark when your eyes flashed red, nor will you."

"You seem awfully certain of that."

Con flashed her a heart-stopping grin. "Because I know you."

"I'm not the same person I was when we were together."

"Nay. You're stronger. You never would have opposed Usaeil back then or even thought to take the throne. You used your pain and became something more."

She lowered her gaze to the floor. "I don't need the compliments."

"I'm stating facts."

Rhi hesitated before she met his gaze. "Thank you."

He waved away her words. "Doona thank me. You should thank yourself."

"You make me sound like some . . . I don't know," she said with a shrug. "But I'm just me. You talked about making mistakes, but I've made millions. Most worse than yours."

He leaned forward to put his forearms on his knees. "Look where you are now. Whether you remain on the throne or no', you've forged one hell of a path. If you question that, look to how the Light have received you as their queen. They adore you."

"Usaeil set the bar pretty low," Rhi quipped with a quirked brow.

Con laughed, which caused her to smile. She loved when he laughed, and it was even better when she caused it.

"Regardless, they love you. You make a good queen," he told her.

Rhi swallowed, unsure what to say next. "I know I told you that you had to remain here, but you don't. Your Kings need you."

"Everyone at Dreagan is fine. I've put Ulrik in charge, and he's doing great. I'm here because I want to be. No' because it'll upset Usaeil or that you demanded it. I'm here because of you."

She glanced away, her heart thumping. "I suppose we should start planning for Usaeil's arrival, but I don't know where to begin."

Con sat up straight. "You've already done it. You have the Queen's Guard as well as the Light Army at the ready. You've notified the occupants of the castle, as well. The only other thing you can do is alert all the Light Fae, but I'm no' sure what good that'll do since Usaeil no doubt has spies roaming around."

"She definitely has spies here," Rhi said with a flat look. "Otherwise, how would she know about me on the throne or us together?"

"True," he admitted. "The first steps have been taken. You need to remember to remain calm when she arrives with the Dark Army. She'll do her best to provoke you."

Rhi slouched back in her chair. "Unfortunately, she does it well."

"You can fight it. You're queen now."

"I don't feel very queenly," she quipped.

Con grinned as he leaned back, stretching his legs out to cross his ankles. "Maybe no' right this minute, but you do anytime you face the Light. You'll do the same when confronted by Usaeil."

"That's all well and good, but what happens when I manage to get riled?" Because she would. It was inevitable when it came to Usaeil.

Con drew in a deep breath and then slowly released it. "We have a couple of options."

"Wait. Before you go on, there's something I need to show you." Rhi got to her feet and waited for him. She wasn't sure why it had suddenly popped into her head to show him the book, but she knew it was the right thing to do.

Con quickly stood. "Lead the way."

"We're not walking there." She held out her hand and waited for him to take it. Once they were linked, she jumped them to the hidden room in the library.

He looked around slowly before meeting her gaze. "I must confess that I found you here the other night. I knew you were inside, but I didna disturb you."

Rhi tugged him to the pedestal that held the book. "This is what I've been reading. I just happened upon the room. The door was left slightly ajar, and when I came in, the words were moving on the page until I touched the tome. Then they fell into place, and I've been coming here to read it ever since."

"It's a verra large book," he said as he leaned from side to side without touching the pedestal or the tome. "It must be important to have been locked in here."

"It's about the Dragon Kings."

His head jerked to her, his black eyes intense. "What about us?"

"A Fae was here long before Usaeil and even before Moreann came to dump the mortals. The writer speaks of the Kings."

A muscle worked in Con's jaw. "The entire book is about the Kings?"

"I'm halfway through, and it's all about the Kings so far. Some pages are about specific dragons, but sometimes, it's just the clans as a whole. There are documented interactions, battles, and even matings."

Con rubbed the back of his neck. "Maybe you should finish reading it. There must be something in there the author didna want to be found if the words moved, and the book was hidden."

"They've not moved since I first found it. It's almost as if the book wanted me to read it. Touch it."

"No," he said with a frown.

Rhi gave him a flat look. "Con. Touch the book."

He paused for a moment before he lightly put a finger on the page. Nothing happened, which made Rhi smile.

"It wants you to read it, as well," she said.

Con flipped a page, his face filled with confusion. "How was a Fae on this realm, and none of us knew it?"

"There's a passage in there about you becoming King of Kings," Rhi said with a smile.

He stepped back from the book, wariness lining his face. "Finish reading it. There might be something important. I'll get with Varek and Merrill to begin strategizing."

"You should have the generals of the army as well as the Captain of the Queen's Guard with us. I can read this tonight."

Con bowed his head. "Then let's get on with it."

CHAPTER THIRTY-FOUR

Dark Palace

The eighth Dark lay dead at Usaeil's feet. She stepped over the body and dusted off her hands as she looked at Coslar. He pulled his gaze from the disintegrating form of the Fae and focused back on her.

"Is that the last?" Usaeil demanded.

Coslar nodded. "It is."

"Good. Are the Dark accepting my leadership now?"

"They are."

"Just what I wanted to hear. My meeting with the generals of the army went swimmingly. We'll be setting out soon for the Light Castle."

Coslar clasped his hands behind his back. "You really think the new queen will bow to you?"

"Never," Usaeil replied with a laugh. "She'll fight me tooth and nail, which is just what I want. I'll give her the option to step aside and let me unite the Light and Dark in an effort to save so many innocents from death."

"The Light will love you for that."

"I'm their queen. Of course they'll love me." When Coslar lowered his gaze, she narrowed her eyes. "What is it? Spit it out."

He lifted a shoulder as he briefly looked at her. "You're not their queen anymore. Rhi is."

"That matters not. They loved me once, they will again. Rhi will bring them death. I'll bring them peace."

"What of the Dragon Kings? Constantine is with Rhi at the Light Castle."

Usaeil lifted her lip in annoyance. "Do you doubt me?"

"I'm merely making sure you've thought of everything."

She laughed. "I've been at this game longer than you've been alive. Trust me, I've thought of every possible outcome. Nothing can trip me up this time. Not Rhi, and especially not Con. Once Rhi is gone, Con will have no choice but to come to me."

"I heard once that if a Dragon King loses his mate, he dies."

Usaeil cut her eyes to him. "Con only thinks Rhi is his mate. When she dies, he won't, and it'll prove that *I'm* his true mate."

"What if you're wrong?"

"I'm never wrong," she stated icily, becoming irritated by the Dark's incessant questions.

He bowed his head in deference. "Of course. How are you planning to take out Rhi so you can get Con to your side?"

"With such elegance that Rhi will never see it coming." Usaeil studied him with narrowed eyes. "Why? Are you worried about being taken with dragon fire?"

"The thought has crossed my mind."

"The Kings won't do anything until Rhi does. Once I goad her into attacking, I'll go straight for her. After that, I'll ensure that the Kings can't hurt anyone."

Coslar's eyes widened in surprise. "You can do that? Share the spell so I can protect myself."

Usaeil smiled as she shook her head. "Maybe one day, but for now, that secret remains with me. You'll need me to protect you, so you need to make sure none of the Dark come after me while we're in battle."

"The Dark will do whatever I need them to do," he stated.

Usaeil rolled her eyes. "Don't feed me that line of bullshit. I know firsthand how conniving and manipulative the Dark can be. Each of you has always been out for yourselves. That's all going to change. Use your power, that's fine, but you need to show your loyalty to *me*. I'm the only one who can truly lead you."

"Our Kings before Balladyn were only about themselves."

"If you value your life, you'll never speak Balladyn's name in my presence again. Do you understand?" she asked, every syllable laced with anger.

Coslar's eyes flashed with something for just a heartbeat before he bent at the waist in a bow. "Yes, my queen."

She snapped her fingers to get his attention. When he looked at her, she motioned for him to straighten. "You look like you can hold your own in battle."

"I can."

"Perfect. I want you at the head of the Dark Army with the generals and me."

His eyebrows shot up in his forehead. "Me? That's quite an honor. Thank you for trusting me."

"I don't trust anyone."

"Then why have me beside you?"

She smiled then. "There will come a time when I need you. If you're there, then you'll be rewarded handsomely. If not, it's no great loss. There are a hundred more just like you out there."

Something dangerous flashed in Coslar's eyes. "Maybe you should get one of them, then. I'm not your lapdog."

"Oh, but you are. You have been since you followed me up the stairs when I first came to take over as queen."

"I agreed to help, but I'm not your slave."

Usaeil let her gaze rake over his hard body. "Slave? No, you aren't that. But you do as I command."

"Because I wish to serve you, not because I have to. There's a difference. You should realize that if you want to hold this throne."

She quirked a brow. "Is that a threat?"

"It's a fact."

"Point taken." She moved closer to him and put a fingernail on his chest before she slowly ran it down his front. "I do like when you try and put me in my place."

He stopped her when she reached his waist, refusing to let her go any lower. "As I said, I'm not your slave."

"Don't you want to share my bed?" she asked seductively.

He grinned and leaned close. Just before their lips touched, he said, "Will I be able to leave it?"

"Are you asking if I'll kill you?"

"Yes."

She laughed softly and cupped his cock and balls with her other hand. "If I wanted you dead, you'd be dead. I wouldn't wait until you're in my bed to do it. Although, that does give me ideas."

Coslar lowered his head to hers. Once more, he pulled away just before their lips met.

Usaeil pouted. "You're really refusing me?"

"Be nicer to me, and I might say yes next time."

She stood with her mouth gaping when he turned on his heel and walked away. No one refused her. Well, no one besides Con. Now, Coslar was? This couldn't be happening.

Was she losing her appeal? Usaeil found a mirror and looked into it. Not even the silver in her hair or her red eyes diminished her beauty. In fact, they made her look even better. What was it, then? She wracked her brain before she began laughing.

"Coslar's playing hard to get, is all. I'm in a position of power, and he wants to feel as if he's making the moves." She rolled her eyes. "Men. Fine. I'll play along. He'll be my puppet before long."

Once she had Con, though, Coslar would be tossed aside. She wasn't going to apologize for it. Con had her heart, and that's just the way it was. Usaeil turned and looked out the window. The sun was setting on another day. Very soon, it would be time for her to take back the Light throne and put Rhi in her place once and for all. The meddling Fae had disrupted too much of Usaeil's life. But she had something in store for Rhi that she'd never see coming.

"It's just what you deserve," Usaeil spoke aloud.

Her thoughts then turned to Con. She couldn't believe that he was back with Rhi. Usaeil wanted to deny it, but report after report had come in stating the fact. Con even joined her when Rhi met with the Fae in the throne room. And he wasn't the only Dragon King there—Merrill and Varek were with him.

Usaeil's stomach churned with the news. She wanted to scream, to shout at the unfairness of it all. But she had taken what was rightfully hers once. She would do it again. This time, she had the Druid magic within her to give her an advantage.

"So long as I stay away from Gemma," Usaeil said with a shudder.

She'd thought to kill the Druid as she had her family, but Gemma proved adept at staying alive. Whatever the Druid had that caused Usaeil to lose the ability to do magic was enough to keep her far, far from the mortal. Thankfully, Gemma's mate, Cináed, would keep her far from the Light Castle. For a time, anyway.

Once Rhi was gone, and the Fae were united under Usaeil's leadership, it would take a few years for the Kings and their mates to welcome her, but welcome her they would. After all, she would be Con's mate and queen, which meant she would be *their* queen.

Usaeil could hardly wait for that. But she needed to keep her eye on her main target—Rhi. She was the one who had messed up everything to begin with. Balladyn was gone, and Moreann was isolated so she couldn't cause any trouble, which left only Rhi, Usaeil's last remaining enemy.

"Soon, old friend," Usaeil said. "Soon, I'll be the one to end your life. Enjoy your time while you can."

PART THREE

If you want to know what honor is, you
need only look to one individual among all
dragons—the King of Dragon Kings.

—UNKNOWN

PART THREE

CHAPTER THIRTY-FIVE

Thick clouds obscured the moon for long moments in time, but it managed to peek through and shine its light upon the land. Con watched it through the glass doors of the balcony, itching to shift and take to the skies.

It hadn't been that long since he'd been in his true form, and he had gone much longer before without shifting. Why then did he feel the need now? He didn't question it, merely opened the doors and strode out onto the terrace.

He looked up and searched the sky until he spotted Merrill's orange scales. Con ran the few steps to the railing, put his foot on it, and launched himself into the air. As he did, he shifted and spread his wings. He beat them to catch a current of air and circled the castle before soaring up into the clouds.

Usually, he used this time to clear his head, but instead, he took the opportunity to think over everything that'd happened the last few days, including his recent talk with Rhi. He wanted to believe that they were moving forward, but he couldn't know that for sure.

What he did believe was that for the first time since

they had been a couple, they were speaking from the heart. No more barriers, no more half-truths. It felt good. Right, even. A huge weight had been lifted from him the moment he'd been able to finally tell Rhi the truth.

Were they past all of it now? He couldn't say for certain. Despite the happiness they'd shared, there was a mountain of pain and heartache between them that would likely come up again. He'd hoped they could hash it all out, but that was asking a bit too much. Besides, there would be things that Rhi might remember later on that she needed to talk about. He understood that.

Just thinking about her made him smile. Without a doubt, she was his mate. Mortals called it a soulmate, and it aptly described what he felt for Rhi—or what any dragon experienced when they found their other half.

He dipped his wing and turned to head back toward the Light Castle. Rhi was in the hidden room of the library, finishing the book. She had wanted to bring it back to her chambers, but Con had cautioned her against it. The book had been locked away in the library for a reason. Perhaps it was better that they leave it there.

The notion that some Fae had been on the realm before he'd become King of Kings was confusing. How had they gotten here? When had they left? And, more importantly, how had none of the dragons known?

His mind halted at the last question. Someone had known. If the writer of the book could describe things in so much detail, they had been involved with the dragons. And yet, Con couldn't for the life of him remember anyone but the dragons being around until the first mortals showed up.

Something didn't make sense, and he hoped he would be able to figure it out soon. Based on what little Rhi had told him, the author had only been intrigued by the dragons. Still, someone must have known about a Fae among them.

He opened his mental link to all the Kings. *"I need each of you to think back to before I became King of Kings. Do any of you remember a Fae being on this realm? And Kellan, double-check all of your records."*

Between Kellan and the other Kings, surely someone could give Con the answers he needed.

"I'll check now," Kellan answered.

Con continued flying in and out of the clouds. He wasn't worried about Usaeil attacking, even if Moreann joined her. The late afternoon and early evening had been spent coming up with several plans to protect not just the castle but also the Fae. They were ready.

The generals had been open to suggestions offered by the Kings, as well as the Queen's Guard. Rhi, herself, had several excellent ideas that Con couldn't wait to see put into action. Though he didn't make light of the situation. When Usaeil arrived, it was going to be intense.

A part of him really wanted Erith to have the Reapers take Usaeil's soul and be done with everything, but that wasn't going to happen. If Erith hadn't done it before Usaeil and Rhi met on the battlefield the first time, she wasn't going to do it now. Though Con wasn't sure why.

Erith's response that Usaeil was Rhi's to take down didn't quite have the same impact as it had before. In fact, it was time to have a chat with Erith about it.

He dove down to the sea, tucking his wings as he did. As the beach approached, he spread his wings, halting his descent as he landed softly upon the shore. He shifted back into his human form, clothing himself in a pair of jeans and a black V-neck tee.

"Erith," he called.

Con watched the dark water coil into waves that foamed white and rolled onto shore. He had called to Death a few times in the past, so he knew she would come if she could.

"This is a surprise," came a feminine voice from behind him.

He turned his head to find Erith walking toward him. "Thank you for coming."

"You knew I would." She tucked a strand of blue-black hair behind her ear.

Gone were her elaborate black gowns. In their place was a mix of black leather and chainmail that would make any Amazon, Celtic, or Norse warrior proud. Though her black sword wasn't on her person, she could call it to her with just a thought.

"Torin was veiled at the meeting to plan for Usaeil's arrival," Erith said. "I know what's going on."

Con nodded. "Rhi and I both knew he would be. You put him here to watch over things. I didna think he needed a formal invite to come to the meeting."

"If you didn't ask me here to tell me of the plans, why did you call for me?"

He blew out a breath and faced her, meeting her lavender gaze as the moon briefly shed its light upon them. "Rhi."

"What about her?"

"You know what. Why your interest in her? Why make certain she's the one who kills Usaeil? You could've removed Usaeil years ago. If anybody's soul deserves reaping, it's hers."

Erith looked at the water and wrapped her arms around herself before softly blowing out a breath. "I'm a goddess. I'm Death. Yes, I could've judged Usaeil and had the Reapers take her soul, but I didn't because she is part of Rhi's path."

"That doesna make sense."

"Because you don't have all the facts."

Con frowned as he stared at Erith, waiting for her to look at him. "Then tell me."

"I can't," she said and sighed loudly. "It isn't time yet."

"What the bloody hell does that mean?"

Her head swung to him at his explosive response. "Some people believe in destiny. Some think we forge our own paths. The truth is that it's a mix of the two. A person is simply born to do certain things, no matter what paths they take in life. You were born to be not just King of Golds but also King of Kings. You knew it deep in your soul."

"So?" Con asked. "I also knew my mate wouldna be a dragon. What about it?"

"Do you wonder why you knew those things with such certainty?"

Con shrugged. "I never thought much about it."

Erith eyed him. "Perhaps you should."

"I doona like cryptic messages. Just tell me what you want me to know."

"I can't," she said with a shake of her head. "I wish I could, but I can't."

"That makes no sense, but I doona care about myself. This is about Rhi. You obviously care a great deal about her. Why are you no' helping her?"

Erith's brows drew together. "Whatever gave you the idea that this is only about Rhi?"

That took Con aback. "You had Daire following her while veiled for months."

"Yes, I did."

"She's the only one you did that to. Who else would this be about?" Then it came to him. He could hardly believe it. His chest grew tight, his heart thumping wildly against his ribs. "Me."

Erith faced him then. "Of course, it's you. Do you think you and Rhi could have a love like you do without your lives being intertwined in a myriad of ways?"

"You never said anything."

"Why would I?"

Con looked above her head while trying to take it all in. "You didna have me followed."

"We were friends. And before you ask, no, I didn't befriend you simply because of Rhi. I came to you because I needed a friend. And so did you."

He nodded and drew in a breath as he looked at her once more. "As my friend, you know how I've suffered without Rhi. I can no' lose her."

"That's not up to me, unfortunately," Erith replied in a soft voice. "Answer the question I posed to you a few moments ago. Why do you think you were so sure about certain things in your life?"

"I suppose because it's my destiny."

"Maybe," Erith said with a nod. "Or, it could be because you'd seen it."

He jerked back as if slapped. "Seen it? I can no' look into the future."

"I didn't say it was magic, Con. I said that maybe you saw some of your path. It could've been in a dream. Or the magic of the realm could've shown you. You might not have seen Rhi's face, but you knew her in an instant, didn't you?"

"The first time I saw her, without speaking to her, I knew she was my mate."

Erith smiled then. "You trust your instincts. It's what

has gotten you and the Kings where you are today. You trusted your gut both before you were King and after. You need to keep trusting it."

"I wanted to know why you wouldn't reap Usaeil's soul, not all of this."

"Usaeil is part of your and Rhi's life. There's no way around it. It's why I told Rhi that she had to be the one to fight Usaeil. It couldn't be you or me or anyone else. It has to be Rhi."

Con twisted his lips. "It's her destiny."

"In a manner of speaking, yes. Everything that has happened to you and Rhi from your very first breaths until now has happened for a reason. You both need to accept that. And just so you know, I *could* intervene and remove Usaeil from the picture."

"Then do it," Con urged.

Erith gave him a sad smile. "If I do, you'll lose Rhi."

"If you doona, I could lose her."

"One is a fact. The other is just a possibility."

How could she say such a thing? Rhi needed to live. He had to have her. Con had lived without her for far too long. He couldn't do it anymore. "Wait. When you say I will lose Rhi, do you mean she'll die? Or that she'll no longer be mine?"

Erith shrugged. "Does it really matter?"

No, it didn't, and she knew it. Con raked a hand down his face. "Rhi is unlike anyone I've ever met. She's endured so much. Things that would have made a weaker individual lose their light long ago."

"But hers stays strong," Erith added.

"That it does."

"Just as you have."

Con shot her a dark look. "Doona bring me into this."

"As I said, your and Rhi's lives are intertwined in

ways you can't even imagine. They have been from the very beginning of time. Even before you were born."

Con could accept that, and, in many cases, it made sense, since they were mates. "And Usaeil? You're telling me she's intertwined with us, as well?"

"Unfortunately."

"What about you?"

At this, Erith grinned. "Oh, yes."

"Then I'm lucky to have a friend such as you by my side."

Her smile faded. "I want to help you and Rhi, but the outcome won't be what you want if I do. I know that isn't what you want to hear, but it's the truth."

He wasn't sure if it was or not. Erith could be hiding more, but what he did know was that she was his friend. She wouldn't willingly hurt him if there was another way. "Thank you."

"I didn't tell you anything."

"Actually, you told me quite a lot. I just need to sort through it all." And he would.

Erith chuckled. "You always did like puzzles."

Before she left, he asked, "Do you know anything about a Fae who was on this realm before I became King of Dragon Kings? One who might have written a book about their time here?"

"I can't say as I do," she said as she turned.

But Con saw the smile that she tried to hide. She knew something about the book, but she wasn't going to tell him. It was just another puzzle for him to figure out.

CHAPTER THIRTY-SIX

Rhi slowly closed the book. She'd read the last few pages three times, but the words hadn't changed. She was shaking as she got to her feet and placed the book back on the pedestal. Her heart thumped wildly as her limbs grew numb from shock.

And desolation.

She wanted to ignore the words she'd read, to disregard them as if they had never been. But she couldn't. The knowledge was now burned into her mind whether she wanted it there or not. How ridiculous that she'd thought reading the book might give her some insight into the Dragon Kings, tell her things she hadn't known. Instead, it had shown her something else entirely, something she wasn't prepared for.

Something she wasn't sure she could accept.

Her first instinct was to go to Con. He always knew how to sort through such issues. But she couldn't do that because then she'd have to tell him what she knew.

Rhi walked from the hidden room and softly shut the door behind herself. The library was quieter than usual in the early morning hours before dawn. Most were not up yet, which made the castle seem almost as if it too slept.

She made it several feet before she had to stop and lean against a bookshelf to compose herself after an onslaught of horror, dismay, and bewilderment bombarded her. There was no way she could go back to her chamber like this. Con wouldn't let up until she told him what was wrong and divulged everything, and she couldn't do that. It was better if he never knew.

She *wished* she didn't know.

But she did. There was no changing that now.

With her hand to her forehead, Rhi closed her eyes and took in calming breaths, but it didn't help. In fact, she became further agitated the more she thought about what she'd read. Her incredulity turned to outrage, and that shifted to fury.

"Rhi."

Her eyes flew open at the sound of her name. She spotted Torin before her, the Reaper's concerned look telling her that he'd been watching her. "What?" she snapped.

"You look like you're going to do something you'll regret later," he said.

She pushed away from the bookshelf, her gaze latched on to him. That's when she knew. "You were in the room with me, weren't you?"

He gave a single nod.

She'd always been aware when Daire was near her. How was it that she hadn't realized that Torin was in the room? Had she been that absorbed by the book? The obvious answer was yes. And that did nothing to calm her.

"So, you know," she stated.

Torin swallowed loudly as his silver eyes glanced away. "I do."

"I can't sit here and do nothing."

"You can't leave, either."

She quirked a brow. "Oh, really? Do you think you can stop me?"

"Honestly, I'm not sure."

Rhi drew in a shuddering breath. "What I read, what was in that book . . . it changes everything. For all of us."

"I know," he said in a soft voice. He shook his head. "Usaeil has had that book in her possession for her entire reign. It was her family's before that."

"She didn't read it."

Torin's look was skeptical. "Are you sure?"

She wasn't, and that irritated her.

"You should talk to Con about this—"

"No," Rhi said before he'd even finished speaking.

Torin's brows drew together. "You're going to keep this from him?"

"For now."

"He's King of Dragon Kings. If anyone can take it, he can."

Rhi shook her head, not wanting to hear it. "Con has too much to deal with as it is. I'm not putting something else on his shoulders."

"Even if it involves you?"

She glared at Torin and lifted her chin. "You may be a Reaper, but that doesn't scare me."

"Maybe not, but you're frightened. Say what you will to anyone else, but I've seen you and Con. You've found each other again, even if you don't want to admit it. And you're terrified of losing him."

Rhi wanted to deny it as she looked at the floor. In fact, she'd accepted her death just a short time ago. But now, well, now that Con had come to her, everything had changed. All she thought about was being with him and the future they could have.

If only Usaeil weren't in the picture.

"There's no shame in it," Torin continued. "You've suffered enough. So has he. Perhaps it's time the whole truth came out."

"Erith knows," Rhi said as she slid her gaze to Torin.

Torin's lips flattened for a moment. "It would explain her interest in you."

"It certainly does." But Rhi's thoughts weren't on Death. They were on someone else.

Torin's look intensified. "Don't. Whatever you're thinking, don't do it, at least not before you talk to Con."

"Why not? Because he might stop me?"

"Maybe," he answered.

"How do you know I wasn't meant to read the book?"

He parted his lips to answer, but then shook his head.

She blew out a breath. "Exactly. When I found it, the words moved all over the page. They stopped for me and allowed me to read them. That means I was supposed to."

"Or it was hidden so you wouldn't find it."

Rhi didn't want to consider that option, but now that he'd said it, she had no other choice. "It doesn't matter now. I know the truth."

"Ignore it," Torin pressed.

She gaped at him. "Why? How does that serve anyone?"

"I don't know," he admitted. "I've got a bad feeling about this."

"Because you know I'm going to Usaeil."

A muscle jumped in his jaw. "Because you're going to Usaeil."

"If you're afraid for me, then come with me. Otherwise, stand aside."

"I could alert Con or Erith," Torin threatened.

Rhi rolled her eyes. "If you were going to, you would've already done it."

Torin turned away in agitation before he faced her once more. "Fine. I'll go with you, and I'll go veiled."

"Don't bother. Usaeil will realize you're there."

"You can't go alone."

Rhi closed the distance between them and forced a smile. "This has always been between Usaeil and me. No one can stop this. Not you, not Erith, and not Con."

"If anything happens to you, Con won't recover from it."

"Do you think it'd be better if he watched it happen? That would only make things worse, and you know it."

"Rhi," Torin said before he sighed. "This is a mistake. We've all banded together to defeat Usaeil. You keeping this to yourself defeats that."

She tucked her hair behind her ear. "Actually, I think this is exactly the right thing to do. It'll keep the Druids on Skye safe, the Warriors and Druids of MacLeod Castle from being involved, not to mention, it'll prevent the Light and Dark from entering into another civil war. Then there are the Dragon Kings. They've been fighting to protect this realm and themselves for so long. It's time they had some peace."

"You're Con's mate. He'll never have peace without you."

She gave him a flat look. "You think I'll be defeated."

"I'm merely pointing out a fact you need to consider."

Rhi didn't bother to answer. There was nothing to say. She knew firsthand how she'd feel if Con were killed, preventing them from being together in this life. He would wait for her, though, so they could be together in the next life.

But she would endure heartache the likes of which might very well kill her.

"Rhi, no," Torin begged.

She flashed him a smile. "I'm Queen of the Light. Don't fear for me."

He turned with her as she walked past him. Her smile faded before she teleported to her island. It had been weeks since she'd come here, but she wasn't visiting for solace. She was here to get herself together and pick a place to call for Usaeil.

Rhi stood in the shack, her eyes going to the nail polish Con had bought for her. She didn't have time to go to Jesse and have her nails done. Black leather replaced her pants, and a solid black shirt covered her torso. Her new armor covered her upper body and shoulders but allowed free movement for her arms. Armored vambraces covered her forearms. Next, she called for her black Christian Louboutin boots with their four-inch heels and silver spikes on the toes.

She pulled her hair away from her face in dozens of tiny braids that then formed one thick plait at the back of her head. Last, she called forth her sword. It filled her right palm, the weight balanced perfectly.

A flash of something caught her attention. She looked at the table and found a curved dagger. Rhi went to inspect it. The moment she saw it, tears gathered in her eyes. She set her sword down and carefully lifted the weapon.

"Thank you," she said as she tucked Balladyn's blade into her left boot.

She picked up her sword again before jumping to the middle of the Sahara Desert. It was a secluded place without any mortals. A good place for a battle where magic could be unleashed without any humans seeing anything or getting involved.

Rhi stood atop one of the sand dunes as the wind whipped around her. Her heart ached for Con, but she never let his name escape her lips. She had to do this alone.

"Usaeil," she called. "Your time is up."

CHAPTER THIRTY-SEVEN

"What the fuck do you mean, she left?" Con bellowed.

Few things caused unease within Torin. Constantine being furious was one of them. Torin pulled his gaze from the King of Kings and glanced at Eoghan, who stood with Erith.

"I tried to dissuade her," Torin began.

Con got in his face, their noses practically touching. "You didna try hard enough."

Torin had spent years hiding his pain—as well as his fury. But he wasn't going to back down, even if it *was* Constantine in his face. "You weren't there," he bit out.

"She's my mate," Con said through clenched teeth.

Torin's gaze narrowed. "And she's also a queen who has a bloody mind of her own."

Con whirled around and put his fist through a panel in the wall, crumbling the granite. He stood there, breathing heavily, his back to everyone.

"Whether you believe it or not, I did try to stop her," Torin said. "As soon as she was gone, I called Eoghan and Erith, and we found you."

Con shook his head of blond waves and sighed. "I

doona blame you. I blame myself. I should've known no' to leave her alone. Rhi can be rash."

"We all can be when we're protecting those we love," Eoghan said.

Con tilted his head to look at Eoghan before he nodded. "Aye."

Torin looked at Erith, who hadn't said anything after he told her that Rhi had read the book. He waited for her to tell Con about it. When she didn't, Torin knew Death was keeping that to herself. But why? Torin couldn't figure it out. Con could handle it. If Death was holding her tongue, that meant there was more that Torin—and Rhi—didn't know.

The King of Dragon Kings, the strongest of all dragons, had two very powerful women shielding him. Torin couldn't help but be a little envious. The one being in all the realm who didn't need protection seemed to have it in spades.

Con put his hands on his hips and faced the others with a loud sigh. "What made her go? I know Rhi. She wouldna leave on her own unless she felt she had to."

"It doesn't matter why she left," Erith finally spoke.

But Con's gaze remained on Torin. He wanted to ignore the Dragon King, to pretend the question hadn't been posed directly to him. Death hadn't said he couldn't say anything, but Rhi had made it clear that she didn't want Con to know. And Erith's silence pretty much said it all.

"Torin?" Con asked, his voice going deep.

Eoghan started toward them, but Torin held up his hand, halting the Reaper. Torin then slid his gaze to Erith.

"Doona look at her," Con said as his eyes moved between them. "I'm asking you."

"But he answers to me," Erith replied. She pressed

her lips together and turned away as she walked slowly around the room. "There is a book—"

Con frowned. "Aye. Rhi showed it to me. I read a few pages of it."

"She finished it," Torin said.

The agitation Con had shown moments before vanished. He became utterly still, no emotion on his face. "And?"

Erith stopped and turned to him, their gazes clashing. "That book was lost long ago on the Fae Realm. I didn't realize that Usaeil's grandfather had found it. He must have brought it to this realm when the Light came. Then, he built the room in the library. Somehow, he was able to hide it from me."

"Why would he want to do that?" Con questioned.

Torin wondered the same thing. He'd never heard of such a book, and usually, something that important was never hidden for long. Yet, this one had been. It seemed impossible.

"Some things are better left unknown," Erith replied.

Con crossed his arms over his chest. "I doona believe that."

"It's out now," Torin said.

Con glanced his way before he narrowed his gaze on Erith. "Since I know how keen you've been to watch Rhi, I'm guessing Torin knows exactly what is in that book."

"He wasn't just here to keep an eye on Rhi. He was here to keep me informed," Erith replied.

Con dropped his arms. "And you didna trust me or Rhi to do that."

"You had more than enough to—" Erith began.

But Con cut her off. "You said you were my friend. I've believed that. But now I'm beginning to wonder what it is you're hiding from me."

Eoghan, who had been listening intently the entire time, took a deep breath and said, "Con, we realize your emotions are running high because Rhi is gone, but that doesn't mean Erith isn't your friend."

Con cut his black gaze to Eoghan and didn't say anything for several moments. Then he returned his attention to Erith. "The book wanted Rhi to read it. Did you know the words were moving when she found it?"

"There is a spell on it that prevents certain people from reading it," Erith admitted.

Torin looked between them. "That means someone tried before Rhi. Usaeil?"

"It doesna matter," Con said. "I doona care what's in the book. I just want to get to Rhi. You can find her," he told Erith.

Death licked her lips. "She wants to do this on her own."

"Would you sit aside if Cael did such a thing? Where is he, by the way?"

Torin and Eoghan exchanged a grin because they knew that Con had backed Erith into a corner that she had no choice but to accept.

"Please. Reconsider. Rhi is strong. She can hold her own," Erith pleaded.

Con shook his head. "I let Rhi go once. I swore I would remain by her side no matter what this time."

"Did you consider that she's doing this because she's protecting you?" Erith asked, her voice rising with her emotions.

You could've heard a pin drop, the room grew so silent. Torin had seen violence before. He'd been a part of it, as well. But the hostility, the utter savagery coming from Con now, made him want to get a safe distance away. Like on another realm.

Torin spotted Eoghan straightening as if he too fought the need to take a step back.

Because if any being could hold their own against Death, it was Constantine.

"The only one who needs protecting is Rhi," Con said in a tone as cold as the arctic. "No' me."

Erith looked at the floor before grudgingly lifting her gaze to Con. "That's not true."

"What are you no' telling me?" Con demanded.

"A lot."

"Then you better start talking, because my patience has run dry."

Torin wasn't sure he or Eoghan should be privy to any of this, but he wasn't going to leave. Not that he thought Death would need him. Erith could certainly take care of herself. She was a goddess, after all.

And Con didn't need him, either. No, Torin stayed because he couldn't make himself leave. Part of it was because he knew what was in the book. The other part was that he was Fae and was rooting for Rhi.

"Erith," Con said in a dangerous tone.

Her lips parted when the door to the queen's chambers was thrown open as Varek strode inside. His gaze landed on Con, though no words were spoken. The Reapers could remain veiled for as long as they wanted. They also had the ability to teleport all over the realm. Still, they couldn't speak telepathically like the Dragon Kings.

Con swung his head to Erith. "We're no' finished here, but right now, we must get ready. The Dark Army has arrived."

With every step, Con kept hearing Torin's voice telling him that Rhi was gone. Con couldn't believe she'd left without talking to him. Whatever was in that damn book had made her toss out all their plans and go after Usaeil herself.

"This is to throw us off," Merrill said when Con finally reached him.

Con looked out over the field, taking in the multitude of Dark Fae waiting to attack. Not so long ago, they'd been led by Balladyn, who had stood behind Rhi and the Kings as she fought Usaeil. Now that same army was here to take over the castle.

"Usaeil isna here," Varek said as he searched the troops. "That willna make Rhi happy."

Merrill frowned as he looked at Con. "Where is Rhi?"

"Gone," Con told them. "She read something and went to challenge Usaeil herself."

Varek shook his head as his lips twisted. "Usaeil must have sent the army here to make sure we wouldna help Rhi."

"Hard to help if we doona know where she is," Merrill added.

Con swallowed, his mind sorting through various events to see which would be the best course of action. He doubted the Dark Army would wait to attack. Rhi might have taken the fight away from the castle to save the Light, but she had put herself in a bad situation. All the Light would know was that the Dark Army had arrived, and their new queen wasn't there to lead them.

"I'm game to attack," Varek said as he rubbed his hands together.

Con shook his head slowly. "No' yet."

"Then, what do we do?" Merrill asked.

"Nothing. This is the Fae's domain, no' ours. I willna step in and act as their leader."

Varek snorted. "Someone needs to."

Con turned on his heel and strode back into the castle where he found the generals gathered together. He stopped before them, waiting for them to notice him. "Your queen has taken the fight with Usaeil away from the castle to limit the number of casualties," he told them.

One snorted, unimpressed by the statement. He replied with a nasally Irish accent. "That hasn't stopped the Dark Army from coming at us."

Con stared at the man. "Has it entered that small mind of yours that Usaeil has done this on purpose to make you nervous? She knows Rhi isna here to lead you, but you doona need your queen. The plans were already laid out, and all of you are aware of them. Now, get your heads out of your arses and protect this castle while your queen is doing her best to safeguard all of you."

Thankfully, one of the generals took charge and began delegating orders. Once the others were gone, he turned to Con and asked, "Will the Kings still aid us?"

"Of course," Con replied.

With that, the general left to get his troops ready. Con then found the Queen's Guard, but to his surprise, they were already corralling the Light into safe places to minimize the chances of them being harmed.

The Fae might live for thousands of years, but they were just like the mortals, more interested in a fight than their own safety.

Con was on his way back to Merrill and Varek when he passed the library. He halted, wondering if he should look at the book. There was a battle brewing. He should be there to help if needed. Actually, he should be with Rhi.

What bothered him was that he knew both Rhi and Erith were keeping something from him. He didn't like that.

Con drew in a breath and pivoted to enter the library.

CHAPTER THIRTY-EIGHT

Usaeil's Manor

Moreann refused to die in this place while being held by Usaeil. The traitorous bitch actually thought she could hold her. But Moreann wasn't the Empress of Lornavon for nothing.

It had taken her days—times when Usaeil had ignored her, thereby giving Moreann the time needed—to slowly but surely break through the spells Usaeil had put in place. It had been difficult. Two had knocked Moreann unconscious. One nearly took her life. Working on all of them had taken years away.

She looked down at her hands that were now wrinkled and spotted with age. When she first discovered the spell to remain immortal, she'd actually thought it would merely slow the aging process. At the time, she hadn't cared if she aged or not. But years of being youthful had changed everything. Now, each time she saw a new wrinkle or found another gray hair, she grew anxious.

The spell took a lot of power to cast and maintain. As much as she loved that it had kept her alive for far longer than anyone else on her realm, the one thing she couldn't do was reverse whatever aging had already taken its toll on her body. Which meant, it would've taken a few hundred years for her to look as she did now.

Just one more reason to hate Usaeil.

"My people need me," Moreann said as she lowered her hands to her sides and lifted her face. "No longer will I be held in this horrible place by some power-hungry, spoiled Fae who doesn't know her place."

Moreann walked to the door and turned the handle. The door swung open, but as she waited, no one rushed into the room. She wasn't fooled. The Trackers were all over the house. The minute one of them spotted her, they'd let Usaeil know.

Let them. Moreann was prepared for a battle with the Fae queen. Moreann smiled and stepped out of the room. She turned and made her way down the hall to the stairs. As she walked past a room with a door closed, she paused. Someone was inside.

Curious, she opened the door and looked within to find a Light Fae lying upon the bed. At first, she thought he was asleep, but it didn't take long for her to realize that something else was going on. He lay unmoving except for the rise and fall of his chest. He wasn't dead, and he didn't look ill, either.

Moreann moved closer and put one finger on his hand. She felt the layers of magic Usaeil had woven over the male like a thick blanket that not even the rays of the sun could penetrate. The same kind of spell she had taught Usaeil how to do when they formed the Others and set the traps for the Dragon Kings.

"Ungrateful bitch," Moreann whispered.

She almost attempted to wake the Fae, but it would take nearly as much magic as she'd used to get free. While the idea of taking the male away from Usaeil would be gratifying, causing weakness within herself when she would need all her strength to fight the Trackers and Usaeil was foolish.

"Good luck," Moreann told the Fae and walked from the room.

She was halfway down the stairs when she spotted the first Tracker. Moreann waved her hand, and the Tracker exploded. The commotion caused more to rush at her. Without breaking stride, she killed each of them with just a flick of her wrist.

By the time she reached the bottom of the staircase, half a dozen Trackers were watching her. She smiled at them, noting their dubious expressions.

"I know there are more of you veiled. I'll let you live if you allow me to leave. Tell Usaeil I've gone. I want her to know. But if any of you come at me, I'll kill you all."

The Trackers held their ground, which she was thankful for because she could feel herself weakening. She needed a place to rest and recharge, and that wouldn't happen until she was out of this house.

She was almost to the door when she felt something. She halted and slowly turned toward a set of stairs leading down. She hadn't noticed them when Usaeil had brought her here, but she hadn't had a chance to see much of the house before she was locked away.

Moreann eyed the Trackers who still hadn't moved as she walked to the stairs. A Tracker there hastily backed away. She kept her eye on him as she descended the steps into the dungeon. Once she was past him, the Tracker raced upstairs with the others.

To Moreann's surprise, she found an old Druid sitting on the floor of a cell as if he were meditating. She studied his long, white beard and hair, waiting for him to notice her. She didn't have time for his games, however. "I know you're awake. Open your eyes."

His lids lifted, and old eyes looked at her.

She studied him as she reached out with her magic to sense his. "You've quite a bit of power. It's rare for Druids to have so much on this realm."

Still, he said nothing.

"Why does Usaeil keep you prisoner?"

He remained silent.

Moreann flattened her lips, her irritation growing. "Surely, you can tell me your name."

He simply blinked in response.

She knew she should leave, but there was something about him that intrigued her, something that held her there. Though she wasn't sure what it was. "I can free you. I'm leaving now. Come with me."

"I want nothing to do with you," he said in a Scottish brogue, his lips lifted in a sneer. "You're responsible for all of this."

She put her hand to her chest and laughed. "That's quite a lot you've put on my shoulders."

"You brought the mortals here. You sought to undermine the dragons and take their realm. You formed the Others and did untold damage to countless generations because you could no' accept that the magic on your realm was dying."

Her smile dropped. "You think to condemn me because I'm trying to protect my people?"

"Did it ever occur to you that magic, like all things, dies? You have no right to take over someone else's realm simply because you want it."

"Of course I can, if they're not strong enough to hold it."

He laughed then and climbed to his feet with ease that belied the age she saw on his face. "But the Dragon Kings were strong enough to hold it. Still, you didna give up. You put together the Others, which should've given you this realm. But it didna. The Dragon Kings still won, and you doona know why. I bet that galls you."

"I was betrayed by those I considered allies. That's why I didn't succeed."

The Druid shook his head, his confident smile in place. "You lost because the magic of this realm thwarted you. And it'll continue to do so. This realm willna be yours."

"But it is mine," she retorted. "You're a descendant of my people, which means we have the same type of blood in our veins. I'm here, my people are here. Nothing can change that now."

"Your people?" He raked his gaze over her as if the mere sight of her turned his stomach. "You tossed *your people* out when they didna have magic. You couldna stand to have them on your realm. They were left without a home, without anything. You thought leaving them here would weaken the Dragon Kings. Instead, it only made the Kings stronger."

It was her turn to laugh. "Oh, I beg to differ. The Kings had to send their dragons away. That was a blow no one saw coming but me."

"You didna weaken the Kings. You unified them. They're stronger now than ever before. There isna anything you can do that will break them apart."

She crossed her arms over her chest. "Look at you, behind bars, yet thinking you're better than I am. I'm the one leaving."

"You think I'm no' able to get free?" he asked with a smile.

"I think if you could, you would."

He chuckled and shook his head. "I've actually been waiting for you."

"Me?" she asked, her brows raised in confusion.

"I've been waiting for you to find me so I could tell my friends."

Moreann couldn't believe she had offered to help such an ungrateful person. "You're delusional. There's no way you're getting out of here, not with the Trackers up there. I was your only way out. As far as I'm concerned, you can rot in here."

He lifted his gaze to the ceiling and nodded. "The Trackers can be fearsome, that's for sure. They also have an uncanny ability to remain veiled for long periods."

"Exactly."

He smiled then.

"What are you grinning about?" she demanded.

"Like I said, I've been waiting for you. I knew when you came down here that all the Trackers would gather together to see what you would do. And they have."

Moreann shrugged, growing tired of his talk. "Whatever. I'm leaving. I imagine when Usaeil returns and finds me gone, she'll take it out on you."

Not even that remark dimmed his arrogant smile.

Moreann turned around, only to find her way blocked by a woman with red hair and green eyes filled with vengeance. Behind her stood five other Druids. Moreann lifted her chin and used her empress voice as she demanded, "Get out of my way."

"Psst," the old Druid behind Moreann said to get her attention. "Did I forget to mention that we're from Skye?"

Moreann's stomach dropped to her feet. She had been surprised by how quickly a few of the mortals had gained magic after she left them on the realm. They had been powerful, and they had all headed to one place—the Isle of Skye. There, they banded together, creating one of the strongest communities of Druids on the realm.

Powerful enough that they gave even her pause.

All this time, she'd believed that her only problem would be the Trackers. She hadn't thought about other Druids hindering her escape.

The redheaded female took a step toward her. "You aren't going anywhere."

"Nice try, but you can't hold me." It was a bluff, but Moreann didn't know what else to do. She couldn't remember the last time she'd been so terrified. The fact that she was still weakened from breaking through Usaeil's spells only added to her fear.

One of the Druids behind the redhead moved around her, his gaze locked on Moreann. "You didna believe our ancestors were good enough for you, but the truth is, you're no' good enough for them."

"The Ancients speak to us," an older woman said as she walked around the redhead and approached Moreann. "They heard Corann and told us where to find him. And you."

Corann. Moreann's head jerked to the side to look at the old man. She knew that name. It was one the Druids had spoken when they looked into the future for her. They had warned Moreann that if she encountered him, he would ruin everything.

Corann gave her a nod. "I've been waiting for this day for a verra long time."

That's when the truth slammed into her. "You let yourself be taken by Usaeil."

Corann shrugged. "I did what had to be done for this realm at the urging of the Ancients."

Moreann looked back at the Druids making their way to her. She stepped back, continuing to move away from the Druids. But there was nowhere for her to go. All too soon, her back hit a wall.

She lifted her hands, gathering her magic. She was

empress. She had found an answer for her people, and she wouldn't let them down. "You don't scare me. I killed the Trackers easily enough. I'll kill you, as well."

"That's no' going to happen," said a teenage boy right before he threw magic at her.

Moreann blocked it. Before she could smile in triumph, the other five blasted Moreann. Once more, she attempted to block the hits, but there were too many. And she was so weak.

Her magic had never abandoned her before, but that's exactly what was happening now. She felt it in her bones. Still, she continued fighting, using whatever magic she could muster to defend herself. Unfortunately, it did nothing to thwart those attacking her.

She fell to her knees, her thoughts turning to her people. What would they do without her? Then, she was on her back, looking up at Corann, who loomed over her.

"Your people will survive," he told her. "And the magic will return to them. It left because of you, because of the spell you cast for immortality. You caused the demise of the magic on your realm. You never thought to look at yourself or your people as the reason for the magic dying out. You believed the answers lay elsewhere. And you thought to take what wasna yours. You forced the greatest Druids of your realm to sacrifice themselves so you could look into the future and find a way to destroy the Kings. Yet those same Druids betrayed you. They lied to you because they saw what you couldn't. All these years, the magic has been teaching you the error of your ways, but you refused to listen."

"I'm listening," she whispered, struggling to draw breath into her lungs.

But it was too late. The last of her magic ebbed away, taking her life with it.

CHAPTER THIRTY-NINE

MacLeod Castle

Isla jerked at the sound of the Ancients in her head, spilling her coffee all over the counter in the process. She hurriedly set aside the pot and rushed out of the kitchen and into the great hall.

"What is it?" Hayden asked when he saw her.

Isla swallowed as she looked at everyone in the room, all who now stared at her. She slowly walked to Hayden, who wrapped an arm around her, sensing that she needed his warmth and comfort.

After a moment, she said, "Something has happened. The Ancients are . . . well, the only way I can describe it is to tell you they're rejoicing."

Sonya pushed back her chair and ran to the door before throwing it open and walking outside. The hall was silent as they waited to see if the trees would once more speak to her. It felt like an eternity before Sonya returned. She gently closed the doors behind her and said, "Moreann is dead."

"Did the trees say anything else?" Broc pressed.

Sonya shook her head of red hair and wrapped her

arms around herself. "They just kept repeating that Moreann is dead."

"Could it be the Kings or Rhi?" Quinn asked.

Fallon shrugged, his lips twisting. "I've heard nothing from them, and the Kings assured me that we would know when it was time for battle."

"Maybe it wasna a planned skirmish," Charon replied.

Isla looked up at Hayden and grinned. "It doesn't matter. One enemy is gone. The founder of the Others is no more, which means the group is no longer a threat to the Dragon Kings or this realm."

"I think we need to determine that for sure," Lucan stated.

Fallon nodded. "Aye. I'll go to Dreagan now."

"I'll come with you," Phelan said as he got to his feet.

Isla called out to Fallon right as he and Phelan teleported away, but it was too late. They hadn't heard her.

Larena wore a frown as she asked, "What is it?"

"The Ancients. They've changed what they're saying," Isla explained.

Cara leaned her elbow on the table. "What now?"

Isla closed her eyes, lulled by the drums and the chanting of the Ancients. No matter how many times she asked them, she still didn't know why they had chosen to speak to only her and not any of the other Druids at the castle, but at the moment, it didn't matter.

"They're . . . cautioning us." Isla frowned as she tried to make out the words. "It sounds like they're saying 'book,' but I can't be sure."

Camdyn ran a hand through his long, black hair, his dark eyes troubled. "Book? What kind of book?"

"I don't know," Isla answered while keeping her eyes closed. "I can't hear them clearly. It sounds like half are still celebrating Moreann's demise, but others are fo-cused on saying something else. Like I said, it sounds like *book*, but it could be anything." She opened her eyes and shook her head as her stomach churned with anxiety. "I can't tell."

Saffron rubbed a hand along Camdyn's back. "Maybe Fallon and Phelan will figure something out."

"I'll see what the trees know," Sonya said.

Gwynn followed her. "And I'll ask the wind."

"I might as well talk to the stones," Evie said as she too walked outside.

The elation Isla had experienced moments ago was gone, leaving her apprehensive and uneasy, all her senses on high alert.

"I've got you," Hayden whispered.

She held onto him tighter. "And I have you."

"Together, we can survive anything. Including what-ever is coming our way."

The problem was, she wasn't sure that whatever the Ancients were upset about was coming for them. Just because the Ancients decided to speak to Isla didn't al-ways mean the issue was with someone or something at MacLeod Castle.

She thought about the Dragon Kings and Rhi, as well as the Fae. With one enemy gone, that left Usaeil. But the ex-Light Queen shouldn't be underestimated. In fact, Isla was beginning to believe that Usaeil was more danger-ous than any other being.

The sight of the mug falling from Eilish's fingers prompted Ulrik into action. He moved quickly, grabbing the cup before it could hit the floor. Some of the hot tea splashed onto his hand, but he barely felt it since his attention was on his mate.

"Babe?"

She blinked and looked at him then at the mug. She flexed her fingers as if bringing feeling back into them. "Thank you."

"What just happened?" he asked in concern.

"I think it was the Ancients. It was so faint that I could barely hear them."

Darcy rushed into the kitchen, out of breath and wild-eyed. "I-I." She paused and swallowed. "Oh, dear."

Ulrik eyed Darcy. He had been responsible for her losing her magic when she helped him break through the binding spell. Ulrik hated that it had happened to her, but he wasn't sorry that he had gotten his magic back. Without it, he'd be dead now.

"Darcy? What is it?" Ulrik pressed.

Warrick's tall figure filled the doorway behind his mate. The moment he spied Darcy, he walked to her and gently held her face in his hands. "Are you all right, love?"

"Yes," she said with a smile. "I heard the Ancients. I couldn't make out what they said, exactly, but I heard them for the briefest of moments."

Eilish said, "So did I."

Ulrik met Warrick's gaze. "I wonder if the other Druids did, as well."

"One way to find out," War said.

It didn't take long for Ulrik to have the Druids and their mates gathered in Con's office. He slid his gaze to Eilish to see that she was still upset by what had happened. The fact that the Ancients had spoken to her and Darcy was good news, but not knowing what they were trying to say wasn't.

"All of you are here because you're either a Druid or have ties to the Druids, specifically those from Skye,"

Ulrik said. "Both Eilish and Darcy heard the Ancients. The Ancients didna speak long, and neither Eilish nor Darcy could discern what they said. Did any of you hear anything?"

Faith shook her head when Ulrik looked her way, but she had her arms wrapped around herself, clearly ill at ease with what was happening. Dmitri remained by her side, his arms around her.

Beside them was Devon, who licked her lips when Ulrik's gaze landed on her. Devon said, "I heard something. It was faint, but it sounded like distant drums."

"The Ancients," Eilish confirmed.

Esther drew in a breath and said, "I heard it, as well. The drums, that is. And right after, I heard voices. But like Eilish and Darcy, I couldn't make out the words."

"Include me in that," Claire replied from her chair where V stood directly behind her. "Woke me from my sleep."

Bernadette raised her hand. "I heard drums, but I thought it was from music somewhere in the house."

Ulrik then turned his eyes to Gemma. Her light blue eyes met his before she said, "I heard them. I also heard what they said."

"What was it?" Eilish asked before Ulrik had a chance.

Gemma shifted her feet and glanced at Cináed beside her. "They said two words. Moreann and dead."

Ulrik didn't rejoice as the others in the office did. The Ancients had a habit of being cryptic instead of just saying what it was they meant. Until he knew for sure that Moreann was dead, he would continue thinking of her as a threat.

He leaned back in the chair, his attention returning to Faith. The link from her father to the Skye Druids was something that hadn't sat well with Faith from the beginning. Ulrik suspected it had something to do with the fact that she had found the wooden dragon from the Others and had brought it to Dreagan, where things had nearly become disastrous.

Dmitri obviously thought so as well because he said over the din of conversation, "Ask Faith again."

Instantly, the office grew quiet. Ulrik slowly released a breath. "Faith? Did you hear the Ancients?"

Her eyes teared up as she looked at him. "I don't want any kind of connection to the Druids. That's what led me to find the wooden dragon and bring it here."

"That's in the past," Dmitri told her. "And that wasna your fault."

Ulrik nodded slowly. "He's right. It wasna your fault. The Others made sure to have it there, knowing you would be the one to find it. No matter what you did, your path would have led you there, but no' just because of the wooden dragon. You found Dmitri, as well."

Faith smiled as she tilted her head to look at her mate. "That's true."

"Let the past go," Dmitri urged her.

She drew in a deep breath and blew it out. Then, she looked at Ulrik. "I heard the drums of the Ancients, but no words."

Every mate at Dreagan who was either a Druid or had a link to the Druids had heard the Ancients. What was it the Ancients were trying to say? Was it that Moreann was dead?

"They'll return, right?" Darcy asked as she looked at the other women. "The Ancients didn't get their message across, so they should return."

Eilish shrugged her shoulders. "I wish I had an answer."

Ulrik heard his name from below and got to his feet.

He said nothing as he strode down the hall to the stairs and looked down to find Fallon and Phelan.

"Is it true?" Fallon asked, looking up.

Ulrik frowned. "Is what true?"

"Is Moreann dead?"

Ulrik straightened and turned to see that everyone had come out of the office behind him. Eilish smiled as she hurried down the stairs, pulling Ulrik after her.

When he reached the bottom, Ulrik asked, "Did the Ancients tell someone that?"

"Isla said they were rejoicing, but it was the trees that told Sonya," Phelan replied.

Eilish smiled as she glanced at the other Druids still on the steps. "We heard the Ancients but couldn't exactly make out what was said."

"The trees don't lie," Gemma said. "If they said Moreann is dead, then she's gone."

He couldn't celebrate yet. Ulrik still had too many unanswered questions.

"I know what you're going to ask," Fallon said. "And I doona know who killed her or how."

There was a knock on the door. Ulrik walked past Fallon and Phelan and opened it to find none other than Corann and Rhona. He was surprised to see them but moved aside so they could enter.

Corann looked at those around him and smiled. "I see the good news has already reached Dreagan."

"You're free," Ulrik said.

Corann smiled and shook his head. "In a manner of speaking."

"What does that mean?" Eilish asked.

Rhona's face was filled with sadness. "Corann was able to communicate with me via his mind. He couldn't show me where he was, however."

"No' while I still had my body," Corann explained.

Ulrik frowned as he looked at the very real person before him. "I doona understand."

Corann laughed softly. "My time here is up. Usaeil took most of my magic and my life, but I managed to keep enough to let Rhona know where my body was. Then, I just had to wait for her to find me to take care of Moreann."

"I had other Druids with me. We were able to get there before Moreann left. We made sure she'll never hurt anyone on this realm or any other again," Rhona replied.

Ulrik couldn't believe that Moreann was dead. As he looked, he saw Corann's body shimmer as if it couldn't hold its shape any longer.

Corann gave a nod to all and then winked at Rhona before he faded.

CHAPTER FORTY

Would it allow him entry? Con wasn't sure the secret door would open for him. But he didn't care if he had to burn the entire castle down with dragon fire, he was going to learn what secrets the book held.

Con took the remaining few steps toward the door. Just as he reached it, there was a soft click as it opened. He put his hand on the door and pushed it open. As soon as he entered, the lights within the room flared to life, but his gaze was focused on the book that was spotlighted on the pedestal.

He shut the door behind him and walked to the tome. As he stood before it, Con wondered why he had been mentioned in the volume. Kellan was still searching his archives as Keeper of History to see if any Fae had been around before Con became King, but so far, he had found nothing.

With a deep breath, Con opened the book. "You let me read you once. I need to again. I need to see what you wanted Rhi to learn."

The turn of the first page had Con holding his breath, but the words didn't move. He quickly scanned until he found where he'd stopped reading the last time. Then, his eyes moving faster than they ever had, he began to devour the words written upon the page.

What had taken Rhi only a handful of hours, took Con merely minutes. When he finished, he clutched the edges of the pedestal with his eyes closed, his heart hammering as his brain tried to come to terms with the truth.

He was shaken to his very core. And the more he thought about it, the more alarmed he became. He wished that Rhi had come to him, but he understood why she hadn't. Con couldn't stand there and try to make sense of it all. He had to *do* something. His eyes flew open as he straightened and strode from the room. The moment he stepped out into the library, Erith stood there.

"Damn you," he said as he glared at her.

"You know as well as I do that sometimes things are out of our control."

He shook his head, anger causing him to stalk to her. She didn't back away, even when she had to tilt her head back to maintain eye contact with him.

"I doona want to hear any more lies," he told her.

She released a breath. "They were never lies."

"Half-truths. Omitting facts. That's lying."

"I didn't have a choice."

He snorted and gave her a scathing look. "You and I both know that's the only thing we do have—free will. You had a choice in whether to befriend me or no'. You had a choice of whether to follow Rhi or no'. You had a choice in what to tell me. You had choice after choice after choice."

"But now you know why Rhi has to be the one to fight Usaeil."

Con turned away before he did something he'd regret. He fisted his hands and faced Erith once more. "I doona agree at all. What you've done is put Rhi in a position she didna ask for."

"It's in her blood! You know that as well as I. You saw it from the very beginning, and don't you dare deny it," Erith said, her lavender eyes sparking with fury.

"What I saw was my mate, the woman I've been waiting my entire life for."

"She still your mate."

Con couldn't remember the last time he'd been so furious. It took every bit of his power to keep his temper in check, but even that was slipping away. "Were you even my friend?"

"How can you ask that?" Erith asked, her face contorted with sorrow and confusion. "Of course, I was. I *am*."

"But you didna tell me about the book."

She threw up her hands. "Why would I? What good would it have done?"

"I would've removed Usaeil myself."

Erith rolled her eyes. "For someone so intelligent, you can be pretty stupid at times. You couldn't have done anything to Usaeil. Up until recently, she was the most beloved queen the Light had ever known. Do you know what they would've done to you? What about Rhi? Do you know what she would've thought of you? And it's not like you could show Rhi the book. Because no matter how righteous you believe you are right now, even you can't deny that you'd have kept it from her."

Con raked a hand through his hair. "You're right. I would've. I can no' imagine what she thought when she read that. And I wasna here to talk to her about it."

"Rhi is strong. Stronger than either of us. I think, deep down, you know that. It's part of what makes her so special."

"I should be with her, helping to fight Usaeil."

Erith smiled sadly and shook her head. "That show-down has been brewing from the moment Usaeil chose her path. Fate has seen to that. There's nothing either of us can do to stop it. And you know that."

"I can no' lose my mate."

She gave him a flat look. "You need to have more faith in Rhi. She killed Usaeil the first time they met. If Moreann hadn't taken her body, Rhi would've cut off Usaeil's head, thereby rendering Usaeil's spell that allows her to come back to life null and void."

"Tell me where my mate is. I know you can find her," Con demanded.

"I won't."

Con looked over her head, searching the area. "Where the bloody hell is Cael? Maybe he can talk some sense into you."

At this, Erith grinned. "Cael is . . . otherwise occupied with his own mission."

"Where is he?" Con asked, eyes narrowed.

"I'm sure you'll find out soon enough. Don't you find it odd that the Dark aren't attacking?"

Con wasn't finished speaking about Rhi. "No doubt Usaeil gave them orders for when to attack. Stop changing the subject."

"You're the one who asked about Cael."

"Stop. Just stop," Con said, more tired than he'd ever been. "I'm no' going to sit around and wait to find out if Rhi can defeat Usaeil a second time, especially when Usaeil has taken Corann, the leader of the Skye Druids as her prisoner. We both know she's no doubt killed him for his magic. Usaeil is powerful on her own. Give her the random juice of a meager Druid, and she's off the charts. Can you imagine how powerful she'll be with Corann's magic within her?"

Erith grinned. "It might make her equal to Rhi."

"Why do you find that humorous?" Con bellowed.

Death's smile faded as her face tightened with anger. "I understand that you're worried about Rhi, but stop for a moment and remove yourself from that connection. What do you see? You, Constantine, King of Golds and King of Dragon Kings, have always been able to remove any emotional ties to see the bigger picture."

"I can no' this time."

"You can. You've been trying to for some time, but the fact that Rhi went out on her own has jumbled everything within you. Take a breath and control your emotions."

Con would rather put his fist through something again, but he couldn't deny that Erith had a point. He never let himself get so emotional because it caused people to make the wrong decisions. Sentimentality had to be removed so one could see all actions and reactions, all options and recourses.

He closed his eyes and drew in a deep breath before slowly releasing it. It gained him some ground, but not nearly enough. It took another six tries before he could find the state of dispassionate detachment he usually resided in. Some called him cold, but it gave him the upper hand in battle, and there was no doubt that he was going to war.

With his eyes still closed, he let his mind's eye see the Dark Army from when he'd been in the queen's chambers. They stood at the ready, much as they had when they followed Balladyn to the Light Castle just a few weeks before. Generals stood at the front of the ranks, but there was another Dark there, as well.

The Light Army were already gathered and waiting for the Dark to make their move. Merrill and Varek were eager to shift and join the fray. Con didn't need to check in with Ulrik. He knew his friend had Dreagan and everyone there safe. Besides, it wasn't Dreagan that Usaeil was after at the moment.

Con's mind briefly touched on the Skye Druids, especially Corann. The moment he thought of the Druid leader, any concern he had vanished. Con didn't linger on that. He would figure it out later. Since he'd heard nothing from Rhona, he had to assume that no more Druids had been taken from the isle.

He debated whether to get in touch with Fallon. The Druids and Warriors of MacLeod Castle were ready to fight, but he didn't want to bring them in. Not because they couldn't hold their own, but because he could leave them to their peace now that the Others had been dismantled. After all, everyone at the castle had earned it.

The fact that Erith was at the Light Castle told him that the Reapers were more than ready to go. Torin was already there, and it wouldn't surprise him to learn that there were other veiled Reapers about.

Finally, his thoughts came to Rhi. If he put aside the fact that she was his mate, he knew how powerful her magic was, how strong she was physically, mentally, and emotionally. Erith had been right. Everything that had happened to Rhi had been to get her ready for this day. All the triumphs, all the trials, all the heartache—it had made her into the mighty, forceful queen that she was now.

Con wanted to protect Rhi because she was his mate, not because he believed she couldn't handle herself. She had proven that she could, time and again—and he'd ignored it many times. Rhi needed no one. She could do anything she wanted, which she had proven by healing the Fae Realm as well as claiming the Light throne.

If he had been smitten with her when she was carefree and mellow, then he loved her beyond all comprehension now as the queen and protector of not just the Light, but of all beings. She didn't need him, but she wanted him. That meant more to him than anything now that he understood it. She had chosen him, not because he was King of Kings, but because she had *seen* him. Just as he had truly seen her all those years ago—and again now.

He opened his eyes and looked at Erith. "Usaeil doesna stand a chance."

"Exactly. I've known that for a long time, but I needed you to see it."

"Does Rhi know?"

Erith shrugged. "I can't guess at her thoughts. Based on what Torin saw, yes, I think she does."

It wasn't Con's duty to go after Rhi. He would remain at the Light Castle and protect her people as she had done for him countless times.

Erith smiled and nodded. "There's the Con I know. Ready?"

"Everything has led to this moment. I thought I'd be going up against the Others and a host of other enemies, but it's just Usaeil."

"I never had any doubt that you and the Kings would prevail."

He chuckled. "Even I wasna sure."

"The Others hit all of you like you've never been hit before. But look where the Dragon Kings are now. You've survived one enemy after another. Ulrik is back at Dreagan where he belongs, and you've told Rhi everything."

"You speak as if we've won."

"You have, in many ways."

"And if Usaeil wins? You know I have to ask. We

wouldna be good leaders if we didna consider all out-comes."

It took Death a few moments before she said, "If Us-aeil wins, then the Reapers are going for her."

"I thought she shielded herself from you."

"I know where Rhi is."

His gaze narrowed on her. "Meaning you're heading there now. If Rhi loses, you'll call the Reapers to take Usaeil right then."

"Yes."

"And Moreann? Xaneth?"

"We won't stop looking for Xaneth. Usaeil is keeping him prisoner somewhere because she wants to hurt him. Killing him would be too easy. As for Moreann—"

Con smiled as Ulrik's words filled his head. "She's dead. The Skye Druids killed her."

"A fitting end for the empress."

Con blew out a breath as he got the rest of the news from Ulrik through their mental link. "Usaeil killed Corann. She has his magic as we feared."

"I'm not worried at all for Rhi," Erith said as she winked at Con.

CHAPTER FORTY-ONE

A shiver of apprehension ran through Rhi as Usaeil appeared before her. The Queen of the Dark wore all black, including the same boots Rhi had. No doubt Usaeil had chosen the outfit and boots to get a rise out of Rhi, but it wasn't going to work. Rhi held in the quip that nearly got past her lips.

Usaeil smiled. "I've been waiting for this moment."

"We've already done this. I won," Rhi stated.

Usaeil smiled wider and shook her head. "You got lucky last time, but as you found out, I have a few tricks up my sleeve. Not to worry. You won't win this time."

"Actually, you'll be the one who discovers that the supposed tricks you have won't work. Your reign is over. Everyone knows it but you."

"Little Rhiannon, who always wanted to run with the mighty," Usaeil taunted. "Someone told you that you had what it took to lead, but we both know the truth. You're scared of everything and look to others for validation. How many times did you come asking for my advice?"

Rage rumbled through Rhi. "You were my friend. Of course I wanted your advice. That doesn't mean I always took it."

"One of your many mistakes. Had you listened to what I told you, you never would've had your heart broken by Con. You wouldn't have been banished, and you wouldn't be about to die."

"That's your problem. You think you can do no wrong."

Usaeil smiled confidently. "I ruled the Light for millennia. I'm Queen of the Dark now. And soon, I'll be Queen of the Fae. I know I can do no wrong. This is my destiny."

Rhi snorted loudly, her grip tightening on the hilt of her sword. "You killed your entire family to take the throne, even though it wasn't meant to be yours."

"And look what I've done for the Light!" Usaeil bellowed, her anger finally showing. "I found us a new home here. I built us a life. And I even found a way to make peace within the Dark."

At this, Rhi laughed. "You? You didn't do shite. That was all Con and the Dragon Kings. You only joined forces with the Kings because you realized that the Fae were about to be tossed from this realm, which meant that your alliance with Moreann as an Other would cease. And it was your grandfather, your family, who built the castle. They got us here. Not you."

"Your point?" Usaeil asked, her expression bored.

Rhi rolled her eyes. "You've been Dark since you had your family killed. Your entire reign as queen has been tainted."

"I never hurt any of you. In fact, I made us strong."

"You destroyed us. You're everything the Light isn't."

Usaeil lifted one shoulder in a nonchalant shrug. "None of you knew. Not even you."

"Balladyn did," Rhi guessed.

The queen's gaze narrowed. "He was getting suspicious, yes. I saw him watching me. I might have let it go, but then I learned that he was in love with you."

"So?" Rhi shook her head. Then she decided it was time to see if Usaeil had read the book or not. "What does it matter who loves me or doesn't?"

Usaeil lifted her chin. "I'm a queen with power, who makes others quake in fear. There isn't anything I can't do. Or men I can't make fall in love with me. I shouldn't be jealous of anyone, much less you."

"Because others respect me? Or maybe it's because you know I can rule better than you."

"That's right. Keep guessing," Usaeil said sarcastically. "You know nothing."

Rhi drew in a deep breath. "Or is it because you know that every time we meet on the battlefield throughout the ages, I always win?"

"You always did think you knew what you were talking about, but it's nothing but gibberish. You try to appear intelligent, but, like always, you've missed the mark."

Rhi nodded, twisting her lips. "Maybe. Tell me, why did you kill every child you conceived?"

"Because I didn't want anyone taking the throne from me."

"You can't live forever."

Usaeil grinned. "Watch me."

Rhi pressed her lips together. "But . . . you didn't kill all your children. There's Thea."

"I might have had a moment of weakness that allowed

her a chance at life as a Halfling in the mortal world, but I found her and killed her."

It was Rhi's turn to smile. "Did you? You're sure of that?"

"Trying to make me doubt myself. How . . . petty."

Rhi shrugged, still grinning. "Did you ever wonder why the Reapers and Death didn't go after you?"

"How do you know about that?" Usaeil demanded.

"I know quite a bit, actually. Answer the question."

Usaeil's nostrils flared as she glared at Rhi. "They didn't come after me because they knew they couldn't best me."

"Bless your heart," Rhi said in a sing-song voice and placed her left hand on her chest. Then she gave Usaeil a flat look. "That's . . . utter shite. You were so wrapped up in yourself, you didn't realize that Thea and one of the Reapers had fallen in love. And it wasn't just any Reaper, it was one of their leaders."

Usaeil's face went blank, then she shrugged. "So?"

But Rhi could see that Ubitch was nervous. "Death is a goddess. That means she's stronger than Con. Let that sink in for a second. Now, tell me, did she not go after you because she couldn't claim your soul? No. She didn't go after you or send any of the Reapers because, apparently, it's my destiny to end your reign. Oh, and as for Thea, she's very much alive."

"I felt the life fade from her."

"That's right. You did," was all Rhi said as she grinned again.

Usaeil's red eyes flashed with fury. "Then how is she alive?"

"You'd need to ask her, although that's pretty impossible because if Thea sees you, she'll kill you. That is if Eoghan, her husband, doesn't do it first."

Usaeil shook her head and rolled her eyes as she laughed. "Trying to get under my skin. Nice try, but it's not going to work."

"The way you're standing with your hands clenched says otherwise."

"Why do you even care about my children?"

Rhi blinked, understanding in that instant that Usaeil hadn't read the book. For all Rhi knew, the queen might not even know of its existence. "It takes someone without a heart to kill the way you have. Women throughout the universe are desperately trying to have children, and you kept getting pregnant and ending the babies' lives as if they meant nothing."

"Because they didn't."

"Oh, but they did. You see, you knew that if even one of those children lived, and you raised it, it would grow tired of waiting for you to die and kill you like you killed your family."

Usaeil confirmed the statement with a nod. "As any good ruler would do."

"Then there's Thea."

"She was half-human. I knew she posed no threat."

"But you didn't want her with the Fae."

Usaeil sighed loudly. "As I said, she was half-human. She didn't belong with us."

Rhi twisted her lips. "She didn't belong with the mortals, either, but that's where you sent her. Although, I have to admit, she was better off in an orphanage than with you."

"You can't hurt me when none of your words mean anything," Usaeil said with a cackle.

"Did you ever think what might happen if one of your offspring was Fae and grew up Fae?"

Usaeil briefly closed her eyes. "I've already answered this. Is this your attempt to kill me with boredom because you're afraid to fight me again?"

"Oh, I'm not afraid to fight you."

"Then let's fight."

"Answer my question," Rhi pressed.

Usaeil threw up her arms in agitation and let her hands slap against her legs. "None of my children besides Thea ever lived, so it doesn't matter. And if one had survived, they would likely come for my throne, and I'd have to kill them. It was better to do it in the womb."

"Or you actually had the child but tossed it into the sea."

Usaeil's face paled. Several seconds passed in silence. "You can't know about that."

"But I do."

"How?" Usaeil demanded through clenched teeth.

Rhi smiled tightly. "Wouldn't you like to know?"

"That child died. I watched it sink beneath the waves."

"You weren't the only one watching that day."

Usaeil's lips thinned as she pressed them together, her chest rising and falling quickly. "Are you telling me that child lived?"

Rhi didn't answer, merely stood there.

"Tell me!" Usaeil shouted, spittle flying from her lips.

Rhi glanced at the ground between them. "You thought you did everything perfectly, made sure that no one had a claim to your throne. Not only did you allow Thea to live, there is also the babe you threw into the sea. And then there're your Trackers, who failed to kill Xaneth."

"You don't need to worry about Xaneth. I've got him taken care of."

"Perhaps. Maybe you don't. His friends are looking

for him. Not only are the Dragon Kings searching, but so are the Reapers."

Usaeil shrugged and blew out a harsh breath. "As if I care. No one will find him, and even if they do, they'll never be able to save him."

"You give yourself far too much credit."

"Really?" Usaeil asked with a laugh. "Were you able to find me? Or the Druids I took from Skye?"

Rhi forced a smile at the mention of the Druids. "You believe that you're more powerful than Death herself, but you kill countless innocent Druids to take their magic so you can stand against your enemies. For someone who thought she had made sure no one would knock her off her throne, you sure have created some very powerful, very pissed-off enemies."

"You say that as if I care. I have Moreann. If we want, we can organize the Others again."

"You can try, but I doubt you will. In case you've forgotten, there is the child we were just discussing."

Usaeil slashed her hand through the air. "That child is dead, and I'm done talking about it."

"Why did you throw it into the sea?" Rhi pressed. "You wanted him or her, didn't you?"

"No."

"Then why didn't you kill it when it was still inside you? Why did you wait until it was born?"

Usaeil tossed her silver locks over her shoulder. "That's how I did it for the first couple of babies. Then, after that, I killed them in my womb."

"Hmm," Rhi said. "You could've strangled it, plunged a knife into its heart, or even smothered it. But you threw it in the sea that fateful day."

"You want me to believe the child is still alive. It isn't."

Rhi raised her brows. "Oh, but it is."

"Then where is it so I can kill it?" Usaeil demanded.

Rhi lifted her sword. "Right here."

CHAPTER FORTY-TWO

Usaeil laughed at Rhi's statement. "You? Do you really believe I'm that stupid?"

"I found the book," Rhi said.

Usaeil's heart skipped a beat. There was only one book Rhi could be referring to—the one hidden in the library. "So?"

"I'm guessing you tried to read it. The moment you touched it, the words began moving."

There was only one way Rhi could know that, and that was if she had indeed found the book. "You think you know so much. When in fact, you know nothing."

"The words returned to normal for me."

The calm way in which Rhi spoke only aggravated Usaeil more. How could the bitch be so calm when her nerves were vibrating with the need to plunge her sword into Rhi?

"I see that surprises you," Rhi replied, a hint of a smile curving her lips. "Ever wonder why you couldn't read it?"

"Again, you think you know what you're talking about."

Rhi tilted her head to the side. "You know the book I'm referring to, right?"

"Of course. My grandfather showed me where he hid it." Usaeil finished the sentence with a roll of her eyes.

"Did you read it?"

Usaeil blew out a breath. "No. I don't care to, either. Now, can we get on with things?"

"That's too bad, because there was so much to learn from it."

"So what if it talks about the Dragon Kings?"

Rhi's grin grew. "So you *did* try to read it."

"My grandfather told me what it was about," she lied, happy that she could cover her arse so quickly.

"I'm fairly certain that he knew neither of you could read it. I bet he tried to tell you that, but you didn't have time to hear him."

It vexed Usaeil that Rhi knew her so well. Instead of retorting with some sarcastic comment, Usaeil merely raised a brow. "If you have something to say, spit it out."

"I already did. I'm the child you threw away."

"As if I'd ever believe such a claim. I knew your parents, Rhi. You forget that. I remember when your mother was pregnant with you, how proud she was. If only she knew the truth about your father."

Rhi's gaze briefly lowered to the ground. "The woman who raised me had been pregnant. She went into labor the same day you threw me out."

"Are we going to fight? Or are you going to bore me with more details?"

"The one who saw you, got me from the sea and brought me to them. There were complications with the delivery. The babe died within her. I was put in its place, and that's all it took to absorb some of her magic."

Usaeil wanted to deny all of it, but she couldn't. Though she didn't believe for a second that Rhi was her daughter. She'd have known if a child of hers had survived.

Rhi blew out a breath. "The book goes into great detail about how the child was saved from the waters."

"And you believe all of this nonsense?"

"Do you know what the beginning of the book was about? The Dragon Kings. The one who wrote the book was here. They saw Con becoming not just King of Golds but also King of Dragon Kings. They spoke about how the dragons lived, the different clans, wars, marriages, and the arrival of the mortals."

Usaeil swallowed, suddenly intrigued. "Who was it?"

"The writer called themselves a Fae."

"It was my grandfather, wasn't it?" Usaeil pressed.

Rhi's brows came together in a frown. "You think your grandfather saved me from drowning and didn't return me to you?"

"Not that," Usaeil said angrily. "I'm talking about the information regarding the Dragon Kings. Who wrote the book."

"Despite all that's happened, you still believe you will be with a King?"

"Not just any Dragon King. Con," Usaeil replied, confidence in every syllable. "I know this game you and he are playing now. Go ahead, play it. But in the end, he'll be mine."

"In the end, you'll be ash."

"Interesting that you aren't telling me you'll have Con."

Rhi laughed and licked her lips. "What happens between Con and me isn't any of your business. It never was."

"You actually think you're good enough to be his queen?"

"I know what my heart feels, and I know that he feels the same. It never had anything to do with being royalty. That's not how Kings are chosen in dragon culture. That was all in your head."

Usaeil cocked out a hip and shot Rhi a look of contempt. "And yet you're claiming to be my child, and thereby royal."

"Royal?" Rhi laughed out loud at this. "Frankly, I'm appalled that I have any connection to you at all. It makes my skin crawl knowing what I do now."

"Then why not keep it to yourself?" Usaeil taunted.

"Because this moment between us, the battle that's about to happen, Fate decided it long before I was even conceived."

Usaeil shook her head. "That's shite. I don't care if you claim to be mine or not, you're going to die."

"Are you not at all interested in who saved me from the sea that day?"

"No," Usaeil replied and called her sword to her. She shot Rhi a dark look. "It's time you died. I can't believe I ever thought of you as a friend."

"Now who's lying? You never wanted to be my friend. The least you could do is admit that."

Usaeil issued a bark of laughter. "You're right. I never liked you. I saw how ambitious you were, which I'll admit, intrigued me. However, I also saw how others looked at you. As if you were this glittering object they desired above all else. You made friends easily, and everyone always wanted to be with you. It's why I made you a Queen's Guard."

"I earned that position."

"No," Usaeil said with a laugh. "I gave it to you so I

could find out more about you. Did you have skills with a sword? Yes. Even Balladyn spoke highly of you, urging me to let you in. How could I refuse the captain of my Guard? Within days of joining, you began talking to me each time you saw me. I saw my opportunity then."

"To realize I wasn't a bad person?"

"To make sure that you never became more than I was. The Light are supposed to worship me, but you kept doing these daring feats, and all anyone could talk about was you. You made them laugh, you awed them, but more than anything, you did things your way."

Rhi pulled a face. "And what's wrong with that?"

"They stopped talking about me. They stopped looking at me. It was all about you."

"Could you be any pettier?" Rhi replied.

Usaeil hated jealousy. No one had ever made her feel it other than Rhi. It grew inside her like a parasite, twisting her once comfortable life into something she hated. There was only one thing that she loathed more than that—Rhi. "I followed you one day. I wanted to see what was so fekking interesting about your life. That's when I saw you and Con together for the first time."

"You're pathetic. You were Queen of the Light. Everyone worshiped you, loved you. Why wasn't that enough? Why did you come after me?"

"Because your light is so damn bright!" Usaeil shouted.

Rhi shook her head, raking her gaze over Usaeil in pity. "You say that as if it's my fault."

Usaeil closed her lips, refusing to say more.

"Do you even know who my father is?"

At this, Usaeil began laughing. She couldn't believe the irony. It seemed too good.

"Something amusing?" Rhi asked.

There was no denying that Rhi was upset by her laughter, but that only made Usaeil laugh harder. Finally, she wiped her eyes and looked at Rhi. "You want to know who your father is? He's the only one you've ever known."

"Why can't you just tell me the truth?" Rhi asked, rolling her eyes.

"Oh, I am. He was at the castle quite a bit, and he was very handsome. I thought I would have to seduce him, but he wanted me as much as I wanted him. Our affair lasted for over a year."

Rhi looked like she might vomit.

Which only made Usaeil happier. "When I discovered that I carried his child, I told him I'd get rid of it if he joined the Others."

"You were already planning to kill me," Rhi said tightly.

Usaeil shrugged. "He didn't know that. He knew if I had the child, then every Light would want to know who the father was, and he didn't want your mother discovering that he was weak. It must sting knowing your father isn't the saint you thought him to be."

"Things make sense now. One of his children died. It was determined that I would take its place and let both of you believe the child the two of you created was gone."

The more Rhi talked like that, the more Usaeil wanted to know who'd intervened. But she couldn't come out and ask. Rhi wanted that, and because of that, she'd keep the truth from Usaeil out of spite.

"For things to happen as you say you read in that stupid book, whoever found you would have to be someone with immense power," Usaeil said. "The Dragon Kings would never stoop so low as to get involved with us in that fashion, and there wasn't a single Fae who had the kind of power I had even then."

"That's because it wasn't a Fae who did this. It was Death," Rhi answered with a smile.

Usaeil's knees threatened to buckle. "No," she whispered.

"Oh, yes," Rhi said with a nod. "She was the one who came and witnessed the dragons and Kings. She wrote down everything. Of course, she was veiled during all of it, so the Kings never knew it was her. She thought of herself as a Fae because she had spent so much time on the Fae Realm."

"Then how did my family come into possession of the book if it was Death's?" Usaeil demanded to know.

Rhi shrugged. "I'm not entirely sure, but I'm guessing it was one of the many things Death forgot about and your family happened to find. There is no title on the book, nothing that would suggest it was anything more than a journal."

"Then why couldn't I read it?"

"My guess is that the pages are infused with Death's magic simply by her touching it. It made sure that anyone against her wouldn't be allowed to read it."

Usaeil flattened her lips. "You're not my child. That babe is long dead. Everything you're saying is a lie."

"I know the truth, and so do you. Denying it won't make it go away. You went to such lengths to ensure that there was never a child who could challenge you for the throne." Rhi lifted her blade and put it in front of her face, the tip facing up. "And yet, here I am, making sure that when this day ends, you'll be nothing but a bad memory that will soon be forgotten."

Usaeil twisted her wrist, letting her sword dance

around her body as she formed an orb of magic in her other hand. "If you believe that, then you don't know me at all."

Usaeil didn't wait for a reply as she threw the ball of magic at Rhi.

CHAPTER FORTY-THREE

Excelling in battle had always come easily to Rhi. Maybe too easily. She had always believed that she had gotten that from her father, but now, she wasn't so sure.

She didn't want to believe the things she'd read in the book, but how could she not? Instinctively, she grew angry with Erith, but it wasn't Death's fault. Erith had written things down in a journal. The only fault Rhi could really place at Erith's feet was that she had pretended to be Fae, though Rhi understood that the goddess had been searching for a place to belong. Rhi might have done the same in her shoes.

Rhi saw the orb of magic coming at her. Usaeil directed it right at her face, but it was if the ball were flying in slow motion. Rhi easily sidestepped it and watched the orb pass by her without doing any damage.

Rhi then returned her gaze to Usaeil to find the Dark's mouth open in a battle cry as she lifted her sword. In that instant, at that very second, Rhi knew she could kill Usaeil. It's what she had come to do. It was her destiny.

But she didn't want to do it.

Not because Usaeil was her mother.

No, this was about everyone else. Rhi found it almost too easy to put aside her own feelings. She realized it must be how Con dealt with situations. It was a gift she'd never had before, and one she wasn't sure she could maintain. But for whatever reason, she was able to do it now.

"The truth has come out."

At one time, Rhi had assumed that voice was the darkness. She wasn't so sure anymore. What she did know was that it had always told her the very things she didn't want to face. Now, however, she had embraced not only the past but also the present.

"You're the thing Usaeil has feared from the beginning. You're the light and the darkness, a Fae strong enough to embrace both and not become Dark. You're what she has always aspired to be. But she was too weak."

Rhi watched as Usaeil charged her in slow motion. It would be easy for Rhi to raise her blade and let Usaeil impale herself on it. It's what Usaeil deserved after the horrific things she had done.

But Rhi didn't do it. She shoved Usaeil to the side before the Dark queen could reach her. Usaeil fell to the ground. At her gasp of outrage, time righted itself.

Usaeil jumped to her feet and faced Rhi. "Resorting to spells now, are we?"

"No," Rhi said. "Not that you'd believe me."

"Of course, I don't believe you. You need to win, and you'll do anything to make sure that happens."

Rhi stepped to the side as they began circling each other. "Those are your motives, not mine."

"You actually expect me to accept that?"

"I don't care what you think."

Usaeil pulled a face. "Aww. If you weren't so desperate for my approval, I might believe you. But we both know how long you've wanted my validation."

"Validation?" Rhi repeated as she laughed. "You're utterly full of yourself."

"You're telling me that you didn't want to be a member of the Queen's Guard to get close to me?"

Rhi shook her head as she looked for an opening to attack. She was just getting ready to pounce when Usaeil shifted, effectively blocking Rhi. "I wanted to become a Queen's Guard to be the first female picked. The Guard is the most lethal, most cunning of all the armies of the Fae. That's why I wanted to be one of them, not because of you."

Usaeil halted, her eyes narrowing. "And you speaking to me?"

"You were the fekking queen! You know how glamorous and stunning you were. There wasn't a single Fae who didn't want to call you their friend."

"You're pathetic."

"I might be, but at least I never deceived anyone as you did with the Light for thousands of years. You're the very thing they have fought against since the first one turned Dark."

Usaeil's crimson eyes flashed dangerously. "You don't know power until you become Dark. You don't know anything until you've tasted power from both sides."

"Is that why you killed the Druids?"

"I'm tired of talking," Usaeil said as she spun and threw several small orbs of magic before swinging out her sword.

Rhi dodged the orbs and flipped over the blade. She landed and lifted her sword. The tip nicked Usaeil's throat before the queen jerked out of the way. "First blood," Rhi stated as she held out her sword so Usaeil could see the blood that dripped to the sand.

Usaeil's lips lifted in a sneer. "You're a babe. You

can't fathom the wars I've been in. You know nothing. Your arrogance is astounding."

"Apparently, I come by it naturally."

Her reply clearly outraged Usaeil. The queen's face turned red, and her nostrils flared.

Rhi grinned and raised her other hand, giving her mother the motion to charge. "What are you waiting for?"

"Why here?" Usaeil asked instead of attacking.

"I wanted to make sure it was just us."

Usaeil shifted, her entire body taking on the stance of someone suddenly wary. "As if I'd believe you."

Without warning, Usaeil sent out a burst of magic that threw Rhi backward. She landed hard on the sand, the impact knocking her breath from her before she began rolling down the dune. Rhi managed to get her feet beneath her and stop herself. When she looked up into the spray of sand, she spotted Usaeil standing at the peak, looking down at her.

"Stay down there. It's where you belong," Usaeil taunted.

Rhi teleported back to the top and slammed the pommel of her sword into Usaeil's mouth. The queen stumbled back two steps as blood spurted from her nose and busted lip.

"Second blood," Rhi stated.

Usaeil wiped her mouth with the back of her hand, healing herself as she did. "I'm finished playing with you. It's time for you to die."

Rhi's heart slowed, thumping deep and even. The world vanished. The past didn't intrude, and the future meant nothing. All she saw was Usaeil—an enemy who had done enough damage for ten lifetimes.

She didn't lift her blade as Usaeil rushed her. Rhi waited until the queen reached her, and then swung up her sword to block the attack aimed at her neck. Usaeil spun and tried a second time.

Rhi parried, their blades clashing loudly in the silence of the desert. Then she leveled her own attack, swinging her sword first one way and then the other, never letting Usaeil know which direction she was coming from. She moved quicker than ever before, completely lost in the battle. She didn't second-guess herself or what her body wanted to do. Rhi instinctively knew what to do at every turn.

Whether Usaeil was on the offensive or the defensive, Rhi knew exactly what to do to block her every move, to the point where Usaeil became furious. Rhi was growing tired, but it didn't matter. She would finish this battle—taking Usaeil's life, no matter how long it took.

Usaeil lunged forward, thrusting her sword. The tip of it caught on Rhi's shirt and ripped it as she spun to the side before knocking away Usaeil's weapon with her blade. Both were too involved in the fight for words. This was to the death, after all, and neither wanted to fall.

The queen didn't retreat this time. She came at Rhi again and again. Rhi ducked one swing and blocked another. Then she had to dive to the side. As she did, she recalled that Balladyn's dagger was in her boot.

She grasped the handle of it as she rolled to her feet and faced Usaeil. The queen's gaze locked on the knife for a moment before she bared her teeth. They charged each other simultaneously. Their swords clashed near their faces as they stared at each other, hatred and contempt passing between them. Rhi then smiled as she felt something warm run over the hand gripping the dagger. Usaeil frowned briefly and then looked down to see that the curved blade was buried in her side.

Rhi's triumph was short-lived as she felt a stinging pain spread from her right hip. When she glanced down, she saw Usaeil's hand holding an orb against her. The magic penetrated her clothes and skin and was even now sinking into her muscle. It wouldn't be long before it reached her bone, and that's when the real pain would begin. It would also mean a significant amount of healing time, something Rhi didn't have.

She was the first to pull away, which made Usaeil smile. As Rhi yanked the dagger from the queen, she twisted the blade, causing as much pain as she could. Usaeil screamed and stepped back before covering her wound with her hand.

Just like when Rhi had busted her nose, the queen used magic to heal herself. It put Rhi at a disadvantage since she was still injured, but Usaeil was clearly allowing her emotions to dictate her actions, and seemingly wasn't aware that she was draining the Druid magic she had taken to strengthen herself for the fight.

The agony of the dark magic running through Rhi caused the calm and control she had to leave. She drew in a deep breath and fought for its return. She managed it just before Usaeil's blade came down on her.

Rhi lifted the dagger and sword to block Usaeil. Then Rhi pushed the queen away with such force that Usaeil fell onto her back, disbelief contorting the features of her face. Rhi was breathing heavily as she stalked to Usaeil. She only took two steps before the queen teleported behind her. Without hesitation, Rhi twisted and dropped to her knee. She saw the direction of her blade and knew she was going to hit her mark.

And she wasn't the only one.

Usaeil quickly teleported just as Rhi expected her sword to make contact. With only air there, Rhi toppled over. She quickly got to her feet and looked around, but Usaeil was nowhere to be found.

"Coward!" Rhi bellowed.

She was breathing heavily, her side aching, but she refused to let any of that into her head. She wracked her brain for where Usaeil would go, and that's when she realized there was only one option for the queen—the Light Castle.

CHAPTER FORTY-FOUR

Tensions were running high. Con and his men weren't affected, but the Fae were another matter entirely. Members of the Dark Army were beginning to twitch, their eagerness for battle apparent in the way they couldn't control their emotions.

The Light Army wasn't much better, but at least they weren't facing the Dark at the moment. They were half-hidden, waiting for the time they were needed.

It was the Queen's Guard who stood before the castle now. They were stoic, composed. They were the elite of the elite, and they were protecting a queen who had once been in their ranks.

Con knew Rhi would be proud of them. He couldn't wait to tell her. But that would have to wait. Several times, his mind had tried to think of the many ways Rhi's and Usaeil's battle might go, but he never let himself finish. The not knowing was killing him, but he'd promised to defend the Light Castle, and that's what he was going to do.

For her.

"They willna last much longer," Varek said as he jerked his chin to the Dark Army.

Merrill crossed his arms over his chest. "Are the Reapers here?"

"We can handle this," Con replied. Even as he said the words, he knew that Torin and the other Reapers were nearby but veiled. It was Erith's way.

Varek's head swiveled to him. "I doona suppose you'll tell us if you learned what Torin wouldna share earlier."

"Oh, he knows," Merrill replied. "Con always finds out."

"Leave it, gentlemen," Con said.

Thankfully, they let the matter drop. Something kept drawing Con's attention to the right side of the Dark Army. He swept his gaze over each Dark, his enhanced senses seeing clearly even at that distance. Again and again, his eyes kept coming to the Dark at the front with the generals.

"Merrill. Varek. Take to the skies. Stay hidden," he ordered.

The two turned on their heels and hurried away. They were discreet enough to shift and take flight. However, the Dark knew that the Dragon Kings were there, which meant they would be looking for them.

"Be wary," Con warned the two via their mental link. *"Seeing one of you may be all it takes to set off this powder keg."*

Varek snorted. *"No thanks to Ubitch."*

"We got this," Merrill said.

But Con wasn't finished with his warnings. *"Ulrik?"*

It took only a second before his friend answered. *"Everything okay?"*

"No' by a long shot. Rhi left and is fighting Usaeil somewhere else."

"I can understand why she'd do that, but it wasna wise for her to go alone."

"Can Rhona tell us where Usaeil kept Corann so we can look into it?"

Ulrik grunted. *"She's already told me. I've no' sent anyone yet."*

"Doona. Things here are . . . complicated."

There was a pause before Ulrik asked, *"Can you tell me?"*

"Rhi found a book hidden in the library."

"Does this have anything to do with you asking if any of us remember a Fae being here?"

"It does. The book is actually more a journal than anything. The author came to this realm before I was even King of Golds. They saw my coronation as King of Kings."

"Erith."

Con grimaced. *"How did you figure it out?"*

"It's easy. Erith has always been your friend. The fact that she saw you before you were a King speaks to why she searched you out and befriended you. I take it that isna all that was in this journal."

"There's information about Rhi."

Ulrik made a sound in the back of his throat. *"I suppose it explains Erith's interest in Rhi."*

"Aye."

"Do I even want to know?"

Con rubbed his fingers on his forehead, making small circles. *"Usaeil gave birth to a girl child and threw her out the window of the Light Castle on the Fae Realm and into the sea. Usaeil watched as the bairn was claimed by the water. What Usaeil didna know was that Erith saw the entire thing."*

"Bloody hell."

"It gets worse. The parents Rhi knew were also pregnant with a child. Erith saved Rhi when she realized the child of the other couple had died in the womb. Erith managed to switch the bairns inside the woman. It's how Rhi absorbed some of her mother's magic."

Ulrik blew out a loud breath. *"Fuck me. Usaeil has always been afraid of someone with a claim to the throne trying to kill her."*

"It's going to happen. This is Rhi's destiny. Erith saw it all when Usaeil threw her out the window like trash."

"Rhi has an actual claim to the throne."

"Aye," Con replied.

Ulrik cleared his throat. *"That's some news. I'd love to see Usaeil's face when she discovers this. And the Light Castle? How are things?"*

"Tenuous, at best," Con explained. *"Be vigilant. I've a feeling things willna wrap up as neatly as we want."*

"When do they ever?" Ulrik replied with a snort.

Con severed the link when he spotted a Dark moving from the front of the army and walking toward the castle. A word from a general brought the Fae back into line. But for how much longer?

No sooner had that thought entered his head than Usaeil appeared before her army. She faced the castle and raised her gaze until she saw him. Despite her black attire, Con spotted the wet spot near her right side, as well as the tiny nick at her throat. Rhi had gotten in some hits.

But where was Rhi?

Con didn't want to worry, but he couldn't help it. Rhi would be here if she were alive. The urge to shift and rain dragon fire on Usaeil and the Dark was nearly too much to resist. A few seconds later, he was glad he didn't when Rhi materialized beside him. The sight of her was like air to a drowning man. Her lips curved up in a smile.

Two heartbeats later, they threw themselves at each other and embraced.

"I knew she hadna bested you," he said.

Rhi pulled back enough to kiss him long and slow. "It isn't over yet. She ran from me."

"Then let's show her what we have."

"Con," she began.

He put a finger to her lips. "Later. There are more pressing matters right now." He looked down and saw her wound as well as the blood that seeped down her side. "Why did you no' tell me?" he admonished as he used his magic to heal her.

"Thank you," she replied with a smile. "I guess I was too intent on kissing you."

He grinned. The loud war cries from below drew their attention. The Dark Army rushed the castle. Con gave a shout to the Queen's Guard, who pulled up their shields and swords in unison. The Light Army poured from either side of the castle onto the battlefield.

"Wow," Rhi said from their vantage point up high in the castle.

Con nodded when the Queen's Guard took the lead as the army fell in behind and to either side of them. They covered significant ground before the Dark reached them.

"It's time," Con said.

Rhi gave him a look.

"You're my queen, as well as Queen of the Light. Prove it."

"Are you sure?"

"Aye," he said right before he stepped onto the railing and jumped.

He shifted and took to the skies. As he flew up and turned around to soar over the castle, Merrill and Varek moved in on either side of him. The three of them flew over the Dark, scattering those in the back who had yet to reach the melee. Just as Con was about to knock a dozen or so with a swipe of his tail, he felt Rhi upon his back.

"Try not to kill the Dark!" Rhi bellowed so he could hear.

While Con didn't agree with her, he passed on her request to Varek and Merrill, who were as confused as he. Until he recalled what Moreann had said about Rhi and Noreen being the ones to unite the Light and the Dark.

He felt her cling to his scales and remembered how they had often flown around Dreagan in such a manner. They had even talked about how effective they could be in battle if she fought upon his back. Con had told her that no Dragon King had ever had someone riding him while in a fight. Up until that moment.

"Where's Usaeil?" Rhi asked.

Con scanned the battle but found no sign of her. He spotted a group of Dark that had managed to separate a Queen's Guard from the others. He dipped his wing and swung around before he flew low over the ground. The guards looked up as they approached and dropped prone to the ground.

The Dark Fae turned and looked at him and Rhi. Their faces said it all. He took out three with his wing while Rhi got two with her sword. It wasn't until he flew around and then over the castle that he found Usaeil. Six Queen's Guards lay dead at her feet, along with an unknown number of the Light Army. She had a large group of Dark behind her, who kept anyone from attacking from anywhere but the front.

Con glanced at Merrill and Varek, who were keeping the Dark scattered except for the small group near Usaeil. He had no way of alerting Rhi to his plans, but he knew she'd catch on quickly.

He released a loud roar that made everyone, including Usaeil, look up. At the sight of Rhi upon his back, Usaeil's face mottled with rage. She redoubled her efforts and killed three more Fae in a blink.

Con landed between Usaeil and the castle, causing the ground to shake. He kept his wings spread and roared again. The Dark with Usaeil were frightened to the point where they scrambled backwards.

"Running from me? Not a very queenly thing to do," Rhi said to Usaeil from atop Con's back.

Usaeil's red eyes flashed angrily as she eyed Rhi. "I came for my castle."

"You mean mine. You lost it. And as your blooded heir, your daughter, I'm laying claim to it."

Con smiled at Rhi's announcement. She might not have wanted the information, but it was Usaeil who didn't want anyone to know.

"You're talking nonsense," Usaeil replied.

Rhi teleported to stand beside Con. "No more running."

"As if you can stop me."

Rhi then looked at Con before she raised her eyes to the sky. He opened a link to Varek and Merrill and said, *"Get a boundary up like we have at Dreagan. Except this time, make sure no Fae can leave."*

With the two of them flying around the castle setting up the spell, Con added his magic from the ground and pushed it outward until it covered the castle and the battlefield. Then he moved it up to meet Varek's and Merrill's magic. When it was finished, Con nodded his head to Rhi.

"No Fae is leaving," Rhi announced. "Light or Dark, you will all remain to watch Usaeil and I fight to the death."

CHAPTER FORTY-FIVE

There was something exhilarating about standing beside Con against an enemy. Rhi had believed that she needed to fight Usaeil on her own, but that wasn't the case at all. Usaeil wasn't just her nemesis, she was everyone's. Even those on the realm who didn't know her.

Rhi looked at Con, his gold scales gleaming in the sunlight. He was a sight to behold. There wasn't a dragon alive who could compare to him—in either form. He was simply untouchable.

And she loved him. She had always loved him. Even when he hurt her, she had held onto the love they'd felt for each other as if it were all she had. Because it had been. That love kept her going. It was too bad it had taken her so long to see it.

Balladyn had known. He'd tried to tell her, but she hadn't listened. And, in the end, she'd hurt him—something she'd never wanted to do. He'd been the only friend she'd ever had, the only one who had been there when she was at her lowest.

"All of you keep forgetting who I am," Usaeil said,

her voice carrying loudly. "I'm queen, and you will obey me."

"Queen? You're not fit to be anyone's queen," Rhi replied. "You lied to every Light here, using glamour to cover what you really are."

Usaeil laughed. "Look who's talking. You, who everyone believed could do no wrong, took up with a Dark. Balladyn, of all people," the queen said with a snort. "It's your fault he's dead."

Con leaned forward and issued a growl to Usaeil that rumbled deep within him. Then his large head swung to her as his purple eyes met hers. Rhi knew that he was trying to tell her that Usaeil was wrong, but she wasn't. Balladyn had been betrayed and left for dead because he knew Rhi. It was because of her that Balladyn had been turned Dark.

"You know it's true," Usaeil said, a broad smile on her face. "You're the one who caused Balladyn to topple from his post as Captain of the Queen's Guard and turn Dark."

Rhi swung her head back to Usaeil. "He wasn't just any Dark. He was their king, a ruler unlike any they'd ever had. One who thought of the Dark instead of personal power. A king who wanted to make the Dark stronger, better. And you killed him."

Usaeil threw back her head and laughed. "If you honestly think the Dark care, then you don't know them at all."

Behind Usaeil, Rhi saw the Darks' attitudes shifting to those of contempt—for Usaeil. Rhi had seen the change Balladyn had instilled in the Dark in the short time he'd been king, and she counted on that to turn the tide. If only her friend could be here to see it.

Rhi continued. "You might think that, but you're

wrong. You see, Balladyn captured me and held me in the dungeons of the Dark Palace with chains, but not just any bonds—the Chains of Mordare."

Usaeil eyed Rhi up and down before briefly cutting her eyes to Con. "He wanted to make sure no one came for you."

"I didn't need anyone," Rhi stated. "I broke the Chains of Mordare."

The gasp from the Dark and Light Fae alike was loud enough to make Rhi pause. It also caused Usaeil to stand straighter.

"Liar," Usaeil said.

Rhi smiled and shook her head. "I'm not. I broke them and caved in a large section of the dungeon."

"It's true!" a Dark Fae in the back shouted.

"Those chains were unbreakable, inescapable by any Fae," Rhi continued. "Until me. Now, they're no more."

Usaeil glanced at Rhi's wound to find it healed. "Stalling?"

"Not at all," Rhi replied. "I'm staking my claim to the throne. I'm also showing everyone why you're the wrong person to lead. The Light are better off without you. I took the throne to call you out, but it was really the news of Con and me that did it. As for the Dark, they had a king, a good one. I know Balladyn was good because he was my friend. He was a legendary warrior for the Light, and he became a savior for the Dark. You betrayed him not once but twice. You couldn't even fight him. You stabbed him in the back, literally. And you took his life."

Rhi heard the Dark grumbling with each of her words, their gazes locked on Usaeil, hatred in their gazes. Rhi glanced at Con to find him noticing the same thing.

"You waltzed into the Dark Palace and claimed their throne," Rhi told Usaeil. "What if they don't want you?"

"Balladyn was nothing. You were his weakness. It's why I asked Taraeth to kill him. I never had any idea that Taraeth would turn him Dark or allow Balladyn to rise in the Dark ranks. It's Taraeth's fault that Balladyn killed him. That's how each King of the Dark takes the throne—through blood. Why is it any different when I do it?" Usaeil demanded.

"Because Balladyn cared about the Dark. You just care about power."

Usaeil rolled her eyes. "This just proves how naïve you are."

"Really?" Rhi asked as she watched the Dark begin to gather around Usaeil.

The queen was too focused on Rhi and Con to take much notice, but the Light did. Those on the battlefield slowly moved away from the Dark, who now had their sights set on someone else.

Rhi locked her gaze with Usaeil's. "We lost our realm due to civil war, and what did you do? You brought the Dark here today to fight the Light."

"Balladyn did, as well."

"Balladyn told the Dark Army they were coming to stand with the rest of the Dragon Kings and me, against you. It wasn't going to be another civil war. That's what *you* wanted."

"So?" Usaeil screamed. "Have you seen some of the Fae?" Usaeil snorted and rolled her eyes dramatically. "We need to be a strong race. If the weakest of the Light and Dark die, then good riddance. Survival of the fittest. I'll do it as often as I see fit. We're Fae! To mortals, we're gods," she said, raising her arms out at her sides.

"And that's why you'll never be queen of anything again," Rhi said.

Usaeil frowned, not understanding. Then she heard

the commotion behind her and turned to see the Dark closing in. Usaeil tried to teleport away, but the shield the Dragon Kings had put up prevented that.

Con nudged Rhi with his wing. She looked behind her and saw the Light rushing for Usaeil, as well. Rhi jumped on Con's back as he leapt into the air. As they rose, she glanced down and saw Usaeil struggling to get free of the Fae surrounding her.

They stabbed her, hit her, and pummeled her with magic until the only thing Rhi saw was Usaeil's hand reaching through the cluster of bodies for help.

Then, even that was gone.

CHAPTER FORTY-SIX

It was over.

Or was it? They had been down this road before, and Con wasn't about to believe anything until he saw Usaeil's body turn to ash.

He swung around and returned to the group of Dark who had surrounded Usaeil. He hovered over them, flapping his wings. Merrill and Varek joined him, and it wasn't long before the Dark took notice.

They scattered like the wind, leaving what remained of Usaeil. Con landed first. Rhi slid from his back as Varek and Merrill descended. Con shifted, and as he did, clothed himself. He found Rhi staring at him. Her expression told him nothing. He held out his hand, and she quickly took it. Her fingers were cold, and he could feel a tremor run through her.

"You did good," he told her.

She glanced at the ground. "It's not over yet."

"Then let's make sure it is."

Con walked them to the broken and partially dismembered body of Usaeil. The queen's red eyes were open and vacant. Most of her skin was gone from her face, and even clumps of hair had been yanked from her head.

"They were vicious," Rhi whispered.

Con tightened his hold. "They had to be. She was vicious in life, in the little regard she had for others."

"The Dark care nothing for life."

"Balladyn started to change that. Progress was slow, and I'm no' sure he even realized the impact he had. I'm no' sure the Dark did, either—until he was gone," Con told her.

Rhi swallowed and licked her lips. "Usaeil isn't disintegrating."

"Because of her spell."

"She could remain like that forever."

Con lifted one shoulder in a shrug. "Or we can make sure she's gone for good."

"I'll do it."

"You doona have to. Merrill and Varek would be happy to douse her with dragon fire."

Rhi's silver eyes met his as she smiled. "Thank you for the offer, but I have to do this."

"She birthed you."

"She was a monster who tried to kill me. Erith gave me life. She gave me a family who loved me. Despite my father's faults, he adored my brother and me. And I know he loved my mother. It would've killed her to know that he'd been unfaithful."

Con brought their joined hands to his lips where he placed a kiss on her fingers. He bowed his head and reluctantly loosened his fingers on hers. Rhi kept her gaze locked with his as she gently pulled her hand away. Then she drew in a deep breath and faced Usaeil.

"*Be ready,*" Con cautioned Merrill and Varek.

He didn't care that it appeared as if Usaeil were dead. Rhi had killed her the first time, and look what had happened. However, Moreann was no longer alive and able to snatch Usaeil's body away at the last minute.

But that didn't mean Con would let his guard down.

He looked around and found every Fae watching Rhi. Even the Dark appeared in awe of her. Not that Con blamed them. Rhi had climbed higher than most, only to hit rock bottom before clawing her way up again, stronger than ever before.

She was devoted to her people, steadfast with those she cared about, and unwavering for those she loved. She was noble, trustworthy, and utterly devoted to whatever she believed in. Whenever a friend was in need, Rhi never hesitated to help however she could, even going so far as to put her very life in danger.

Rhi was one in a million.

A breeze blew in, lifting the ends of her hair that hung from the ponytail. She stared down at Usaeil for a long moment before she called her sword to her. Con tensed. He covered Usaeil with magic so no one could take her from the area. His gaze lowered to Usaeil. Her end had been a painful one, but after all the deaths she'd caused, she'd reaped what she sowed.

Suddenly, Rhi lifted her sword above her head, holding it with both hands. Then she let out a battle cry and sliced downward. The blade cut through Usaeil's neck cleanly. The former queen's head rolled toward him, her red eyes seeming to look straight at Con.

Rhi turned on her heel and returned to his side. Then, her silver eyes met his. "Burn her."

He issued a nod to Merrill and Varek. Both Kings drew in deep breaths before directing dragon fire onto Usaeil's body. The heat didn't bother Con, but he saw sweat soon covering Rhi. It was over as quickly as it had begun, however. When the Dragon Kings closed their mouths, there was nothing left of Usaeil but ash.

What remained of the Queen's Guard moved forward, and using magic, they directed the ash away from the castle. When the last bits were finally gone, the guard turned as one to Rhi and lowered to one knee, their heads bowed, and their right fists held over their hearts. Con smiled as he looked at Rhi. The Light would only flourish under her leadership.

"Please, rise," Rhi said to the guards. Then she turned toward the castle and the Light who watched her. "A new era has begun for the Light." A cheer went up, but Rhi ignored it as she then turned to the Dark. "I can say the same for the Dark. Because we are more than Light or Dark. We are Fae!" she declared as she turned to speak to all of them.

As more cheers broke out, Rhi looked at Con, a wide smile on her lips. He took her hand and pulled her to him. He held her close as he realized how lucky he was to have her.

"You're amazing," he told her.

She chuckled and leaned back to look at him as she locked her arms around his neck. "I learned from the best—you."

"A compliment?" he teased. "I'm no' sure what to do with that."

Her black brows rose as she gave him a stern look that was ruined by her grin. "Get used to it, because I'm going to shower you with them."

"Only if I can do the same."

"You better. Because flattery will get you everywhere."

They both laughed as he gazed at her. Con shook his

head. "I love you. I've always loved you. You may no' believe th—"

"Shhh," she told him as she put a finger on his lips to silence him. Her expression was serious as she briefly dropped her gaze to his chest before meeting his eyes again. "I know why you ended things. It was the right thing to do. I see that now. I should've seen it long ago."

"You were hurt," he said as he moved her finger away.

"Maybe. But I knew you. I knew how much you loved me. I should've realized that you'd never do anything that drastic without a very good reason."

Con gave a little shake of his head. "I put my brethren before you."

"As you should have."

"You were my mate. You should have come first."

She smiled softly and cupped his cheek. "But you aren't just any Dragon King, my love. You're *King* of Dragon Kings, and that means your people will always come first."

"You're my people. You're my heart, Rhiannon. When you're with me, I'm a better dragon, man, and leader. You call me on my mistakes and help me achieve the peace I never thought possible. I know I've a lot to do before I can win your heart again, and I understand that."

She pulled back, her face creased in a deep frown. "Excuse me? Did you not just hear what I said? I'm yours. I've always been yours. Even before we knew each other, I was yours. I just waited to find you. Then I had you for a little while, but I had to lose you again because the path I needed to walk had to be taken alone."

"It shouldna have been that way."

"It doesn't matter. None of that matters now because

we're together. I love you. So much. You can't even fathom how much."

He grinned and gave her a soft, lingering kiss. "I have an idea."

"Con," Varek called through their mental link.

Con looked up and saw that the Dark weren't sure what to do. One of the generals made his way to them. Con blew out a breath. "We'll have to finish this later. Right now, we need to let the Dark return home."

"Yes," Rhi said as they faced the general.

The Dark stopped before them and bowed his head, first to Con and then to Rhi. In a thick Irish accent, he said, "I'm Reland, a general of the Dark Army, and I've come to ask that we be allowed to return to the palace."

"Who will take the throne?" Rhi asked.

Reland shrugged, his lips twisting. "A handful wanted it, and had the strength to take it, but Usaeil killed them."

"Your feelings about Balladyn were clear," Con said.

The general ran a hand through his short, black and silver hair. "I didn't like his tactics at first. Balladyn kept his intentions hidden, but looking back, I believe he did it because he knew that the Dark wouldn't want to go in the direction he pointed us."

"I'm sure there are many who are glad he's gone," Rhi said.

Reland shook his head slowly. "Not as many as you might think. Balladyn was good for us. He was honest. When we followed him here the first time you fought Usaeil, he gave us the option of fighting or not. No ruler of the Dark has ever done that before. For a long time, we were nothing but the evil ones, the ones who betrayed each other to get to the top. He showed us there was another way."

"And yet, he was betrayed," Con pointed out.

The general paused as he looked at the ground. "Bal-ladyn's rule might have been short, but it will have a last-ing effect on all of us."

Rhi drew in a breath and asked, "I may call on some of you at a later date for a meeting. I hope you attend."

"It would be an honor," Reland said as he bowed with a flourish.

As the general walked away, Con looked to his Kings to begin removing the shield. Once it was done, the Dark jumped back to the Dark Palace.

"What are you planning?" Con asked Rhi.

She shrugged and wrapped her arm around his waist. "You'll have to wait and see."

"I'm no' the patient sort."

Rhi giggled as he rested an arm across her shoulders. "Looks like this will be a good time to learn."

"Minx," he teased with a grin.

"Oh, you've not seen anything yet."

Their banter came to an end when they started toward the castle. Fae were pouring out, trying to get Rhi's at-tention while they all shouted her name.

A female Queen's Guard moved before the Fae and raised her hand. "Silence!"

To Con's surprise, the Light listened. He leaned close to Rhi and said, "She's good."

"Her name is Selos, and I agree. I've been watching her these past few days."

"Meaning?"

"I'm going to make her Captain."

Somehow, Con wasn't surprised.

Rhi teleported them both to her chambers. It wasn't long before there was a knock on the door, and Merrill was calling Con's name.

"Enter," Rhi beckoned.

Selos opened the door for Merrill and Varek. Merrill shot the Fae a frown as he walked past her and into the room. Con hid his grin.

"I kept telling her you'd want to see us," Merrill said as he shook his head. "But she didna believe me."

Varek rolled his eyes. "Imagine that."

Rhi laughed and walked to the sofa to sit. She took off her boots and set her feet on the coffee table, crossing one ankle over the other.

"I've already told Ulrik the news," Varek said.

Con walked to stand beside the sofa. "I appreciate that. Is all good at Dreagan?"

"Appears so. It also looks as if things are fine here," Merrill added.

Varek grinned wickedly. "I'm sure you two want some *alone time*."

"We certainly do," Rhi said and looked up at Con.

He chuckled as he gazed down at her. "You two can return to Dreagan."

Rhi frowned as she dropped her feet to the rug and stood. "You're sending them to Dreagan?"

"The Light are safe."

"I wanted us to go to Dreagan."

Now he was confused. "You're the queen. You need to remain here."

"You're King of Kings. You should be at Dreagan. Besides, you've spent enough time here."

He reached for her, pulling her to him. "What's going on?"

"I know I'm Fae, but I don't belong here."

"You've always loved the castle."

She sighed and flattened her hands on his chest. "I may love the castle, but it's not where I want to live. I want to live at Dreagan."

"The Light need their queen here."

"And the Kings need their King at Dreagan," she argued.

Con glanced up, intending to tell Varek and Merrill to leave, but the two were already gone. "Rhi, what's going on?"

"I'm not going to be queen."

He studied her for a long moment before he nodded slowly. "You're thinking about what Moreann said regarding you and Noreen."

"I am."

"That was one of many paths you could've taken. It's no' the one you're on now."

"Why can't it be?" she countered. "Think about it. Both the Light and Dark are set up perfectly for there to be a council to govern both. It makes sense, and hopefully, it will stop us from constantly fighting the other."

He rubbed his hands up and down her arms. "There will always be Light who will fight the Dark and vice versa. That will never change."

"I know. The council will help with that. I'm not saying it'll be easy. In fact, the easy road would be to find someone to take the Dark throne. But I know in my gut that the right decision is to set up a council."

Con drew in a breath. "If that's what you think, then I'll help out in any way you need."

"Right now, all I can think of is that I'm finally back in your arms. I don't care about the past or the years we lost. All I want to think about is right now and that you love me."

"There is one other thing I would like for you to think about."

She cocked her head to the side. "What's that?"

"Becoming my mate. I've waited my entire life for you."

"Constantine, King of Dragon Kings, just tell me when to be there to make it official."

He ran the pads of his fingers along her cheek. "Right now."

She laughed and rose up on her tiptoes to kiss him. "I'm fairly certain those at Dreagan will want more time. Besides, I need to shop."

"Come naked for all I care. I only want you there."

"Just try and stop me," she said with a smile.

CHAPTER FORTY-SEVEN

The silence in the hall was deafening after she'd finished speaking. Rhi stared at the elders of each family that she had called together. There was surprise on some faces, while others looked confused, and even more who didn't bother to hide their anger.

"The Dark and Light have battled for too long," she said. "The Fae Realm was nearly destroyed."

"You mean it *was* destroyed," someone corrected her.

Con stood beside her. She'd thought he might speak up, but he had yet to say anything. Still, she was glad that he was there.

"The Fae Realm is healing. I . . . I began it. There is a habitable portion that is larger than all of Ireland. It's enough for the Fae to return."

One of the females crossed her arms over her chest. "How are we to believe you?"

"Go look for yourself. I've built two new doorways right from this castle to the Fae Realm. One will lead you inside the healed area, and the other to the outside so you can see that it is the Fae Realm," Rhi told them.

"Why would we go back there?"

Rhi glanced at Con. "This was never our world. We came here because we had nowhere else to go. The Dragon Kings allowed us to stay, but even then, we attacked them. The Light have had an alliance with them for some time, but the Dark continued to cause trouble. For those who want to return to the Fae Realm, I say we let them."

"For them to destroy it again?"

Rhi searched the crowd to find who asked the question, but she couldn't determine who it was. "Hopefully, we have all learned from the past. But that is also what the council is for. Instead of the Light and Dark being separate with two different rulers always trying to outdo each other, why not join the two races. It won't be easy, but it can be done." When no one replied, Rhi continued. "A specific number of seats will be determined."

A man in the front asked, "An even number of seats? That would make it difficult to break a tie."

"There would indeed have to be an odd number of seats," Rhi replied.

A woman in the back shook her head in agitation. "You want me to accept that the Dark would have more seats than us?"

"The Dark will say the same," Rhi retorted. She lifted her chin. "Take a page from the mortals. There will be elections, with the terms of those sitting on the council rotating so no one remains for centuries. Not all elections will be held at the same time. They'll be staggered."

The man in the front said, "That sounds good, but that still doesn't address who will make up the odd number."

"I think the best way to do it is if the Dark and Light vote together. We're not going to have the Dark decide theirs and then we decide ours. No. It should all be done together, and the top . . . seven votes will be our council.

Once the council is determined, then those on it will cast their votes on who the head council member is."

Rhi waited to get flack, and for several moments, there was nothing. When arguments did arise, it was the idea of the Light and Dark voting together. The fact that the elders only had that to bicker about was trivial compared to the rest.

"First step accomplished," Con whispered.

She cut her eyes to him and shot him a smile. She had wanted to wait until after they were mated before she called the elders together, but Con had talked her into doing it before they left the Light Castle. In the end, he'd been right.

"Will you sit on the council?" someone asked.

Rhi faced the crowd once more and parted her lips, unsure of how to answer.

It was Con who said, "If she's voted in, of course, Rhi will. When has she ever abandoned the Fae?"

She wanted to throw herself at him and kiss him until the morning. Instead, she gave him a bright smile and mouthed, "*I love you.*"

Rhi hadn't intended to sit on the council, but Con was right. If she was voted in, she would do it.

"I suppose you should talk to the Dark now," the stern woman said. "I doubt they'll go for it, but if they do, then we'll give it a try."

Rhi could hardly believe her luck. She turned away as the elders filed out. She bit her lip and giddily grasped Con's hand as they walked toward her chambers. "Can you believe that worked?"

"Of course."

"Now, I just need to have Noreen talk to the Dark."

Con halted and faced her. "Sweetheart, *you* have to go to the Dark. They doona know Noreen. They know you."

"Ugh," she said and rolled her eyes as her shoulders drooped. "Why do you always have to be right?"

"Because I am." He kissed the top of her head. "Ready?"

She widened her eyes at him. "Now?"

"No time like the present."

She grumbled but teleported them both outside of the Dark Palace. The guards at the door glanced at each other before one rushed inside.

"That doesn't bode well," Rhi rumbled.

Con laughed softly. "It'll be fine."

Once more, he was right. It looked as if Rhi would have to get used to telling him that. In less than thirty minutes of their arrival, the elders from the Dark families stood in the palace. She, Con, and the generals of the Dark Army stood on the stairs to be seen.

Rhi spent the next twenty minutes going over everything she had spoken to the Light about—even the part about the Fae Realm. It was difficult to tell what the Dark were thinking since most wore surly expressions.

"You healed the Fae Realm?" someone asked.

Rhi turned her head in the direction of the voice. "By accident."

"Is it true you're Usaeil's daughter?" someone else asked.

She blew out a breath. "It's true. I have a claim to the Light Throne, and I've taken it, but only to call Usaeil out to answer for her crimes. I don't want to be queen, and I believe the way the Light and Dark have been governed all these millennia is wrong. It's time to forge a new path."

"Who counts the votes?" a male asked.

Rhi shrugged. "I'm sure we can set something up to ensure it's fair."

"What about having the Dragon Kings count them?" the same male questioned.

Con stood with his arms crossed over his chest. He bowed his head to the male Dark and said, "The Kings would help if asked."

"Would it be fair, though?" a female toward the middle asked. She pointed her finger between Rhi and Con. "After all, rumor has it she's going to be your mate."

"She has been my mate for a verra long time, but we've no' made it official yet. That will happen soon. The point, I believe, is that you want to know if we'll be impartial. We can be."

Rhi licked her lips. "The Light have agreed to try this. Are all of you willing, as well?"

There was silence before the Dark began to talk among themselves, including the generals, who walked down the stairs to be with the others. Rhi turned to Con and wrinkled her nose. She couldn't tell how it was going, and she was afraid to get her hopes up.

Finally, the general who had spoken to her at the battle walked up a few steps and stopped before her and Con. "It's been decided that we're also willing to try this council."

Rhi smiled at everyone. "Thank you. It's going to be an uphill battle at first, but we can do this. I know it. Start collecting names of those who would like to be on the ballot for the council. I'll make sure the Light do the same.

Her steps were light as they walked from the Dark Palace. "I can't believe that went so well."

"You're a natural. Doona be surprised if you're voted onto the council," Con warned her.

She shrugged. "As you said, I won't abandon my people."

"And if they return to the Fae Realm?"

Rhi shrugged, not sure what to say since she hadn't thought of that. "I don't know."

"We'll deal with whatever happens."

She eyed him. "You're entirely too good to me."

He turned her to face him. "Actually, I just want to get this over with so we can have some time alone."

She tsked. "Why didn't you say so?"

In the next blink, she had them at Dreagan. They stood in the middle of Con's bedroom. The walls were painted white, except for one that was matte black. It was the wall that had the bed against it. The bed was a modern piece of black wood with a simple white comforter. The floors were dark wood with a large rug of white and gray. No one had ever realized that she wore black because Con had always favored it. It had been her secret, but one he had always known.

"It's about time I have you back in my bed," he said, right before he claimed her mouth in a fiery kiss.

CHAPTER FORTY-EIGHT

He woke with a smile for the first time in centuries. Con realized that he had a pillow in his arms and reached for Rhi, only to find the bed empty. His eyes flew open as he sat up to make sure she wasn't in the bed.

"Over here, stud."

His head swung toward the sound of her voice, and he found Rhi sitting naked with her legs tucked against her in one of the big, overstuffed, gray chairs. She wore a soft smile, her eyes heavy-lidded.

"I thought to find you in bed with me," he said as he threw his legs over the side of the mattress and stood. He then started toward her.

She chuckled and held out her hand for him. Once he reached her and took it, she pulled him down beside her and kissed him. "I've not slept that deeply in some time, but I woke at dawn and wanted to watch the sunrise."

"You should've woken me."

She shook her head of long, black hair. "You looked too adorable."

Adorable? No one had ever called him that. He wrapped

his arms around her and held her against him. "Tell me this isna a dream."

"It isn't. I'm here. We're together. Finally."

"Aye. Finally."

They grew quiet, each soaking in the moment. It was Rhi who broke the silence. "Being here with you feels like we were never apart, but yet I know I'm a much different person."

"You've been through quite a bit. Of course, you've grown."

"You saw the darkness in me."

He pulled her away to look into her silver eyes. "I did, but you were strong enough no' to let it take you."

"Knowing who my birth mother is, makes me wonder why the darkness didn't take me?"

"You have no control over who your parents are. No one does. You became more than either of them, and that proves that blood doesna always matter."

She glanced away. "I don't ever want to become Usaeil."

"You willna. You're too strong."

"And my father?" she asked, her brows raised. "I thought he was a good man, but he cheated on his wife with Usaeil and joined the Others."

Con pulled her back against his chest and wound a strand of her thick hair around his finger. "I can no' speak to your father's involvement with Usaeil. What I can guess is that she forced him into the Others because of their affair. Maybe he wanted to join them on his own. Maybe he didna. We'll never know. But more importantly, it doesna reflect on you. The decisions and actions of your parents were never yours. You shouldna have to pay for them."

"Usaeil was my mother." Rhi shuddered, her voice cracking.

"Nay, love. Your mother was the woman who raised you and loved you."

Rhi tilted her head to look up at him, tears shining in her eyes. "She was the best mother."

"Exactly. Usaeil was never a mother. She simply birthed you."

"Erith," Rhi said, her face tightening.

Con blew out a breath. "You want to talk to her."

"I . . . don't know. Part of me wants to ask her why she saved me, and another part says it doesn't matter."

"Whatever you want. You get to decide."

Rhi nodded and tightened her arms around him. "I love you."

"And I love you."

"Everyone is going to have a million questions."

He chuckled. "I doona think so. They'll smile and nod, and I'll get quite a few *told-you-so's*, but I think that'll be it."

"I still can't believe I'm here."

Con heard the smile in her voice, and his lips turned up at the corners. He kissed the top of her head. "It's where you've always belonged. And it's where I've always wanted you."

"It's where I've always wanted to be."

"Con?"

The sound of Ulrik's voice in his head made Con's lips tighten. *"Be there shortly."*

"It's all right," Rhi said as she looked up at him. "You are King of Kings, and you're needed."

He frowned as he gazed at her. "How did you know?"

"You tensed. I knew we wouldn't have a lot of time, and that's expected. We have eternity."

"You're amazing."

She nodded as she sat up. "I'll remind you of that often."

He chuckled as he got to his feet and dressed for the day. He reached for the cufflinks to find Rhi standing beside him, holding the dragon head cufflinks and dressed in a tight-fitting black shirt tucked into black leather pants, black stiletto heels on her feet.

"Let me," she said as she put on first one cufflink and then the other. Then she stepped back and smiled. "There. Handsome as always. No one can wear a suit like you, babe."

He grinned and reached for her hands. "No one can wear anything quite like you."

"I do like the way you think," she replied with a grin before giving him a quick kiss.

They walked from the chamber, hand-in-hand. The moment they reached the stairs and looked down, they spotted everyone. He and Rhi exchanged a smile before he kissed her. Shouts of joy rose from below.

"They approve," Con said, his face still close to hers.

She nodded and touched his cheek. "They're excited to finally see you happy."

He tugged her beside him as he made his way down the stairs to the main floor. Con stopped a few steps from the bottom and let his gaze roam around the room and the press of bodies as the Dragon Kings and mates squeezed in.

"I want to thank all of you for keeping Dreagan safe. Usaeil is no more. Two of our enemies are now gone, and we've managed to come out ahead once more. Our friends and allies have a lot to do with that. Unfortunately, we lost Corann. He was a good friend to all, and he'll be sorely missed. I believe Rhona, who he chose as his predecessor, will fill the role nicely." Con paused and looked at Rhi. "There is news on the Fae front, as well. Would you like to tell them?"

Rhi smiled and nodded. Her gaze searched for Noreen until she found the Dark Fae. "Moreann told us that in one scenario, we helped to develop a council for the Fae that would unite the Light and the Dark. That has stuck with me since I heard the words. Yesterday, with Con's help, I began the first step in that journey. Both the Light and Dark have agreed to give it a try. I would love your help."

"As if you need to ask," Noreen replied with a bright smile. "It would be my honor."

Rhi then found Shara. "You, as well. This won't be an easy process, but I believe it's the next evolution for the Fae."

"I'll help in any way I can," Shara stated.

Con looked at the crowd once more. "The Dragon Kings have always been guardians of this realm. That will never change as long as one of us is here. We've won the day against the Others, and that has made us stronger. We've each endured more than anyone should, but, again, it's because Fate chose each of us. We will celebrate because we deserve it, but we'll never let our guard down. No' only do we have Orun in the dungeon, but the weapon is still missing. We're no' any closer to learning about the dragons, either. We all want answers. However, we're going to lend V and Claire our support as the delivery date draws nearer." Con licked his lips and slid his gaze to Rhi for a long moment. "It may be our destiny no' to have bairns, but there's a verra good chance the magic of the realm may be on our side now. Only time will tell."

V bowed his head to Con. Claire smiled at him as

she rubbed her belly. "Thank you," she said. "No matter what happens, Vlad and I have each other and a family we know will support us. For that, we both thank you."

Con cleared his throat as he found the Kings he wanted to call out, standing near each other. "That brings me to my next bit of news. V, Royden, and Cain. Is it time?"

The three Kings smiled at their mates and nodded.

Royden was beaming when he said, "Just tell us when."

"We've been waiting on your return," Cain said.

Con had expected such answers. "Is tonight too soon?"

"No," Claire, Annita, and Noreen replied in unison.

"Looks like we have a triple mating ceremony tonight," Con announced. "Everyone knows what to do."

Ulrik cleared his throat loudly. "And what about your ceremony?"

Rhi smiled and ducked her head before she looked at Con.

He raised his brows in question, and she shrugged in reply. He looked at the others. "We can do it tonight, as well."

"That willna do," Kellan stated from the back.

Con frowned and opened his mouth to ask why, but he didn't get a chance as Ulrik spoke.

"You're King of Dragon Kings," Ulrik said. "Your ceremony with your mate will be held separately from the others'."

Con nodded in agreement. "But only if we can do it soon."

"Like tomorrow," Rhi added.

Ulrik laughed as he crossed his arms over his chest. "Leave it to us. Con needs to get things ready for tonight, and Rhi, I'm sure you need to shop."

"Actually, I don't," she said.

Con jerked his head to her. "You don't?"

She just smiled in return. "Nope."

"Do you have a dress?" he prodded.

Rhi faced him and pointed a finger at his chest. "Oh, no. You don't get to ask me any such questions. You'll have to wait until tomorrow to find out."

"I sure hope that means you can help me," Annita said.

Rhi laughed and nodded. "I will never pass up a shopping trip. Come on, girls. We have planning to do."

As she pulled away from him, Con held her hand and tugged her back. He then gave her a languid kiss and gently ended it. "Doona be gone long."

"Just try and keep me away, lover," she whispered.

"If you're no' here, I'll come looking for you."

"Now that's a promise I can live with," she replied with a wink.

Con watched her leave with the other mates, uncaring that the Dragon Kings stared at him. He was happy, and he let it show.

Once the women were gone, he turned back to his brethren, just now noticing that Henry wasn't among them. "We need to decide what to do with Orun, and quickly. I doona like him here."

CHAPTER FORTY-NINE

It was time. There was no longer any denying it. Melisse wished there was another way, but there wasn't. She had known it for weeks and had tried to ignore the facts, but that was no longer an option.

She honestly wasn't sure what would happen to her. That was part of the reason she had stayed away from Dreagan to begin with. Yet the magic of the realm kept insisting. She could no longer refuse.

Henry was nowhere around. She wasn't sure if she was happy about that or not. It would be nice if she wasn't alone, but Henry was mortal. There was a very real chance he could get hurt, or worse, killed. She liked him too much to put him in that kind of position. Not to mention, he was important in the grand scheme of things as the JusticeBringer.

Melisse smiled at the thought of Henry. He had been determined to find out who she was, and no matter how she attempted to dissuade him, he had nevertheless persisted. She didn't regret sharing her secret with him. Henry wasn't like the other humans she had encountered. He saw the world differently. It could be because of his training as a spy, but she believed he would've seen things differently regardless of that training. It was because Henry was special.

Proof of that was his being the JusticeBringer, which went hand-in-hand with his sister being the TruthSeeker. The two of them were part of a lineage that the magic had set up the moment the humans set foot on this realm.

Actually, before that. Though no one but Con knew that.

For so long, she had despised the Dragon Kings. Now, she wasn't sure what she felt. She had learned so much since escaping, and now she was going back to the very place she had been held prisoner. The time for free will was running out quicker than grains of sand through her hand. Getting onto Dreagan wasn't the issue. It was the next part that kept tripping her up.

Melisse walked along the invisible boundary on the back side of Dreagan. Two miles and a thick forest separated the border from the nearest road. She touched the trees as she walked, her mind going over what she had to do. A loch came into view. She stopped at the edge, her skin feeling too tight over her muscles and bones.

All those years trapped and unmoving, she had dreamed of all the ways she'd make those who held her pay. She'd heard every word the Dragon Kings, especially Con, spoke. She learned about the world around her, heard how it was evolving and growing. Yet all the while, she was imprisoned and unable to do anything.

The loch was stunning, the water a bright blue against the vibrant green of the surrounding forest and the craggy mountains that rose up on one side. The sky was filled with dark clouds that looked about to drench the area in rain. She drew in a deep breath and smelled the dampness in the air.

Her heart pounded, eager for the next step. But she hesitated. The last time she had given in, she had been a young child. That's when the last King of Kings had discovered her and locked her away. Thousands upon thousands of years had passed since then. She had grown into an adult, all while locked away in Constantine's mountain.

She couldn't blame him exactly. He had only done what the last King of Kings had told him to do. Con had never harmed her, but he hadn't freed her, either. He hadn't asked her for her side of the story. Then again, she likely wouldn't have in his place. But that didn't excuse him.

Melisse closed her eyes and drew in a deep breath before she shifted. The pain was fleeting, barely a thought before she was in her other form—a dragon. She opened her eyes and smiled. The world looked crisper, the smells were more invigorating, the sounds sharper.

She unfurled her wings and moved them up and down. Turning her head, she looked back as she swung her tail from side to side. Her violet scales glistened as the first drops of rain fell from above. All she wanted to do was take to the skies, but she made herself wait. The Kings had kept their existence a secret for a reason. Melisse had no wish to begin the war again—not now, at least.

She tucked her wings as she walked into the loch. Then she dove beneath the water and swam toward the barrier that cut through half the loch. The moment she passed through the magic, she felt it move over her.

The Kings hadn't been aware when she left Dreagan, and they wouldn't know when she returned. She could've come back any way she wanted, but this was the route she had chosen.

Melisse rose to the surface and swam toward the other

shore. Once there, she looked up at the clouds gathered overhead. The rain was coming down at a steady pace now, but it wouldn't hide the color of her scales. The Kings would spot her for sure. That is if she took to the sky.

She inwardly chuckled as she looked at the path between the two mountains before her. She could fly between mountains over a large section of Dreagan, making sure never to crest the top of them. Which meant, it was possible that she could get close to Dreagan without being seen.

Without hesitation, Melisse jumped into the air and spread her wings. She faltered once, twice before she caught a current. It was instinct for her to climb high, but she caught herself before she rose over the top of the mountain. Instead, she shifted downward, gliding between the mountains. The feel of the wind on her scales was unlike anything else. She'd never felt so free, so . . . powerful.

As she wove through the mountains, she knew she would be flying more than she would walk from now on. There was nothing else like it, and she couldn't believe that the Dragon Kings limited how often they took to the skies.

But she wasn't going to feel sorry for them. Not after what they had done to her.

Melisse felt the magic call to her. She wanted to go to the Dragonwood, but to do so would bring her into the open and allow the Kings to see her before she was ready. But the magic was adamant. She knew better than to ignore it. After all, she had ignored the pull to return to Dreagan for weeks and look what that had gotten her.

With a sigh, Melisse turned back toward the Dragonwood. There was too much distance from the last mountain and the forest for her to fly. She would have no choice but to return to her human form and walk it.

She reached the last mountain and landed a bit awkwardly. There was much she had to learn. After a small hesitation, she shifted and stood shivering in the rain. Melisse used her magic to clothe herself, including a raincoat. She pulled the hood up to hide her hair and started toward the woods.

Her strides were long and steady as she ate up the distance. She didn't breathe normally until she was within the Dragonwood. She stopped beside an old oak and leaned against it with her eyes closed.

"What do you want of me?" she asked the magic.

There was no answer, like usual. Melisse opened her eyes and pushed away from the tree as she walked to the source of all the magic on the realm. It took her a while as she maneuvered through the forest and past a waterfall.

When she reached it, she kneeled beside it and placed her hands on the ground. Magic pulsed beneath her palms like a heartbeat. No words were spoken, but none were needed. Instead, the magic passed feelings *through* her. It calmed her racing heart and eased her anxiety. She drew in a deep breath as the magic spread through every part of her. She had no idea how long she remained there or why the magic wanted her, but it didn't matter. She was utterly at peace now with what she had to do.

Melisse once more opened her eyes. "Thank you," she told the magic as she straightened and got to her feet.

Then she turned toward Dreagan Manor. It was time.

Henry wasn't sure why he'd felt the overwhelming need to come to the Dragonwood. Especially when he knew that Con and Rhi were in the manor, but he'd come anyway.

He ignored the rain as it soaked through his clothes and ran down his face. He wandered through the woods, trying to figure out why he was out there instead of inside where it was dry.

Then he saw her.

Melisse.

He'd just happened to look to the side and saw a flash of violet. Henry had tripped over a root, but he still didn't take his eyes from her as he reached out blindly to grab hold of anything that would keep him from falling. Luckily, his hands found a tree that kept him upright.

The sight of Melisse stole his breath. He hadn't known she could shift into a dragon, but he'd known with a sense of certainty he couldn't explain that it was her. And when she shifted into human form, his knowledge had been confirmed. The sight of her naked, even for just a heartbeat, caused his balls to tighten, and need to rush through him as hot as fire.

He'd been shocked when she threw up the hood to her raincoat and started straight toward him. He hadn't moved, hadn't so much as breathed when she walked past him in the Dragonwood.

His eyes followed her until he had no choice but to forget that she was there or follow her. He trailed her, ensuring that he kept enough distance between them so that she wouldn't notice him.

The rain helped to shield the noise he made, though he was surprised that she didn't know he was there. If she was a dragon, then her senses should be as enhanced as the Kings'. He deduced that she must be focused on something and too enthralled to notice.

When she stopped and went down on her haunches before placing her hands on the ground, he realized it must have something to do with the magic of the realm.

He couldn't feel it like the Kings could, but he'd heard them speak about it being in the Dragonwood. That must be why Melisse had come.

He was glad to see her, especially since she was all he could think about since their last meeting. He'd wanted to go to her, to learn more, but too much had been going on at Dreagan for him to do that. Now, she was here. He was so happy about it that it took him a moment to realize that it might not be a good thing that she was at Dreagan.

His smile faded. Whatever reason she might have for hating the Kings, they had been good to him and his sister. The Dragon Kings had saved them both, and he owed them more than he could ever repay.

But then there was Melisse. He wasn't sure what he felt for her, but it was unlike anything he'd ever experienced before. She was important, not just to the Dragon Kings but also to the race of dragons in general. Of that, Henry was positive.

Though, again, he wasn't sure how or why.

Con had told him that he had no desire to hurt Melisse, but Henry wasn't sure if Melisse felt the same about him and the other Kings. There was no way he could stand against her since he wasn't a dragon, but he *could* talk to her.

He moved out from behind the tree so when she stood and turned toward him, her gaze met his.

"Henry," she whispered.

Even from the distance, he heard her. Not with his ears, but with his mind and heart. He smiled at her, deliriously happy to see her again—no matter why she was at Dreagan. Her steps were hesitant and slow at first when she started toward him. He also moved to her until they met in the middle. All the while, his lips were curved into a grin.

"What are you doing here?" she asked as she looked around.

He chuckled. "I could ask the same of you. Don't worry. No one else is here."

Melisse swallowed. "How long have you been out here?"

"I saw you. The real you."

Her whitish-silver eyes lowered, and her gaze dropped briefly to the ground. "I don't know what the real me is."

"What do you mean?" he asked with a frown. "Aren't you a Dragon Queen? That's how the Kings shift into human form. I just thought . . . well, that you had to be a Queen.

She shook her head as she smiled sadly. "No."

"Then . . . what are you?"

"Half-dragon. Half . . . something else."

"You don't know what your other half is?"

Her chest expanded as she drew in a breath. "No."

"Con might. You should ask him. Or is that why you're here?"

Her unusual eyes held his for a long, silent moment. "I'm not here to talk to Con."

"Then why are you here?"

"There is something I have to do."

He sidestepped when she attempted to walk around him, effectively blocking her. "No matter what you might think, the Dragon Kings have been good to me. Con especially. He gave me a home here. I can't let you hurt them."

"You can't stop me."

"Don't make me choose between you and them."

She cocked her head to the side. "I'm not asking that."

"Aren't you?"

CHAPTER FIFTY

It was really happening. Rhi could hardly contain her excitement. She was bursting at the seams, but she held it all in check as Claire, Annita, and Noreen searched for their gowns. Rhi had always loved to shop, but what she enjoyed more than anything was shopping for others. And she was good at it, too. She really looked at people, learned them and their quirks, the things that set them apart. Then she found styles that she thought matched them.

With all the Druids, as well as Shara and herself, they were more than capable of fashioning dresses out of magic. But that's not what any of the mates had done before, and it wasn't what the three wanted now.

Instead, they were at a shop in Milan. The mates separated and began searching the store. Rhi kept herself apart, not to shop for her own gown, but because she wanted to look through the dresses on her own.

Claire had found only a handful of gowns to match V's copper color. But Rhi had spotted something in the back that she wanted to take a closer look at. As soon as she pulled the sleeveless gown out, she knew it belonged to Claire.

The others were helping Claire zip up a different gown, so Rhi silently hung the dress with the others for Claire to try on and turned to see how Annita was faring.

Beige should be an easy color, and it was. The problem for Annita was finding something that fit her style. Rhi was up for the challenge. She searched for the next twenty minutes before she found the perfect dress. Rhi hurriedly added it to the ever-growing stack of Annita's options and then went to check on Noreen.

"I don't know," Noreen said as she stared at herself in the mirror, wearing a sleek navy gown. "I like them all."

"But do you *love* any of them?" Lily asked her.

Noreen shook her head. "Love? No."

"Try on another," Sabina urged.

When Noreen went back into the dressing room, Rhi winked at the women there and hurried back to the racks of dresses. She found the one for Noreen almost immediately. Rhi put her finger to her lips when she returned with it and hung it before the last two Noreen had to try on.

Grace smiled at Rhi as she reached for the dress and handed it to Noreen. "Try this one."

Rhi sat on one of the many chairs and waited for Noreen to come out. As she did, she glanced toward Claire's dressing room. The gown she'd chosen was no longer hanging outside, which meant that Claire had brought it in to try on. Same with Annita.

There was a gasp from those around her. Rhi swung her head and found Noreen walking from the dressing room. She went to the mirrors, a huge smile on her lips. Rhi nodded with approval at the gown. The navy dress had a sweetheart neckline covered in navy beading. It was sleeveless and hugged Noreen's body to her waist, where the skirt dropped into a full A-line with layers of tulle. The same beading at the neckline was also around the waist and hip area.

"I love it," Noreen stated with a bright smile, her red eyes alight with excitement.

Lily jerked her head toward Rhi. "Rhi was the one who found it."

Noreen whirled around. "Thank you so much."

"It was my pleasure," Rhi replied.

"Noreen has her gown," Grace told the others.

Jane pulled back the curtains of Claire's dressing room and said, "Ta-da!"

Everyone looked in Claire's direction as she walked out in Rhi's pick. The copper satin conformed to Claire's figure to perfection, molding over the slight baby bump. The neckline was twisted before the satin molded to Claire's body. Along the hips, more of the fabric twisted into a larger knot, and the skirt fell gently in folds to the floor. Claire walked out with her head high and a smile on her face. When she turned toward the mirror, everyone caught sight of the small train on the gown.

"This is my dress," Claire announced. "Who picked it out? Because I thought we had all the copper dresses in the store."

Rhi raised her hand.

"You're amazing," Claire said and blew her a kiss with her hands.

Rhi winked in return.

"What about Annita?" Noreen asked as she and Claire went to stand by each other.

"She's coming," Iona said from the other side of the dressing room curtains.

Rachel looked at Rhi. "Did you pick a dress for Annita?"

"I did," Rhi replied.

Sammie rubbed her hands together. "Which one was it?"

Rhi laughed and shook her head. "We'll have to wait and see which one she picks."

It wasn't the dress Annita came out in. It wasn't the next four she tried on, but Rhi spotted the gown she had chosen as one of the two remaining. She said nothing as Annita came out in the next to the last dress, still not happy.

Noreen and Claire remained in their gowns as they waited for Annita. There was silence as Iona came out with an armload of gowns that Annita didn't like.

Then, from inside Annita's dressing room, she gave an excited shout before saying, "Someone zip me. Please!"

Sammie rushed inside and let out a little squeal herself before she threw open the curtains and stepped aside for Annita to come out.

Rhi nodded in approval. The beige gown was one-shouldered, the left arm covered in sheer fabric with a large bell sleeve. It was hand-embroidered with champagne-colored sequins and stones along the neckline and the single sleeve. More of the sequins and stones were sprinkled on the right side of Annita's waist before it appeared as if the gems shot out in all directions before fading. The skirt was slim and fell in five ruffled layers, each one longer than the last.

"That is your dress," Claire stated.

Noreen nodded. "It's so beautiful."

Annita twirled around. "I love it so much."

Gianna put all three women together and then looked at Rhi. "These are all the gowns you picked, aren't they?"

"I like to shop," Rhi said with a shrug.

Before she knew it, Annita, Noreen, and Claire were hugging her. There was laughter all around before the women changed back into their regular clothes and purchased the gowns.

Only then did Rhi find every mate staring at her. "What?" she asked.

Cassie said, "It's your turn to find a gown."

"I don't need one," Rhi told them. "I've had mine."

Lexi's eyes widened. "How long have you had it?"

"Since Con and I were first together, and he told me he wanted me as his mate."

"Can we see it?" Darcy asked.

Rhi smiled and shook her head. "Not until tomorrow. We need to get back to Dreagan so Noreen, Annita, and Claire can begin getting ready."

"Ugh. My hair," Claire stated with a wince.

Sophie looped her arm with hers. "We've got you covered. We've got all three of you covered."

"I need shoes," Annita said, wrinkling her nose.

Alexandra perked up. "I know just the place. Come on, girls."

They left the shop and made their way down the street to another store. In minutes, Alexandra had all three future mates sitting down as she looked around the store. Five minutes later, Annita had a gorgeous pair of Jimmy Choo's, the high-heeled mules embellished with rhinestones across the arch.

For Noreen, Alexandra chose a pair of navy Sophia Webster's Coco Crystal Glitter Pointed-Toe pumps with crystal beaded stiletto heels.

Claire put on a pair of Valentino Garavani Rockstud T-strap copper stilettos that matched her gown so perfectly, it seemed as if they had been made for each other.

And when the others turned to her, Rhi shook her head. "I've got the shoes, as well."

With nothing else to do, they bought the shoes and teleported back to Dreagan to begin readying themselves for the mating ceremony.

Rhi ducked out and made her way to Con's room. He was most likely in his office, but she wanted just a few minutes alone to soak up being back at Dreagan as his mate—not his ex.

She walked inside the chamber. Closing the door softly, she started toward the bed when Con said, "I've been waiting forever for you to come home."

She whirled around, a smile on her face. "Home. I like the sound of that."

He rose from the chair and made his way to her, sliding his hand into her hair and gripping it. "I want you at the ceremony tonight."

"You know it's against the rules."

"I doona care. I want you by my side."

She smiled and gave him a stern look. "I'll be at the afterparty."

"You've been to other ceremonies. Need I remind you that you went veiled? No one but me will know you're there." She tried to kiss him, but he pulled back, all teasing gone. "I really want you with me."

She wound her arms around his neck. "Then I'll be there, but you can't let any of the others know. I want them to believe I've been waiting for them at the party afterward."

"I promise," he murmured before he kissed her.

She sank into him, drowning in the desire he fanned so easily. "I should go help the mates."

"Forget them," he said as he lifted her in his arms and carried her to the bed. "I'm the one who needs you."

She looked up at him from the bed and removed their clothes with just a thought. "I'm all about being needed."

"Then you'll be set for eternity, sweetheart."

CHAPTER FIFTY-ONE

Con straightened the tux jacket as he looked at himself in the mirror. He'd wanted to keep Rhi in bed for hours, but they had only gotten a short time together before she left to help the mates get ready. After she left, he took a long shower and readied himself for the night. The ceremony wasn't for a few hours yet, but he still needed to get gifts for Claire, Annita, and Noreen.

His gaze lowered to the kilt he wore. At one time, he had donned one every day in the mortal world and had enjoyed it. The Scots were not only determined and steady, they were also loyal and resilient. A combination that made him happy that they were the people who called his land home.

Con thought of the upcoming ceremonies and could hardly contain his excitement for his own. He found himself twisting the dragon head cufflinks and thought of Erith. She wasn't a dragon or a mate, but she was a friend. If it hadn't been for her, Con never would've found his mate. Erith had saved Rhi and allowed her to grow up in a household where she was loved and cherished, a place where they had pushed her to achieve her dreams instead of holding her back.

Then there were the Reapers—including Balladyn. And he couldn't forget Henry. Even Xaneth, if the Light Fae could be found. What he wanted to do went against every tradition of the Dragon Kings, but maybe it was time to change a few things.

Con walked from his chamber and made his way downstairs. He heard the women's laughter drift down from their rooms, and he knew all of them were having a grand time. He didn't need to check on the Kings, but he went looking for one in particular. He found V with the Silvers. Con paused in the doorway of the dimly lit cavern and watched V silently stare at the four dragons that had been sleeping since the war with the mortals.

"I'm all right," V said in a soft voice.

Con moved to stand beside him. "Are you?"

"Will we be hurt if Claire loses the babe? Aye. Will we be devastated if the bairn is stillborn? Without a doubt. But we'll still have each other."

Con turned his head to look at V. "Claire might no' survive this. I've watched some human couples be torn apart by such tragedies."

"We've talked about how we'll handle things if the worst happens." V blew out a breath and shook his head before he looked at Con. "I worry about Claire pulling away if the bairn dies. I can get through it if I have her, but if I doona . . ."

"I understand. Did you tell her this?"

V nodded slowly. "We spoke about it while you were at the Light Castle. She said she didna want to wait until after the bairn before we mated."

"Is she fearful for her life?"

"I doona think so. I believe it's more to show me that no matter what, she wants to be mine forever."

Con drew in a breath. "Claire is strong. You're strong. If the two of you can lean on each other, then you'll get through this. And if a miracle happens—"

"Doona," V interrupted him, his face lined with anxiety. "I can no' allow myself that hope. I need to prepare for the worst."

"I understand."

V sighed loudly. "Good."

"While I'm glad you shared this, that isna why I sought you out."

That's all it took for V to face him, his gaze clear. "What do you need?"

"An idea came to me earlier. I've been mulling it over, and before I went to Rhi with it so she could put the idea before the Fae, I wanted to talk to you."

"It's about our dragons," V stated, no anger in his voice.

"Aye. Rhi has proposed that with the Fae Realm healing, the Fae could return there to live. I've not said we're kicking them out, nor has anyone asked what we want to do. I left it open on purpose."

V's smile was slow as he crossed his arms over his chest. "You want to ask the Fae if our dragons can live there."

"Exactly. We'd be able to get to and from there easily. It would keep our dragons close, and the relationship with the Fae would be crucial for both them and us."

"You're right. There's just one catch."

Con's lips twisted ruefully. "We need to find the dragons first."

"They could all be dead."

"I doona want to think about that."

"I can no' help but think about it. It's been a verra long time. Because of that, if they are alive, they could now be somewhere they doona wish to leave in order to start new again."

"Or they could be somewhere that's no' ideal and we give them a place that is."

V's brow furrowed. "With the Fae."

"They can no' come here, and we can no' take the human mates away from their world."

"Nay, we can no'." V dropped his arms and blew out a long breath. "If you can convince the Fae to accept this plan, then I'll look for the dragons."

Con started to turn away and then paused. "No matter what happens with the bairn, everyone at Dreagan will be here for you and Claire."

"I know," V said and faced the Silvers once more.

Con left the cavern and walked around the manor. The house was more alive than ever. It was large enough to hold all the Dragon Kings and then some. And, if need be, they could add on to the manor.

That is if all the Kings and their mates continued to live here. There was plenty of room on Dreagan land for each of them to have a home of their own, much like the Warriors and Druids had done at MacLeod Castle.

The manor was still the heart of Dreagan, and it always would be. Con found himself back in Dreagan Mountain, this time walking the many tunnels. He recalled the first time he'd come to the area and had felt the magic. He'd known then that this was where he wanted to be.

From that day on, Dreagan had been his home, the place where he knew he would rule the dragons and raise a family of his own. He no longer knew for sure if he might have a family. It was enough that he was about to claim his mate. At one time, when he'd chosen the Kings over her, he'd believed that he had lost Rhi forever. Now, in a twist of Fate that he'd never seen coming, she was his once again.

He touched one of the dragon carvings he had cut into the stone while building the manor. It seemed like it just happened yesterday, but in reality, it was lifetimes ago. So much had changed since then. *He* had changed.

And yet, so much had stayed the same.

He walked to the back entrance of the mountain and stood looking out at the sky that was even now darkening for the coming evening. The rain had abated, but he could smell more on the way.

So many times, Con had stood in this exact spot, waiting for his brethren to return. Each of them had endured heartache that had brought them low, and had somehow found the strength to keep going, to keep putting one foot in front of the other.

Ulrik, his best friend and the brother he never had, was the one who had suffered the most. No one would ever truly understand how much it had taken out of Con to not only bind Ulrik's magic but also banish him from Dreagan. The war with the mortals had left scars on all of them.

Every King had a story to tell regarding those they'd lost, the horrors they witnessed, and the weight of watching the dragons cross the dragon bridge that took them away from this realm. Con still remembered when he nearly told the Kings to follow their dragons over the bridge. Because what was a King without their clan?

Many Kings healed as much as they could when they took to their mountains and slept the centuries away. But not Con. He'd raged alone, doing anything and everything he could not to go mad from loneliness and second-guessing every decision he made.

Days passed and turned into weeks, then months and years. Before he knew it, a century was gone, then a millennium. It was all a haze as he struggled to face each new day.

Those were the darkest of times for him. His thoughts had been bleak, his rages violent. If it weren't for the spell that kept the Kings from feeling anything for the humans, he knew he likely would've killed every one of them, wiping the realm of their existence for good.

But he continued to live, continued on—for his brethren. He'd promised to lead them, to give them a place they could call home and live. And that's precisely what he'd done with Dreagan.

He'd watched the first of the Kings, Hal, find his mate. Then, one after another, the Kings fell in love, expanding their family, opening it to include mortals, Druids, and Fae. Con might have had his doubts about taking humans as mates, but they had stood beside their Kings and Dreagan with more strength than Con had given them credit for.

Three more Kings were mating tonight. He was happy for them, even if he was thinking more about his own ceremony than theirs. Though, who could blame him? He'd waited an eternity to claim Rhi as his.

"I thought I'd find you here," Ulrik said as he walked up beside Con.

Con grinned at his friend. "We've come a long way."

"Aye. All thanks to you."

"I can no' take all the credit. Each King had a hand in this, even you."

Ulrik snorted and crossed his arms over his chest as

he widened his stance. "I did more damage than anything. If you hadna stopped me, I would've killed all the humans. I wouldna have come back from that."

"I know."

"You know what I've never understood?"

"What's that?"

"Why did the magic no' chose another King when I attacked the mortals? My heart wasna pure that day."

Con shook his head, his lips flattening. "You've always been purer of heart than anyone I've known, and I think the magic knew that. You were betrayed. You retaliated."

"I didna act like a King."

"If the magic truly thought that, then it would've pushed another silver dragon to challenge you, but none did. That tells me everything I need to know."

Ulrik twisted his lips and looked out over the land. "I had to walk that path. It's what brought me home to Dreagan and allowed me to find Eilish. I accept and understand that."

"We all have a path to walk. Me, included."

Ulrik's gold eyes slid to him. "The magic was right in choosing you as King of Kings. You're the best man I know."

Con lowered his gaze to the ground as he smiled at the compliment. "It's good to have you home."

"It's good to see you happy," Ulrik replied with a smile.

Con looked at him and laughed. "It sure is."

"There's something else I want to know."

"What's that?"

"Where do you get the jewelry you give the mates?"

Con jerked his chin to the silver cuff on Ulrik's wrist. "Take me to my mountain, and I'll show you."

"Easy enough."

No sooner had Ulrik touched him than they were in Con's mountain. He started walking through the tunnels with Ulrik following him until he came to a small chamber off to one side. A chest rested on the floor. Con kneeled beside it and opened it to reveal a mass of glittering jewels in all shapes and sizes.

"Bloody hell," Ulrik said in a shocked whisper.

Con glanced at him with a smile. "Dreagan is sitting atop a plethora of gems just waiting to be found. The years I was alone, I found some. Others I . . . picked up here and there."

"You mean you took them from the mortals," Ulrik said with a laugh.

Con shrugged and lifted a diamond the size of his palm. "I never stole anything. For the longest time, they would toss aside the gems, not seeing the beauty in the rough stones."

"But you did."

"As dragons always do."

Ulrik smiled, nodding. "Now I know where the stones come from, but what about the jewelry itself?"

"Let's start with V. As the King of Coppers, finding a gemstone of that color isna easy. I could give Claire a band of copper. Perhaps hammered as a bracelet. But I doona think that fits her."

"Then what would?"

Con searched until he found a nearly five-carat copper zircon gem. He pulled out the round stone and held it up for Ulrik to see. "This. As a necklace, set in rose gold."

Ulrik's brows shot up. "That certainly suits Claire more than hammered copper."

"Aye. Then I simply create what I see in my mind."

Con closed his eyes and used his magic to craft the rose gold necklace with the zircon.

"It's beautiful," Ulrik said and took the finished necklace from Con.

He created a velvet box and handed it to Ulrik to put the necklace in. "Take care of that while I search for Annita's gift."

"Here it is," Con said in triumph a moment later as he held up the cluster of druzy that sparkled. "I'll put this in a ring for Annita."

After he created it, Con handed it and another velvet box to Ulrik.

For Noreen, Con couldn't decide which of the navy stones to give her. He held up the lapis lazuli as well as a dark sapphire for Ulrik to see. "I'm leaning toward the lapis for Noreen."

"The sapphire is beautiful, but I, too, think the lapis. Another ring?"

Con shook his head and split the large stone in half with a thought. "Earrings with platinum wire wrapped around them."

"Aye. I can see Noreen wearing them."

Con handed the earrings and box to Ulrik and started to close the lid, but he hesitated. He'd thought to craft Rhi's gift later, but he wanted Ulrik's opinion.

"What is it?" Ulrik asked as he set the third box on the floor next to him.

Con licked his lips. "Rhi's gift."

"About that," Ulrik said. "I and the other Kings have a request."

CHAPTER FIFTY-TWO

The hours flew by. Rhi had kept herself busy helping Annita, Claire, and Noreen choose how to wear their hair and finish getting ready. No one had asked if she was going to the ceremony, because everyone knew that only the Kings and the mates were allowed. Rhi wasn't sure how she felt about breaking the rules this time when she hadn't thought twice about it in the past.

Maybe it was because Con had asked her when he hadn't allowed anyone else to break them before.

"You all right?" Annita asked her.

Rhi smiled. "I'm just thinking about tomorrow."

"Your ceremony is going to be glorious. I wish you'd shown us your gown," Noreen said.

Rhi felt all eyes on her. The three women had opted to get ready together instead of in separate rooms. She smiled and coyly said, "Tomorrow night will be here soon enough. Let's focus on these three ladies tonight."

And just like that, Rhi ensured that there would be no more talk of her upcoming ceremony.

There was a knock at the door and then she heard Con's voice. Rhi's heart picked up as she turned when someone opened the door for him. Their gazes met, and they smiled at each other.

Con cleared his throat and looked at the three women about to become mates. "It's nearly time. I'd like a few moments alone with each of you, please."

One by one, the women left the room. Rhi followed Jane out and paused beside Con. He bent and gave her a quick kiss. She looked back at the three women and shot them a wink before she went to Con's bedroom.

She snapped her fingers, and a gold and black twenties-inspired flapper gown with rhinestones and fringe covered her. She completed the look with a pair of black Valentino stilettos with gold studs.

Rhi left her hair down and parted it to one side so that it fell in waves around her. She added a gold rhinestone headband to complete the look. She teleported downstairs in time to see Claire, Annita, Noreen, and Con descend the stairs.

Con winked at her. The moment everyone was out of sight, Rhi veiled herself and teleported into the cavern. She kept to the side away from anyone and watched as Claire entered first, followed by Annita, and then Noreen, with Con bringing up the rear.

Rhi had witnessed several mating ceremonies. She didn't listen to the words this time, nor did she look at the couples. Her gaze was on Con as she thought about the next night and the two of them standing here.

It would feel like an eternity before their time came. They had already waited for so long, what was a few more hours? At least that's what she'd thought at the time. Now, she wished she were up there right now with the rest of them.

All too soon, the ceremony was over. Claire winced when her dragon eye tattoo appeared on her left shoulder. Annita bit her lip, and Noreen sucked in a breath. And, just like that, the three women were now immortal, living for as long as their Kings did.

Con's voice boomed through the cavern, announcing the newly mated couples. As everyone congratulated them, Con looked right in her direction. She smiled, even though he couldn't see her, because that's what he did to her.

She jumped to the party area and waited for everyone to arrive. It didn't take long. In fact, Con was one of the first to enter. He drew her into his arms and held her close.

"I couldn't help thinking about us tomorrow night," she confessed.

He chuckled and pulled back to look at her. "I had a difficult time remembering what I was supposed to do and say because of the same thing."

They shared a laugh and began to sway as the music started up.

"Is this what you want?" he asked.

She nodded, still smiling. "Definitely."

"Good."

"And you?"

"Without a doubt."

She rose up and gave him a kiss. "Our time will be here soon enough."

"You look gorgeous. You could wear that tomorrow."

Rhi shot him an appalled look. "Bite your tongue. I've got something even better."

"Better than that?" he asked in disbelief. "I doona believe it."

"Just wait."

"I doona think I can."

She giggled.

"We could do it now. Everyone is here," he suggested.

Rhi considered it, then caught sight of some of the Kings whispering as they glanced in Con's direction. "We can't do that."

"Why no'?" he asked with a frown.

"Because you've gone out of your way to make each of the ceremonies you performed for the Kings and their mates special. They want to do the same for you."

"For us," he corrected with a smile.

Rhi nodded. "Us. We can't take that away from them."

"I suppose no'."

"But we don't have to remain here all night."

Con's black eyes heated with desire. "Just what I wanted to hear."

"Your chamber?"

"*Our* chamber."

She smiled. "Our chamber?"

"Aye. And fast. I need inside you now."

CHAPTER FIFTY-THREE

"I don't like this."

Melisse looked at Henry as they walked through the back entrance of the mountain just as the sun came up. "I said you didn't need to be involved."

"As if that was going to happen," he retorted sharply.

She halted and turned to face him. "I told you I'm not here to hurt Con."

"I want to believe you, but since you won't tell me what you *are* doing here, I'm not leaving you alone."

"You know I can make you, right?" she stated.

His hazel eyes were unwavering as they held hers. "Then do it," he dared.

"I don't want to." And she didn't. But she also didn't want him there just in case things went . . . badly. Because there was a really good chance they could.

"Then stop threatening that. This is my home. The people here are my family. Esther might be my blood relative, but everyone else is my friend, which makes them family. I won't allow you to hurt anyone."

Her nostrils flared as she lifted her chin, irritation getting the best of her. "You're a mortal, Henry. You might be the JusticeBringer, but you can't do anything to stop me."

"Thanks for reminding me of my shortcomings," he snapped.

"I'm not trying to hurt you."

"Trust me, I know my limits better than anyone," he replied sarcastically. "I don't need you throwing them in my face."

Melisse wished she had chosen her words more carefully, but there wasn't time for that. She shook her head and turned around to continue walking. "I can't do this now. We'll talk later."

She heard Henry's sharp intake of breath as if he were about to yell. She whirled around, her hand up. Right before she sent the magic, she hesitated. That's when she realized he had tested her. He hadn't been about to alert the Kings. He had wanted to see what she would do.

"And here I thought I meant something to you," he said derisively. He raked his gaze over her and shook his head.

Melisse lowered her arm to her side. "You do. Otherwise, I wouldn't let you be here."

"Last time I'm asking. What are you doing here? It's bad enough the Kings weren't alerted to your arrival. I won't remain silent if you plan to harm any of them."

"I've told you repeatedly to trust me."

"Yet you've given me no reason to."

Melisse felt the magic pushing her to hurry. "I'll tell you everything once I finish. I can't wait any longer. I'm sorry."

She spun and began running through the tunnels. Melisse quickly outdistanced Henry with her speed. She could sense the anxiety of the magic as it propelled her faster and faster through the corridors.

"Con!" Henry bellowed from behind her, his voice dimming as she put more distance between them. "Banan! Anyone! Down here, now!"

Melisse pumped her legs faster as she sped through the tunnels that twisted and turned in a maze. She wasn't sure where she was going. All she had was the magic guiding her lower into the mountain, urging her onward—until, finally, she reached her destination.

Her breathing was ragged, her chest rising and falling rapidly when she slowly walked the last few steps and looked inside the small chamber. No bars signaled that it was a prison, but there didn't need to be with the magic running across the entryway, preventing the prisoner from escaping.

Melisse's gaze locked on the man kneeling in the middle of the chamber facing her. She'd never seen him, but she knew who it was—Orun, the *drough* who had come with Moreann to wipe out the Dragon Kings. The Druid had his eyes closed and his head tilted back with his elbows bent and his fingers together, palms facing up.

That's when she realized that he was using magic. She knew very little about the Druids, but given the urgency of the magic of the realm and how it was pushing her, she guessed the spell was nearly finished. She didn't know what it was, and it didn't matter. He had to be stopped.

Melisse heard a rumble through the tunnel and glanced to one side to see Con leading the charge toward her. Her head swiveled in the other direction to find more Kings coming. She returned her gaze to Orun, who lifted his head and looked directly at her as the last word formed. She had no idea how she knew this, only that she did.

There wasn't room for Melisse to shift in the narrow passage. She hadn't used her power as a weapon ever, but she trusted the magic of the realm to lead her. It had brought her here in time. She had to trust it now, just as she had to trust her instincts.

Her magic surged within her, fierce and violent, and without another thought, she directed all of it at Orun. The force of it was unlike anything she'd ever felt before. It was terrifying and invigorating. She parted her lips and released a battle yell as she threw up her arms, her palms outstretched toward Orun. The Druid never finished the last word. Instead, it turned into a scream of agony that lasted merely a heartbeat before there was nothing but silence.

Melisse closed her eyes. She'd never killed before, and she didn't like the emotions churning within her now. She felt sick at taking a life, but she also knew it had been the right thing to do to save those at Dreagan. How could something so wrong also be right? She wasn't sure she could ever come to terms with it.

Dimly, she realized that the rumble of the Kings coming for her had stopped. Was she dead? Maybe she hadn't killed Orun. Perhaps the Kings had gotten to her.

A hand gently touched her arm as another was placed on her back.

"It's over, Melisse."

Constantine. Of course, he would be the one who spoke. So, she wasn't dead. Yet. She drew in a shuddering breath and lowered her arms. Slowly, her eyes opened to look within the cavern, but there was nothing left of Orun.

Her head turned to Con. "He was casting a spell to kill Claire's bairn and ensure that none of you ever had children."

A King with long, dark hair and ice blue eyes pushed through the others and came to stand next to Con. "Let me be the first to thank you. You saved my mate, and for that, I'm in your debt."

Melisse cut her eyes to Con, but the King of Kings' face revealed nothing. She licked her lips and bowed her head to V.

Con stared silently at her for a moment before his lips turned up in a grin. "I'm sure all of you are wondering who this is. Her name is Melisse. She's the weapon I've kept secret since I became King of Kings."

She couldn't believe that Con had told the others who she was. "Why are you telling them?"

"Because it's time. It's been time." Con looked at the gathered Kings. "Melisse is half-dragon, half-Dark Fae. The first King of Kings learned of her existence and imprisoned her."

Laith shook his head in confusion. "Why would he do that? Melisse is proof that the blood can mix."

"Wait. Dark Fae?" Tristan asked. "How is that possible? I didna think any Fae came before their world was destroyed."

Melisse felt Con's gaze on her. She was waiting with bated breath to hear his answer because this was something she didn't know, either.

Con took in a deep breath. "How do you think the Fae knew of this realm when theirs was destroyed? They sent envoys to find places they could go if there was ever a need. A female Dark came here. The King of Kings found her first, and they struck up a friendship. He kept her secret, refusing to let anyone know that she was on the realm. They became lovers, and she bore him a child. Melisse."

"Why imprison Melisse, though?" Arian pressed.

"No dragon, much less a King, had ever had offspring with another species," Con told them. "The Dark were powerful, and the King of Kings wasna sure of the mix between the two races. The Dark left Melisse here at the King's insistence and returned to the Fae Realm. The

King kept Melisse hidden and watched her grow for the next six years until he saw the strength of her magic."

Melisse swallowed and kept her gaze straight ahead instead of looking at the others. She knew this part. She remembered it all too well.

Con's black eyes briefly lowered to the ground. "That fateful day, the King realized that Melisse had such a powerful mix of dragon and Fae magic that she could destroy all of us, even the Kings, if she wanted."

"You're telling me her father fucking imprisoned her instead of teaching her about us, instead of loving her and including her?" Rhys asked, outraged.

Melisse's eyes burned with tears. She had asked herself those same questions over and over. She'd wondered what it was about her that had made her so unwanted, so unlovable. For millennia, she'd been locked in the mountain, hearing the world around her, but never being able to take part.

Con nodded. "Aye. He did that, and it wasna long before he was no longer King of Kings. I believe the magic of the realm made that decision. However, Melisse's imprisonment didna end there. The first King told the next about Melisse, and that King of Kings also decided to keep her where she was. Tarel did the same. He told me it was better to be safe than sorry when he gave me the task of guarding her. They were the last words he spoke to me before he died, so I couldna question him. But I wasna sure of any of it. I had to keep her a secret, but I began digging into things. It was a slow process since no one knew of her existence, and I didna know the name of the Fae or even how to get to the Fae Realm. Then, my investigation was interrupted by the arrival of the mortals, and eventually, our war with them."

"That's how you knew we'd be able to shift when the mortals arrived," Sebastian said.

Con nodded slowly.

Melisse wasn't sure if she believed Con. She wanted to. She remembered the many times he had come to visit her, especially after the dragons had been sent away, and the other Kings had taken to their mountains. Sometimes, Con would just sit with her. Other times, he told her how the humans were developing. Though he never talked about himself, she heard the loneliness in his voice. Both of them had been prisoners at that point. Some of her hate and anger had dissipated during that time.

"Then he couldna free her when the rest of the Kings were hiding," Kellan continued. "Just in case what Tarel told him was true."

Melisse met Con's black gaze. "And the years since? Why didn't you free me then?"

"I've no excuse," he answered. "I should have, and for not doing so, I ask your forgiveness. I know I doona deserve it, but I'm hoping that someday, you'll be able to give it. You showed your true colors when you left Dreagan and didna attack. And especially what you did for Claire, V, and their bairn today."

"I still want to know how she got free," Darius asked.

Everyone looked to Melisse. She drew in a deep breath and shrugged. "I don't know. The magic my father used always kept me frozen in place, unable to move. I could hear the world, and even see Con when he ventured to his mountain, but no matter how I tried, I couldn't use my magic to free myself. I . . . I've always felt the magic of the realm. It's what led me here to Orun this morning. It's been even stronger over the last few months. It began when Ulrik returned to Dreagan. Suddenly, the magic holding me was gone. I got as far from Dreagan as I could after I got free because nothing was going to make me a prisoner again."

"None of us want that for you," Ulrik said.

Con faced her and held her gaze. "We've all much to make up for. Dreagan is our home, and we're opening it to you, as well. Live here with us or no'. It's your choice. Regardless, you can visit anytime."

"Are you serious?" she asked, unsure if she could believe him.

Con's lips turned up in a smile. "I am. Tomorrow night is my mating ceremony with Rhi. I'd verra much like if you came."

"All right," she said, searching the crowd of faces for Henry, but he was nowhere to be found. She wasn't sure if it was a good idea to stay at Dreagan or not. Melisse distrusted all of them, but she wanted to talk to Henry, maybe try and explain everything.

If he let her, that is.

"Good. Decide the rest later. There's no reason for you to hide anymore," Con told her. "Explore Dreagan and the manor as you see fit. I'm sure Henry will be happy to show you around."

Melisse wasn't sure what to say, so she remained silent. The Kings each came up to her, introducing themselves. There were so many. She knew names from listening to Con but remembering the faces that went with each would take some time.

She called out to Con as he walked away. "Who is the King of Violets?"

"There isna one," Con said as he stopped and looked back at her. Then he shot her a grin. "I believe the magic of this realm has chosen its first Dragon Queen."

CHAPTER FIFTY-FOUR

"You're smiling."

Rhi opened her eyes and looked down at Jesse, who was finishing up Rhi's pedicure. "I am."

"I've not seen that in some time," the Texas native said. Then she frowned. "Actually, you've not been in here for weeks. I was beginning to worry."

"Life happened," Rhi said in way of explanation.

Jesse waggled her dark brows. "But you're happy now?"

"Oh, yeah."

"By that glow and the color you chose for your nails, I'm thinking wedding."

Rhi simply smiled.

Jesse's eyes widened. "Are you serious?"

"It's been a long time coming, but yes."

The nail tech jumped to her feet and hugged Rhi. "I'm so very happy for you."

"Don't worry. I'll be a regular again for my nails."

"Good to hear." Jesse sat back down and reached for the nail polish. "The Scottish collection is pretty popular here. Think they'll come out with an Irish one?"

Rhi shrugged. "Maybe. You know I'll buy it, just like I bought the entire Scottish collection. The man I'm marrying is a Scot."

"Oh, wow," Jesse said with wide eyes.

"He's so amazing. Don't get me wrong, he can be an ass, but his intentions are always good."

Jesse finished with Rhi's toenails and then moved her to do her nails. She applied the OPI color You've Got that Glas-glow, a pinky shade that went on neutral for Rhi. Instead of a design, all she wanted Jesse to do was put Glitzerland, a metallic gold, along her cuticles to create a semicircle.

"I hope I get to see pictures," Jesse said.

Rhi finished paying and gave Jesse a hug. "I promise you will."

Rhi strode from the salon and walked a few blocks before ducking behind a building and teleporting back to Dreagan. She arrived in her and Con's bedroom chamber and looked around. Con had woken her that morning with his hands and mouth. Their lovemaking had been slow and fiery, leaving them grasping at each other as they climaxed together.

They then lay entwined and watched the sun rise before Con was suddenly called away. He'd left in such a hurry that she hadn't had time to tell him her plans for the day.

Her gaze went to where she'd left him a note. It was still there, but below her message he'd written:

I cannot wait to see you tonight. I love you.

Always yours,

C

Rhi pressed the note to her chest and closed her eyes as she smiled. There was a knock at the door that drew her attention. She folded the letter and set it aside so she wouldn't lose it, then she went to open the door.

Shara smiled in greeting. "I came earlier, but I think you were gone."

"Yep," Rhi said and held up her hands, wiggling her fingers to show her nails. "Had to get these taken care of."

"Ohhh. Gorgeous. We've already had breakfast. Everyone wanted to come up here, but I thought just one of us would do."

Rhi laughed and stepped aside, motioning for the Fae to enter. "Thank you for that. There are quite a few mates now."

"You're telling me. I was the sixth."

"And I'll be the,"—she paused and counted—"the twenty-seventh."

Shara laughed, nodding. "And there are still Kings who aren't mated."

"I know. I don't think it'll be long for them. By the way, do you know why Con had to run out so early this morning?"

The Fae's face scrunched with worry. "Actually, I don't. But he wasn't the only one. All the Kings left."

"Hmm. Since no one has said anything, I'm guessing all is good?"

Shara shrugged and wrinkled her nose. "We can only hope after all the shite we've been through."

"I know Con returned to our chambers. That must mean whatever crisis it was got worked out."

"It better have. Your ceremony is going to be the biggest of them all. Nothing should interrupt that."

Rhi shifted nervously as she glanced at the clock on the wall. "I've got hours yet."

"I know you don't need any of us to get ready. You're the epitome of a fashion expert, and you have magic, but you helped yesterday. We would all love to be here if you need us."

"Oh, I'm going to need everyone." Then she turned in a circle and said, "And look at these chambers. There is plenty of room for everyone to get ready right here. So, bring everyone up. We'll even have lunch here."

Shara's smile was wide as she rushed to the door. "I'll tell them now."

Rhi blew out a breath and then laughed. It was really going to happen. She was going to be Con's mate. But until the ceremony was finished, and the tattoo was on her arm, she would be wary of anything—or any*one*—interrupting things.

In no time, the mates filled the chamber. An assortment of makeup was brought in that would make cosmetic hoarders everywhere jealous.

They looked through various eyeshadows as they ate a lunch of sandwiches and champagne. And at every turn, Rhi was asked again and again about her dress, but she refused to tell or show them.

When lunch was finished, she sat in a chair and let the others begin applying her makeup. They had asked if she wanted to go more neutral or glamorous, and her answer was that she didn't know.

Normally, she could pick out every detail of a look, but not today. She was excited and nervous all at the same time. She would suddenly smile, thinking about Con and the vows they had spoken to each other so long ago. When that happened, the group would *awww* in unison.

There was no mirror in front of her, so Rhi had no idea what her makeup looked like, but she wasn't worried. The mates had her back, and she had theirs. They were family.

Lily stepped back and put the cap on the lipstick. "Wow."

"I honestly didn't think you could look more beautiful, Rhi," Eilish stated. "But you do."

Devon nodded. "Damn, girl. Just . . . *damn*."

Rhi smiled giddily. "I want to see."

Lily shook her head of black hair. "Not yet. It's time for your hair."

"How would you like to wear it?" Gemma asked.

Rhi glanced at the clock and found that nearly two hours had already passed, which meant that it was getting closer to the time for the ceremony. "I don't care."

Alexandra lifted a long lock of Rhi's wavy, black hair. "It depends on what the dress looks like."

"Fine," Rhi said with a laugh. "I'll tell you that it's strapless, but that's all you're getting."

Sophie smiled at Alex. "That's really all we need."

Rhi closed her eyes and let her mind wander as the others began messing with her hair. Their talk, and the feel of them touching the thick locks, was soothing, allowing her to rest in an almost meditative state.

She had been listening for the darkness inside her, but it hadn't made a peep since Usaeil died. Con had told her it wasn't the darkness, that it was her inner voice. Rhi knew that wasn't true. The voice *had* been the darkness. Whether that changed or not, she couldn't say.

The journey that she'd taken had been full of ups and downs, the road rocky, and sometimes, she had no choice but to crawl when she couldn't walk. She'd reached heights in her life that she'd never thought to achieve, and she'd hit rock bottom more times than she wanted to think about.

But she always pulled herself back up, dusted off, and continued onward as her parents had taught her.

So many times, she'd believed that Fate was against her, but that hadn't been it at all. The truth—as simple as it was—was that she'd had a journey to take. She had to walk a path only she could so she could become the woman she was. Someone who had never thought darkness could come into her world. But she hadn't just encountered it, she had touched it, let it inside her, and used it to defeat Usaeil the first time.

Rhi was both light and dark. There was no doubt. Now, she was both—ying and yang.

Rhi felt a soft touch on her shoulder. Her eyes opened to find the room silent as death. She looked up at Denae, her whisky-colored eyes probing.

"What is it?" Rhi asked.

Denae shook her head and shrugged. "Just wanted to see if you were all right. You looked asleep."

"Resting," Rhi told her. She didn't move her head when she felt the slight tug from someone working with her hair.

Denae laughed and leaned back against the wall. "I couldn't rest on my ceremony day. I was a ball of nerves."

"Why do you think I'm resting?" Rhi said with a wide grin.

The others laughed in response.

Rhi drew in a breath. "I think we need more champagne."

"I'm on it," Kinsey announced as she jumped up and rushed to the door.

Sabina followed her. "I'll help."

"How is it coming?" Rhi asked those working on her hair.

Denae smiled. "I wouldn't do it justice by trying to explain. I had no idea Alex had mad skills as a hairstylist."

"I can do anyone else's hair, just not my own," Alex said with a chuckle.

Rhi snorted. "Oh, please. I've seen your hair. It's gorgeous."

"So is yours. Annnnnnd, I'm done," Alex stated.

Alex, Bernadette, and Esther moved to stand next to Denae. The four of them stared at Rhi until she frowned.

"I'm getting a little freaked out by the silence and stares."

Bernadette wiped at the corner of her eye. "You're always beautiful, but today . . . Well, you're stunning. And this is without the dress."

"Oh, for Heaven's sake," Esther said. "At least show us the shoes."

Alex rubbed her hands together. "Oh, please. I'm dying to see if I've guessed which shoes you've chosen."

Rhi moved a lock of hair that had fallen across her eye. She could tell that some of her hair was down, but she had no idea about the rest. She was dying to find a mirror and look, but she made herself wait.

"Fine. I'll show you the shoes," she announced.

Kinsey came in with a bottle of champagne and Sabina on her heels. "Shoes? Did someone say shoes?"

"Rhi is going to show us hers," Elena announced.

Standing, Rhi turned her chair to face the majority and motioned the other four to join. Then she called the box of shoes to her.

"I knew it!" Alex shouted when she spotted the light brown box.

Rhi laughed and took off the top of the Christian Louboutin box. Then she folded back the red tissue paper and lifted the Grotika Spiked Clear pump. Glittering gold crystals mixed with gold spikes on a clear, pointy toe with a golden leather back and finished with the renowned—and Rhi's favorite—red sole. She held it one way and another, letting everyone get a look at it.

"It's Rhi to perfection," Grace said.

Rhi ran her hand along the side of the shoe. "I knew as soon as I saw them that I had to have them."

"If those are your shoes, your dress is going to be fabulous," Faith replied.

Rhi put the shoe back into the box and handed it to Esther to pass around. Then Rhi looked at the clock. Another few hours had passed, but it was still too early for her to get ready.

"What is it?" Eilish asked.

Rhi twisted her lips and held out her empty glass of champagne to be filled as the bottles made the rounds. "I want it to be time, but I've still got at least an hour to kill."

"Actually, you don't."

Rhi blinked. "What does that mean?"

Instead of answering, Eilish nodded to Denae, who turned to the others. "It's time, ladies."

Half of them rose and hurried out the door without a word.

Rhi looked from Eilish to Denae and back again. "What's going on?"

"The Dragon Kings would like to see you before the ceremony," Denae explained.

Rhi's frowned deepened. "Um . . . okay."

"It's fine," Eilish said with a wave of her hand. "Con visited each of us beforehand and spoke to us, and since it's his ceremony, the Kings would like to do the same for you. Since there are so many of them, it's going to take a while."

"Oh. That sounds . . . nice," Rhi said with a smile.

Denae beamed. "I thought so. Unfortunately, that means we've got to get ready, too. Half of us are doing that now. When they return, the rest of us will dress and hurry back."

Rhi sat back, listening as idle conversation started up. It was nice to be a part of something so wonderful. She laughed at the jokes, giggled at the antics of some of the Kings, and threw in ideas for upcoming date nights.

Before she knew it, the first half of the mates returned. They each sparkled in gowns the color of their King. Rhi looked at the time and noted that it had only been twenty minutes since they departed.

"Magic," Shara said as she walked past her.

Rhi laughed, realizing that she hadn't thought about them using magic. Eilish gave her a wink as she left with the second half. Rhi finished off a second and third glass of champagne before the remainder of the mates returned. They stood together, one big family that had seen both hard and glorious times.

"I'm really happy to see my friends find such amazing women as their mates," Rhi said. "Each of you brings something unique and special to your relationship, and therefore, Dreagan. I'm lucky to have all of you."

It was Lily who said, "We're the lucky ones to call you our friend."

"Stop," Claire said as she wiped at her eyes. "I'm going to cry."

Sophie chuckled. "You're going to cry anyway."

"I know," Claire whined and sniffed loudly. "Why

do you think I have waterproof makeup on? I don't want black marks down my face."

Rhi laughed at the two of them, but inside, she feared what was to come with Claire, V, and their child. It could be something wonderful, or it could be something terrible. The fact that Usaeil was involved meant it could be either. No one said anything. They didn't need to. No one was more aware of the situation than Claire and V.

"All right," Darcy said. "It's time we see that dress."

The mates began chanting, "Dress. Dress. Dress," until Rhi finally threw up her hands and got to her feet.

"All right. I'm getting it," she said with a laugh.

She set aside her champagne flute and walked into the dressing room. Just as she shut the door, there was a knock, and Cassie poked her head inside.

"You're going to need these," she said as she held out the box of shoes.

Rhi smiled and took the box. Only after the door was shut again did she release a breath. She kept herself turned away from the full-length mirror in the room and removed her clothes. Then she put on the sexy champagne-colored lingerie she knew Con liked so much. Next, she sat on the round stool in the middle of the dressing room and put on her shoes. Rhi stood and took several deep breaths. Only then did she call the dress to her.

Her gaze lowered to the full skirts. The sight of them made her smile. She'd had this gown for so long, but nothing had altered her love of it. It was classic, elegant, and withstood time.

Slowly, she turned to face the mirror. She locked gazes with her reflection and could only blink in surprise. They had put very little makeup on her, focusing on accentuating her eyes, making them look even larger, and her lashes longer. The barest hint of color was on her cheeks and lips. It was perfect in every way.

Her gaze then moved to her hair. The front and sides had been pulled back and pinned so the locks fell softly around her shoulders. The back was loose, or at least some of it was. A turn of her head showed that Alex had put a small braid on either side of Rhi's head.

Finally, she looked at her gown. She'd never tried it on until now. She hadn't been sure how everything would look when it all came together, but Rhi knew that she'd made the right decision.

She walked to the door and opened it. Without announcing herself, she stepped out. The room grew quiet as the mates noticed her. Then, everyone started talking at once. Rhi could only laugh as she listened to their compliments.

It was Eilish who whistled to get everyone's attention. "As much as I want to stay and chat with Rhi like the rest of you, we can't. It's time."

Rhi waved as the mates began filing out. She liked having them there, and now that they were leaving, she wanted them back.

"We're going to the cavern," Eilish told her. "Con will be there, as well."

"And the Kings?"

Eilish's smile grew. "Con walked each of us in. They're going to walk you in."

"Oh," Rhi said, taken aback by the gesture.

Eilish shot her a dubious look. "Did you really think they would do any less? They adore Con. They adore you. This is their way of showing it." Eilish gave her a quick hug. "I'll see you soon."

Once the Druid walked out, Hal came in, followed by Guy, Banan, and then Kellan. It took her a moment to realize that they were in the order of who had found their mates, with the single Kings coming in last. As they filed in, Rhi remained standing. She met each of their gazes, smiling as she did. They took up much more of the chamber than the mates had.

Rhys spoke first. "There was a time I didna think you and Con would reconcile. I'm pleased more than you could ever know that hope prevailed, and you will be our queen."

"Aye," they agreed in unison.

Ulrik then stepped forward. "Life hasna always been easy. Yet, you never let any of us down. You risked your life, time and again, for everyone at Dreagan. You did it no' just because you loved Con, but because you were our friend. We may no' have always told you, but we saw the effort, we noticed the sacrifices. No one deserves happiness more than you and Con."

She blinked to hold back the tears. She had to look away before she cried. When she returned her gaze to Ulrik, he held something behind his back.

Ulrik grinned at her. "Con has put a lot of thought into the gifts he has given each of the mates, as he will for the Kings who have yet to find their other halves. I saw for the first time yesterday just what he goes through when he decides on a piece of jewelry for the mate in question. And it made me think of you."

Rhi frowned. "I don't need anything from you all except friendship and love."

"You've got that and more," V replied.

Darius nodded. "Con is King of Dragon Kings. You, as his mate, will be our queen."

Ulrik then went down on one knee as he pulled his hands around and showed her what he had been hiding.

Rhi gaped at the crown that glittered with so many

gemstones it blinded her. It was made of various colored metals as well as having a stone for every color King. The colors were arranged in such a way that they faded from one set to another. And in the center of it all was a large, oval, champagne-colored stone the size of her palm.

She could find no words as Ulrik got to his feet and walked around her to set the crown on her head. It was heavy, a reminder of what she would now help Con carry as his mate.

One by one, each of the Kings came to her and bowed their heads, letting her know they welcomed her into the family. It was all she could do to hold back the tears. Ulrik was the last, and after his bow, he held out his arm. Once she looped her hand in the crook of his elbow, they proceeded from the chamber.

The two of them followed the rest of the Kings down the stairs, moving through the conservatory and into Dreagan Mountain and the cavern where all mating ceremonies were conducted.

As the entrance loomed, Ulrik leaned close and asked, "Ready?"

"I've been ready for this my whole life," she answered, giddy with pleasure and excitement.

He chuckled as they walked into the cavern. Rhi's gaze immediately went to Con, who stood at the front. He beamed at her, his excitement palpable.

"I told you he never stopped loving you," Ulrik whispered before they reached Con.

She didn't get a chance to answer as Con took her hands and kissed her, which brought cheers from everyone.

CHAPTER FIFTY-FIVE

Beautiful didn't begin to describe Rhi. Con felt choked with emotion when he saw her walk into the cavern. The sight of his mate, his beloved, made his heart nearly burst.

The strapless ballgown showcased her ample breasts and faded from a soft cream at the neckline to a deep gold at the hemline. The dress glittered with rhinestones and sequins that grew progressively thicker as the gold deepened.

Then he saw the crown.

Con's gaze jerked to Ulrik, who stood in the place Con usually did to preside over the ceremonies.

"I'm barely holding it together to keep from crying," Rhi warned. "If either of you say anything, I'm going to lose it."

Con chuckled and quickly blinked to fight the emotion that choked him. He looked out over the cavern to the Dragon Kings and nodded. He couldn't find the words to thank them, but he would later.

Ulrik cleared his throat. "I always knew that one day, one of us would be up here when it was Con's time to be mated. I'd hoped it would be me saying these words."

His gaze slid to Con and held there for a heartbeat. "I'm beyond grateful to be home at Dreagan and back with all of you. And, Con, you're my brother. You always have been, and you always will be."

Con heard Rhi sniff and saw a lone tear fall down her cheek. He squeezed her hands, causing her to look at him. Then he smiled. She returned it and gave his hands a squeeze, as well.

"It's now time to officially welcome Rhi as mate to Con." Ulrik asked, "Constantine, do you bind yourself to Rhiannon? Do you vow to love her, protect her, and cherish her above all others?"

Con could barely contain his joy. "Without a doubt."

"Rhi, do you bind yourself to Constantine, King of Golds and King of Dragon Kings? Do you swear to love him, protect him, and cherish him above all others?"

"Absolutely," Rhi announced in a clear voice.

Con watched as Rhi's lips parted and surprise flashed in her eyes at the brief pain of the dragon eye tattoo forming on her upper arm.

Ulrik smiled at them. "The proof of your vows and your love marking Rhi as Con's for eternity!"

A loud cheer erupted in the cavern. Con pulled Rhi close and kissed her, but he ended it sooner than he wanted. "I have something for you."

The cavern began to quiet, but Con didn't care if anyone witnessed or not. He'd wanted to wait until he and Rhi were alone to give her this, but he couldn't. He wanted her to have it now. He'd crafted the ring years ago when he'd sunk so low without her, hoping against hope that one day he might be able to give it to her. He pulled the velvet box from his suit pocket and opened it so she could see the ring inside. Her hands went to her mouth as her eyes widened.

She looked up at him. "It's gorgeous."

He took the ring from the box then reached for her hand. The emerald-cut gold moissanite gem was three carats and set in rose gold metal. The band also had smaller, pave moissanite gems that encircled it.

"You had my heart before I knew you existed. You will have it for all eternity," he vowed.

She put her hands on his chest and said, "We said our vows long ago. I never stopped loving you or wanting you. And I never will. I was yours from the start of creation. Together, we can do anything."

"Together," he murmured before he kissed her once more.

The cheers of the Kings and mates was deafening, but it was time for a celebration unlike anything Dreagan had seen in thousands of years.

Con wanted nothing more than to continue kissing her, but he made himself stop until they could be alone later. He met her sparkling silver gaze and said, "I invited some friends."

"You did?" she asked with a small frown. "Who?"

He jerked his head to the side. "Take a look."

Rhi followed his gaze. He knew the moment she spotted the Druids and Warriors from MacLeod Castle. She gasped and waved at them.

"Keep looking," he urged.

Her gaze swung to him, surprise in her eyes. "The Reapers?"

"All of them."

There was a brief pause before her head turned back to the Reapers and their mates.

Then Balladyn stepped forward. The once Captain of the Queen's Guard and King of the Dark walked to them. Balladyn bowed his head to Con, then looked at

Rhi. "You outshine the moon this night. You and Con deserve all of this and more."

Con looked at Rhi to see her dash away a tear.

"Stop," she ordered Balladyn with a small laugh. "You're going to make me cry."

He chuckled, his smile wide as his red eyes slid to Con. "You'll never know how grateful I am for the invitation. I owe you."

"You owe me nothing," Con said.

Rhi grabbed Balladyn when he went to turn away. "Not without a hug."

Whatever jealousy Con might have had for the Fae was gone now that Rhi was his once more. Balladyn and Rhi had leaned on each other when they had no one else. It was a special kind of bond that would forever link them.

Balladyn met Con's gaze once more, and he knew that they hadn't seen the last of the Fae-turned-Reaper. And Con was just fine with that.

After Balladyn returned to the other Reapers, Rhi looked at Con. "I can't believe you invited them. It's against the rules."

"I am King of Kings. If anyone can . . . adjust . . . the rules, it's me," he told her with a smile. "Besides, they're our friends and allies. Why should they no' be a part of such a celebration."

"I'm very glad you adjusted the rules."

"They are no' the only ones here."

Rhi laughed, shaking her head and causing the light to bounce off the many jewels in her crown. "More?"

"Of course." Con searched the room until he spotted Henry, then he motioned the mortal forward.

When Rhi saw Henry, she shot Con a wide smile. "Now, this is special."

Con didn't say more until Henry was nearly upon them. Con let his gaze move slowly over the cavern until he had everyone's attention. "I doona think the Dragon Kings have had a more loyal friend than Henry. He has done more than I ever expected a mortal to do for us. Because of that, I tasked Henry with finding the weapon that went missing from Dreagan. I omitted much of the information I knew about the weapon because my instincts told me that Henry was the one to find it. And I wasna wrong.

"I kept a secret from the moment I became King of Kings. One that I was never sure about. I shouldna have kept putting off learning the truth. For that, I owe someone an apology. I can only ask for forgiveness and hope that they might forgive me someday. You see, the secret I kept was about the weapon the previous King of Kings believed would destroy no' just the dragons but the Kings, as well. The weapon, however, is a person—half-dragon, half-Dark Fae. And our first Dragon Queen. Melisse," he called.

Henry remained on the step below Con as the crowd parted, and Melisse strode forward with her head held high. She was still unsure about being at Dreagan, but Con knew she only needed time to see that she was welcome among them.

"Is this why you left early this morning?" Rhi whispered.

Con nodded and leaned his head toward her. "I didna have a chance to tell you."

"This is amazing." When Melisse reached them, Rhi held out her hand and grasped Melisse's. "I'm very happy to meet you. Our first Dragon Queen. This is cause for celebration."

Melisse frowned briefly. "It doesn't bother you that I'm half Dark?"

Rhi chuckled and shared a look with Con. "As my King has so often told me, everyone has both light and darkness inside them. It's up to each individual to figure out which they want to feed the most."

For the first time, Melisse's lips curved into a smile. She bowed her head and dipped into a curtsey, looking from Rhi to Con. "Thank you."

Con took a deep breath as Rhi linked her fingers with his once more. "This ceremony has always been for Kings and their mates only. Until tonight, no outsiders were allowed in. I decided to change that no' only because we defeated our enemies with the help of our allies, but also because those allies are our friends. The Warriors and Druids, the Reapers and their women, Death and Cael, Henry, and even Melisse. The Dragon Kings might have guarded this realm on our own before, but now, we do it with friends. And I believe that makes us even stronger."

Everyone cheered and clapped. As the applause died down, Con took Rhi's hand to lead her out of the cavern and to the party area within the manor.

"Speaking of Erith and Cael, I don't see them," Rhi said.

Con waited until they were out of the cavern before he said, "They were here during the ceremony. I'm no' sure where they went."

But he found them as he and Rhi walked into the ballroom. Con didn't have to direct Rhi toward them, she moved that way herself. Death wore one of the black gowns she used to favor with her hair pulled away from her face. Cael had his arm around her, dressed in all black, as well.

"I wasna sure you'd remain," Con said to them.

Cael's purple gaze met Con's. "Erith wanted to talk to you two alone."

Rhi quirked a brow. "So you left the ceremony and came to the party, which makes no sense."

"I wasn't sure you'd want me here at all," Erith told her.

Con watched his mate as Rhi's nostrils flared. There were things that both women needed to say to each other, and there was no time like the present.

"You should've told me," Rhi stated.

Erith drew in a breath and nodded. "I know you feel that way, but it isn't something I could just blurt out."

"But you knew when you had Daire follow me," Rhi argued. "You could've told me then."

"You wouldn't have believed me, nor did I think you were ready to hear it. Besides, things would've turned out drastically different if you had known last year versus finding out now. I knew I would never be the one to tell you the truth. I knew you would figure it out on your own." Erith shrugged. "When I went into the sea to save you, you weren't struggling. You weren't anxious or afraid. You were floating as if in utter peace. I saw the light within you, and while I couldn't see the path you'd walk, I knew you had to live."

Rhi looked away and swallowed loudly. Con held her hand tighter, sensing the struggle within her.

Death continued. "From the moment I took you from the sea, I never stopped watching your life. I was there the day you and Con met. I saw the two of you fall in love, I witnessed the vows you exchanged, and, yes, I saw when it all fell apart." Erith closed the distance between them and grasped Rhi's free hand. "I was with you when you returned to the Fae Realm to die, but I didn't protect you. I didn't need to. You did it all on your own without even realizing it. I didn't need to send for Con, either. He came on his own. That's how deep the love between the two of you runs."

Rhi's head swung to him as she gave him a watery smile as tears overflowed and fell down her cheeks. "He is rather wonderful."

Con wiped away a tear. "You're the one who is wonderful."

"What I'm trying to tell you," Erith said with a sniff, "is that I've always been on your side. You may not believe that, but it's the truth. I've been on both of your sides."

Con flashed her a smile. "Thank you for that. You came when I needed a friend the most. If you had done nothing more than save my mate, I would still call you a friend."

"Thank you," she told Con. Erith's lavender gaze moved to Rhi. "I know you're hurting now, and I'll answer any questions you may have. After . . ." She paused to look at Cael, who gave her a nod. "There is something else I have to tell you."

"Why did you have Daire follow me?" Rhi asked.

Erith released Rhi's hand and smiled. "Because I knew you were walking a line between the light and darkness. I also knew you were strong enough to ignore the darkness, but if I thought you were struggling, then I needed to know so I could get the one person who could help you—Con."

Rhi swiveled her head to him and smiled. "Con's right. You are a friend to us." Rhi returned her gaze to Death and smiled. "Thank you for saving me. Thank you for giving me to the family you did. Thank you for caring enough to look out for me and for being there for Con when I couldn't."

Erith smiled and glanced at Cael. "Actually, you might want to thank Cael, as well. He went undercover at the Dark Palace to await Usaeil's arrival. Then he made sure he was the one she turned to for information."

"As if I was going to sit on the sidelines after everything she'd done," Cael quipped.

Con grinned. "Well done."

"I thought you might have guessed, since you kept looking at me on the battlefield," Cael said.

"There was something about the Dark that kept drawing my attention, but I didna guess it was you," Con said.

"It was easy getting close to Usaeil. Too easy," Cael said with a frown. "You'd think she would've been less trusting, but she was the opposite."

"It wasn't that she trusted," Rhi replied. "It's that Usaeil believed that even if someone did betray her, she'd be around to punish them. It never entered her mind that she could be bested."

Con shrugged as he gazed down at Rhi with love. "That was her downfall."

"Your enemies are vanquished," Erith said. "What will you do now?"

Con shook his head and glanced at the growing crowd behind him. "This realm has too much magic and many beings who are powerful. Do you really think we'll get any peace?"

"For a while, but you're right. There will always be someone who thinks they can best us," Cael said.

Rhi faced Con. "Enough of that talk. Tonight, we're celebrating a Dragon Queen as well as our mating. I want laughing and dancing all night long."

"I'm all yours," Con said.

She led him into the middle of the room as music began to play. Con pulled her into his arms and held her tightly as they swayed with the music.

"You are everything to me," he told her.

She gazed up at him with so much love that his heart skipped a beat. "And you are everything to me."

"My Queen."

"My King. Now and always."

EPILOGUE

"Erith," Cael said as they watched Rhi and Con dance.

She swallowed. "Not tonight. Let them have this night."

He took her hand and turned her to face him. "It's time. You said that when we came here tonight. You could've told them yesterday."

"Look at them," she insisted. "They're deliriously happy. They deserve the time."

Cael's purple eyes held hers. "You're scared to tell them."

"No."

"Aye," he stated. "You're Death, my love. A fekking goddess."

She glanced at the couple once more. "They forgave me about Rhi's secret."

"They need to know," he pressed.

"I know," she relented. "Give them a little time to enjoy themselves."

"You've got thirty minutes. If you don't tell them, I will."

For the next twenty-nine minutes, Erith watched the

couple dance, gaze into each other's eyes, talk to people, laugh, and kiss. She wanted to do anything but what she was about to do, but she had no other choice. Like Cael had said, it was time. It was past time, actually.

With a lift of her hand, she got Con's attention and called the couple over. Rhi was laughing at something Con said when they reached her and Cael.

"You don't have a drink," Rhi told her. "You need one."

Erith waved away her words. "I was hoping I could have a quiet word with the two of you before we left."

"What is it?" Con asked.

Cael shook his head. "Your office might be better."

Con's smile faded as his black eyes slid to her. "Can this no' wait?"

"It's waited too long, actually," she admitted.

Rhi gave a firm nod. "You mentioned earlier that you had something to tell us. I forgot about it until now. Is this it?"

"Yes."

Con put a hand on Rhi's back. "Follow us."

The walk through the manor and up to Con's office felt like it took an eternity, but it also seemed entirely too short. Erith kept thinking about all the different reasons not to tell the couple the news she had. As if reading her mind, Cael brought their linked hands to his mouth and kissed the back of her fingers.

"It'll be fine, love."

But she knew it wouldn't. It was the reason she had kept putting this off. She might be a goddess, but she was scared. Cael had been right earlier.

All too soon, they were inside Con's office, the door shut, keeping everyone out. The silence was deafening after the loud music and conversation at the party.

"Forgive me for being direct, but I'd like to get back to our mating party," Con said.

Erith drew in a deep breath and then slowly released it. "I understand."

"Then what is it?" Rhi asked when Erith didn't continue.

Cael said, "Give her a moment, please. This isn't easy."

"Is there trouble for you? The Reapers?" Con asked, concern on his face.

Erith felt the tears well, and despite blinking, one fell onto her cheek. She was standing there terrified, and all Con thought about was that she might be in some kind of trouble. "Nothing like that," she said and swiped away a tear. "I've kept secrets for so long. I was so relieved when Rhi finally discovered who she really was. I don't like secrets, but sometimes, there is no getting away from them. Once you have them, you see for yourself how they can destroy people."

"You said secrets," Con said in a quiet voice. "Plural."

She nodded, holding Cael's hand tighter.

Rhi set her glass of champagne down on Con's desk. "How many more?"

"One," she answered.

Con's black eyes held hers. It was Rhi who asked, "Involving who?"

Erith squeezed her eyes closed as more tears gathered. "You and Con."

For a minute, silence filled the room. Erith had already gone this far, there was no turning back now. She licked her lips and moved her gaze to Rhi. "When you ventured to the Fae Realm after Con ended things, I told you I followed you. There were still a few Dark there, and they attacked you. You were caught unawares and were badly wounded."

"And you did nothing?" Con demanded.

Cael glared at Con. "Let her finish."

Erith tried to swallow, but her mouth was dry. "Just as I was coming to your aid, the Dark left. You were unconscious, and I was about to take you to my realm when I felt it."

"What?" Rhi asked in a whisper.

Another tear fell down Erith's face. "Life."

Rhi's brows drew together in confusion. She reached for Con as her knees buckled. He grasped her, holding her up as tears welled in her eyes.

"As soon as I felt it, I realized I had a choice to make. I could save you," Erith said, "or I could save your child."

It was like all the air went out of Con. "Child?"

More tears fell down Erith's face. "I knew Rhi was strong enough to survive, so I took the baby."

"No," Rhi said. "I wasn't pregnant. I would've known."

"You were just a few weeks along," Erith told her. "You wouldn't have known."

Con and Rhi held each other, their gazes locked on Erith. It was Con who asked, "Did the child live?"

"Yes. I made sure of it with my magic."

Rhi let out a choke as she turned her head against Con as she cried.

Beside Erith, Cael remained still and stoic, giving her his strength for what was still to come.

"Why did you no' tell us?" Con asked, his own eyes filling.

Erith shook her head. "I can give you a multitude of reasons, and none of them will be sufficient for either of you. It wouldn't be for me if I were in your place. I did what I did out of love for both of you and the children."

"Children?" Rhi's head snapped up.

"You were having twins," she explained. "A boy and a girl."

A muscle in Con's jaw jumped. "Where are they?"

"I raised them on my realm for a while until I realized it wasn't enough. Both kept trying to leave, so I let them guide me to where they wanted to go, knowing I wouldn't let anything happen to them. That's when they brought me to where your dragons are."

All the color drained from Con's face. "The dragons are alive?"

"Very much so," Cael answered.

Erith smiled. "And being ruled by your children."

Rhi and Con embraced, speaking softly to each other. Several moments passed before Rhi lifted her head and wiped at her eyes. She asked, "Do the children know of us?"

"They do. They know everything. In fact, they've been here a few times and have seen both of you," Erith said.

Con gazed at Rhi as she gave him a nod. He then looked at Erith. "Show us our children. Give us that, at least."

As if she could refuse such a request. Erith released Cael's hand and stepped to the side. She held an arm out, palm up as she swung it in a big circle. Each time she did, lavender sparks flew as the magic coursed from her into the window she created. The gray haze faded as the spell finished and the opening cleared to reveal the other realm.

The sound of dragons roaring deafened her, but Erith didn't look through the window. She watched Con and Rhi to see the couple's gaze riveted on the sight before them. Erith knew the instant they saw the twins. A smile pulled at Con's lips as more tears escaped Rhi's eyes as she covered her mouth with her hand.

"Take us to them," Rhi said.

"Take me, as well," came a deep voice from behind them.

Erith's head jerked to the door to find Vaughn standing there, staring into the window to the dragon realm and the twins.

Henry stood in the still house and listened to the distillation of the whisky. He no longer needed to track the Dark or look for Usaeil.

Or search for the weapon.

There was nothing for him to do now, nothing for his mind to focus on.

Except for the fact that he was the JusticeBringer.

Esther and Nikolai had gone to the Isle of Eigg for answers. Maybe it was his turn to see what he could dig up on his birth parents. He hadn't cared one way or another before, but now . . . there was nothing else for him to think about.

It was either his past or Melisse, and Melisse had made it clear how she thought of him. A human with no magic.

He had a title—JusticeBringer—and he was supposed to have some sort of destiny, but what? He had no idea what he was supposed to do now. There was no way he could go back to the mortal world now that he'd lived at Dreagan.

Nor could he remain without doing *something*. He needed a mission. Otherwise, he was going to lose his mind.

Without warning, he felt Melisse near. He hadn't spoken to her since Con and Rhi's mating. She'd tried to get his attention to talk to him, but he'd made certain that wouldn't happen. Not because he didn't want to talk to her, but because he needed to figure out who he was before he did.

He was tired of being lost, of not knowing what it was he was meant to do. Everyone kept talking about how detrimental he and his sister were to governing the Druids. Still, so far, all he'd managed to do was see how Usaeil had killed a Druid. There had to be something more.

And he was going to find it.

Without looking at Melisse, he turned and walked out of the manor. It was time he got some answers for himself.

ACKNOWLEDGMENTS

A special shout-out to everyone at SMP for getting this book ready, including the amazing art department for such a stunning cover that matches the character to perfection. Much thanks and appreciation go to my exceptional editor, Monique Patterson.

To my amazing agent, Natanya Wheeler, who is on this dragon train with me.

A special thanks to my children, Gillian and Connor, as well as my family for the never-ending support. I also can't be remiss in thanking Charity and J.S. for all the incredible support, graphics, laughter, and ideas.

Last, but not least, G.

Hats off to my incredible readers and those in the DG Groupies FB group for keeping the love of the Dragon Kings alive. Words can't say how much I adore y'all.